HE IS
LEGEND

HE IS LEGEND

AN ANTHOLOGY CELEBRATING
RICHARD MATHESON

EDITED BY
CHRISTOPHER CONLON

TOR®

A TOM DOHERTY ASSOCIATES BOOK

NEW YORK

This is a work of fiction. All of the characters, organizations, and events portrayed in these stories are either products of the authors' imaginations or are used fictitiously.

HE IS LEGEND: AN ANTHOLOGY CELEBRATING RICHARD MATHESON

Originally published by Gauntlet Press

A Tor Book
Published by Tom Doherty Associates, LLC
175 Fifth Avenue
New York, NY 10010

www.tor-forge.com

Tor® is a registered trademark of Tom Doherty Associates, LLC.

ISBN 978-0-7653-2614-0 (trade paperback)
ISBN 978-0-7653-2613-3 (hardcover)

First Tor Edition: September 2010

Printed in the United States of America

COPYRIGHT ACKNOWLEDGMENTS

CONTENTS

Editor's Note

One Saturday afternoon when I was twelve, my father took me to a flea market near our home. There, in someone's box of used books, I found a battered Bantam paperback called *Third from the Sun* (with its flea-market price, fifteen cents, scrawled in crayon above the words). The cover showed a curious half-man, half-bird creature cooking the disassembled parts of a human being in a frying pan. A hot orange sun burned overhead. Bats flapped about in the background.

I bought the book.

Little did I know this moment marked the beginning of a journey for me into the worlds of Richard Matheson that would still be going on today, more than thirty years later.

For this celebration I asked some of today's finest writers to create new stories set within Richard Matheson's fictional worlds—sequels, prequels, variations—or to more generally utilize classic Matheson themes. The result, I hope you'll agree, is phenomenal—the closest thing we're likely to get to a new collection of Richard Matheson tales (since he essentially retired from writing short stories in the early 1970s), and a first-rate anthology in its own right.

This doesn't mark the end of my Mathesonian journey, not by a long shot. But it's a major milestone on a trip which began all those years ago with a fifteen-cent used paperback—which, by the way, I still own.

—Christopher Conlon
2008

FOREWORD

MATHESON THE MASTER
RAMSEY CAMPBELL

I hope not to offend Richard Matheson by suggesting that he is arguably the greatest living writer of modern horror fiction, and certainly among the most innovative. Of course he has worked in different fields, but I'd like to concentrate on that one, not least because it often overlaps the other territories he explores. Along with Fritz Leiber, Ray Bradbury and Charles Beaumont, he brought the American genre into everyday settings and everyone's life. His importance has yet to be fully appreciated. Let me work on its pedestal.

His first published tale, "Born of Man and Woman," achieves a great deal in a remarkably small space. It gives a voice to a monster, not least in its prose style, and although our experience is confined to his, we may conclude that his vision is less restricted than that of his parents. There's compassion without sentimentalism, and I mean to praise the tale by saying that it's nasty, brutish and short. "Dress of White Silk" restricts our viewpoint with the young narrator's language, the better to pace various revelations, while "Drink My Red Blood" uses the spare style of a school reading book to convey its obsessed protagonist's limitations. Horror fiction had rarely seen such a burst of experiment. More were to come.

Although many of his early short stories were science fiction, terror was often at their heart. "Lover When You're Near Me" recalls C. L. Moore's "Shambleau" in its appalled extraterrestrial eroticism; both stories challenged the limits of genre publication in their day. "The Curious Child" may end reassuringly, but it's the oppressive sense of mounting panic that lingers in the mind, while "The Edge" takes us there and leaves us, like its luckless everyman victim, teetering helplessly. "Return" uses time travel to update the ghost story in a way that's both poignant and disturbing, adjectives that equally apply to "The Test," a tale I won't spoil by description. "Witch War" and "The Likeness of Julie" gift teenage girls with extrasensory powers. These two stories are all the more chilling for the nonchalance of their psychics, and the combination of character and the psychic has none of the mediaeval caricaturing of adolescence to be found in *The Exorcist* and its many clones, despite preceding that novel by decades. "Trespass" may be seen to prefigure in more modern terms a famous supernatural novel of the sixties. "Legion of Plotters" is a seminal study of paranoia, and "The Distributor" makes paranoia its cold heart. As for "Shipshape Home," it ends on a high note of terror, a line of dialogue that has stayed with this reader for fifty years or more, and the same can be said of the spectral "Long Distance Call." But the most sustained terror in his work is to be found elsewhere.

That brings me to the novels. "You may be in at the birth of a giant," says the blurb on the back of my yellowing Gold Medal paperback of *I Am Legend*, and if anything, that's an understatement. The novel didn't just revolutionise vampirism by observing that its progression would be geometric (one of several Matheson insights to be developed by Steve King); it turned the protagonist's entire world into a nightmare and sustained it at book length. Like its successor, *The Shrinking Man*, it relieves the intensity of the central situation with flashbacks no more reassuring than uneasy dreams. Indeed, Scott Carey's entire tale resembles one, and its psychological resonances are profound. *A Stir of Echoes* begins with a séance and inflicts a ghost on the reluctant hero, but its considerable power resides in the oppressive clammy sense of suffering from an uninvited wild talent and in the suburban secrets his psychic power uncovers. Matheson continued to create terse terrors in the early seventies, whether reinventing the lethal doll motif in claustrophobic terms ("Prey") or producing the definitive nightmare of road rage ("Duel"). However, my vote for his ultimate achievement in horror goes to *Hell House*.

It resembles Shirley Jackson's masterpiece, of course, even in its title. Four researchers occupy a haunted mansion—"the Everest of haunted houses"—and are beset by phenomena both spectral and psychological. While it lacks the delicacy of Jackson's novel, it is considerably more terrifying. Indeed, it was the last piece of fiction that (back in the early seventies) I regretted staying up alone at night to finish. I'd thought the idea of fearing to look over your shoulder in those circumstances was a publicist's exaggeration, but the last hundred pages or so of *Hell House* proved me wrong. Thank you, Richard!

It was filmed two years after publication, just too early to benefit from the taboo-breaking of *The Exorcist*. The author's screenplay toned down or omitted the rawer elements from which the book gains much of its power. It could be faithfully filmed now, but I suspect the author might prefer it not to be. He has admitted in interviews that he doesn't much like horror, Poe included. I can't disbelieve him, but I do have to make an effort to believe, given how he helped bring Poe to the screen.

At the time those Roger Corman films were decried for including bland young actors for teen appeal—even Jack Nicholson is pretty colourless in *The Raven*. In retrospect, though, it's striking how little their presence compromises the funereal visions of *House of Usher* or *The Pit and the Pendulum*. If Matheson faithfully conveyed Poe's doomed Gothic romanticism, he improved on Dennis Wheatley (who certainly needed it) in *The Devil Rides Out*. His version of *Dracula* is unfairly neglected, and more entitled to be described as Bram Stoker's than the Coppola film (which seems influenced by it). On the non-supernatural front, *Fanatic* (retitled *Die! Die! My Darling* in America, to Richard's disgust) is as suspenseful as its forties precursor, *My Name Is Julia Ross*. The films based on Matheson's adaptations of his own work range from the very effective (the by no means incredible *Shrinking Man*, the justly celebrated television film of "Prey") to the compromised (*The Last Man on Earth*).

One other project promised to be ideal: his adaptation with Charles Beaumont of Fritz Leiber's great modern supernatural novel *Conjure Wife*. However, it was filmed in England by Sidney Hayers, to which end it was revised by George Baxt, who had written *Circus of Horrors* and *Payroll* for Hayers. Like *Hellraiser*, the film takes place in a vague mid-Atlantic setting, neither quite American nor entirely British, and the rampant gargoyle of the novel and of the original script is transformed into a stone eagle that flaps through the final reel (giving the film its title *Night of the Eagle*, though in America it borrowed Merritt's title *Burn, Witch, Burn*). In many ways the film is a good piece of work, but it could have been a great one.

My imagination has been much enriched by my many encounters with Richard's work, and the same can be said of my field. If I've concentrated on that field in this skimpy essay, be aware that there is far more to him. I'm sure those aspects of his work will be celebrated by writers more competent to do so than I am. Let the celebration commence. Here's to Richard Matheson, one of the glories of all his genres.

Ramsey Campbell
Wallasey, Merseyside
9 July 2007

THROTTLE

A Tale Inspired by "Duel"

BY JOE HILL AND STEPHEN KING

"Duel," Richard Matheson's 1971 tale of a motorist being pursued on the highways by a crazed truck driver, attained legendary status when it was filmed by a young Steven Spielberg. For their take on the theme, Joe Hill—author of the bestseller *Heart-Shaped Box*—teams up with his father, Stephen King, who has written over fifty phenomenally successful novels and story collections, including *Lisey's Story* and *Duma Key*. Their first-ever collaboration, an event in itself, gets this Matheson celebration off the starting line at full throttle.

THROTTLE

They rode west from the slaughter, through the painted desert, and did not stop until they were a hundred miles away. Finally, in the early afternoon, they turned in at a diner with a white stucco exterior and pumps on concrete islands out front. The overlapping thunder of their engines shook the plate glass windows as they rolled by. They drew up together among parked long-haul trucks, on the west side of the building, and there they put down their kickstands and turned off their bikes.

Race Adamson had led them the whole way, his Harley running sometimes as much as a quarter-mile ahead of anyone else's. It had been Race's habit to ride out in front ever since he had returned to them, after two years in the sand. He ran so far in front it often seemed he was daring the rest of them to try and keep up, or maybe had a mind to simply leave them behind. He hadn't wanted to stop here but Vince had forced him to. As the diner came into sight, Vince had throttled after Race, blown past him, and then shot his hand left in a gesture The Tribe knew well: *follow me off the highway*. The Tribe let Vince's hand-gesture call it, as they always did. Another thing for Race to dislike about him, probably. The kid had a pocketful of them.

Race was one of the first to park, but the last to dismount. He stood astride his bike, slowly stripping off his leather riding gloves, glaring at the others from behind his mirrored sunglasses.

"You ought to have a talk with your boy," Lemmy Chapman said to Vince. Lemmy nodded in Race's direction.

"Not here," Vince said. It could wait until they were back in Vegas. He wanted to put the road behind him. He wanted to lie down in the dark for a while, wanted some time to allow the sick knot in his stomach to abate. Maybe most of all, he wanted to shower. He hadn't got any blood on him, but felt contaminated all the same, and wouldn't be at ease in his own skin until he had washed the morning's stink off.

He took a step in the direction of the diner, but Lemmy caught his arm before he could go any further. "Yes. Here."

Vince looked at the hand on his arm—Lemmy didn't let go, Lemmy of all the men had no fear of him—then glanced toward the kid, who wasn't really a kid at all anymore and hadn't been for years. Race was opening the hardcase over his back tire, fishing through his gear for something.

"What's to talk about? Clarke's gone. So's the money. There's nothing left to do. Not this morning."

"You ought find out if Race feels the same way. You been assuming the two of you are on the same page even though these days he spends forty minutes of every hour pissed off at you. Tell you something else, boss. Race brought some of these guys in, and he got a lot of them fired up, talking about how rich they were all going to get on his deal with Clarke. He might not be the only one who needs to hear what's next." He glanced meaningfully at the other men. Vince noticed for the first time that they weren't drifting on toward the diner, but hanging around by their bikes, casting looks toward him and Race both. Waiting for something to come to pass.

Vince didn't want to talk. The thought of talk drained him. Lately, conversation with Race was like throwing a medicine ball back and forth, a lot of wearying effort, and he didn't feel up to it, not with what they were driving away from.

He went anyway, because Lemmy was almost always right when it came to Tribe preservation. Lemmy had been riding six to Vince's twelve going back to when they had met in the Mekong Delta and the whole world was *dinky dau*. They had been on the look out for tripwires and buried mines then. Nothing much had changed in the almost forty years since.

Vince left his bike and crossed to Race, who stood between his Harley and a parked truck, an oil hauler. Race had found what he was looking for in the hardcase on the back of his bike, a flask sloshing with what looked like tea and wasn't. He drank earlier and earlier, something else Vince didn't like. Race had a pull, wiped his mouth, held it out to Vince. Vince shook his head.

"Tell me," Vince said.

"If we pick up Route 6," Race said, "we could be down in Show Low in three hours. Assuming that pussy rice-burner of yours can keep up."

"What's in Show Low?"

"Clarke's sister."

"Why would we want to see her?"

"For the money. Case you hadn't noticed, we just got fucked out of sixty grand."

"And you think his sister will have it."

"Place to start."

"Let's talk about it back in Vegas. Look at our options there."

"How about we look at 'em now? You see Clarke hanging up the phone when we walked in? I heard a snatch of what he was saying through the door. I think he tried to get his sister, and when he didn't, he left a message with someone who knows her. Now why do you think he felt a pressing need to reach out and touch that toe-rag as soon as he saw all of us in the driveway?"

To say his goodbyes was Vince's theory, but he didn't tell Race that. "She doesn't have anything to do with this, does she? What's she do? She make crank too?"

"No. She's a whore."

"Jesus. What a family."

"Look who's talking," Race said.

"What's that mean?" Vince asked. It wasn't the line that bothered him, with its implied insult, so much as Race's mirrored sunglasses, which showed a reflection of Vince himself, sunburnt and a beard full gray, looking puckered, lined, and old.

Race stared down the shimmering road again and when he spoke he didn't answer the question. "Sixty grand, up in smoke, and you can just shrug it off."

"I didn't shrug anything off. That's what happened. Up in smoke."

Race and Dean Clarke had met in Fallujah—or maybe it had been Tikrit. Clarke a medic specializing in pain management, his treatment of choice being primo dope accompanied by generous helpings of Wyclef Jean. Race's specialties had been driving Humvees and not getting shot. The two of them had remained friends back in The World, and Clarke had come to Race a half a year ago, with the idea of setting up a meth lab in Smith Lake. He figured sixty grand would get him started, and that he'd be making more than that per month in no time.

"True glass," that had been Clarke's pitch. "None of that cheap green shit, just true glass." Then he'd raised his hand above his head, indicating a monster stack of cash. "Sky's the limit, yo?"

Yo. Vince thought now he should have pulled out the minute he heard that come out of Clarke's mouth. The very second.

But he hadn't. He'd even helped Race out with twenty grand of his own money, in spite of his doubts. Clarke was a slacker-looking guy who bore a passing resemblance to Kurt Cobain: long blond hair and layered shirts. He said *yo*, he called everyone *man*, he talked about how drugs broke through the oppressive power of the overmind. Whatever that meant. He surprised and charmed Race with intellectual gifts: plays by Sartre, mix tapes featuring spoken word poetry and reggae dub.

Vince didn't resent Clarke for being an egghead full of spiritual-revolution talk that came out in some bullshit half-breed language, part Pansy and part Ebonics. What disconcerted Vince was that when they met, Clarke already had a stinking case of meth mouth, his teeth falling out and his gums spotted. Vince didn't mind making money off the shit, but had a knee-jerk distrust of anyone gamy enough to use it.

And still he put up money, had wanted something to work out for Race, especially after the way he had been run out of the army. And for a while, when Race and Clarke were hammering out the details, Vince had even half-talked himself into believing it might pay off. Race seemed, briefly, to have an air of almost cocky self-assurance, had even bought a car for his girlfriend, a used Mustang, anticipating the big return on his investment.

Only the meth lab caught fire, yo? And the whole thing burned to a shell in the space of ten minutes, the very first day of operation. The wetbacks who worked inside escaped out the windows, and were standing around, burnt and sooty, when the fire trucks arrived. Now most of them were in county lockup.

Race had learned about the fire, not from Clarke, but from Bobby Stone, another friend of his from Iraq, who had driven out to Smith Lake to buy ten grand worth of the mythical true glass, but who turned around when he saw the smoke and the flashing lights. Race had tried to raise Clarke on the phone, but couldn't get him, not that afternoon, not in the evening. By eleven, the Tribe was on the highway, headed east to find him.

They had caught Dean Clarke at his cabin in the hills, packing to go. He told them he had been just about to leave to come see Race, tell him what happened, work out a new plan. He said he was going to pay them all back. He said the money was gone now, but there were possibilities, there were contingency plans. He said he was so goddamn fucking sorry. Some of it was lies, and some of it was true, especially the part about being so goddamn fucking sorry, but none of it surprised Vince, not even when Clarke began to cry.

What surprised him—what surprised all of them—was Clarke's girlfriend hiding in the bathroom, dressed in daisy print panties and a sweatshirt that said *CORMAN HIGH VARSITY*. All of seventeen and soaring on meth and clutching a little .22 in one hand. She was listening in when Roy Klowes asked Clarke if she was around, said that if Clarke's bitch blew all of them, they could cross two hundred bucks off the debt right there. Roy Klowes had walked in the bathroom, taking his cock out of his pants to have a leak, but the girl had thought he was unzipping for other reasons and opened fire. Her first shot went wide and her second shot went into the ceiling, because by then Roy was whacking her with his machete, and it was all sliding down the red hole, away from reality and into the territory of bad dream.

"I'm sure he lost some of the money," Race said. "Could be he lost as much as half what we set him up. But if you think Dean Clarke put the entire sixty grand into that one trailer, I can't help you."

"Maybe he did have some of it tucked away. I'm not saying you're wrong. But I don't see why it would wind up with the sister. Could just as easily be in a Mason jar, buried somewhere in his backyard. I'm not going to pick on some pathetic hooker for fun. If we find out she's suddenly come into money, that's a different story."

"I was six months setting this deal up. And I'm not the only one with a lot riding on it."

"Okay. Let's talk about how to make it right in Vegas."

"Talk isn't going to make anything right. Riding is. His sister is in Show Low today, but when she finds out her brother and his little honey got painted all over their ranch—"

"You want to keep your voice down," Vince said.

Lemmy watched them with his arms folded across his chest, a few feet to Vince's left, but ready to move if he had to get between them. The others stood in groups of two and three, bristly and road dirty, wearing leather jackets or denim vests with the gang's patch on them: a skull in an Indian headdress, above the legend **The Tribe • Live on the Road, Die on the Road.** They had always been The Tribe, although none of them were Indian, except for Peaches, who claimed to be half-Cherokee, except when he felt like saying he was half-Spaniard or half-Inca. Doc said he could be half-Eskimo and half-Viking if he wanted, it still added up to all retard.

"The money is gone," Vince said to his son. "The six months too. *See it.*"

His son stood there, the muscles bunched in his jaw, not speaking. His knuckles white on the flask in his right hand. Looking at him now, Vince was struck with a sudden image of Race at the age of six, face just as dusty as it was now, tooling around the gravel driveway on his green Big Wheels, making revving noises down in his throat. Vince and Mary had laughed and laughed, mostly at the screwed up look of intensity on their son's face, the Kindergarten road warrior. He couldn't find the humor in it now, not two hours after Race had split a man's head open with a shovel. Race had always been fast, and had been the first to catch up to Clarke when he tried to run, in the confusion after the girl started shooting. Maybe he had not meant to kill him. Race had only hit him the once.

Vince opened his mouth to say something more, but there was nothing more. He turned away, started toward the diner. He had not gone three steps, though, when he heard a bottle explode behind him. He turned and saw Race had thrown the flask into the side of the oil rig, had thrown it exactly in the place Vince had been standing only five seconds before. Throwing it at Vince's shadow maybe.

Whisky and chunks of glass dribbled down the battered oil tank. Vince glanced up at the side of the tanker and twitched involuntarily at what he saw there. There was a word stenciled on the side and for an instant Vince thought it said SLAUGHTERIN. But no. It was LAUGHLIN. What Vince knew about Freud could be summed up in less than twenty words—dainty little white beard, cigar, thought kids wanted to fuck their parents—but you didn't need to know much psychology to recognize a guilty subconscious at work. Vince would've laughed if not for what he saw next.

The trucker was sitting in the cab. His hand hung out the driver's side window, a cigarette smoldering between two fingers. Midway up his forearm was a faded tattoo, **Death Before Dishonor**, which made him a vet, something Vince noted, in a distracted sort of way, and immediately filed away, perhaps for later consideration, perhaps not. He tried to think what the guy might've heard, measure the danger, figure out if there was a pressing need to haul Laughlin out of his truck and straighten him out about a thing or two.

Vince was still considering it when the semi rumbled to noisy, stinking life. Laughlin pitched his ciggie into the parking lot and released his air brakes. The stacks belched black diesel smoke and the truck began to roll, tires crushing gravel. As the tanker moved away, Vince let out a slow breath, and felt the tension begin to drain away. He doubted if the guy had heard anything, and what did it matter if he had? No one with any sense would want to get involved in their shitpull. Laughlin must've realized he had been caught listening in and decided to get while the getting was good.

By the time the eighteen-wheeler eased out onto the two-lane highway, Vince had already turned away, brushing through his crew and making for the diner. It was almost an hour before he saw the truck again.

Vince went to piss—his bladder had been killing him for going on thirty miles—and on his return he passed by the others, sitting in two booths. They were quiet, almost no sound from them at all, aside from the scrape of forks on plates, and the clink of glasses being set down. Only Peaches was talking, and that was to himself. Peaches spoke in a whisper, and occasionally seemed to flinch, as if surrounded by a cloud of imaginary midges . . . a dismal, unsettling habit of his. The rest of them occupied their own interior spaces, not seeing each other, staring inwardly at who-knew-what instead. Some of them were probably seeing the bathroom after Roy Klowes finished chopping up the girl. Others might be remembering Clarke face down in the dirt beyond the back door, his ass in the air and his pants full of shit and the steel-bladed shovel planted in his skull, the handle sticking in the air. And then there were probably a few wondering if they would be home in time for *American Gladiators*, and whether the lottery tickets they had bought yesterday were winners.

It had been different on the way down to see Clarke. Better. The Tribe had stopped just after sunup at a diner much like this, and while the mood had not been festive, there had been plenty of bullshit, and a certain amount of predictable yuks to go with the coffee and the donuts. Doc had sat in one booth doing the crossword puzzle, others seated around him, looking over his shoulder, and ribbing each other about what an honor it was to sit with a man of such education. Doc had done time, like most of the rest of them, and had a gold tooth in his mouth in place of one that had been whacked out by a cop's nightstick a few years before. But he wore bifocals, and had lean, almost patrician features, and read the paper, and knew things, like the capital of Kenya and the players in the War of the Roses. Roy Klowes took a sidelong look at Doc's puzzle and said, "What I need is a crossword with questions about fixing bikes or cruising pussy. Like what's a four letter word for what I do to your momma, Doc? I could answer that one."

Doc frowned. "I'd say 'repulse,' but that's seven letters. So I guess my answer would have to be 'gall.'"

"Gall?" Roy asked, scratching his head.

"That's right. You gall her. Means you show up and she wants to spit."

"Yeah and that's what pisses me off about her. 'Cause I been trying to train her to swaller while I gall her."

And the men just about fell off their stools laughing. They had been laughing just as hard the next booth over, where Peaches was trying to tell them about why he got his nuts clipped: "What sold me on it was when I saw that I'd only ever have to pay for one vasectomy . . . which is not something you can say about abortion. There's theoretically no limit there. *None*. Every jizzwad is a potential budget buster. You don't recognize that until you've had to pay for a couple of scrapes and begin to think there might be a better use for your money. Also, relationships aren't ever the same after you've had to flush Junior down the toilet. They just aren't. Voice of experience right here." Peaches didn't need jokes, he was funny enough just saying what was on his mind.

Now Vince moved past the cored out, red-eyed bunch, and took a stool at the counter beside Lemmy.

"What do you think we ought to do about this shit when we get to Vegas?" Vince asked.

"Run away," Lemmy said. "Tell no one we're going. Never look back."

Vince laughed. Lemmy didn't. He lifted his coffee halfway to his lips but didn't drink, only looked at it for a few seconds and then put it down.

"Somethin' wrong with that?" Vince asked.

"It ain't the coffee that's wrong."

"You aren't going to tell me you're serious about taking off, are you?"

"We wouldn't be the only ones, buddy," Lemmy said. "What Roy did to that girl in the bathroom?"

"She almost shot him," Vince said, voice low so no one else could hear.

"She wasn't but seventeen."

Vince did not reply and anyway no reply was expected.

"Most of these guys have never seen anything that heavy and I think a bunch—the smart ones—are going to scatter to the four corners of the earth, as soon as they can. Find a new purpose for being." Vince laughed again, but Lemmy only glanced at him sidelong. "Listen now, Cap. I killed my brother driving blind drunk when I was eighteen. And when I woke up I could smell his blood all over me. I tried to kill myself in the Corps to make up for it, but the boys in the black pajamas wouldn't help me. And what I remember mostly about the war is the way my own feet smelled when they got jungle rot. Like carrying a toilet around in my boots. I been in jail, like you, and what was worst wasn't the things I did or saw done. What was worst was the smell on every-one. Armpits and assholes. And that was all bad. But none of it has anything on the Charlie Manson shit we're driving away from. Thing I can't get away from is how it stank in the place. After it was over. Like being stuck in a closet where someone took a shit. Not enough air, and what there was wasn't any good." He paused, turned on his stool to look sidelong at Vince. "You know what I been thinking about ever since we drove away? Lon Refus moved out to Denver and opened a garage. He sent me a postcard of the Flatirons. I been wondering if he could use an old guy to twist a wrench for him. I been thinking I could get used to the smell of pines."

He was quiet again, then shifted his gaze to look at the other men in their booths. "The half that doesn't take a walk will be looking to get back what they lost, one way or another, and you don't want any part of how they're going to do it. 'Cause there's going to be more of this crazy meth shit. This is just beginning. The tollbooth where you get on the turnpike. There's too much money in it to quit, and everyone who sells it does it too, and the ones who do it make big fucking messes. The girl who tried to shoot Roy was on it, which is why she tried to kill him, and Roy is on it himself, which is why he had to whack her forty fucking times with his asshole machete. Who the fuck besides a meth-head carries a machete, anyhow?"

"Don't get me started on Roy. I'd like to stick Little Boy up his ass and watch the light shoot out his eyes," Vince told him, and it was Lemmy's turn to laugh then. Coming up with deranged uses for Little Boy was one of the running jokes between them. Vince said, "Go on. Say your say. You been thinkin' about it the last hour."

"How would you know that?"

"You think I don't know what it means when I see you sittin' straight up on your sled?"

Lemmy grunted and said, "Sooner or later the cops are going to land on Roy or one of these other crankies and they'll take every- one around them down with them. Because Roy and the guys like him aren't smart enough to get rid of the shit they stole from crime scenes. None of them are smart enough not to brag to their girlfriends about what they been up to. Hell. Half of them are carrying rock right now. All I'm saying."

Vince scrubbed a hand along the side of his beard. "You keep talking about the two halves, the half that's going to take off and the half that isn't. You want to tell me which half Race is in?"

Lemmy turned his head and grinned unhappily, showing the chip in his tooth again. "You need to ask?"

The truck with LAUGHLIN on the side was laboring uphill when they caught up to it around three in the afternoon.

The highway wound its lazy way up a long grade, through a series of switchbacks. With all the curves there was no obvious place to pass. Race was out front again. After they departed from the diner, he had sped off, increasing his lead on the rest of The Tribe by so much that sometimes Vince lost sight of him altogether. But when they reached the truck, his son was riding the guy's bumper.

The ten of them rode up the hill in the rig's boiling wake. Vince's eyes began to tear and run.

"*Fucking truck,*" Vince screamed, and Lemmy nodded. Vince's lungs were tight and his chest hurt from breathing its exhaust and it was hard to see. "*Get your miserable fat ass truck out of the way!*" Vince hollered.

It was a surprise, catching up to the truck here. They weren't that far from the diner . . . twenty miles, no more. LAUGHLIN must've pulled over somewhere else for a while—but there was nowhere else. Possibly he had parked his rig in the shade of a billboard for a siesta. Or threw a tire and needed to stop and put on a new one. Did it matter? It didn't. Vince wasn't even sure why it was on his mind, but it nagged.

Just past the next bend in the road, Race leaned his Softail Deuce into the lane for oncoming traffic, lowered his head, and accelerated from thirty to seventy. The bike squatted, then *leaped.*

He cut in front of the truck as soon as he was ahead of it—slipping back into the right hand lane just as a pale yellow Lexus blew past, going the other way. The driver of the Lexus pounded her horn, but the *meep-meep* sound of it was almost immediately lost in the overpowering wail of the truck's air horn.

Vince had spotted the Lexus coming and for a moment had been sure he was about to see his son go head on into it, Race one second, roadmeat the next. It took a few moments for his heart to come back down out of his throat.

"*Fucking psycho,*" Vince yelled at Lemmy.

"*You mean the guy in the truck?*" Lemmy hollered back, as the blast of the air horn finally died away. "*Or Race?*"

"*Both!*"

By the time the truck swung through the next curve, though, Laughlin seemed to have come to his senses, or had finally looked in the mirror and noticed the rest of The Tribe roaring along behind him. He put his hand out the window—that sun-darkened and veiny hand, big-knuckled and blunt-fingered—and waved them by.

Immediately, Roy and two others swung out and thundered past. The rest went in twos. It was nothing to pass once the go-to was clear, the truck laboring along at barely thirty. Vince and Lemmy swept out last, passing just before the next switchback. Vince cast a look up toward the driver on their way by, but could see nothing except that dark hand hanging out against the door. Five minutes later they had left the truck so far behind them they couldn't hear it anymore.

There followed a stretch of high open desert, sage and saguaro, cliffs off to the right, striped in chalky shades of yellow and red. They were riding into the sun now, pursued by their own lengthening shadows. Houses and a few trailers whipped by as they blew through a sorry excuse for a township. The bikes were strung out across almost half a mile, with Vince and Lemmy riding close to the back. But not far beyond the town, Vince saw the rest of The Tribe bunched up at the side of the road, just before a four-way intersection—the crossing for Route 6.

Beyond the intersection, to the west, the highway they had been following was torn down to dirt. A diamond shaped orange sign read CONSTRUCTION NEXT 20 MILES BE PREPARED TO STOP. In the distance, Vince could see dump trucks and a grader. Men worked in clouds of red smoke, the clay stirred up and drifting across the tableland.

He hadn't known there would be roadwork here, because they hadn't come this way. It had been Race's suggestion to return by the backroads, which had suited Vince fine. Driving away from a double homicide, it seemed like a good idea to keep a low profile. Of course that wasn't why Race had suggested it.

"What?" Vince said, slowing and putting his foot down. As if he didn't already know.

Race pointed away from the construction, down Route 6. "We go south on 6, we can pick up I-40."

"In Show Low," Vince said. "Why does this not surprise me?"

It was Roy Klowes spoke next. He jerked a thumb toward the dump trucks. "Bitch of a lot better than doing five an hour through that shit for twenty miles. No thank you. I'd rather ride easy and maybe pick up sixty grand along the way. That's my think on it."

"Did it hurt?" Lemmy asked Roy. "Having a thought? I hear it hurts the first time. Like when a chick gets her cherry popped."

"Fuck you, Lemmy," Roy said.

"When I want your think," Vince said, "I'll be sure to ask for it, Roy. But I wouldn't hold your breath."

Race spoke, his voice calm, reasonable. "We get to Show Low, you don't have to stick around. Neither of you. No one's going to hold it against you if you just want to ride on."

So there it was.

Vince looked from face to face. The young men met his gaze. The older ones, the ones who had been riding with him for decades, did not.

"I'm glad to hear no one will hold it against me," Vince said. "I was worried."

A memory struck him then: riding with his son in a car at night, in the GTO, back in the days he was trying to go straight, be a family man for Mary. The details of the journey were lost now; he couldn't recall where they were coming from or where they had been going. What he remembered was looking into the rearview mirror at his ten-year-old's dusty, sullen face. They had stopped at a hamburger stand, but the kid didn't want dinner, said he wasn't hungry. The kid would only settle for a Popsicle, then bitched when Vince came back with lime instead of grape. He wouldn't eat it, let the Popsicle melt on the leather. Finally, when they were twenty miles away from the hamburger stand, Race announced that his belly was growling.

Vince had looked into the rear view mirror and said, "You know just because I'm your father doesn't mean I got to like you." And the boy had stared back, his chin dimpling, struggling not to cry, but unwilling to look away. Returning Vince's look with bright, hating eyes. Why had Vince said that? The notion crossed his mind that if he had known some other way to talk to Race, there would've been no Fallujah and no dishonorable discharge for ditching his squad, taking off in a Humvee while mortars fell; there would've been no Dean Clarke and no meth lab and the boy would not feel the need to be out front all the time, blasting along at seventy on his hotshit jackpuppy when the rest of them were doing sixty. It was him the kid was trying to leave behind. He had been trying all his life.

Vince squinted back the way they had come . . . and there was that goddamn truck again. Vince could see it through the trembling waves of heat on the road, so it seemed half-mirage, with its towering stacks and silver grill: LAUGHLIN. Or SLAUGHTERIN, if you were feeling Freudian. Vince frowned, distracted for a moment, wondering again how they had been able to catch up and pass a guy who'd had almost an hour lead on them.

When Doc spoke, his voice was almost shy with apology. "Might be the thing to do, boss. Sure would beat twenty miles of dirt bath."

"Well. I wouldn't want any of you to get dirty," Vince said.

And he pushed away from the side of the road, throttled up, and turned left onto 6, leading them away toward Show Low.

Behind him, in the distance, he could hear the truck changing gears, the roar of the engine climbing in volume and force, whining faintly as it thundered across the plain.

The country was red and yellow stone, and they saw no one on the narrow, two-lane road. There was no breakdown lane. They crested a rise, then began to descend into a canyon's slot, following the road as it wound steadily down. To the left was a battered guardrail, and to the right was an almost sheer face of rock.

For a while Vince rode out front beside Lemmy, but then Lemmy fell back and it was Race partnered beside him, the father and the son riding side by side, the wind rippling Race's movie star black hair back from his brow. The sun, now on the western side of the sky, burned in the lenses of the kid's shades.

Vince watched him from the corners of his eyes for a moment. Race was sinewy and lean, and even the way he sat on his bike seemed an act of aggression, the way he slung it around the curves, tilting to a forty-five degree angle over the blacktop. Vince envied him his natural athletic grace, and yet at the same time, somehow Race managed to make riding a motorcycle look like work. Whereas Vince himself had taken to it because it was the furthest thing from work. He wondered idly if Race was ever really at ease with himself and what he was doing.

Vince heard the grinding thunder of a big engine behind him and took a long lazy look back over his shoulder just in time to see the truck come bearing down on them. Like a lion breaking cover at a watering hole where a bunch of gazelles were loafing. The Tribe was rolling in bunches, as always, doing maybe forty-five down the switchbacks, and the truck was rushing along at closer to sixty. Vince had time to think *He's not slowing down* and then LAUGHLIN slammed through the three running at the back of the pack with an eardrum-stunning crash of steel on steel.

Bikes flew. One Harley was thrown into the rock wall, the rider— John Kidder, sometimes known as Baby John—catapulting off it, tossed into the stone, then rebounding and disappearing under the steel-belted tires of LAUGHLIN's truck. Another rider *(Doc, no not Doc)* was driven into the left lane. Vince had the briefest glance of Doc's pale and astonished face, mouth opening in an **O**, the twinkle of the gold tooth he was so proud of. Wobbling out of control, Doc struck the guardrail and went over his handlebars, flung into space. His Harley flipped over after him, the hardcase breaking open and spilling laundry. The truck chewed up the fallen bikes. The big grill seemed to snarl.

Then Vince and Race swung around another hard curve side by side, leaving it all behind.

The blood surged to Vince's heart, and for a moment there was a dangerous pinching in his chest. He had to fight for his next breath. The instant the carnage was out of sight, it was hard to believe it had really happened. Hard to believe the spinning bikes hadn't taken out the speeding truck, too. Yet he had just finished coming around the bend when Doc crashed into the road ahead of them. His bike landed on top of his body with an echoing clang. His clothes came floating after. Doc's sleeveless denim jacket came drifting down last, ballooning open, caught for a moment on an updraft. Over a silhouette of Vietnam in gold thread was the legend: **WHEN I GET TO HEAVEN THEY'LL LET ME IN BECAUSE I'VE ALREADY BEEN TO HELL IRON TRIANGLE 1968.** The clothes, the owner of the clothes, and the owner's ride had dropped from the terrace above, falling seventy feet to the highway below.

Vince jerked the handlebars, swerving around the wreck with one bootheel skimming the patched asphalt. His friend of thirty years, Doc Regis, was now a six-letter word for lubricant: *grease*.

He was face down, but his teeth were glistening in a slick of blood next to his left ear, the goldie among them. His shins had come out through the backs of his legs, poles of shining red bone poking through his jeans. All this Vince saw in an instant, then wished he could *un*-see. The gag muscles fluttered in his throat and when he swallowed, there was a burning taste of bile.

Race swung around the other side of the ruin that had been Doc and Doc's bike. He looked sideways at Vince, and while Vince could not see his eyes behind his shades, his face was a rigid, stricken thing . . . the expression of a small kid up past his bedtime, who has walked in on his parents watching a grisly horror movie on DVD.

Vince looked back again and saw the remnants of The Tribe coming around the bend. Just seven now. The truck howled after, swinging around the curve so fast that the long tank it was hauling lurched hard to one side, coming perilously close to tipping, its tires smoking on the blacktop. Then it steadied and bore on, striking Ellis Harbison. Ellis was launched straight up into the air, as if bounced off a diving board. He almost looked funny, pinwheeling his arms against the blue sky—at least until he came down and went under the truck. His ride turned end over end before being swatted entirely aside by the eighteen-wheeler.

Vince caught a jittery glimpse of Dean Carew as the truck caught up to him. The truck butted the rear tire of his bike. Dean highsided and came down hard, rolling at fifty miles an hour along the highway, the asphalt peeling his skin away, his head bashing the road again and again, leaving a series of red punctuation marks on the chalkboard of the pavement.

An instant later the tanker ate Dean's bike, bang, thump, *crunch*, and the lowrider Dean had still been making payments on exploded, a parachute of flame bursting open beneath the truck. Vince felt a wave of pressure and heat against his back, shoving him forward, threatening to lift him off the seat of his bike. He thought the truck itself would go up, slammed right off the road as the oil tanker detonated in a column of fire. But it didn't. The rig came thundering through the flames, its sides streaked with soot and black smoke belching from its undercarriage, but otherwise un-damaged and going faster than ever. Vince knew Macks were fast—the new ones had a 485 power-plant under the hood—but *this* thing . . .

Supercharged? Could you supercharge a goddamn *semi*?

Vince was moving too fast, felt his front tire beginning to slurve about. They were close to the bottom of the slope now, where the road leveled out. Race was a little ahead. In his rearview he could see the only other survivors: Lemmy, Peaches, Roy. And the truck was closing in again.

They could beat it on a rise—in a heartbeat—but now there *were* no rises. Not for the next twenty miles, if his memory was right. It was going to get Peaches next, Peaches who was funniest when he was trying to be serious. Peaches threw a terrified glance back over his shoulder, and Vince knew what he was seeing: a chrome cliff. One that was moving in.

Fucking think of something. Lead them out of this.

It had to be him. Race was still riding okay but he was on autopilot, face frozen, fixed forward as if he had a sprained neck and was wearing a brace. A thought struck Vince then—terrible but curiously certain—that this was how Race had looked the day in Fallujah that he drove away from the men in his squad, while the mortar rounds dropped around them.

Peaches put on a burst of speed and gained a little on the truck. It blasted its air horn, as if in frustration. Or laughter. Either way, the old Georgia Peach had only gained a stay of execution. Vince could hear the trucker—maybe named Laughlin, maybe a devil from Hell—changing gears. Christ, how many forward did he have? A hundred? He started to close the distance. Vince didn't think Peaches would be able to squirt ahead again. That old flathead Beezer of his had given all it had to give. Either the truck would take him or the Beez would blow a head-gasket and *then* the truck would take him.

BRONK! BRONK! BRONK-BRONK-BRONK!

Shattering a day that was already shattered beyond repair . . . but it gave Vince an idea. It depended where they were. He knew this road. He knew them all, out here, but he had not been this way in years, and could not be sure now, on the fly, if they were where he thought they were.

Roy threw something back over his shoulder, something that twinkled in the sun. It struck LAUGHLIN's dirty windshield and flew off. The fucking machete. The truck bellowed on, blowing double streams of black smoke, the driver laying on that horn again—

BRONK-BRONK! BRONK! BRONK-BRONK-BRONK!

—in blasts that sounded weirdly like Morse.

If only . . . Lord, if only . . .

And yes. Up ahead was a sign so filthy it was only barely possible to read it: CUMBA 2.

Cumba. Goddam Cumba. A played-out little mining town on the side of a hill, a place where there were maybe five slots and one old geezer selling Navajo blankets made in Laos.

Two miles wasn't much time when you were already doing eighty. This would have to be quick, and there would only be one chance.

The others made fun of Vince's sled, but only Race's ridicule had a keen edge to it. The bike was a rebuilt Kawasaki Vulcan 800 with Cobra pipes and a custom seat. Leather as red as a fire alarm. "The old man's La-Z-Boy," Dean Carew had once called the seat.

"Fuck that," Vince had replied indignantly, and when Peaches, solemn as a preacher, had said, "I'm sure you have," they all broke up.

The Tribe called the Vulcan a rice-burner, of course. Also Vince's Tojo Mojo El Rojo. Doc—Doc who was now spread all over the road behind them—liked to call it Miss Fujiyama. Vince only smiled as though he knew something they didn't. Maybe he even did. He'd had the Vulcan up to one-twenty and had stopped there. Pussied out. Race wouldn't have, but Race was a young man and young men had to know where things ended. One-twenty had been enough for Vince, but he'd known there was more. Now he would find out how much.

He grasped the throttle and twisted it all the way to the stop.

The Vulcan responded not with a snarl but a cry and almost tore out from under him. He had a blurred glimpse of his son's white face and then he was past, in the lead, riding the rocket, desert smells packing his nose. Up ahead was a dirty string of asphalt angling off to the left, the road to Cumba. Route 6 went past in a long lazy curve to the right. Toward Show Low.

Vince looked in his right-hand rearview and saw the others had bunched, and that Peaches still had the shiny side up. Vince thought the truck could have taken Peaches—maybe all the others—but he was laying back a little, knowing as well as Vince did that for the next twenty miles there were no upgrades. Beyond the turn-off to Cumba, the highway was elevated, and a guardrail ran along either side of it; Vince thought miserably of cattle in the chute. For the next twenty miles, the road belonged to LAUGHLIN.

Please let this work.

He let off the throttle and began squeezing the handbrake rhythmically. What the four behind him saw (if they were looking) was a long flash . . . a short flash . . . another long flash. Then a pause. Then a repeat. Long . . . short . . . long. It was the truck's air horn that had given him the idea. It only *sounded* like Morse, but what Vince was flashing with his brake-light *was* Morse.

It was the letter R.

Roy and Peaches might pick it up, Lemmy for sure. And Race? Did they still teach Morse? Had the kid learned it in his war, where squad-leaders carried GPS units and bombs were guided around the curve of the world by satellite?

The left turn to Cumba was coming up. Vince had just time enough to flash R one more time. Now he was almost back with the others. He shot his hand left in a gesture The Tribe knew well: *follow me off the highway.* Laughlin saw it—as Vince had expected—and surged forward. At the same time he did, Vince twisted his throttle again. The Vulcan screamed and leaped forward. He banked right, along the main road. The others followed. But not the truck. LAUGHLIN had already started its turn onto the Cumba spur. If the driver had tried to correct for the main road, he would have rolled his rig.

Vince felt a white throb of elation and reflexively closed his left hand into a triumphant fist. *We did it! We fucking did it! By the time he gets that fat-ass truck turned around, we'll be nine miles from h—*

The thought broke off like a branch as he looked again into his rearview. There were three bikes behind him, not four: Lemmy, Peaches, and Roy.

Vince swiveled to the left, hearing the old bones crackle in his back, knowing what he would see. He saw it. The truck, dragging a huge rooster-tail of red dust, its tanker too dirty to shine. But there was shine fifty or so yards in front of it; the gleam of the chromed pipes and engine belonging to a Softail Deuce. Race either did not understand Morse, didn't believe what he was seeing, or hadn't seen at all. Vince remembered the waxy, fixed expression on his son's face, and thought this last possibility was most likely. Race had stopped paying attention to the rest of them—had stopped *seeing* them—the moment he understood LAUGHLIN was not just a truck out of control, but one bent on tribal slaughter. He had been just aware enough to spot Vince's hand gesture, but had lost all the rest to a kind of tunnel vision. What was that? Panic? Or a kind of animal selfishness? Or were they the same, when you came down to it?

Race's Harley slipped behind a low swell of hill. The truck disappeared after it and then there was only blowing dust. Vince tried to catch his flying thoughts and put them in some coherent order. If his memory was right again—he knew it was asking a lot of it; he hadn't been this way in a couple of years—then the spur-road ran through Cumba before veering back to rejoin Highway 6 about nine miles ahead. If Race could stay in front—

Except.

Except, unless things had changed, the road went to hardpan

dirt beyond Cumba, and was apt to drift across sandy at this time of year. The truck would do okay, but a motorcycle . . .

The chances of Race surviving the last four miles of that nine-mile run weren't good. The chances of him dumping the Deuce and being run over were, on the other hand, excellent.

Images of Race tried to crowd his mind. Race on his Big Wheel: the Kindergarten warrior. Race staring at him from the back seat of the GTO, the Popsicle melting, his eyes bright with hate, the lower lip quivering. Race at eighteen, wearing a uniform and a fuck-you smile, both present and accounted for and all squared away.

Last of all came the image of Race dead on the hardpan, a smashed doll with only his leathers holding him together.

Vince swept the pictures away. They were no help. The cops wouldn't be, either. There *were* no cops, not in Cumba. If someone saw the semi chasing the bike, he might call the State Police, but the closest one was apt to be in Show Low, drinking java and eating pie and flirting with the waitress while Travis Tritt played on the Rock-Ola.

There was only them. But that was nothing new.

He thrust his hand to the right, then made a fist and patted the air with it. The other three swung over to the side behind him, engines clobbering, the air over their straight-pipes shimmering.

Lemmy pulled up beside him, his face haggard and cheesy-yellow. "*He didn't see the taillight signal!*" he shouted.

"*Didn't see or didn't understand!*" Vince yelled back. He was trembling. Maybe it was just the bike throbbing under him. "*Comes to the same! Time for Little Boy!*"

For a moment Lemmy didn't understand. Then he twisted around, and yanked the straps on his righthand saddlebag. No fancy plastic hardcase for Lemmy. Lemmy was old school all the way.

While he was rooting, there was a sudden, gunning roar. That was Roy. Roy had had enough. He wheeled around and shot back east, his shadow now running before him, a scrawny black gantry-man. On the back of his leather vest was a hideous joke: **NO RETREAT NO SURRENDER.**

"Come back, Klowes, you dickwad!" Peaches bellowed. His hand slipped from his clutch. The Beezer, still in gear, lurched forward almost over Vince's foot, passed high-octane gas, and stalled. Peaches was almost hurled off, but didn't seem to notice. He was still looking back. He shook his fist; his scant gray hair whirled around his long, narrow skull. *"Come back you chicken-shit DICK-WAAAAD!"*

Roy didn't come back. Roy didn't even *look* back.

Peaches turned to Vince. Tears streamed down cheeks sun-flayed by a million rides and ten million beers. In that moment he looked older than the desert he stood on.

"You're stronger'n me, Vince, but I got me a bigger asshole. You rip his head off; I'll be in charge of shittin' down his neck."

"Hurry up!" Vince shouted at Lemmy. *"Hurry up, goddamn you!"*

Just when he thought Lemmy was going to come up empty, his old running buddy straightened with Little Boy in his gloved hand.

The Tribe did not ride with guns. Outlaw motorheads like them never did. They all had records, and any cop in Nevada would be delighted to put one of them away for thirty years on a gun charge. One, or all of them. They carried knives, but knives were no good in this situation; witness what had happened to Roy's machete, which had turned out as useless as the man himself. Except when it came to killing stoned little girls in high school sweaters, that was.

Little Boy, however, while not strictly legal, was not a gun. And the one cop who'd looked at it ("while searching for drugs"—the pigs were always doing that, it was what they lived for) had given Lemmy a skate when Lemmy explained it was more reliable than a road-flare if you broke down at night. Maybe the cop knew what he was looking at, maybe not, but he knew that Lemmy was a veteran. Not just from Lemmy's veteran's licence plate, which could have been stolen, but because the cop had been a vet himself. "Au Shau Valley, where the shit smells sweeter," he'd said, and they had both laughed and even ended up bumping fists.

Little Boy was an M84 stun grenade, more popularly known as a flash-bang. Lemmy had been carrying it in his saddlebag for maybe five years, always saying it would come in handy someday when the other guys—Vince included—ribbed him about it.

Someday had turned out to be today.

"Will this old sonofabitch still work?" Vince shouted as he hung Little Boy over his handlebars by the strap. It didn't look like a grenade. It looked like a combination Thermos bottle and aerosol can. The only grenade-y thing about it was the pull-ring duct-taped to the side.

"I don't know! I don't even know how you can—"

Vince had no time to discuss logistics. He only had a vague idea of what the logistics might be, anyway. *"I have to ride! That fuck's gonna come out on the other end of the Cumba road! I mean to be there when he does!"*

"And if Race ain't in front of him?" Lemmy asked. They had been shouting until now, all jacked up on adrenaline. It was almost a surprise to hear a nearly normal tone of voice.

"One way or the other," Vince said. "You don't have to come. Either of you. I'll understand if you want to turn back. He's my boy."

"Maybe so," Peaches said, "but it's our Tribe. Was, anyway." He jumped down on the Beezer's kick, and the hot engine rumbled to life. "I'll ride witcha, Cap."

Lemmy just nodded and pointed at the road.

Vince took off.

It wasn't as far as he'd thought: seven miles instead of nine. They met no cars or trucks. The road was deserted, traffic maybe avoiding it because of the construction back the way they had come.

Vince snapped constant glances to his left. For a while he saw red dust rising, the truck dragging half the desert along in its slip-stream. Then he lost sight even of its dust, the Cumba spur dropping well out of sight behind hills with eroded, chalky sides.

Little Boy swung back and forth on its strap. Army surplus. *Will this old sonofabitch still work?* he'd asked Lemmy, and now realized he could have asked the same question of himself. How long since he had been tested this way, running dead out, throttle to the max? How long since the whole world came down to only two choices; live pretty or die laughing? And how had his own son, who looked so cool in his new leathers and his mirrored sunglasses, missed such an elementary equation?

Live pretty or die laughing, but don't you run. Don't you fucking run.

Maybe Little Boy would work, maybe it wouldn't, but Vince knew he was going to take his shot, and it made him giddy. If the guy was buttoned up in his cab, it was a lost cause in any case. But he hadn't been buttoned up back at the diner. Back there, his hand had been lolling out against the side of the truck. And later, hadn't he waved them ahead from that same open window? Sure. Sure he had.

Seven miles. Five minutes, give or take. Long enough for a lot of memories of his son, whose father had taught him to change oil but never to bait a hook; to gap plugs but never how you told a coin from the Denver mint from one that had been struck in San Francisco. Time to think how Race had pushed for this stupid meth deal, and how Vince had gone along even though he knew it was stupid, because it seemed he had something to make up for. Only the time for make-up calls was past. As Vince tore along at eighty-five, bending as low as he could get to cut the wind resistance, a terrible thought crossed his mind, one he inwardly recoiled from but could not blot out—that maybe it would be better for all concerned if LAUGHLIN *did* succeed in running his son down. It wasn't the image of Race lifting a shovel into the air and then bringing it down on a helpless man's head, in a spoiled rage over lost money, although that was bad enough. It was something more. It was the fixed, empty look on the kid's face right before he steered his bike the wrong way, onto the Cumba road. For himself, Vince had not been able to stop looking back at the Tribe, the whole way down the canyon, as some were run down and the others struggled to stay ahead of the big machine. Whereas Race had seemed incapable of turning that stiff neck of his. There was nothing behind him that he needed to see. Maybe never had been.

There came a loud *ka-pow* at Vince's back, and a yell he heard even over the wind and the steady blat of the Vulcan's engine: *"Mutha-FUCK!"* He looked in the rear-view mirror and saw Peaches falling back. Smoke was boiling from between his pipestem legs, and oil slicked the road behind him in a fan shape that widened as his ride slowed. The Beez had finally blown its head-gasket. A wonder it hadn't happened sooner.

Peaches waved them on . . . not that Vince would have stopped. Because in a way, the question of whether Race was redeemable was moot. Vince himself was not redeemable; none of them were. He remembered an Arizona cop who'd once pulled them over and said, "Well, look what the road puked up." And that was what they were: road-puke. But those bodies back there had, until this afternoon, been his running buddies, the only thing he had of any value in the world. They had been Vince's brothers in a way, and Race was his son, and you couldn't drive a man's family to earth and expect to live. You couldn't leave them butchered and expect to ride away. If LAUGHLIN didn't know that, he would.

Soon.

Lemmy couldn't keep up with the Tojo Mojo El Rojo. He fell further and further behind. That was all right. Vince was just glad Lemmy still had his six.

Up ahead, a sign: WATCH FOR LEFT-ENTERING TRAFFIC.

The road coming out of Cumba. It was hardpan dirt, as he had feared. Vince slowed, then stopped, turned off the Vulcan's engine.

Lemmy pulled up beside. There was no guardrail here. Here in this one place, where 6 rejoined the Cumba road, the highway was level with the desert, although not far ahead it began to climb away from the floodplain once more, turning into the cattle chute again.

"Now we wait," Lemmy said, switching his engine off as well.

Vince nodded. He wished he still smoked. He told himself that either Race was still shiny-side-up and in front of the truck, or he wasn't. It was beyond his control. It was true, but it didn't help.

"Maybe he'll find a place to turn off in Cumba," Lemmy said. "An alley or somethin' where the truck can't go."

"I don't think so. Cumba is nothing. A gas station and I think a couple houses, all stuck right on the side of a fucking hill. That's bad road. At least for Race. No easy way off it." He didn't even try to tell Lemmy about Race's blank, locked-down expression, a look that said he wasn't seeing anything except the road right in front of his bike. Cumba would be a blur and flash that he only registered after it was well behind him.

"Maybe—" Lemmy began, but Vince held up his hand, silencing him. They cocked their heads to the left.

They heard the truck first, and Vince felt his heart sink. Then, buried in its roar, the bellow of another motor. There was no mistaking the distinctive blast of a Harley running full out.

"He made it!" Lemmy yelled, and raised his hand for a high-five. Vince wouldn't give it. Bad luck. And besides, the kid still had to make the turn back onto 6. If he was going to dump, it would be there.

A minute ticked by. The sound of the engines grew louder. A second minute, and now they could see dust rising over the nearest hills. Then, in a notch between the two closest hills, they saw a flash of sun on chrome. There was just time to glimpse Race, bent almost flat over his handlebars, long hair streaming out behind, and then he was gone again. A second after he disappeared—surely no more—the truck flashed through the notch, stacks shooting smoke. LAUGHLIN on the side was no longer visible; it had been buried beneath a layer of dust.

Vince hit the Vulcan's starter and the engine bammed to life. He gunned the throttle and the frame vibrated.

"Luck, Cap," Lemmy said.

Vince opened his mouth to reply, but in that moment, emotion, intense and unexpected, choked off his wind. So instead of speaking, he gave Lemmy a brief, grateful nod, before taking off. Lemmy followed. As always, Lemmy had his six.

Vince's mind turned into a computer, trying to figure speed versus distance. It had to be timed just right. He rolled toward the intersection at fifty, dropped it to forty, then twisted the throttle again as Race appeared, the bike swerving around a tumbleweed, actually going airborne on a couple of bumps. The truck was no more than thirty feet behind. When Race neared the **Y** where the Cumba bypass once more joined the main road, he slowed. He had to slow. The instant he did, LAUGHLIN vaulted forward, eating up the distance between them.

"*Jam that motherfuck!*" Vince screamed, knowing Race couldn't hear over the bellow of the truck. He screamed it again anyway: "*JAM that motherfuck! Don't slow down!*"

The trucker planned to slam the Harley in the rear wheel, spinning it out. Race's bike hit the crotch of the intersection and surged, Race leaning far to the left, holding the handlebars only with the tips of his fingers. He looked like a trick rider on a trained mustang. The truck missed the rear fender, its blunt nose lunging into thin air that had held a Harley's back wheel only a tenth of a second before . . . but at first Vince thought Race was going to lose it anyway, just spin out.

He didn't. His high-speed arc took him all the way to the far side of Route 6, close enough to the bike-killing shoulder to spume up dust, and then he was scat-gone, gunning down Route 6 toward Show Low.

The truck went out into the desert to make its own turn, rumbling and bouncing, the driver down-shifting through the gears fast enough to make the whole rig shudder, the tires churning up a fog of dust that turned the blue sky white. It left a trail of deep tracks and crushed sagebrush before regaining the road and once more setting out after Vince's son.

Vince twisted the left handgrip and the Vulcan took off. Little Boy swung frantically back and forth on the handlebars. Now came the easy part. It might get him killed, but it would be easy compared to the endless minutes he and Lemmy had waited before hearing Race's motor mixed in with LAUGHLIN's.

His window won't be open, you know. Not after he just got done running through all that dust.

That was also out of his control. If the trucker was buttoned up, he'd deal with that when the moment came.

It wouldn't be long.

The truck was doing around sixty. It could go a lot faster, but Vince didn't mean to let him get all the way through those who-knew-how-many gears of his until the Mack hit warp-speed. He was going to end this now for one of them. Probably for himself, an idea he did not shy from. He would at the least buy Race more time; given a lead, Race could beat the truck to Show Low easily. More than just protecting Race, though, there had to be balance to the scales. Vince had never lost so much so fast, six of The Tribe dead on a stretch of road less than half a mile long. You didn't do that to a man's family, he thought again, and drive away.

Which was, Vince saw at last, maybe LAUGHLIN's own point, his own primary operating principal . . . the reason he had taken them on, in spite of the ten-to-one odds. He had come at them, not knowing or caring if they were armed, picking them off two and three at a time, even though any one of the bikes he had run down could've sent the truck out of control and rolling, first a Mack, and then an oil-stoked fireball. It was madness, but not *incomprehensible* madness. As Vince swung into the lefthand lane and began to close the final distance, the truck's ass-end just ahead on his right, he saw something that seemed not only to sum up this terrible day, but to explain it, in simple, perfectly lucid terms. It was a bumper sticker. It was even filthier than the Cumba sign, but still readable.

PROUD PARENT OF A CORMAN HIGH HONOR ROLL STUDENT!

Vince pulled even with the dust-streaked tanker. In the cab's long driver's-side rearview, he saw something shift. The driver had seen him. In the same second, Vince saw that the window *was* shut, just as he'd feared.

The truck began to slide left, crossing the white line with its outside wheels.

For a moment Vince had a choice: back off or keep going. Then the computer in his head told him the choice was already past; even if he hit the brakes hard enough to risk dumping his ride, the final five feet of the filthy tank would swat him into the guardrail on his left like a fly.

Instead of backing off he increased speed even as the left lane shrank, the truck forcing him toward that knee-high ribbon of gleaming steel. He yanked the flash-bang from the handlebars, breaking the strap. He tore the duct-tape away from the pull-ring with his teeth, the strap's shredded end spanking his cheek as he did so. The ring began to clatter against Little Boy's perforated barrel. The sun was gone. Vince was flying in the truck's shadow now. The guardrail was less than three feet to his left; the side of the truck three feet to his right and still closing. Vince had reached the plate-hitch between the tanker and the cab. Now he could only see the top of Race's head; the rest of him was blocked by the truck's dirty maroon hood. Race was not looking back.

He didn't think about the next thing. There was no plan, no strategy. It was just his road-puke self saying *fuck you* to the world, as he always had. It was, when you came right down to it, The Tribe's only *raison d'etre.*

As the truck closed in for the killing side-stroke, and with absolutely nowhere to go, Vince raised his right hand and shot the truck-driver the bird.

He was pulling even with the cab now, the truck bulking to his right like a filthy mesa. It was the cab that would take him out.

There was movement from inside: that deeply tanned arm with its Marine Corps tattoo. The muscle in the arm bunched as the window slid down into its slot, and Vince realized the cab, which should have swatted him already, was staying where it was. The trucker meant to do it, of course he did, but not until he had replied in kind. *Maybe we even served in different units together,* Vince thought. *In the Au Shau Valley, say, where the shit smells sweeter.*

The window was down. The hand came out. It started to hatch its own bird, then stopped. The driver had just realized the hand that had given him the finger wasn't empty. It was curled around something. Vince didn't give him time to think about it, and he never saw the trucker's face. All he saw was the tattoo, **DEATH BEFORE DISHONOR**. A good thought, and how often did you get a chance to give someone exactly what they wanted?

Vince caught the ring in his teeth, pulled it, heard the fizz of some chemical reaction starting, and tossed Little Boy in through the window. It didn't have to be a fancy half-court shot, not even a lousy pull-up jumper. Just a lob. He was a magician, opening his hands to set free a dove where a moment before there had been a wadded-up handkerchief.

Now you take me out, Vince thought. *Let's finish this thing right.*

But the truck swerved away from him. Vince was sure it would have come swerving back, if there had been time. That swerve was only reflex, Laughlin trying to get away from a thrown object. But it was enough to save his life, because Little Boy did its thing before the driver could course-correct and drive Vince Adamson off the road.

The cab lit up in a vast white flash, as if God Himself had bent down to take a snapshot. Instead of swerving back to the left, LAUGHLIN veered away to the right, first back into the lane of Route 6 bound for Show Low, then beyond. The tractor flayed the guardrail on the right-hand side of the road, striking up a sheet of copper sparks, a shower of fire, a thousand Catherine wheels going off at once. Vince thought madly of July 4th, Race a child again and sitting in his lap to watch the rockets' red glare, the bombs bursting in air: sky-flares shining in his child's delighted, inky eyes.

Then the truck crunched through the guardrail, shredding it as if it were tinfoil. LAUGHLIN nosed over a twenty foot embankment, into a ravine filled with sand and tumbleweeds. The wheels caught. The truck slued. The big tanker rammed forward into the back of the cab. Vince had shot beyond that point before he could brake to a stop, but Lemmy saw it all: saw the cab and the tanker form a V and then split apart; saw the tanker roll first and the cab a second or two after; saw the tanker burst open and then blow. It went up in a fireball and a greasy pillar of black smoke. The cab rolled past it, over and over, the cube shape turning into a senseless crumple of maroon that sparked hot shards of sun where bare metal had split out in prongs and hooks.

It landed with the driver's window up to the sky, about eighty feet away from the pillar of fire that had been its cargo. By then Vince was running back along his own skid-mark. He saw the figure that tried to pull itself through the misshapen window. The face turned toward him, except there was no face, only a mask of blood. The driver emerged to the waist before collapsing back inside. One tanned arm—the one with the tattoo—stuck up like a submarine's periscope. The hand dangled limp on the wrist.

Vince stopped at Lemmy's bike, gasping for breath. For a moment he thought he was going to pass out, but he leaned over, put his hands on his knees, and presently felt a little better.

"You got him, Cap." Lemmy's voice was hoarse with emotion.

"We better make sure," Vince said. Although the stiff periscope arm and the hand dangling limp at the end of it suggested that would just be a formality.

"Why not?" Lemmy said. "I gotta take a piss, anyway."

"You're not pissing on him, dead or alive," Vince said.

There was an approaching roar: Race's Harley. He pulled up in a showy skid stop, killed the engine, and got off. His face, although dusty, glowed with delight and triumph. Vince hadn't seen Race look that way since the kid was twelve. He had won a dirt-track race in a quarter-midget Vince had built for him, a yellow torpedo with a souped-up Briggs & Stratton engine. Race had come leaping from the cockpit with that exact same expression on his face, right after taking the checkered flag.

He threw his arms around Vince and hugged him. "You did it! You *did* it, Dad! You cooked his fucking ass!"

For a moment Vince allowed the hug. Because it had been so long. And because this was his spoiled son's better angel. Everybody had one; even at his age, and after all he had seen, Vince believed that. So for a moment he allowed the hug, and relished the warmth of his son's body, and promised himself he would remember it.

Then he put his hands against Race's chest and pushed him away. Hard. Race stumbled backward on his custom snakeskin boots, the expression of love and triumph fading—

No, not fading. *Merging.* Becoming the look Vince had come to know so well: distrust and dislike. *Quit, why don't you? That's not dislike and never was.*

No, not dislike. Hate, bright and glowing.

All squared away, sir, and fuck you.

"What was her name?" Vince asked.

"What?"

"Her name, John." He hadn't called Race by his actual name in years, and there was no one to hear it now but them. Lemmy was sliding down the soft earth of the embankment, toward the crushed metal ball that had been LAUGHLIN's cab, letting them have this tender father-son moment in privacy.

"What's wrong with you?" Pure scorn. But when Vince reached out and tore off those fucking mirror shades, he saw the truth in John "Race" Adamson's eyes. He knew what this was about. Vince was coming in five-by, as they used to say in Nam. Did they still say that in Iraq, he wondered, or had it gone the way of Morse Code?

"What do you want to do now, John? Go on to Show Low? Roust Clarke's sister for money that isn't there?"

"It could be there." Sulking now. He gathered himself. "It *is* there. I know Clarke. He trusted that whore."

"And The Tribe? Just . . . what? Forget them? Dean and Ellis and all the others? Doc?"

"They're dead." He eyed his father. "Too slow. And most of them too old." *You too*, the cool eyes said.

Lemmy was on his way back, his boots puffing up dust. He had something in his hand.

"What was her name?" Vince repeated. "Clarke's girlfriend. What was her name?"

"Fuck's it matter?" He paused then, struggling to win Vince back, his expression coming as close as it ever did to pleading. "Jesus. Leave it, why don't you? We *won*. We *showed* him."

"You knew Clarke. Knew him in Fallujah, knew him back here in The World. You were tight. If you knew him, you knew her. What was her name?"

"Janey. Joanie. Something like that."

Vince slapped him. Race blinked, startled. Dropped for a moment back to ten years old. But just for a moment. In another instant the hating look was back; a sick, curdled glare.

"He heard us talking back there in that diner parking lot. The trucker," Vince said. Patiently. As if speaking to the child this young man had once been. The young man he had risked his life to save. Ah, but that had been instinct, and he wouldn't have changed it. It was the one good thing in all this horror. This filth. Not that he had been the only one operating on filial instinct. "He knew he couldn't take us there, but he couldn't let us go, either. So he waited. Bided his time. Let us get ahead of him."

"I have no clue what you're talking about!" Very forceful. Only he was lying, and they both knew it.

"He knew the road and went after us where the terrain favored him. Like any good soldier."

Yes. And then had pursued them with a single-minded purpose, regardless of the almost certain cost to himself. Laughlin had settled on death before dishonor. Vince knew nothing about him, but felt suddenly that he liked him better than his own son. Such a thing should not have been possible, but there it was.

"You're fucked in the head," Race said.

"I don't think so. For all we know, he was going to see her when we crossed his path at the diner. It's what a father might do for a kid he loved. Arrange things so he could look in, every now and then. See if she might even want a ride out. Take a chance on something besides the pipe and the rock."

Lemmy rejoined them. "Dead," he said.

Vince nodded.

"This was on the visor." He handed it to Vince. Vince didn't want to look at it, but he did. It was a snapshot of a smiling girl with her hair in a ponytail. She wore a CORMAN HIGH VARSITY sweatshirt, the same one she had died in. She was sitting on the front bumper of LAUGHLIN, her back resting against the silver grill. She was wearing her daddy's camo cap turned around backwards and mock-saluting and struggling not to grin. Saluting who? Laughlin himself, of course. Laughlin had been holding the camera.

"Her name was Jackie Laughlin," Race said. "And she's dead, too, so fuck her."

Lemmy started forward, ready to pull Race off his bike and feed him his teeth, but Vince held him back with a look. Then he shifted his gaze back to his boy.

"Ride on, son," he said. "Keep the shiny side up."

Race looked at him, not understanding.

"But don't stop in Show Low, because I intend to let the cops know a certain little whore might need protection. I'll tell them some nut killed her brother, and she might be next."

"And what are you going to tell them when they ask how you happened to come by that information?"

"Everything," Vince said, his voice calm. Serene even. "Better get moving. Ride on. It's what you do best. Keeping ahead of that truck on the Cumba road . . . that was something. I'll give you that. You got a gift for hightailing it. Not much else, but you got that. So hightail your ass out of here."

Race looked at him, unsure and suddenly frightened. But that wouldn't last. He'd get his fuck-you back. It was all he had: some fuck-you attitude, a pair of mirrored sunglasses, and a fast bike.

"Dad—"

"Better go on, son," Lemmy said. "Someone will have seen that smoke by now. There'll be Staties here soon."

Race smiled. When he did, a single tear spilled from his left eye and cut a track through the dust on his face. "Just a couple of old chickenshits," he said.

He went back to his bike. The chains across the insteps of his snakeskin boots jingled . . . a little foolishly, Vince thought.

Race swung his leg over the seat, started his Harley, and drove away west, toward Show Low. Vince did not expect him to look back and was not disappointed.

They watched him. After a while, Lemmy said: "You want to go, Cap?"

"No place to go, man. I think I might just sit here for a bit, side of the road."

"Well," Lemmy said. "If you want. I guess I could sit some myself."

They went to the side of the road and sat down crosslegged like old Indians with no blankets to sell and watched the tanker burn in the desert, piling black oilsmoke into the blue, unforgiving sky. Some of it drifted back their way, reeking and greasy.

"We can move," Vince said. "If you don't like the smell."

Lemmy tipped his head back and inhaled deeply, like a man considering the bouquet of a pricey wine.

"No, I don't mind it. Smells like Vietnam."

Vince nodded.

"Makes me think of them old days," Lemmy said. "When we were almost as fast as we believed we were."

Vince nodded again. "Live pretty—"

"Yep. Or die laughin'."

They said nothing more after that, just sat there, waiting, Vince with the girl's picture in his hand. Every once in a while, he glanced at it, turning it in the sun, considering how young she looked, and how happy.

But mostly he watched the fire.

RECALLED

A Sequel to "The Distributor"

BY F. PAUL WILSON

In this story F. Paul Wilson speculates on the eventual fate of Theodore Gordon, Richard Matheson's destructive protagonist who wrecked the lives of his neighbors in the classic 1958 tale "The Distributor." Mr. Wilson is the author of more than thirty novels, including the long-running Repairman Jack series (*The Tomb, Legacies*, and many more) and his Adversary Cycle (including *The Keep*, made into a feature film in 1983, and *Nightworld*).

RECALLED

Time to move.

Monday, April 26

Another town, another rental in another peaceful, unsuspecting neighborhood.

That was the easy part. As for the rest . . . it used to be so much simpler.

Listen to me, he thought. I sound like an old fart.

Well, he *was* an old fart. He'd been at this for decades, but instead of becoming routine, it had grown increasingly difficult. And he knew the problem wasn't with him.

The world had changed.

Used to be reputations could be ruined with a mere hint of impropriety—adultery, drunkenness, wantonness, porn peeping. Now it was anything goes. Only incest and pedophilia seemed to lack champions in the mass media, and it was anyone's guess as to how long before their paladins appeared and hoisted their flags.

People daily bragged on TV about what in the good old days would have had them afraid to show their faces in public. And nowadays the love that once dared not speak its name would not shut up.

But other, newer taboos had arisen from what used to be a matter of course.

And the ability to improvise was the greatest asset of an effective distributor.

The last town had been a quiet little place in central Jersey known as Veni Woods. He'd called himself Clay Evanson there, a name he'd used before, way back when. Just last week, before arriving here in Wolverton, a quaint little town on Long Island's south shore, he decided to use another alias from the past: Theodore Gordon.

Every night before his arrival he'd closed his eyes and made the name his own. He was Theodore Gordon. All other names faded. He was Theodore Gordon and no one else.

After a little research, he found a furnished rental in the racially mixed Pine View Estates development on the eastern end of town. It had come down to a choice between that and another area half a mile west, but when he saw a woman wearing a striped hijab get out of a Dodge SUV on Fannen Street in Pine View and let herself into one of the houses, his decision was made.

He'd spent last Thursday night introducing himself around. As usual, he was a widower—not quite two years since his poor, dear Denise passed—and a financial consultant who worked from home, renting with intent to buy. Seven other houses made up this block of Fannen Street. He met the McCuins and their sullen fifteen-year-old son, Colin; the very Catholic Fabrinis and Robinsons; the waspish Woolbrights; the irreligious Hispanic Garcias with their noisy dog; the Muslim Rashids; and the very black Longwells. He made a point of inquiring at each stop about the best Internet access in the area. This induced Mr. Robinson and Mr. Woolbright to brag about the wi-fi networks they'd installed in their homes. Theodore had been hoping for one; two was a blessing.

Over the weekend he'd used his digital Nikon with the telephoto lens to snap photos of as many of his neighbors as possible as they worked in the garden or mowed the lawn, washed the car, or collected the mail. Between shoots he'd wandered Fannen Street, saying hello, helping unload a van, or transplant a bush. In the process he'd managed to see most of the backyards.

Since the Catholics held the majority, he'd attended mass at St. Bartholomew's yesterday morning, making sure he introduced himself to Father Bain in sight of the Fabrinis and Robinsons.

Tonight he'd be ready to go. He'd made starting on Monday a tradition.

The Pine View houses all sat on well-wooded half-acre lots. Four of the homes on this block—the Longwell, Woolbright, Rashid, and Fabrini places across the street—backed up to the woods that lent the development its name. His place sat directly across from the Rashids; the Robinsons were stage left on the corner, the Garcias next door to the right, and the McCuins next door to them on the far corner.

He spent the daylight hours observing the comings and goings and refining his notes. Mr. Robinson and Mr. Rashid carpooled. This was Mr. Rashid's week to drive. Theodore watched Mr. Robinson open the rear door to Mr. Rashid's car, place his briefcase on the seat, then take the passenger seat in front. Mrs. Rashid, a secretary at the grammar school, drove Robinson's girl, Chelsea, to school along with her own daughter, Farah, both ten.

Theodore noted the times of the comings and goings of everyone on the block. Today's were all consistent with last week's.

He admired consistency.

During the course of the day he used his laptop to access Mr. Robinson's wi-fi network next door, but could not enter the system due to a firewall. He would work on breaching that during the week. Firewalls were handy in that they gave people a false sense of security. He'd try the Woolbrights tonight.

Shortly before midnight he wound his way among the pines behind the houses across the street until he came to the rear extreme of the

Woolbrights' property. There he turned on his laptop and slowly made his way closer to the darkened house, stopping every dozen feet or so to see if he could access the wi-fi signal from their home network.

He could, and when it was good and strong, he tapped in and discovered that Mr. Woolbright had accommodatingly left his computer on and his webmail program open. Theodore had found this increasingly common over the years. Folks liked to hop out of bed and check their email before running off to work, and didn't want to fuss with all that log-in nonsense.

Theodore found that Mrs. Woolbright's password was also stored and so he switched over to her account and logged in to the *Village Voice*'s online classified site. There he used her email address to apply for membership. He waited for the verification email, then followed the instructions. As soon as he was officially registered, he placed an ad as Mr. Woolbright in the *men-seeking-men* category. He described himself as "rich and horny and into young stuff. Send a picture or no go."

That done, he turned off his computer and crept to the tool shed by the fence between the Woolbright and Robinson properties. Easing open the door, he slipped a couple of gay porn magazines inside, then re-closed it.

When he returned home he removed a tray of ice cubes from his freezer and carried it to the extra bedroom on the second floor. He raised the window and the screen about twelve inches, then pulled his Firestorm High Performance slingshot from the night table drawer. He popped an ice cube out of the tray, loaded it into the sling, then winged it toward the wooden doghouse where Daisy, the Garcias' short-furred bitch mutt, spent her nights. Theodore had become expert with the slingshot over the years, and rarely missed, even at this distance.

The cube shattered against the doghouse, startling Daisy to full-throated wakefulness. She rushed out with a howl that progressed to frenzied barking. Finally, after inspecting the six-foot picket fence that defined the perimeter of her domain, she quieted down. With some satisfied gruffs, growls, and grumbles, she returned to her abode.

Theodore gave her time to settle down, then let fly another cube.

As Daisy repeated her howls and barks, he heard Mr. McCuin shout from a window on the Garcias' far side, "For Christ sake, Garcia, shut up that goddamn mutt or bring her inside!"

Theodore closed the screen and the window.

He made an entry in his ledger and went to bed.

A good start.

Tuesday, April 27

He waited until 9:30 A.M., watching the various carpool and solitary departures, before knocking on the Woolbrights' door. He'd learned last Thursday that Mrs. Woolbright was a stay-at-home wife.

She looked pale and uncertain when she answered. Perhaps she had received some disturbing emails. He gave her his brightest smile.

"Good morning, Mrs. Woolbright. My lawnmower seems to be on the fritz and I was wondering if I might borrow your husband's."

"My husband's?" She blinked and paused, as if she were translating the words. "Oh, yes. I suppose so. It's around back in the shed."

"Could you show me?" To underscore his probity, he added, "I'll walk around the side and meet you there."

They converged at the shed in the backyard.

"It's in here." She pulled open the doors.

"Thank you."

He waited for her to notice the magazines, then realized they weren't there. He poked his head in and looked around, but they were gone.

He took hold of the lawnmower handle and pulled it out, wondering if they had slipped beneath. But no . . . no magazines.

"Did your husband come out to the shed this morning?"

"What? No. He was running late. Skipped breakfast and ran. In a big hurry to get to . . . the city."

"Yes. I'm sure. I'll be sure to have it back by tonight."

She only nodded, looking distracted.

Theodore wheeled the mower across the street. Where were those magazines? He'd ponder that while he mowed the grass—something he hadn't counted on. He always hired a lawn service whenever he moved into a new town, but he'd put it off because of the Woolbrights. Today he'd planned to be so upset by the sight of those magazines that he'd forget about the mower. But now that he had it, he was obliged to use it.

He turned off the mower. Finally. He'd forgotten what a noisy, monotonous chore it was. Plus he was no spring chicken. He was puffing a little and had wet rings in his armpits. He'd clean off the mower—always be a good neighbor—and wait for Mr. Woolbright's return before wheeling it back across the street. Might catch an earful of domestic strife along the way—though not as much as there could have been had she found those magazines. Someone had taken them. But who?

He saw the mail truck pull up to his box. Even though he'd never receive anything but flyers and contest come-ons at this address, he'd introduced himself to the mailman, whose name was Phil. He waved and Phil waved back.

After the mail truck moved on, Theodore slipped into the backyard and stood behind the big rhododendron next to the post-and-rail fence that divided his property from the Robinsons'. The bush shielded him from the street. Once he was sure no one was in line of sight, he climbed over the fence. In the old days he would have hopped it, but he wasn't as spry or as flexible as he used to be.

He hurried to their back door. When helping Mr. Robinson transplant a spirea on Saturday, he'd noted that the back door lock was a Schlage. He inserted a Schlage bump key, gave it a twist as he tapped it with a little rubber hammer, and he was in. He'd seen no evidence of an alarm system on his introductory visit, so no worry about disarming that.

He hurried upstairs and had no problem locating Chelsea Robinson's room—pink wallpaper, posters of the latest boy group. He went to her dresser and found her underwear drawer. He removed a pair of panties—pink, of course—and stuffed them into his pocket.

Then he was on his way down the stairs, out the way he'd come in—making sure to lock the door behind him—and back over the fence.

Five minutes from leaving his yard to returning. And no one the wiser.

Now that he had the panties, he could pick which photos of Chelsea to print out.

He watched the Rashid house until all was dark except for the glow of a TV from the master bedroom. He'd printed out half a dozen photos of Chelsea—close ups of her face, and crops centered on her flat chest and her little rump. With these trapped under his shirt, and the panties in his pocket, he stole across the street and into the Rashids' backyard. On Sunday he'd helped carry bags of wood-chip mulch from the van to the rear, and had made note that the backdoor to their garage was secured by another Schlage. No surprise. Development builders invariably used the same hardware on their houses.

A tap and a twist of the bump key and he was in. He opened the rear passenger door of Mr. Rashid's Volvo sedan and placed the photos and the panties on the floor where the pink could not fail to catch Mr. Robinson's eye. Then he would see the photos beneath.

Theodore pulled out a penlight and snooped around until he came upon an expensive-looking socket wrench set. He tucked that under his arm and slipped back outside, locking the door behind him.

Before heading for the Longwell house, he detoured to the Fabrinis' front yard where he pulled up every geranium Mr. Fabrini had planted over the weekend and scattered them across the front lawn.

He strolled the starlit street to the other end of the block where he slipped into the back of the Longwells' corner lot and hid the wrench set under the deck.

Back home, he slung ice cubes at Daisy's doghouse until Mr. McCuin screamed again from his window.

After making his daily entry in the ledger, he went to bed.

Wednesday, April 28

Theodore had set his alarm to be sure he'd be awake to see Mr. Rashid pick up Mr. Robinson. He'd given himself enough time to make coffee first.

So now, steaming cup in hand, he sat by his front picture window to wait and watch.

Right on time, Mr. Rashid pulled out of his garage and backed into the street. Equally punctual, Mr. Robinson strode from his front door to the Rashid sedan. He opened the rear door . . .

. . . now we begin . . .

. . . and placed his briefcase in the rear . . .

. . . here we go . . .

. . . then slammed the door and slipped into the passenger seat. Mr. Rashid gunned the car and off they went.

Theodore found himself on his feet, staring through the window. How could Robinson have missed the panties and the pictures? Impossible. Unless . . .

Unless they weren't there.

He focused on the yard next to the Rashids where he'd pulled all the geraniums last night . . . where the lawn should have been littered with dead or dying plants.

But wasn't. At least it didn't appear so from here.

He threw on some clothes and hurried outside, slowing as he reached the sidewalk. Had to be calm. Had to appear to be going for a morning stroll, a constitutional, as they used to say back in the day.

But his inner pace was anything but leisurely as he passed the Fabrini yard and saw that each and every geranium he'd torn out last night had been replanted. He might have convinced himself that he'd dreamed what he'd done but for the orange petals and scattered clumps of potting dirt here and there on the lawn.

He heard a garage door rolling and saw Mr. Fabrini smiling and waving as he backed out of his driveway.

"Good morning!" he called. "Beautiful day, isn't it?"

Theodore nodded. "Yes. Beautiful."

Another wave, another smile—"Have a good one!"—and Mr. Fabrini was on his way, acting nothing at all like a man who'd been forced to spend his first waking hours repairing mindless vandalism. Theodore had been all set to tell him that he'd glanced out his window last night and thought he'd seen the McCuin boy in the front yard, but no point now.

Someone was on to him.

Hard to see how that was possible. He knew no one in town, especially on this block, and no one knew him.

Or was he wrong about that?

He supposed it was possible. In fact, statistically it might even be inevitable that after all these years he would run into someone from a previous distribution point.

But he was always so careful, so circumspect. How could some-one connect him with the unfortunate incidents that occurred during his brief stays?

He couldn't avoid the possibility that someone had. Judging

from the missing porn magazines, the replanted geraniums, and what he had to assume were the missing panties and photos, the possibility looked more like a certainty.

Someone was undoing his work. And that meant someone was following him around, watching his every move.

But who?

He was sure he would have noticed.

It had to be someone with good tracking skills—and other skills as well. Theodore had locked the Rashids' garage door behind him. To remove the panties and photos, the one shadowing him would have to be adept at lock picking.

Who, damn it?

He took a deep breath and told himself to be calm. He prided himself on never becoming upset, never emotionally involved. This was a job, and he a professional.

And a professional could always outthink an amateur.

He spent the rest of the day planning and making a few purchases. Mid-afternoon he placed one call using his untraceable ATT Go Phone.

"Mrs. Woolbright?" he said when she answered, dropping his voice an octave. "Sorry to bother you. This is Harold Mapleton with the Suffolk County parole board."

"Parole board? I have nothing to do with the parole board."

"Of course you don't, Mrs. Woolbright. But your neighbor, Cletus Longwell, does. I'm his parole officer."

"What? He's on parole? For what?"

"Grand theft. But he won't be on parole much longer. His three years will be up next month and I'm just calling to see what kind of neighbor he's been. Any reported thefts around the neighborhood? Anything missing from your premises?"

"No . . . not that I know of."

"Well, good. But ask around, will you? Just in case. Sorry to bother you. Have a nice day."

Shortly before midnight he took his laptop into his yard and tried again to access the Robinsons' wi-fi network but couldn't find the signal.

Frustrated, he took up his position in the extra bedroom and set the Garcia dog to barking until Mr. McCuin screamed from his window.

After that he made a ledger entry but did not go to bed.

Thursday, April 29

Around 1:30 Theodore slipped outside and into the overcast night. He paused in the deeper shadows of the arbor vitae flanking his front door and scanned the neighborhood.

Was someone out there now, watching, waiting to undo his work?

Thursday was garbage pickup day in Pine View Estates. Everyone on the block except Theodore had their cans waiting at curbside. Fannen Street lay empty before him. Still, he had a feeling of being watched. Real? Or paranoia?

He had to assume someone was watching, but could not let that disrupt his schedule. He'd made adjustments to prevent that.

He crossed the street to the Fabrini house and emptied a can of Speed Weed, a fast-acting herbicide, on the geraniums. Nobody was going to save them now. Then he walked to the other end of the block, took the lid off the McCuin garbage can, and left the Speed Weed container on top in plain sight.

Before leaving, he dropped the lid on the grass, pulled a baggy from his pocket, and emptied a dog turd onto it.

Next he stopped back at his place and picked up a ten-quart plastic container and a wrench. Mrs. Robinson always left her car parked in the driveway. Theodore wriggled beneath it and felt around for the drain plug on the crankcase. When he found it he loosened it and let the oil empty into the container. When it was completely drained, he took the container and the plug and carried them across the street, making sure to spill a little oil every six-to-eight feet or so along the way to the Fabrinis' driveway. He left everything in their backyard.

He wondered how far Mrs. Robinson would get before her engine seized up and self-destructed.

Though tired when he returned to his house, sleep was not in tonight's equation. He set himself up in his front window—where he had a pair of Leica night-vision binoculars and a carafe of hot coffee waiting—and settled in to watch. He had no view of the McCuin house; he could see the Fabrinis' front yard but not their back where he'd left the oil and drain plug.

But he could see the Robinson car, right next door, not a hundred feet away. If anyone tried to undo Theodore's work there, he'd spot them and identify them with the help of his binocs. Then he'd start some countermeasures of his own.

Theodore yawned in the dark and checked his watch. Four A.M. Did his quarry suspect that the car was under surveillance? If so—

He felt a cool breeze around his ankles. Where was that coming from?

His chest tightened. He kept all the windows closed. Had someone opened one?

He rose and walked to the stairs. No flow from the second floor. He moved through the dark dining room to the even darker kitchen—

And froze when he saw the back door standing open. He'd locked that, he was sure of it.

His heart pounded as he pushed it closed and scanned the backyard. It hadn't opened itself. What had the intruder wanted? Had he taken anything? What if he was still out there?

Theodore's heart rate doubled as a terrifying possibility struck: What if he was still in the house?

He flipped on the kitchen lights. Nothing out of place, nothing obvious missing.

He turned on all the lights on the first floor. No sign of anyone. But what about the second floor? Had he sneaked past while he'd been on sentry duty?

Was he after the ledger? It catalogued all his work. If it fell into the wrong hands—

He dashed upstairs, flipping every light switch within reach as he moved. He fairly leaped into his bedroom, turned on the lights, then dropped to his knees and jammed his hand between the mattress and box spring.

There. The ledger. He pulled it out. Safe.

But why—?

Diversion!

He ran back to the living room and peered at the Robinson car. It stood alone, just as he'd left it.

Relieved but still unsettled, he turned out all the lights and resumed his watch until dawn.

As the neighborhood came alive, Theodore wheeled his garbage can to the curb. There he made a show of stretching and yawning as he glanced down the block toward the McCuin place. He was pleased to see the lid still off their container. He couldn't see the herbicide can but didn't expect to at this distance.

Across the street he saw Mr. Fabrini scratching his head as he looked at one of his gardens. Theodore wandered over.

"Beautiful morning, isn't it?" he said in a most neighborly way.

Mr. Fabrini turned but didn't smile. "What? Oh, hi, Mister Gordon."

"Theodore, please."

"Right. Yeah, beautiful for us maybe." He pointed to the bed of wilted, shriveling geraniums. "But not for these things. Yesterday they were perfect. Today . . ."

Theodore knelt and touched a browning leaf. He rubbed it between his fingers, then sniffed.

"Hmm."

"What?"

Theodore tore off the leaf and handed it to Fabrini.

"Smell."

Mr. Fabrini did and made a face. "It smells . . . chemical."

"Right. Like Round Up or some other weed killer."

Mr. Fabrini looked dumbfounded. "Weed killer? But who . . . ?" His voice trailed off.

Theodore leaned closer. "I saw someone in your yard last night. At the time I thought it was you. Now I'm not so sure."

"It wasn't me, I can tell you that. Did you see his face?"

"No, but he looked young . . . like a teenager." He let his gaze drift toward the McCuin house.

Mr. Fabrini followed and said, "You don't think it was Colin, do you?"

Theodore backed away a step, as if the conversation had just entered taboo territory. "I'm not pointing any fingers. Like I said, I didn't see a face." He clapped Mr. Fabrini on the upper arm. "Don't take it personally. Some kids have a lot of anger to work out of their systems." With that he turned and waved. "Have a nice day."

Mr. Fabrini's drive to work would take him past the McCuin house. He'd be looking at it. He'd see the Speed Weed can—if it was still there. If someone had interfered and removed it, no matter. A seed had been planted.

As he crossed the street he glanced at the blacktop, searching for the trail of oil he'd left. Where—?

He stopped and stared at a discolored spot on the pavement. It might have been an oil splotch at one time, but now it was . . . something else. It looked like someone had sprayed it with a detergent solution, emulsifying the oil . . . erasing the trail.

When? When had this happened?

He jumped at the sound of a toot. When he looked around he saw Mr. Rashid smiling and waving from his car. Theodore realized he was standing in the middle of the street.

He managed a smile and stepped toward the curb. As he did he glanced at the Robinson car and almost tripped when he saw the puddle of oil spreading out from beneath it. Where had that come from?

Unless . . . while Theodore had been searching the house for an intruder, perhaps his nemesis had tried to replace the drained oil. But that wouldn't have worked because of the missing drain plug. Whatever he added would have ended on the driveway.

Standing next to the vehicle was a very angry-looking Mr. Robinson.

"What the hell?" he was saying. "What the fucking hell?"

"My goodness," Theodore said, walking over to him. "It looks like you've sprung a leak."

He was looking at the oil. It didn't look fresh at all. In fact it looked well used, ready for a change.

"Leak, hell. The plug's missing. Somebody *did* this."

Theodore put on a shocked expression. "Someone from around *here*?"

"Who knows? But why me?" He looked past Theodore and waved to Mr. Rashid. "Be right there, Munaf."

Theodore made a point of looking up and down the block. "Maybe it was simply opportunity. After all, you are the only one who leaves a car out overnight. Has anyone ever complained about that?"

Robinson made a face. "No. And as for—" He broke off and stepped around to the front of the car, pointing at the driveway. "I'll be damned. Look at this—footprints."

Theodore did look, and hid his shock as he saw clear imprints of treaded footprints—sneakers, most likely—leading from the oil slick, across the driveway, and into the grass between Theodore's house and the Robinsons'.

"They head toward your place."

He started across the grass. Theodore, hiding his alarm, followed to his front walk where Robinson stopped, pointing. "They go right to your front door."

He was right. They were fainter here, but no mistaking them.

He wheeled on Theodore. "What the hell's going on, Gordon?"

Theodore didn't have to feign shock. "You can't think *I* had anything to do with this!"

Robinson pointed to the prints. "What else am I supposed to think?"

"I barely know you. Why would I do this? And I don't own any shoes with soles like that. And have a little respect for my intelligence. Would I be dumb enough to leave a trail right to my front door?"

"Maybe you're a dumbass, what do I know? But I do know there's been some strange shit going on lately."

"Like . . . like what?"

"Like someone hacking into Herb Woolbright's computer system and signing him up for a gay website or classified or some such shit. Herb's about as gay as I am. That convinced me to shut mine down. Yesterday Munaf found his socket wrench set gone, and now my car." He fixed Theodore with a narrow-eyed glare. "Nothing like this ever happened around here before you moved in."

Nothing like this had happened to Theodore so early. Later in a job, when a neighborhood was falling apart, suspicion naturally drifted to the newcomer, but by then he was packing up to leave. This was only day four.

But he held his ground.

"I won't stand here and be spoken to like this. And I warn you, if you slander me with these lies, you'll be hearing from my lawyer."

He turned and stomped to his front door. But once inside, he slumped against the door, mind racing, thoughts whirling.

He went to the window and watched Mr. Fabrini pull out of his driveway and coast down the block. He slowed as he passed the

McCuin house—within a few feet of their open garbage can—but he didn't stop to inspect it, merely drove on.

Theodore ground his teeth. His nemesis had most likely removed the herbicide can. Blocked at every turn. Nothing like this had ever happened before.

An unfamiliar sensation began to burn in his gut: uncertainty. What to do? Abort?

Theodore spent the rest of the day debating it, finally deciding on no—he'd never aborted a job and wasn't about to blemish his record now.

He went to his front window and looked out. The commuters were all home by now, eating dinner or having a drink with their spouses. Well, not everyone. Look at this . . .

Across the street, at the far end of the block, he saw Mr. Rashid and Mr. Longwell in what looked like animated conversation— perhaps even an argument.

He decided a stroll might be in order.

As he neared, he saw Mr. Longwell's usually placid black face contorted in anger.

"So, you're missing something from your garage, and what's the first thing you do? You think of the neighborhood nigger? Is that it?"

Mr. Rashid looked offended. "I have never used the N-word in my life!"

The N-word . . . really, the world had become pathetic.

"You came to me looking for stolen property. Why me? Why not your buddy, Robinson?"

"Because he isn't on parole for robbery!"

Mr. Rashid looked instantly regretful for saying that, while Mr. Longwell gaped in shock.

"What? What did you say? Me? On parole? Where'd you hear that bullshit?"

"Your parole office called Jean Woolbright yesterday and—"

"My *parole* officer?" He stared at the Woolbright house. "I know she never liked us living next door, but I never thought she'd stoop to this. Is she insane?" He glanced at Theodore. "What are you looking at?"

Theodore had hoped his bold stare would trigger just that remark.

"Sorry. I couldn't help overhearing."

"This doesn't concern you."

"Well, I am a member of this community now. Perhaps, as a disinterested third party, I might help mediate this disagreement." Before either could object he turned to Mr. Rashid. "You are apparently missing something, and you think Mister Longwell might have it." He turned to Mr. Longwell. "Since I'm sure you don't, why not let Mister Rashid check your grounds and, say, your garage and—?"

"Nobody's snooping through my property without a search warrant, so you both can go to hell!"

So saying, he turned and stomped back into his house.

"My, my," Theodore said. "You'd think if he had nothing to hide he'd want to clear this up."

Mr. Rashid nodded. "Yes. You'd think he would."

He shook his head and walked away toward his home.

Thinking that this job could yet be salvaged, Theodore continued his walk. Even if his nemesis had removed the wrench set from the Longwell yard, Mr. Longwell's refusal to let Mr. Rashid look would be perceived as a sign of guilt.

He began to whistle.

Around 11:30 he began his nightly task of inciting Daisy. Finally, just shy of midnight, he heard Mr. McCuin shout, "I'm gonna kill that dog if you don't shut it up!"

Just what Theodore had been waiting for.

He waited until Daisy calmed down, then whacked her dog house with another ice cube. As she renewed her frenzied barking, Theodore shut the window and went down to the kitchen refrigerator. He pulled out the nice piece of sirloin he'd been saving. He removed a box of mole poison from under the sink. The label said each tablet contained 1.0 mg. of strychnine. He estimated Daisy's weight at thirty pounds. A dozen tablets would be plenty.

Just to be sure, he cut fifteen angled slits into the meat and pressed a pellet into each.

Thursday, April 29

At exactly 3 A.M. he tossed the meat over the fence so that it landed near Daisy's house. She came out with a howl but stopped when she caught the scent of the meat. She was on it in an instant, wolfing it down in a single gulp.

Good dog.

Next he pulled out another can of Speed Weed and used it to write on Mr. Longwell's lawn. He'd thought of using gasoline to burn the word into the grass, but decided this would be more discrete.

Under normal circumstances he would hide the box of poison in the McCuin garage and the empty herbicide can in the Rashids' bushes, but his nemesis would undoubtedly remove them.

He returned home and stood on his front steps where he surveyed dark and slumbering Fannen Street. He sent out a challenge:

Let's see you undo these.

He was up early the next morning, waiting. At 7:10 he heard Mr. Garcia's distraught wail.

"Daisy? Oh, my God, Daisy!"

Theodore immediately stepped out onto his rear deck and called over the fence.

"Mister Garcia? Is anything wrong?"

"It's Daisy! She's not breathing!"

"Oh, dear. Quick! Bring her around front and I'll get my car and take you to the vet."

Never pass up an opportunity to be a good neighbor.

Theodore comforted the sobbing Mr. Garcia on the way home. Daisy's corpse lay draped across his legs.

"Was the vet sure she was poisoned? Who would do such an awful thing?"

Mr. Garcia's tear-stained face contorted into a mask of rage. "I have a pretty goddamn good idea."

Theodore glanced at Daisy. He'd had nothing against the dog. He had nothing against anyone. Collateral damage.

"Oh, dear," he said as he turned onto Fannen Street and saw the police car. "What's happened here?"

He slowed and watched Mr. Longwell pointing to the browned letters spelling *NIGGER* on his lawn, then down the street toward the Rashid house.

A hate crime was such a terrible thing.

He intended to spend the rest of the day making notes in his ledger and quietly planning his next moves—a productive way to while away the time before Mr. McCuin and Mr. Rashid came home to the inevitable confrontations with, respectively, Mr. Garcia and Mr. Longwell.

A knock on the door interrupted him. He found Phil the postman glaring at him. He thrust something into Theodore's hands.

"What do you think you're doing, Gordon?"

Theodore looked down and started when he saw the two gay porn magazines he'd left in Mr. Woolbright's shed. They'd been wrapped in clear plastic and addressed to someone he'd never heard of. The return address was his.

"I don't care what you're into, but you oughta know you can't mail something like that so it's out there for everyone to see."

He turned and strode back to his truck before Theodore could answer. He stared at the magazines. They must have been in his mailbox. He closed the door and dropped them on the dining room table. He stood there thinking.

What was happening now? Had the contest moved to another level, with his nemesis switching from defense to offense?

He went to the window where he saw Phil, the postman, across the street talking to Mrs. Woolbright. Theodore saw him pointing his way.

Perhaps it was indeed time to abort. He'd make that decision tonight after seeing how things went with the McCuin-Garcia and Longwell-Rashid bouts.

Shortly after six, Theodore positioned a chair at his front window, hoping for some fireworks. He was about to seat himself when he heard a sound. He whirled and saw a man standing behind him, but had only a glimpse before a fist smashed into his gut. He doubled over and turned away. Two more blows followed, one to each kidney, driving him to his knees and then onto his side, writhing in agony.

"That was for the dog," said a voice.

When Theodore's pain-blurred vision cleared, he saw a man sitting in a chair, looking down at him. He was average height, average build, average features, with brown hair and eyes. Theodore thought he was the most nondescript man he had ever seen.

A silenced, small-caliber pistol rested on his thigh, pointed in Theodore's direction.

"I'm really pissed about the dog," he said in a flat tone. "That was the last straw. I'm seriously thinking of kneecapping you for that."

Kneecapping? A vision of that almost made him forget the agony in his kidneys.

"No, wait. Who are you? Do I know you? Why are you doing this?"

"You don't know me, and I'm here because someone's paying me to be."

"Paying? Who—?"

"Remember Nelson Pershall, former resident of Veni Woods, New Jersey?"

Mr. Pershall . . . was that what this was about?

"I've never heard of Veni Woods. I don't even like New Jersey."

"You did a good job of pretending to when you were living there and calling yourself Clay Evanson."

How did he know all this?

"Ridiculous!"

Slowly, painfully, he started to push himself off the floor but the intruder kicked him back down.

"I prefer you flat on your belly. Anyway, Nelson Pershall hung himself after being caught in a kiddie-porn sting. His computer was loaded with graphic photos."

"If you're looking for sympathy for a pedophile, you're in the wrong house."

"His daughter swears he wasn't. He lived alone and ran a website that published poetry by codgers like himself."

"What does a daughter know about a parent's hidden life?"

"That's what I thought at first. But she said he was something of a techie and had set up a wi-fi network in his house. Someone could have been using his computer without him knowing it. Sound familiar?"

Theodore said nothing. That was exactly what had happened. He'd even triggered the police sting through Mr. Pershall's computer. But he certainly wasn't admitting it to this thug.

"She said she suspected a man named Clay Evanson. Told me her father's neighborhood had been friendly and peaceful until shortly after this clown arrived. Before he moved on, two people were dead—her father and a woman killed by her husband for cheating—a house had burned to the ground, one man had been arrested for assaulting his next-door neighbor, and another arrested for a hate crime. Are we seeing a pattern here?"

Theodore felt ice sludging through his gut.

"I haven't the faintest idea what this has to do with me. I've never heard of this Clay Evanson. And this woman is obviously paranoid."

"Yeah, that's pretty much what I thought, but she wanted me to fix it and she had the fee. Since I had the time, I took the job. Funny thing was, the day I started, you moved out. So I followed you here. And all of a sudden you're Theodore Gordon. I decided to stick around." He shook his head. "Whoever you really are, you're one sick bastard."

"You're mistaken, I tell you. I—"

"Shut up." He cocked his head. "Listen. Sounds like your neighbors. Let's take a look."

He grabbed Theodore by the back of his neck and hauled him into the chair he'd set up by the window. He was stronger than he looked. Theodore felt the muzzle of the pistol press against the base of his neck.

"Ever wonder what it's like being a quadriplegic? Do anything stupid and you'll find out."

Through the picture window he saw Mr. Robinson between Mr. Rashid and Mr. Longwell. The side window was open so he could hear their angry words. Normally it would be music to his ears. Mr. Fabrini and Mr. Woolbright came out of their houses to try to calm things down. Mr. McCuin joined them.

Suddenly, seemingly from nowhere, Mr. Garcia was racing across the street. He took Mr. McCuin down with a flying tackle. It took three men to pull him off.

"Hold it, guys," Mr. Robinson shouted. "Hold it for just one goddamn minute!" When the men calmed, he said, "Look at us. We were never like this. What's going on here?"

"I can tell you what's going on," Mr. Longwell said, pointing a finger at Mr. Rashid. "He calls me a thief and writes 'nigger' on my lawn!"

Mr. Robinson said, "Hold it! Hold it! Do you know what kind of abuse Munaf gets? He gets called a 'towel head' or a 'terrorist' or— you'll like this one, Cletus—a 'sand nigger.' You really think he's gonna write 'nigger' on your lawn? And by the way, I heard the story about Cletus's parole and asked a friend in the DA's office to do a little checking. The call was a lie."

"Who'd do something like that?"

"Look around," Mr. Robinson said. "Who's not here?"

Theodore held his breath as all heads swiveled his way.

"All this started after Gordon moved in. And I'm pretty damn sure he drained my crankcase."

"And that homo classified I got signed up for," Mr. Woolbright said. "Phil told Jean he had gay porn in his mailbox today."

"But why?" Mr. Garcia said.

"Why don't we go ask him?"

The muzzle pressed harder against his spine.

"That's what *I* want to know. Why? That ledger of yours—looks like you're writing reports. Who are they going to?"

He had the ledger! How—?

How didn't matter. Everything was falling apart. And he was asking the question Theodore never would answer. Never.

"I don't know what you're talking about."

The muzzle pressed deeper into his flesh, then was removed.

"If we had time, you'd tell. But things are moving faster than I'd planned. Robinson is sharp, and you're about to have some very angry people on your doorstep."

"I'll talk to them, reason with them."

"No amount of talk will calm them after they see what's in your garage."

"My garage?"

"Yeah. I raised the door halfway. Front and center is Rashid's wrench set. But there's also an empty can of Speed Weed, some strychnine-containing rat poison, and Robinson's drain plug along with pink panties and photos of his daughter."

Theodore felt as if his bones were dissolving.

"What do you think Robinson is going do when he sees all that?" the intruder continued. "Oh, and I called the vet. I said I was from poison control and he told me it looked like the Garcia dog died from strychnine. So I called Garcia—again as poison control—and told him to make sure he didn't have any strychnine-containing pest control around. How do you think he'll react when he sees that box of rat poison?"

Theodore closed his eyes and trembled.

"You're busted, pal. I'd love to have more time with you, but I don't want to be here when company comes calling. Have a nice day."

Rising on wobbly legs, Theodore turned and faced him. He found his voice. "You'd make a good distributor."

"Is that your game?"

Game? It wasn't a game. It was serious business.

"Who would I be working for?"

Theodore shook his head.

A gloved hand shot out and smashed against his jaw, rocking his head back and sending him to the floor.

"Just in case you thought I'd forgotten about the dog."

Theodore lay there, groaning. After a moment he heard the back door open and close. And then he heard the voices in his front yard.

"What if he's not home?"

"He's always home—haven't you noticed?"

"Maybe he—hey! That's my wrench set! What's it doing—?"

The voices moved toward the garage.

"Speed Weed! That kills grass, doesn't it?"

"And geraniums too."

"What's this? Pictures of Chelsea and—oh shit!"

"Rat poison! The motherfucker!"

An angry babble rose as someone began pounding on the door.

Theodore struggled to his feet and stumbled upstairs.

Exposed . . . bad enough, but losing the ledger was the final humiliation.

He was finished. Nothing to do now but bow out and avoid further embarrassment.

He jumped at the sound of smashing glass. Something had crashed through the front window.

His shaking fingers removed the cyanide capsule from its container. He put it between his teeth and bit hard.

Time to move.

I Am Legend, Too

A Prequel to *I Am Legend*
BY MICK GARRIS

Filmed three times—most recently for the 2007 Will Smith version—*I Am Legend* (1954), the tale of Robert Neville's one-man stand against a world of vampires, is among Richard Matheson's most enduringly popular novels. But what were the events that led to Neville's lonely and terrifying situation? Acclaimed Hollywood writer and producer Mick Garris (*Riding the Bullet, Desperation, Masters of Horror*) finds the answer in this powerful prequel.

I AM LEGEND, TOO

June, 1975

"Happy birthday, Bob," he toasted aloud, finishing with the voice inside his head: *you sanctimonious, hypocritical prick*.

"I'll drink to that," Bob replied, and there was no doubt he would keep true to his word. Again and again and again. He really was developing into a bit of a lush, if you wanted to be honest about it. Ben had begun to notice some time ago that the evening martini at the Neville house had spread to the late afternoon and beyond. He was sure that there was Stolichnaya in the morning V8 before the carpool to the plant, too. Drinkers always imagine that vodka has no smell, but if you're a teetotaler, as indeed Ben had been since going on the program, the reek of alcohol was a pungent one.

Ben tried to look away and unconcerned when Neville leaned in and kissed Freda just a little bit too long. He tried not to notice Freda's blush when she looked to see if her husband had noticed. She brushed Neville's hand away as it slipped along the cool round slope of her bottom.

Ben Cortman seethed, his face burning in embarrassment, resentment bubbling away with its nasty acid against the walls of his stomach. Bob Neville had a beautiful wife of his own, damn it—a former Miss Inglewood, for Christ's sake!—but he just couldn't keep his hands to himself. He wondered if Virginia had noticed her husband's wandering hands and lips. She was a bright woman;

she had to know. But when he looked across the living room through the crowd of good old Bob's celebratory friends, there was the lovely frosted blonde in the low-cut satin dress, laughing at somebody's horrid dirty joke, covering little Kathy's ears with her long delicate hands. Who knows? Maybe they were the kind of couple into the car-keys-in-the-hat parties on the weekends.

God, how Ben wanted a piece of that.

But that's what differentiated man from beast, right? Wanting something that wasn't yours, yet not taking it. He had to admit it, though; if Virginia ever climbed into the kip with Ben, no amount of cracker crumbs would be cause for dismissal. He watched her take a long, luxuriant drag on her Virginia Slim, releasing a cloud of delicate smoke that hovered and promised rain.

Rain on me, Virginia, Ben dreamed. *Rain all over me.*

Fat chance, literally. Ben had been a pretty good-looking guy back in school, but with his work behind a desk at the Delphi plant, he had started to spread out a little. And he had inherited his father's gene for a gleaming scalp; even though he wasn't yet forty years old, his hair clogged the shower drain every morning. With his expanding girth, he was starting to look a little like Oliver Hardy. Maybe he should grow a little moustache . . .

He sipped his Martinelli's bubbling cider and cast another smoky glance at Freda and Bob, both laughing just a little bit too hard. Bob had it all: the best-looking wife in the suburbs, the nicest ranch house on the *cul de sac*, a beautiful and precocious little girl, the foreman job at the plant, all his goddamn blond hair, and a supernaturally flat stomach. Women smiled when he walked into a room; nobody noticed when Ben did.

The smile on Freda's face was just a bit too flushed, her look to Ben just a little too cautious. He knew for certain she'd been unfaithful to him.

Bob Neville had them all fooled; everybody thought he was the nicest guy on the planet with his good cheer, his shaggy blond hair, his knowledge of classical and pop music, his command of the room. He'd even fooled Ben for four of the five years he'd known him and carpooled with him to the plant. But in the last year or so, though, he'd seen how it was all about Bob, what he did, what he thought, what he wanted. If Bob Neville thought *Dog Day Afternoon* was a better movie than *Jaws*, it was fact not opinion. If he was devoted to the exercise regimen of Jim Fixx, then by God, you'd die early if you didn't run five miles a day, too.

Okay, so he was a smart, handsome, funny, likable guy with a position on the way up at Delphi. It didn't make him man of the year in Ben's book. If he heard one more joke about how the old Jew got a bent back by stooping down to pick up pennies off the sidewalk, one more "cheap" wisecrack, one more jape about his prominent nose, he'd just scream. If he saw Neville kiss his wife and try to stick his slimy little tongue into her mouth again, he swore to God he'd kill the bastard.

But he was sure Bob had no idea how he felt. Tomorrow he'd be driving the Pontiac to the plant again, Bob popping in the annoying classical 8-tracks that he *just had to hear*, big grin on his face, sucking on that goddamn pretentious pipe and pontificating on everything from movies to politics to the nice can on the new secretary, and Ben would just drive in silence all the way to Torrance.

So he just sat there and watched his wife—cute, but putting on a little weight herself, if one was to be brutally candid about it—be charmed to blushing by her neighbor. Happy goddamned birthday, Bob.

Ben couldn't even look at Neville when he walked over to speak to Freda.

"Stay here if you like, but I'm going home to bed." He didn't mean to sound like such a martyr, but he really did want to get to sleep. It wasn't the weekend, after all, and he had a lot of work at the plant to get to in the morning.

Freda made a sad-baby face. "Are you sure, honey?"

"I'm really bushed. I've got a lot to do tomorrow."

"And I've got a lot to do *tonight*!" Neville interjected, somehow turning it into a dirty joke. Ben cringed inside, but his face chuckled for him.

"Just one more drink and I'll be right home, okay?"

"Suit yourself. Happy birthday, Bob."

"Sweet dreams, Cortman."

Ben wanted to flip him the bird, but merely turned and left the house for his own.

Ben Cortman stepped out of the steaming bathroom, toweling dry what was left of his hair. He sat on the foot of his bed and looked down in horror at the roll of fat that rested on his lap. Jesus, where did that come from? He stood and looked at the tubby stranger staring back at him from the full-length closet mirror, filled with disgust and self-loathing. He threw on his pajama bottoms and T-shirt and quickly scuttled under the covers and away from Mirror Ben's prying, accusatory eyes.

He settled back into the linens and piles of pillows, picking up his book from the nightstand. He knew that one day he'd make his way all the way through RAGTIME, everybody always saying how great it was and all, but he couldn't imagine that day would come anytime soon.

Anger blocked his ability to read. His eyes scanned Doctorow's words, but his brain could only imagine Freda and Neville liplocked, conjoined at the groin, rutting like farm animals, squealing like ejaculating pigs. He knew it was madness, but Ben just couldn't help it. He threw the book across the room, and the night went silent. He would not sleep this night.

Thanks a lot, Bob.

And then . . . a sound. *Bang!* Against the door.

Freda must be drunker than he thought. Well the hell with her. Let her find her own way to bed. He turned to his side and pretended he was asleep.

He heard another couple of inebriated clunks before the front door came open with a crash that jolted Cortman into a sitting position. Jesus, what was in that last drink?

Silence returned, and Ben's ears were pricked. He sure as hell wasn't going to call out to her, the way she was melting like cheese all over that son of a bitch all night. But what was she doing? He couldn't hear a thing. She must just be standing in the middle of the living room, reeling in a slow, private martini dance.

The quiet seemed to last for minutes, but probably didn't. Then, the single *creak* of a footstep. She's coming, Ben thought, and eased back down under the covers, turning his back to the bedroom door, waiting.

And waiting.

He heard the floor creak again, and the door to the kitchen *screeee* inquisitively open, followed by another long beat of silence. Soft footsteps crossed the living room again and found their way into the darkened hallway. Ben Cortman just grew increasingly disgusted and annoyed as he waited for his wife's sloppy, intoxicated entrance.

Boom! He jumped as she obviously lost her balance and fell against the wall. Instinctively, Ben started up to help her, but thought better of it. The hell with her; let her bruise her leg if she wants to drink so much and put on such a grotesque public display. He started to get concerned when there was no sound following it: no *ouch*, no further footfalls for some long moments. He got up on his elbow and looked down the dark hallway, but couldn't see a damned thing. Then he heard her brush against the wall as she stood again, her slow and unsteady gait shambling at last toward the connubial bed.

Ben resumed his possum sleep position as Freda's lovely, petite feet shuffled across the acrylic pile wall-to-wall carpet they'd put in last summer, generating static electricity with every step. He even heard it crackle distantly in the summer quiet of the night.

He heard her stop in the doorway, but he'd be damned if he was going to turn and face her. He really didn't have anything to say to her tonight. So he lay there in lathered silence, his heart pounding "In-A-Gadda-da-Vida" as he waited for her to ask him if he was awake. She never asked.

All right, that's enough, Ben thought. He turned to face her and the music, a venomous snarl on his dour face.

"I hope you know what a fool you made of yourself in front of our friends . . ."

But the figure silhouetted in the doorway did not respond. Or even move.

She just stood there, a hand resting gently on either side of the entrance, holding the body as steady as it could, though it could not keep it from weaving just a little bit.

Ben waited for an answer, but it became apparent there was no answer coming. Furious, he leaned over and switched on the bedside lamp, snapping the room into a blaze of electric yellow light and hard black shadow.

Ben gasped and pushed back against the headboard: the woman frozen in flashbulb brightness in the doorway was not his wife, Freda, but someone, something, infinitely more upsetting.

The woman was of Freda's height, but that was their only similarity. This woman had long, red tangles of hair framing her face and clumped against her shoulders. She stood completely naked before him, a boldness of stance that seemed completely unaware of her nudity. But the immediate flash of the shamelessly slender naked body, the prominent nipples reaching out from the tiny, withered apples of her breasts atop the protruding ribcage of her desiccated chest, was curdled by the bright crimson-brown splotches that could only have been blood covering her chin and neck. The shock of this strange woman, standing unexpectedly starkers before him, threw Ben completely off-guard, and his eyes kept flicking between the thatch of her Bermuda triangle and the rusty, shiny, sticky crimson sludge that smeared her face.

The first thing that pierced the confusion of this monstrous naked vision in his doorway was that it was someone from the party, that good old Bob Neville had sent her over as some kind of sick joke. But looking at this horrid creature with the blood all over her face, some shreds of some kind of uncooked meat caught in the yellow canines extruding from her hanging brain-dead mouth, the milky veil of cataract covering eyes that once had been a very pale green, was all it took to tell him this was real. And awful.

Ben's mouth worked like a grounded fish, opening and closing without saying anything. Finally, words came out: "Who are you?"

The total lack of intellect was a silent answer. The dead redhead cocked her face to one side, considering the interrogation as if her life depended on it.

Too late.

As she took a step into the bedroom, almost losing her balance as she let go of the doorway, the stench of her death preceded her. Cortman gagged on the fecal scent of rotted flesh and a sluiced-open intestine. He pushed himself back up against the headboard as she drew closer, fear collecting in the pit of his stomach and pulling his penis back inside his body like the head of a frightened tortoise.

"Go away!"

It stopped her for a moment, but only a moment, before she crossed the tiny bedroom and climbed onto the Cortman bed and the corpulent Cortman body, filled to the brim with fresh blood and meat. Cortman's scream felt silly and girlish as it tore out of his throat; he'd never screamed before, not for real, and it felt phony to him. But it didn't stop the vile naked woman from pouncing with surprising agility onto his face, and tearing into his throat with those foul, browning fangs in her mouth. The screams filled with Cortman's blood and gurgled and choked and sputtered.

The dead woman sucked with ferocious power, nursing blood from his pulsing, ragged throat, filling her mouth and gulping it down with a beastly and anguished hunger. And in moments, Ben Cortman was dead.

Freda was not only feeling no pain when she returned from the birthday party, but was flushed and giggly and filled with a warm, girlish rush of desirability. Bob Neville was so funny and smart and handsome, and she knew she would meet him tomorrow night at the Stardust Motel down near the airport. She knew there was no future in it, but sometimes you had to do something to make the present worthwhile, didn't you? She loved Ben, of course, just as she knew Bob loved Virginia. But this thing with Bob had nothing to do with love. Sometimes you just have to feel pretty, to feel desired, to know that someone handsome and charming wanted you, even with the extra ten or fifteen pounds you'd put on in the last couple of years. Maybe it took a few drinks to lubricate the possibilities, and she felt so lonely drinking when Ben couldn't anymore. Bob wasn't so judgmental about that sort of thing; how could he be, the way he put it away? But it was just for fun, a little bit of joy now and then. Is that so wrong?

She dreaded going into the bedroom; she knew Ben would be lying in wait for her there, all pissed off and waiting to castigate her just for having a couple of drinks and a good time. Wasn't that what a party was for, old Mr. Party Poopy Cortman?

She stood at the front door, hoping Ben would have fallen asleep, but knowing better. She'd have to face the music sooner or later, so she might as well get it over with.

She opened the door and stepped into the darkened living room, listening. Not a sound, no lights from down the hall. A hopeful sign.

She closed the front door and locked it behind her, the breath of the California summer night at her heels. She was too woozy to even go in and take a shower. She just wanted to collapse into bed and sleep until tomorrow night, when she could be with Bob and pick up where they left off. She giggled naughtily at the thought, and made her way down the hallway, indecent schoolgirl fantasies in a dirty dance across her cortex.

She held her breath as she reached the bedroom door. Good, she thought, closed, but not tight. She wouldn't have to risk turning the knob.

She eased the door open and gazed at the mountain of Ben, motionless under the covers. The blush of guilt washed over her as she stared at the silent hill of her husband as he lay asleep beneath the sheet. Clouded by the cheering martinis traversing her brain, she felt sorry for Ben. Even though she was his wife, Freda thought, she was probably his only true friend. Not a very good friend right now, she considered; and certainly not a very good wife.

His body never budged. He must really be sleeping hard. Probably had to take the pills.

"Honey?" she ventured. "You sleepin'?"

No reply.

Her mood dropped into the cellar. Alcohol made her go melancholy.

Freda wove her way across the room, suddenly very dizzy, and sat on the corner of the bed.

"Sorry I'm so late, sweetheart."

He was sleeping so deeply he didn't even snore, and somehow that touched her. She reached up to the top of the sheet and gently slid it down, revealing the crown of his head and his closed eyes. He looked sort of sweet in his sleep, and it made her smile fondly. Just moments before, she was filled with resentment over his controlling ways, his disdain for anything that was fun, his moodiness, but now, she looked at his face in repose and remembered the eager young man she married. She reached up to stroke the fringes of hair on his scalp. She frowned when she didn't even feel a heartbeat.

No longer needing a pulse, the late Ben Cortman lurched up and grabbed his wife by the hair, pulling her head back to reveal the object of his desire: the pulsing blue artery beneath the ceramic white skin of her throat. Pounding as deeply and loudly as a tympani, it transfixed him with an insatiable hunger he'd never felt before, a hunger that screamed even louder than his wife, a hunger that overwhelmed him, flooding his brain with a crimson explosion of light and desire.

His canines had lengthened and sharpened in death, with a

ravenous hunger all their own. They clamped onto that delicate, ivory throat with an urgent, rapist's zeal, ripping it open and spattering the wall—and Cortman's face—with sanguinary life, cooling as it ran down the wallpaper into quivering emptiness. Torn asunder, the flesh jacket that contained Freda's soul was evacuated, its sea of life slurped dry by a voracious husband.

Letting out a final, pitiful mewl, Freda Cortman was done.

January, 1976

Cortman's brain had lost most of its human functions since his death. It ran atavistic, incomplete but functional, if only just barely. Reasoning was just beyond its ken, but it retained emotional connections in its primary memory mode. It wanted—needed—food, and had to hide from the light of the sun.

He had lain for months next to the evacuated corpse of Freda, unfulfilled, starving, but inert. He knew hunger, but not how to slake it. In the first days of death, day and night were the same. The bodies lay atop the bed and its stiff, browned linens, utterly devoid of inquisitiveness and desire. Undead, but as good as plain old dead, the heavy curtains above the bed pulled tightly shut. Dead, dark, and silent, the clocks long since unwound, time stopped.

And then, a visit from the creature who began this whole neighborhood chain of events entered the bedroom with a crash, and it awoke something within Ben's inert, lizard brain. His eyes opened and remembered hate as he looked up from the bed into the mad, bloodthirsty eyes of Robert Neville.

Animal Ben, the one that ran only on instinct, death having robbed him of reason, reared back from the man who had despoiled his wife. Maybe he didn't even know that's what good old Bob had done, but he knew he hated this blond-maned bastard who stood before him.

He turned his head to see the stiff corpse of the Freda-thing lying next to him, their hands joined in a death grip of dried blood and gore, then tore his hand away from hers to protect his eyes from the bright light behind the door.

Then, Bob Neville lifted a long, wooden dowel, its leading edge filed down to a murderous point, over his head and dared to slam it into Freda's chest!

Rapist! Murderer!

Somewhere in the back of his sodden, decayed brain, Cortman recalled that this monster standing over him in his own home had stolen his mate, and now, here he was, penetrating her again, this time with ultimate finality. As Neville slammed the wooden stake home, Freda awoke with the same horrid scream with which she had gone to her death . . . and then, as all must, collapsed into ashes and rust-colored dust.

Neville, horrified by the disintegration of the woman's body that he had so coveted just weeks before, took a step back as he watched it catch up with the weeks of atrophy it had avoided in that place between life and death. And as he stepped back, Ben Cortman, shedding the corpulence that weighted him down in life, sprung from the bed and leaped at the impossibly live and rosy-cheeked interloper.

Neville shouted, kicking Cortman away from him and charging out the bedroom door. Cortman, slow and clumsy since he'd died, climbed awkwardly to his feet and lunged at the door, but fell to the carpet when he reached it. The last rays of the winter sun reached into the hallway from the living room windows and seared his eyes with overwhelming brightness and pain. He rolled back into the darkness as Neville ran from the house.

Neville regretted his quick escape from the Cortman house in the days to follow. He could have destroyed his old neighbor once and for all that evening, and saved himself the grief of the Cortman-thing's nightly attacks. But such was not to be.

Cortman sought the secret darkness, the quiet place where he could sleep alone, take the blood-things to feed upon, then sleep as the angry, vengeful sun beat down upon a dying world. It was a place no one else would find, secret and silent, a long forgotten bomb shelter from a much more fearful time. Each morning, just before the dawn sun threatened to leach the undead life from his newly blood-gorged body, the Cortman thing would slink away, retracing a secret path to its subterranean habitat, falling into a blind-but-wide-eyed slumber, not even so much as a heartbeat to disturb its repose.

And then, after the sun fell, hatred would reanimate him, the primal loathing for the man that brought him to this drew him out into the open night to seek to destroy him. Each night, instinct drew him back to the end of the cul de sac, resurrecting him over and over and over to seek out and destroy the thing that had so destroyed him. He may no longer be man, merely legend, but he could hate. And one day, the hatred that animated the meager re-mains of Ben Cortman would destroy the Neville thing that ruined his life.

TWO SHOTS FROM FLY'S PHOTO GALLERY

A Sequel to *Somewhere in Time*
BY JOHN SHIRLEY

John Shirley's "Two Shots from Fly's Photo Gallery" takes the time travel conceit from Richard Matheson's classic 1975 fantasy novel *Somewhere in Time* and invents a new hero who journeys to a very different destination for a very different reason. Mr. Shirley is the author of numerous successful novels, including *Crawlers* and *In Darkness Waiting*, and has written for film (*The Crow*) and television (*Star Trek: Deep Space Nine*).

TWO SHOTS FROM FLY'S PHOTO GALLERY

I tell myself I had no way of knowing Becky would kill herself, that night. It was *morning*, really, when she did it. At about 3:30 in the morning, July 16th, 1975, Rebecca Clanton, the young woman I had married not so long before, took a header off the roof of her sister's high-rise apartment building.

She'd come to see her sister Sandra on a visit. Just to stay overnight, supposedly just to spend time. But Sandra said that Becky hardly spoke, that night—just smoked, and nodded now and then, as Sandra talked about whatever offered to fill the silence. Then Sandra went to bed. And in the dead hours of the morning, as Sandra slept, Becky got up from the sofa bed, went to the kitchen, wrote out a brief suicide note, and took the elevator to the roof. Had probably come there to do just that, leave a note where someone who mattered would find it. It was just too lonely to kill herself alone at home, somehow. With me out of town . . .

She got a good running start and dived off the roof right down into the empty swimming pool behind the building. I saw the body before Sandra. I was back early, the next morning, went over to Sandra's to pick my wife up, heard people on the sidewalk talking about the dead woman in the pool. Went to look, knowing who it would be.

And somehow I still see it in my mind's eye. Becky's splayed, broken, blood-laced body centered in the blue rectangle of the pool as if in a picture frame.

Me, I was out of town when she died. I was in Albuquerque, for a conference on Billy the Kid. I write westerns—well, I've published only one novel, but a good many nonfiction books about the old west. *Henry McCarty AKA William Bonney AKA Billy The Kid* was one of mine, from the University of New Mexico Press; *The Murder of Morgan Earp* was another. My day job was teaching American History at a minor college, but I spent so much time on research trips to ghost towns and pioneer cemeteries covered with weeds, I was always on the verge of losing the job.

I took Becky on a research trip to a particular cemetery in Cobalt Dust, Arizona. She affected to be interested, but when she saw the skeletons, pulled partly out of the yellow dirt by the tree roots muscled into the forgotten old graves, she got a faraway look in her eyes, and went back to the motel. And that night she said, "I have to wonder why you want to spend so much of your time with the dead."

They weren't dead to me, I told her. It was like I traveled in time, when I did the research. Like I had one foot in the Old West.

She shook her head, then, and muttered something about arrested adolescence and macho fixations and wouldn't say any more.

The night she died I was in an Albuquerque bar arguing with another member of the Wild West History Association about whether or not Billy the Kid would really have gotten that amnesty from governor Lew Wallace if he'd been more cooperative. I remember realizing it was almost midnight, and I had promised to call Becky at her sister's that night. So I called, piling a double handful of quarters in the pay phone, and her sister answered, her every syllable iced. "She's gone to bed. Naturally."

"I see. Are you sure she's asleep, Sandra? I got caught up in an academic discussion . . ."

Just then the noise level in the bar peaked. Someone giggled and someone else dropped a glass and everyone applauded as it broke. Someone whooped drunkenly.

"Yes I can hear the academic discussion going on," Sandra said. "Becky's gone to bed. I'm not going to get her up. She's been feeling down and she needs her rest. Goodbye." And she hung up.

She's been feeling down . . .

She'd talked about suicide more than once. Becky was a pale woman with curly black hair, full lips, a face that showed a hint of Native American ancestry. She'd grown up in Arizona. She had a wistful smile, an air of nonchalant resignation. She wore long dark old-fashioned dresses, and black-spangled old lady's feathered hats she found in second hand stores.

I first found Becky in Bisbee, where her mother owned a souvenir shop for tourists hunting remnants of the Old West. Becky sat behind the counter, using the same resigned expression for attending to a customer as just staring out the dusty, flyblown window. A small record player, set up behind the cash register, was playing "Oh! Sweet Nothin'" by the Velvet Underground, not very loud. It was only later that I learned the name of the song.

"Afternoon," I said. "You're Miss Rebecca Clanton?"

She nodded. "You're that guy from the university?"

"College. North San Diego College of the Humanities."

"I got your postcard. Researching a book on the Clanton gang, you said?" She shook her head apologetically. "I don't know anything about my ancestors. I meant to write you back about that. Sorry you made the trip to glorious Bisbee, if you came to talk to me."

She gave out with that wistful smile. Immediately, I wanted to take her in my arms and comfort her. And kiss those large soft lips.

"Lots of times, people know more about their family than they realize. Or they remember that an aunt has some old letters or . . . Could I take you to dinner and just see if anything comes to mind?"

She looked at me doubtfully. "What's your name?" she asked.

"It's Bill Washoe."

"'Lonesome Cowboy Bill.'" She smiled. Sort of smiled. "Lonesome Cowboy Bill" was a song from the same Velvet Underground album. "Okay, Lonesome. Let's go, as soon as I ring this lady up . . ."

I was right, there was Clanton history to be gleaned from Becky. Turned out that her great-grandmother had been shacked up with Billy Clanton—the same Billy Clanton, cowboy and some-time rustler, who'd been shot to death, along with Frank and Tom McLaury, by the Earp brothers and Doc Holliday in a small vacant lot near the OK Corral on October 26, 1881. Ike Clanton's younger brother, Old Man Clanton's youngest kid, Billy had fallen for a mixed-race dance hall girl and sometime prostitute named Isabella Chavez, a girl whom some called "Issy" or "Easy"; she was said to be a quarter French, a quarter black, a quarter Indian, a quarter Chinese—but no one knew for sure.

That much Becky knew. The rest I gleaned, a little later, from county records, a smirking columnist in a frontier newspaper, and a letter, found by a Bisbee county clerk in a family Bible, alluding to the affair.

Billy had gotten Issy knocked up, and had promised he'd marry her, but hadn't made good on it, and it was said that just before the gunfight Ike had been trying to talk him out of the marriage. Then they'd gotten on the wrong side of the Earp brothers, in Tomb-stone, and Billy had been shot down. Isabella had her child, and had given the boy, William Jose, Billy Clanton's surname. The local registrar had stretched a point and made the name official, though she'd never been married to Billy Clanton. Billy's bastard child, William Jose Clanton, had married one Dolores Plainville. Dolores bore a boy, James Isaac Clanton, who'd married Rebecca's mother Louella. Rebecca revealed that William Clanton the Second had deserted Dolores early on, and "Jimmy Ike," as Becky's dad had been called, had deserted Becky and her Mom when she was three.

"We don't have any papers going all the way back to Billy," said Becky, over a steak salad, which was the only kind of salad they had in that Bisbee restaurant. *The Happy Widow*, the restaurant was called. She picked at the lettuce around the beef, leaving the meat alone on her plate when she'd done. "So a lot of these gun-fighter history guys, they don't take my family name too seriously. Mom tried to get them interested, so we could sell some stuff. She got an old pistol and said it was Billy's. She actually bought it in a pawn shop."

"You think your mom would talk to me?"

"If you can get her out of the bars long enough. And offer her money. But she'll just make stuff up. I'm pretty sure the Clanton thing is real though. I look at a picture of him, of Billy Clanton, and he looks like us. And . . . he was shot down. That's almost like saying he was in my family. We're all shot down one way or another. Not always by guns. He was shot down young. My granddad ran off to avoid the draft—and maybe to get away from family—and he was killed when they tried to arrest him. And my dad, we haven't heard from him since he left, but my cousin says dad's in prison over in Texas." She shrugged. "They all just run off and get shot or put in jail somewhere."

"Do they? You've had some bad luck with your family. Maybe you should . . . make another one."

I felt my face redden, when I said that. A stupid, blurted, clumsy thing to say. It just came out. But understand: I'm not a good-looking guy, I'm shaped like a salt shaker, I'm short, I've got a bald spot, a nose like a tuber. Not a lot of experience. And I had been thinking about going to bed with her since I saw her sitting behind the counter, gazing sadly out the dirty window . . .

She gave her almost-smile, then, and looked at me with something close to real interest. Finally she said, "My sister's the one who's done the best—she got out of Bisbee. She's in San Diego, she teaches school."

"San Diego!"

"I know—that's where you're from. Well, she got divorced. But she's dating a guy. And she likes teaching, I guess. Do you like rock music?"

I pretended to be a lot more interested in rock music than I was and expressed a liking for Janis Joplin.

"There's a concert, up in Phoenix I'd like to go to this weekend," she said, with a somewhat theatrical wistfulness. "The Cactus Ridge Festival, but I can't really afford to get there and back."

"In fact," I lied, without hesitation, "I'm planning to go to that same concert . . . So, uh, if . . ."

I remember walking in the desert dusk, hand in hand with Becky.

It was yet another cemetery. This one she didn't mind—it was Boot Hill, in Tombstone, Arizona, carefully preserved: the town lived on entirely through tourism.

At this hour the wooden tombstones were darkening to silhouettes, seemed like something grown from the sandy dun earth like the cacti, the small twisted desert trees. We saw Les Moore's grave: "no Les, no more." We had to look close, in the fading light, to see the grave-marker of Billy Clanton.

Murdered in the Streets of Tombstone.

I'd brought Becky to get a picture of her with the Clanton marker, for inclusion in my book. And because I thought the trip was my best shot for getting her into bed. She'd been pretty warm during the concert, and afterward, she squeezed my hand before rushing into the house. The trip to Arizona meant two rooms in the motel, but the rest of the time we were together, and now, gazing down at Billy's grave, she let me take her hand and keep holding it.

She seemed almost happy. With its constant references to her ancestor—to her martyred ancestor, in the view of anti-Earp historians—Tombstone made her feel important. When I introduced her as Billy's great-granddaughter, much was made of her. She was interviewed and photographed for the local paper.

"It's funny," she said, gazing down at the grave. A prickly pear cactus, beginning to bud, was sprouting from the spot corresponding to Billy Clanton's heart. "I feel almost happy—because I'm part of a famous tragedy . . ."

"Some say it was a tragedy, some say it was Earp and Holliday heroics . . ."

"I can't go with heroics. And if Billy'd lived he might've married

Isabella, and then . . . maybe things would've been better in my family."

That planted the seed of what was to come. It started me thinking about her therapeutically. It occurred to me that if I helped her, made her feel better about herself, she'd feel more attachment to me.

As if reading my thoughts, Becky turned to me, as the cemetery caretaker shouted at us that they were closing for the night; she turned her face to me—tilting it down, because she was a little taller. She leaned closer, and she let me kiss her.

Then she put her arms around me, and whispered in my ear, "You give me hope."

That night in bed she gave me hope, too.

Nine days later, Becky's mother was dead. Out on a drunk, the old woman had stumbled into the street, and had been run over by a Ford pickup hauling beer kegs.

Becky hadn't been close to her mother, but the death seemed to backhand her, emotionally; it sent her reeling. "She wasn't much good, but she loved me best she knew how," Becky said, at the funeral. Becky and I were the only ones attending that cut-rate funeral. "She was all I had. Every Sunday morning, hangover or not, she made me breakfast . . ."

I told her, "I'll make breakfast for you, on Sunday." And that seemed to help. We got closer, then, Becky and I. We went to more concerts, we went on trips—I fought with the college administration to get the time. She came out to visit San Diego . . . and when I popped the question, she said yes. She only thought about it for an hour or two.

We got married in San Diego. And at the wedding, which we held at the Hotel del Coronado, one of the guests was my Uncle Roger who brought his "partner"—a rather taciturn man, a doctor named Crosswell. While we were waiting for the bride to come out, we started talking about the Coronado, a landmark built in 1888, and about old hotels, and I said how visiting old places, for me, could feel like time travel, and the doctor stared at me—and asked, rather suspiciously, what had prompted the remark. Roger looked at him and said, "He doesn't know about Collier. Almost no one does. Forget it."

But when my uncle wandered off to get a drink, I pressed Crosswell, my journalistic instinct piqued, and he muttered something, rather grumpily, about having a transcription of certain tape recordings by a Richard Collier who'd stayed at this hotel, and allegations of Collier's experiments in time travel. References to Collier's obsession with one Elise McKenna.

Then out came Becky in her wedding dress, really smiling for once, and drove away all thoughts of my being anywhere, anytime, but right there.

We were happy for as long as Becky was capable of being happy, which was a week or so, and then we were happy sporadically for a time . . . and then only I was happy. Just happy to be married to her. And after a while, when I realized I was alone in my gladness, neither of us were happy.

It all came down to the implicit tragedy of Becky's life—of life itself, in Becky's view. If we went on a walk, Becky was sure to notice a dead bird in the gutter; if we went to the beach she saw only the trash on the sand and a bird pecking out the eyes of a dead fish; if we went to Disneyland she pointed out the wasteland of parking lot and the high prices and the long lines; she speculated on the exhaustion and resentment of the people dressed as Goofy and Mickey. At home, she listened to a great deal of Tim Buckley and the Velvet Underground and she re-read *The Bell Jar*. Reading

The Bell Jar more than once should be in some clinical psychology book as a warning sign.

"Don't you see?" she'd say to me. "I'm doomed. It's in my blood to be doomed. Some people are born losers—it's built into their chromosomes. You've hitched your wagon to a falling star . . ."

She started sleeping twelve, fourteen hours a day, and not getting out of bed when she did wake up. The house fell into a piled-up disorder like a postmodern sculpture representing her depression. She started talking about suicide. Suicidal depression had been a black tsunami poised over her, just before we'd met— and then my intercession had let her run from it, for a time. But it couldn't be outrun for long, she insisted. The giant black wave was falling on her at last. Perhaps, Becky suggested, we could die together . . .

I went to see my Uncle Roger, but really it was to talk to Crosswell. "You're a physician, Doctor Crosswell—do you know somebody good for this kind of illness?"

He recommended a Doctor Hale Vennetty. I went to see him, for a consultation about my wife. He was a tall pale dour psychiatrist with a phlegmatic, fatalistic air, and he was convinced that once a person was "imprinted" by their childhood, that imprint was their destiny and there was little to be done, though electroshock could be tried. He was interested in Becky's case, since it had an affinity with his pet theory, evolved mostly to account for cyclic ghetto miseries: parental abandonment led to a tendency to abandon one's own children, as if the abandoner were re-enacting the despair of their own childhood. It was a vicious circle that spiraled through the generations, abandonment leading to abandonment. "In fact," he chuckled, "the only way to change it, really, once the imprint has happened, would be to travel back in time and persuade someone who started the cycle of abandonment not to do it . . ."

He made me feel it was hopeless. I went to two more doctors— one of whom suggested an experimental new drug, something called an "antidepressant." I was planning to persuade Becky to sign on for the experimental therapy program . . .

I'd talk to her about it, I decided, right after I got back from Albuquerque.

Then she was dead. And I was alone.

I would grieve, I decided. I would find someone else. Someone healthier.

But I drank a great deal of beer, and overate, and put on forty pounds, becoming even less attractive. Worse, I was dogged by a self-loathing—not an attractive quality. But I couldn't shake it.

I just kept thinking *I could have saved her*, after all. If I had stayed with her. If I hadn't gone on that trip. I'd known she was at risk for suicide—but I went anyway. Because she was becoming a burden to me. I'd wanted time away from her.

I tried blaming it on her sister Sandra. *If only she'd let me talk to Becky that night, I might've cheered her up.*

But it didn't take. I blamed myself. I spent much of 1975 and most of 1976 blaming myself.

By degrees, I became fixated on Vennetty's theory, his cycle of abandonment. Then I remembered Crosswell's story about Collier. The recordings. The tale of time travel . . .

Crosswell wouldn't talk about it. But I had a key to my uncle's house because I fed their four cats when they were out of town. I let myself in one day and searched the file box in the den Crosswell used for an office. It took me all of five minutes to find the manila envelope, at the back of the lowest drawer, with the transcription of the tapes. I took it home and read it with a mixture of dread, disbelief and growing excitement.

The description of the method used for time travel had an eerie verisimilitude for me. On rare occasions, as I'd hinted to Crosswell, I'd experienced something of the sort myself. In the little ghost towns I'd visited, I had felt, sometimes, for perhaps just a second, that the veil of the ages had drawn back, and I'd glimpsed the town in its teeming heyday; had smelled the reeking mules and the reeking prospectors, had blinked in the rising dust . . . before it had faded away. I had almost, *almost* traveled in time.

Collier's process was the same method, crystallized by fanatical dedication. It was a psychological, then a psychic, process. You surrounded yourself with artifacts of the era you wanted to travel to. You dressed for the era. You visualized the era. You fixed the date and time in your mind. You repeated, over and over again, the time, the place, the destination you wanted to travel to. You visualized, you visualized, you visualized. And since the quantum uncertainty hidden at the heart of the universe is penetrable by mind itself, a persistent man might just project himself into the past through sheer force of will . . .

Was it really possible? Was it possible I could project myself a year into the past, and stop Becky's death?

The apartment Becky had died in had grim associations for Sandra and she'd recently given it up. I rented it, splurging my tiny savings to do it, and sat on a chair in the bedroom, staring at a newspaper from the day before Becky had died. It hadn't been easy to get hold of that newspaper. Then I tried for hours to travel back to that night . . .

Now and then, there was a flicker. I almost went. The room would shift, Sandra's old furniture would start to appear. Once I thought I glimpsed Becky. But the trouble was, 1975 was too much like 1976. It wasn't different enough, somehow, for the mind to find its bearings. I kept slipping back to my own time.

But I had confirmed that time travel was possible. I had gone into the past—if only for a moment.

And there was one other possibility for saving Becky. Suppose . . .

Suppose I took seriously what Doctor Vennetty had suggested facetiously. Suppose I traveled back to the time of the Old West's Billy Clanton—and stopped him from being there, in Tombstone, that October day in 1881. He was reputed to be a pretty good-natured kid, over all. With any luck, if he weren't shot down in the OK Corral fight, he'd marry Isabella, and he'd stay with her, and raise that child, and the cycle of abandonment would be broken, and that child's children would not be marked with despair, would not be imprinted, and Rebecca Clanton would not be seeded with depression—and suicide.

I freely confess, I wasn't quite in my right mind, in those days. I felt haunted by Becky, as if some black light shimmering from her despair had settled over me, an invisible cloak I always wore. It drew itself over my eyes, and made me see things in extremes.

Forgetting about Becky, letting her go, was not an option. I had to save her—or die myself.

So I went to Tombstone, Arizona, in October 1976. Went there in period costume. It isn't strange to dress in the manner of the 1880s, there. No one even stared at my frock coat, the watch and chain on my waistcoat, the silk top hat. I rented a room in a bed and breakfast, a tourist-outfitted building that had existed in 1881. The room was already furnished with the right antiques. My pockets were heavy with silver dollars wrapped in outdated paper money. I'd sold my car to get enough money to buy the antique funds from a numismatist. I even had a small, loaded pistol, circa 1979, hidden in my coat.

I decided I should try to go right to the morning the gunfight happened, so that there were fewer variables to deal with—and because, since I was a historian of the Old West, that day was already firmly fixed in my mind. I had visited it many times in my imagination, reading and rereading accounts of the gunfight and the events leading up to it. I had the edge, a jump on visiting Tombstone, Arizona, October 26, 1881.

I locked myself in my antiquated room, set up my own tape recorder, and recorded the words over and over again . . . "October 26, 1881 . . . it is 9 in the morning, the morning of the OK Corral gunfight, in Tombstone Arizona . . . October 26, 1881 . . . it is 9 in the morning . . ." And in the background is music, not too loud, a tape loop of tunes recorded by contemporary folk musicians on acoustic instruments, only songs that were extant in 1881. "Camptown Girls . . ." "The Man on the Flying Trapeze . . ."

I hid the tape recorder in a cabinet, behind me, so the sight of the technology wouldn't take me out of my contemplation of 1881. Battered and tape-looped, it droned the words and the music over and over again. I repeated the words with it, growing hoarse, listening to it when I napped.

It took me three days, scarcely resting, with only a few breaks to eat dried food and drink bottled water, for the process to really begin. On my few visits to the men's room, down the hall, I encountered tourists who stared at me suspiciously. They'd heard the mantra-like drone from my room, the interminable music . . .

October 26, 1881 . . . it is 9 in the morning, the morning of the OK Corral gunfight, in Tombstone Arizona. Picturing this room, that day. The street outside, what it must have been like. Envisioning faces familiar to Tombstone in those days—faces I knew from old tintypes and photographs. Wyatt Earp, Doc Holliday, Big Nose Kate Elder, Mayor Clum, George Parsons, Fred Dodge. Seeing them in my mind's eye. *October 26, 1881 . . . it is 9 in the morning . . .*

And then what Collier had called "the absorption" began. Suddenly I was drawn inward, caught up in a drifting sensation, and a mounting disorientation. The rented room seemed distant, detached. The sound of my droning voice, those songs, became thick, distorted, as if I were going deaf. Then I ceased to hear them—and heard, instead, a shouting from the street, the clatter of horse's hooves. The tinkle of a cheap piano.

The sounds of Tombstone, October 1881.

The officiating lady of the whorehouse was a stout woman with a sausage-curled coif of flaming red hair that contrasted vividly with her blowsy blue dress. She was leaning back in a rocking chair on the front porch, smoking a pipe, her pale thick-ankled left leg cocked over her right knee. She didn't seem particularly surprised to see me, a stranger, walk out of her house—the house I had time traveled to—though she hadn't marked my entrance.

"Now did that Marissa bring herself a man up there without consulting me?" she asked, almost rhetorically, as she frowned at her pipe, knocking its dottle clear on the railing. "If she done that, the wicked vixen owes me three dollars and no mistake . . ."

"Here is your three dollars, ma'am, and good day to you," I said, my voice trembling as I laid the worn silver dollars on the porch railing beside her.

She scooped up the money. "Why these coins has traveled some, worn to a nub." She chuckled and went back to singing wordlessly to herself. I stepped out into the October morning, into the smell of sage and horse dung and leather . . .

Believe, I told myself, feeling dreamlike as I stepped off Fifth Street and onto Allen, in Tombstone Arizona of October 1881. *Believe!*

I turned left, passing the Golden Eagle Brewery, striding by several shops including a hostelry, Campbell and Hatch Billiards, the Cosmopolitan Hotel, the Eagle Meat Market, Hafford's Saloon . . . *Believe in this. This is no dream.* These creaking wagons pulled by oxen and horses; that stagecoach arriving; these weary ladies of the night blinking in the morning light as they stumped blearily to their beds in their high-button shoes. And this shopkeeper, with the flaring mutton chops and the red gaiters, opening up his emporium; the smell of alkali dust and new-cut lumber and the smell of horses and the raw rich scent of privies, many privies, blowing in on the sharp desert wind . . . *It's no dream!*

But it was the dream of every Old West historian. To actually visit Dodge City or Virginia City or Tombstone—back then. And this day of days, the day of the most storied gunfight of the Old West! I could get the truth about the gunfight—no one would ever believe me, of course, but *I'd* know. I'd know who started the fight, and if indeed the Clantons and McLaurys had not even drawn their weapons. That's what the *Tombstone Nugget* had claimed, but the town's more Earp-friendly newspaper, the *Tombstone Epitaph*, had insisted the shooting affray was a straight-up gunfight with Frank McLaury and Billy Clanton drawing first . . .

Too bad I didn't bring a camera back with me, a Polaroid, say, or—

The streets of Tombstone rippled; I seemed to glimpse a Cadillac glimmering into visibility, asphalt appearing under my feet . . .

No! Don't think of things like that! *Focus.* Be here. There's only here and now—October 26, 1881!

I saw an apothecary's shop, then, across the street. *Focus on that.* An old-fashioned apothecary's shop. *You have a plan. You must go there and make a purchase . . .*

I went into the shop, and found the apothecary's assistant, a sallow, sleepy-eyed, greasy-haired woman in a long black dress, and I instantly suspected her of being a laudanum addict. No matter. I made my enquiry and, wordlessly, she sold me what I needed to carry out my plan.

I stepped out to the wooden sidewalk, shivering in the chill wind, and looked fiercely around, trying to fixate on something that would keep me in this time. I focused on a man walking unsteadily along, across the dusty street, a man in a sombrero. He was a plump-faced white man with an oiled mustache and a small pointed beard; the silver and black sombrero didn't seem to go with his stained frock coat, his tall black boots. Then I recognized him. It was Ike Clanton, full up with liquor. He'd been drinking all night long.

I understood the dark, intent look on his face, too. There was fear and anger, perfectly mixed, in that expression, the whole framed by the sullen stupidity of alcohol. I knew what was behind that look . . . and how it would lead to the Gunfight at the OK Corral. Ike would lead me to Billy—and I could prevent Billy from getting killed. I could see to it that Becky's ancestor had some kind of father around.

But I didn't dare think about my wife too much, not consciously—I had to keep my plan to save her in the back of my mind. If I thought about Becky, I'd be thinking about the time she had lived in, and that would propel me out of 1881. I'd be flung forward to the 1970s.

I had to think about this day in 1881. The events about to unfold . . .

Earlier that year, March 15, 1881, the stage had been robbed, and Bob Paul had been killed. The Earps had learned that the robbers were local ne'er-do-wells, surnamed Leonard, Head and Crane. But the stage robbers had made good their getaway. Wyatt Earp knew that members of the "cowboy gang," Ike Clanton and the McLaury brothers, Frank and Tom, were close acquaintances of the stage robbers. Wyatt went to Ike and the McLaurys, told them he'd see they would get the reward money on the quiet, with Earp taking credit for the arrest, if they'd help him find Leonard, Head and Crane. Ike had agreed, telling Wyatt Earp where he thought the stage robbers were holed up. But two of the robbers were killed by the Hasslet brothers before Wyatt could get there, Crane fled the territory—and the whole deal between the Earps and the cowboys fell apart.

Ike was afraid that the leader of the cowboy gang, Curly Bill Brocius, would find out he and the McLaurys had played along with Wyatt Earp. He felt he had to keep his standing in the gang by noisily blustering and damning the Earps, and Wyatt's friend Doc Holliday. Accusations flew back and forth between the Earp faction and the Clanton/McLaury gang.

Holliday, former dentist turned gunfighting gambler, had breezed into town from Tucson, at the request of the Earps, Big Nose Kate in tow. That morning in 1881—the very morning I arrived in old-time Tombstone—Ike had told the bartender at the Oriental that if the Earps and Holliday showed on the street, "the ball would open" and they would have to fight.

Probably Ike was just putting on a drunken show. Ranting. Not really anticipating that all the animosity would really bust out into a gunfight. But it would. The fight would be called the Gunfight at the OK Corral.

But it was staring at a drunken Ike Clanton in the belligerent flesh, in that moment, that fixed me rock-solid in October 26, 1881. Ike glowered at me and swaggered unsteadily off down the wooden sidewalk.

I followed him, hoping he'd bring me to his brother Billy. A block down, Ike slipped into the Grand Hotel, where he kept a room, to catch a little fitful sleep, perhaps. Not knowing where else to go, and knowing that Ike would eventually meet up with his brother Billy—for they were both there at the OK Corral gunfight—I went into a café next door to the Dexter Livery and Feed, across from the hotel, to keep an eye out for Ike.

I ate a hearty breakfast, the food remarkable for its rich taste in some way I could not identify. I over-tipped the owner so there'd be no complaint if I was there for some time, telling the man with the handlebar mustache I might have to wait for some hours, watching the street, as a friend was coming on a mule all the way from San Simon. Looking over the silver dollars, he winked and said I was to make myself comfortable . . .

I hadn't been able to find out, in my research, where Billy Clanton had first been seen in Tombstone that day. So I sat at the window, drinking coffee—it was as if I'd never tasted coffee before!—and watched the street, the dour shopkeepers and ladies in their stately dresses, silver miners on a day off, cowboys riding through from outlying ranches. I sat there glorying in it all, fascinated with the town's quality of newness, of enterprising energy . . .

About half an hour before noon, his eyes red, his face pale, Ike emerged from the Grand Hotel, swaying, now carrying a Winchester rifle, a pistol on his hip. He wandered down the street, seeming to have no definite destination, and I followed—and was unsurprised when he went into a saloon. I ambled into the saloon, stepping over a sleeping drunk, the man's urine soaking the sawdust spread on the floor. I posted myself at the bar, the other end from Ike, hoping to see Billy Clanton arrive. Perhaps I should ask around town for Billy, head him off before he found Ike. Find Billy Clanton, head him off—and save my girl from suicide. Save Becky from being imprinted by abandonment. But suppose, wandering around town looking for Billy, I missed him?

Meanwhile Ike was muttering threats to anyone who'd listen and knocking back whiskey.

Around noon I looked at my goose-egg watch and knew that about now Marshal Virgil Earp, after all too little sleep, was being awakened by Deputy Marshal Andy Bronk. "There is likely to be Hell, Virgil," Bronk would tell him. Virgil, his head pounding, would go out to see about all these threats made against himself and his brothers.

Minutes later Virgil found Ike outside the very saloon I was in—I watched the encounter through the window. A cold wind was blowing, searching through the half open door, when Virgil stepped up behind Ike and grabbed the Winchester. Ike snatched at his pistol and Virgil neatly "buffaloed" him, cracking his own six-shooter over Ike's head, knocking him down. (My historian's heart was pounding—that was Virgil Earp himself, a big man in a dark suit with a bushy ginger mustache, and the slender man with the black mustache joining him was his younger brother Morgan!).

"I heard you were hunting for me, Ike," Virgil said, staring down at the fallen Ike.

"I was," Ike said, holding his head. "And if I'd seen you a second sooner you'd be dead . . ."

"You're under arrest for carrying firearms within city limits."

I knew what would happen then. Ike would be dragged by Virgil and Morgan Earp into Judge Wallace's court. There'd be an altercation there, with Wyatt Earp arriving and calling Ike a "damned dirty cow thief," and adding, "You have been threatening our lives and I know it . . ."

"Fight is my racket, and all I want is four feet of ground," Clanton would respond.

The judge would merely fine Ike, and his weapons would be sent over to his hotel room. As the Earps left the court, they'd encounter Tom McLaury outside, who'd come to check on Ike. Wyatt Earp would demand to know if McLaury was heeled, and Tom would say that he'd fight Earp anywhere, if he wanted it. Still furious from the encounter with Ike, Wyatt would pistol-whip Tom McLaury for his impertinence, knocking him to the ground. And so the fury on both sides would build.

Billy Claiborne would find Frank McLaury and Billy Clanton at the bar of the Grand Hotel and tell them that Wyatt had pistol-whipped Tom . . .

That was it! That's where Billy would be, having come in with Frank McLaury. *The Grand Hotel.* From there, trying to avoid trouble with the Earps—who after all were local lawmen—Frank McLaury would take Billy to the OK Corral, to get their horses. At the OK Corral they'd encounter Tom McLaury, his head bandaged, with the same idea, and then Ike would stumble up to them, unknowingly doom them with his drunken nattering about the Earps, keeping them in the vacant lot next to Fly's Photo Gallery and the OK Corral a few minutes too long . . .

And local men, having heard talk of a gunfight all night and day, would see the Clantons and McLaurys gathered near the OK Corral, talking earnestly, Frank and Billy with hands on their guns, and suppose them making ready to fight the Earps. And those helpful townsmen would warn the Earps and Holliday that the outlaws were massing for a fight—when in fact they were probably going to leave town—and the Earps and Holliday, assuming Ike's threats were real, would come marching down the street to "make a fight."

In a gunfight lasting about thirty seconds, three men would be shot dead by the Earps and Holliday: Frank McLaury, Tom McLaury, Billy Clanton. In Billy's case, it took him a while longer than the others to die.

That's how it would happen, inexorably—unless I could get Billy Clanton out of the line of fire.

I made my way to the bar of the Grand Hotel, getting there before Billy and Frank arrived. I ordered a sarsparilla—no one looked askance at that, for it was still early—and watched the doorway.

Could I really bring myself to do it? Rather than witnessing this cornerstone of gunfighter history, I'd be interfering with it—perhaps stopping it, maybe sending perturbations down the river of time. I might affect history in bigger ways than I intended—for all I knew, if he wasn't killed in the gunfight Billy Clanton might get it into his head to assassinate a President.

Unlikely. These were minor players on the stage of history. No great large-scale change would come about.

But the urge to witness the gunfight was strong. Perhaps I could witness it as it had been known to happen—and then come back again, and change it next time. Perhaps . . .

But here was Billy Clanton, walking through the door, coming into the room with me. I knew him instantly—and I saw echoes of my Becky in his face. I could not let him be shot down. I could not forget my mission to save Becky. He was a living reminder of my purpose.

Both men were dressed in suits for a visit to town, Frank's a bit too small for him, Billy's a tad too large. Billy was but nineteen years old—a fresh-faced boy, smiling, glad to be in town.

The smile would fade when another "cowboy gang" member name of Claiborne came in, with news of Wyatt Earp's pistol-whipping of Tom. I had to intercept Billy Clanton quickly—tell him that I was a friend of his brother Ike, and Ike was out in the alley with urgent news, wanting to see him alone. I'd take him out there and bring out the ether I'd bought at the apothecary's, and I'd grab him from behind, dose him before he knew what was up, drag him somewhere and keep him safe. Maybe the gunfight would go on without him, maybe not, but he would be safe.

I strode over to them—Frank McLaury, a dark, bearded man, and Billy a hulking, fresh faced youth. Billy was taking off his Stetson, wiping dust from his eyes. "Blowin' out there, mister. Say, do I know you?"

"Why, no sir. My name is Billy too, Billy Wells. I have lately become a business partner with your older brother, Mr. Isaac Clanton—and he waits without. He has information he would impart to you, and only to you."

"Ike and me have no secrets from Frank, mister."

"Well sir, he was hoping Frank here would watch the front door, while you and I go out back to talk with Ike. For the Earps are coming."

"Are they now?" McLaury rumbled. "And I'm to watch for them? I'll do 'er, then. But keep your hand on your Colt, Billy, you don't know this man."

Billy shrugged and gestured for me to lead the way. My heart hammering, one hand going into my pocket for the bottle of ether, I led the way out the back, into the dirt alleyway. Billy came out alone with me. And stared at the man already waiting out there. We both stared at him. I was more shocked by the man's presence than Billy was.

It was myself. Another me. Dressed just the same. The only difference was, this version of me, this Bill Washoe, had not shaved in a day or two, and his hair looked lank.

"What the blue blazes have we got here?" Billy said wonderingly. "Your twin! And I never saw two men more alike. And where's my own brother? What's afoot?" His hand went to his gun.

"Ike will meet you at the OK Corral," said the other, unshaven Bill Washoe. "There's been a change my twin here didn't know about. You'll talk with Ike there. It's an emergency—you boys are in danger!"

Billy backed away from us, not wanting to turn his back till he had to—then he hustled through the door. "Frank!" he shouted, as he went in. "We got to go to the OK Corral!"

I was too busy staring at myself, this other version of myself—too busy just trying to cope—to interfere with Billy. Finally, I managed, "What . . . uh . . . ?"

"I'm you," said this other me, stating the obvious with an apologetic shrug. "From a little bit in your future—your future a little later than the Bill Washoe of 1976 that you were, when you came here. I tried to get here earlier in the day but somehow—I was drawn here, and now, to this exact time and place. Probably by you. There's some kind of psychic magnetism between us—and you reached peak intensity here when you met Billy Clanton. This is the point where you started changing events."

Bill Washoe of 1976! The wooden walls of the buildings around us wavered, and began to seem distant. The sounds from the street became murky, distorted . . .

"Don't!" I said. "I am here—*here* in October 26th, 1881!" I looked down the alley to the side street and saw a buggy going by with a lady in a bustle sitting up very straight in it, buggy whip in hand. *1881.* Renewed by my focus on that distinct feature of the time, the alley reified, became more definite.

The later me made a suggestion. "There's a secret Collier didn't know, for staying in the past—pain." He . . . the other *I* . . . raised his hand and I saw he had a badge in it, an antique US Marshall's badge from this era—he'd held it so tightly it had bloodied his hand. He squeezed it there again so that fresh blood dripped. "Once you're in the past, pain fixes you there, if you sustain it with something from this time." He tossed me a like badge. I caught it. "Squeeze it till it hurts, cuts your hand. That'll keep you as I tell you what I must . . ."

I squeezed it till the pain came, and he went on.

"Billy stayed with Isabella, because of what I did—what you want to do. You succeeded, once so far, in keeping him safe from the gunfight. So he married Isabella, and her son did a bit better, and stayed with his wife and so on. And Becky's father stayed with the family. That much you accomplished. Some behavior is imprinted—but some is inherited. Like the tendency to cruelty. And it can be carried on both by imprinting and by genes. Billy's got a cruel streak. He *abused* Isabella, and his son abused *his* wife and child and . . . and Becky's father carried it even farther."

Blood was dripping from my hand . . . 1881 stayed firmly in place, stuck on the thorn of my pain . . . and my growing fear.

"He raped Becky." The two of me said it, together. As I realized and he simply explained. Becky's father stuck around—and that was even worse. The other Bill Washoe spoke on, alone: "When I . . . when *you* . . . got back from Tombstone, it was hard to find Becky. You . . . and I . . . established that she hadn't committed suicide— but where was she? We were no longer married. But she was out there, alive somewhere—I found her in Phoenix, found her by ha- rassing her sister till she told me what had happened to her. Sandra got away from the family before dad returned from jail—and it seems Becky's father made her his little sex slave. Eventually, she ran away, only to become a junkie. To pay for the heroin, she fell into prostitution. She was stoned out—so she wasn't careful. She got serum hepatitis, and syphilis. Got very sick—very, very sick— and when I left the future to come back here again, she was dying. Our Becky was dying very slowly. It was too late to treat the syphilis and she was . . . Oh, God, *she would have been far, far better off dead."* The other Bill Washoe swallowed hard, and went on, "I came back to stop you from saving Billy. If you'd left it alone, she would have had some happiness. And it would have ended quickly, at least, in that empty swimming pool . . ."

I stared. "I don't care," I said at last. A terrible momentum was on me. My sense of purpose had a life of its own. "I can go back to our time—I can perfect time travel and I can go back to save her from her father and . . . and . . ."

"No, no you can't. I've tried. You can't travel in time endlessly— you go mad if you do. Maybe I have gone mad. I'm not even sure I'm talking to you now. You seem real enough . . . I mean—*I* seem real enough . . ."

I shook my head emphatically. "I'm not going to lose my focus. I'm going after Billy and I'm going to save him. Stop him from the OK Corral fight. Then I'll do something about her father—I'll save her from that life too! I'm going after Billy now—don't try to stop me." I started for the OK Corral.

"No!" The other, later Bill Washoe stepped in front of me. He was reaching for his pistol . . .

I drew mine first. I outdrew myself. I think I—he—had been drinking . . .

And I shot him down. Shooting myself down felt kind of good, really.

The other Bill Washoe lay there in a pool of blood . . . I was aware of the portly, aproned bartender coming to the door behind me, staring . . .

The dying man looked up at me and said, hoarsely, "You slowed Billy down already . . . you, trying to stop him . . . from before . . . time has inertia . . . it's . . . psychic, what we do. Our minds will . . . and you will . . . you must . . ."

He didn't finish saying it. His eyes went glassy and his let out a final breath—and died. But I soon knew what he was trying to say. Because in a few moments I felt a long, icy shiver pass through me, as his consciousness left him . . . and merged with mine.

We were the same person. The same soul. The spirit has its own thermodynamics, its own "law of conservation of matter"— so our souls merged. *And I knew what he knew.* What he'd been through, since he'd gone back to our time, poured into me, when our souls combined. His memories became mine.

And the most aching of his memories asserted itself: *Rebecca Clanton lying in the hospital bed, covered in sores, foaming at the mouth, her face the color of rancid butter, her wrists raw in the restraints, as a droning doctor explained that it was too late for antibiotics, too late for her, too late . . .*

It would be a slow, horrible death. A murder, really—by her father. By extension. And maybe, by me. Maybe I'd murdered her with my interference.

I saw the other Bill Washoe had been right. I knew what had to be done. I had slowed Billy Clanton down, interfered with the original pattern. Things would be a little different. He would be a tad later getting to the OK Corral, and even more on his guard now. Maybe he wouldn't die in the gunfight . . .

I ignored the shouting bartender, and I ran to the OK Corral.

The OK Corral was actually a long strip of land between Allen and Fremont Streets. I ran through the corral, past horses and water troughs, and climbed the fence, coming to the narrow strip alley behind Camillus Fly's Photo Gallery, a small building which stood behind Camillus Fly's Boarding House. I still had my gun in my hand—and I saw the adversaries lined up in the eighteen-foot-wide lot, with Tom McLaury to one side, standing behind a horse, his hand on a Winchester in its saddle scabbard; Doc Holliday, a small ash-blond man with a black mustache, bringing a shotgun from under his gray cloak; beside him were Virgil, Morgan—and there was Wyatt, with a droopy sandy mustache: a tall, almost skinny man in a long black coat, wide brimmed black hat. He was just pulling a pistol from his coat as Billy Clanton—not standing where I thought he'd be, historically, but now half hidden behind a post—drew his pistol and fired, at the same time as Earp. But Earp fired at Frank McLaury, hitting him in the stomach—McLaury already had his gun out, while Ike Clanton shrieked that this must stop, and he tried to grab Wyatt Earp's gunhand, saying he was not armed himself, and Earp shouted, "The fight has commenced! Go to fighting or get away!" and shoved him so that Ike turned and stumbled into Fly's boarding house, as the wounded McLaury shot Virgil in the leg, knocking him down, and Doc fired at Tom McLaury with the shotgun before Tom could get that Winchester free, hitting him twice, then dropping the shotgun to pull a silvery pistol, with which he fired at Billy—

But the bullets hit the post, and Billy wasn't hit yet—my interference had been just enough. He was going to get away! He was turned sideways—and he was aiming carefully at Wyatt Earp . . .

Firing from the corner of Fly's Photo Gallery, out of sight of the Earps and everyone else, I shot Billy Clanton, twice.

I shot the son of a bitch down myself. Saw him spin and fall.

Then I drew back under cover and let go of the bloody badge, and as the pain ebbed, I thought about 1976. I thought about disco, and hollow-eyed Vietnam vets . . .

The last of the shooting died away. Billy was lying on the

ground screaming in pain . . . his voice becoming distant, distorted . . . the wall beside me wavered . . . and then became solid again. And it stayed that way.

I looked around, and realized that I was going to stay in this time. Pain and my interference, intertwining me with this time, had fixed me here.

There was shouting from the lot beside Fly's boarding house. Someone was saying, "Was there shots, too, from back there?"

I turned and stumbled away, around the corner, through the Corral, between buildings, almost blindly, till I found myself approaching a group of men behind the bar where I'd shot . . .

Where I'd shot myself dead.

I expected to find them marveling at the bartender's story—how a man had shot his twin and the twin had vanished. For surely the body would not remain in this time.

But there it was—six men turned to stare at me, and the portly bartender pointed. "Why it's the killer himself! Look at his face and the man dead before you! He is the spitting image! He has killed his own twin brother!"

"They even wear the same clothing!"

Guns were pointed at me then and, numbly, I dropped my own.

Now I sit in the territorial jail awaiting execution. The gallows has long been built—I watched from my jail cell window as they used the gallows for a couple of renegade Apaches just last week. I have asked for this sheaf of paper and this pen so that I could write this account, to seal in an envelope and give to the exasperated man appointed as my lawyer. I wish I had the clip from the *Nugget* to include—but it exists in my own time. Old West historians routinely read the pioneer newspapers, and I remember once, in my time, reading in the *Nugget*, with some bemusement, about the man who killed his own twin, in Tombstone, and how the man would say only, "Is it a murder for a man to kill himself? I cannot explain, gentlemen, you would not understand." I said the same yesterday, and never remembered the article till I spoke those words. The story about twin murdering twin had been buried in all the excitement about the "OK Corral fight," scarcely noted. I'd assumed the article a fabrication, not uncommon in frontier newspapers looking to amuse the public. Especially when it was revealed that neither man had identity papers, and the surviving man would not reveal his name. Surely it was a story someone had made up . . .

I chuckled then—and I laugh sadly, now, thinking about it.

I will ask my lawyer to send this to a certain library archive in San Diego, which exists even in this time, the envelope addressed to "Doctor Crosswell"—who does not yet exist—in the hopes it may find its way to him someday. Someone should know what I had in common with Richard Collier. Not just time travel—but love lost.

Perhaps there's an afterlife. Perhaps I'll meet Becky there, her burden lifted at last.

The only thing certain, though, is that at dawn they will hang me for murdering myself.

I might've made up a story about my psychotic twin, and shooting him in self-defense, to save my life—a gun was found on him, after all. But I didn't have the heart for it. You see, Bill Washoe was an arrogant man, who did too little for the woman he loved when she was alive. Who did all the wrong things once she was gone. So I was glad to shoot Bill Washoe dead. And it will be a good thing when he has been marched to the gallows and hung.

For he deserved it.

THE DIARY OF LOUISE CAREY

A Variation on *The Shrinking Man*

BY THOMAS F. MONTELEONE

The Shrinking Man, a seminal Richard Matheson novel from 1956 that became an equally seminal film, is surely one of the most beloved fantasy stories of the twentieth century. Mr. Matheson told us what happened to Scott Carey; but what was it like to be Louise, Scott's wife? Thomas F. Monteleone, author of many successful novels (*Night of Broken Souls, Eyes of the Virgin*) and editor of the celebrated *Borderlands* anthologies, provides a surprising answer.

THE DIARY OF LOUISE CAREY

Sunday

Scott went out on the boat with Marty. Beth is playing with Ginny at her house. So I have the whole house, the whole day, to myself. Hate to say it, but it feels damn good.

How come nobody tells you how deadly *dull* marriage can be? I feel like I'm *pretending* half the time. All those women on TV—selling refrigerators and appliances or playing the wives of nice-enough guys—all wearing spiffy dresses and salon hairstyles. Is that all there is? I feel like I'm trapped in a Peggy Lee song. And it's not "Fever."

If I knew it would be like this, would I get married anyway?

Probably not, sister. Not even for Beth?

Well, maybe. When she's good, Beth is the best thing in my life.

But nobody told me how much *time* kids take. Day and night. No break. Ever. For *me*.

Scott gets the best of it. Gone all day, then just a few hours of play time before he puts her to bed. Beth seems to like him a lot more than me. And why not? I'm the bad guy all day long. He comes in the door all smiles and hugs. So how come she listens to *him* more than me? Him and his deep voice, hands on hips, and she snaps right to it.

Me, I get the rolling eyes and that sassy *no!*
I just want to smack her sometimes.

Monday, The Following Day

Scott's skin still burning from yesterday. He's such a stubborn ass he won't go to the doctor. Doesn't want to waste the money. Never seems to feel that way when he's buying a good bottle of scotch.

Monday, A Week Later

Marty called me today. He's been doing it a lot lately. He says he's calling about Scott. But I wonder.

Like I can really *do* something about his brother. I mean, they've known each other all their lives. Marty always knew Scott's a hothead. Terrible under pressure. What can *I* do?

You can hold my hand—that was Marty joking on the phone. Right.

Tuesday, The Following Day

They were out spraying the neighborhood this morning. Gypsy moths and Japanese beetles. Scott was getting ready to leave for the office when he saw one of the trucks going down the other side of the street. "Look at those donkeys, can you imagine how stupid you have to be to take a job like that?"

Yeah, my husband and the fancy company he thinks he owns. If it wasn't for Marty, their little business would be in the red.

I had to laugh when he was backing the car out of the driveway. He stopped to move a trashcan out of the way—just as the spray truck turned the corner. He caught it full blast.

That night his skin was on fire. So bad I actually felt sorry for him. Till I tried to put some cream on his back and he went nuts on me. Screaming and yelling like I was trying to hurt him.

He makes me so *angry!*

Wednesday, Two Weeks Later

Marty called today.

The younger brother. He's taller and looks like he could've been an actor. He's single and he speaks softly all the time.

He wants to meet with me. To talk about Scott and the business. I said yes.

Thursday, Two Weeks Later

Marty had been right—something *is* wrong with Scott.

But nobody could talk him into seeing a doctor until last night. When Scott asked me why I was wearing high heels . . . and I *wasn't*.

I can still see the look of shock in his eyes when he realized he was shorter than . . . *before*.

Doctor Wilson couldn't figure it out. A man almost six feet tall doesn't suddenly become five-eight.

Unless he's shrinking.

They told Scott they needed to do more tests and he blew up. Right there in the office. He told them he wasn't going to be their guinea pig and pay for the privilege.

Just when I was starting to feel bad for him, he had to go and embarrass me in front of the doctor. There's only one thing worse than a mean man . . . a mean *little* man.

Monday, Four Weeks Later

Don't know how much more I can take of this.

Scott is getting crazier by the day. Marty keeps calling—says Scott is having trouble doing his work.

Worse at home with me. He tore up the special insurance papers when I told him we might need it. Him and his pride and his manhood. To see him strutting around like a little Napoleon I want to laugh in his face.

Now that I can look him square in the eye . . . I just might.

And Marty keeps calling.

Saturday, Five Weeks Later

I feel like some kind of freak . . .

Until last night, it had been one of those things nobody wanted to talk about. But it was always there—like the elephant in the corner of the room. Neither one of us had the nerve to say it—we're not the same without the sex.

And the funny thing is—I don't miss it. Not with him acting like a monster half the time. And I've tried to let him know it. Like changing into my nightgown in the bathroom. Wearing baggy sweaters and housedresses. No makeup in the house. If he doesn't get the message, he is just being dumb.

He spends most of his time around the house with Beth, which is fine with me.

But I know he wants me.

I can see the way he looks at me. And finally last night, finally, he said something. I had to make believe . . . like I had no idea . . . like I was one of those dopey women in taffeta on TV.

He was sitting on the couch and when he put his arm around me, it was like being with my 12-year-old son—if I had one, that is. Oh God . . .

But it got worse.

When he crawled up on me, I felt creepy . . . like those people who like kids.

But he didn't seem to notice. And again, I almost felt sorry for him.

I could barely feel him and his little *thing* inside me, and I wanted to grab him and pull him away. I wanted to scream and tell him how awful this was, but he lost himself, and it was finally over.

He didn't say a word. And neither did I.

We both knew—like I said—it was finally over.

Monday, Seven Weeks Later

I agree with Marty. He can't have Scott in the office any longer. He doesn't want him dealing with clients. Too distracting. Too weird.

So now he's home all the time, and I can't stand it. He's angry all the time. He's three and half feet tall and he looks like a little boy.

But there's more.

Scott keeps saying his brother will keep him on the payroll, but Marty told me different: if Scott can't contribute to the business, he's got to get that insurance to kick in . . . or I'll have to go out and find work, or . . . maybe something else.

Something that would be good for everybody.

I know what Marty wants. And I don't mind saying it—I'm starting to think I do too.

Wednesday, A Week Later

Dealing with the flat tire was a mess. I almost laughed when Scott told me he was too little to get the jack and the tire out of the trunk.

But the worst part was the part about the homo who picked him up. That was just sad.

It makes me realize the truth—I'm living with a freak. And maybe it would have been best if he'd gone off with that other odd man who picked him up.

Just ride off and never come back.

Tuesday, Two Weeks Later

I should hate myself for feeling like this . . . but I can't help it!

I can't stand to be in the same room with him. Every time I look at him, I want to smack him. We never leave the house together, we hardly ever talk unless we're arguing.

The only good thing lately—another writer interviewed him today. They paid us good money for the article in *Look*. Of course, he didn't want to do it, but I put my foot down. The money was way more important than any of his puny feelings.

Monday, Two Weeks Later

The first article about him showed up today. When he saw the pictures, he tore the page into little pieces. I couldn't blame him— they made him look like a scary little doll.

Later, when I came back from the grocery, I found him in the bedroom. He was standing in front of the floor-length mirror.

Wearing his pinstripe suit jacket. It sloped off his shoulders all the way to the floor. Like a little boy playing dress-up.

Except he was crying.

He looked so ridiculous, I got the giggles. I honestly didn't mean to. I couldn't help it. It just came over me. I had to run from the room so he wouldn't hear me.

But I didn't run fast enough . . .

Thursday, Five Weeks Later

We had to move. After the spread in *Look*, people wouldn't leave us alone. Scott got his gun out of his old Army footlocker and started cleaning it. He swore he was going to shoot the next idiot who knocked on the door.

He was so upset, he scared me. Marty came last night and took the bullets out of it. Didn't let Scott know.

By the way, speaking of Marty . . . the apartment he found us is a dump. Low rent neighborhood makes the money last longer, he told me.

Marty says he can find us a better place, but he said I know what I'd have to do to make that happen . . . that's the way he put it.

I hate this place. We'll see.

Friday, One Week Later

He's only three feet tall now. He's losing an inch every week.

What happens when he runs out of weeks?

Nobody knows he lives here because he *never* goes out. Fine with me. It's weird to think he used to be my husband. Even Beth thinks it's funny now—when he tries to tell her what to do, she just giggles.

We had another fight about Beth. He doesn't think I'm backing him up as a father. He got so mad, he stomped out of the house in his little Buster Brown shoes.

When he didn't come right back, I felt guilty so I got in the car with Beth to look for him. Then something happened.

I turned a corner and stopped the car. Down the block, at the edge of the playground, some kids were beating up a little boy. And just as I put the car in gear to drive down there and stop them, I realized it was Scott . . .

I took it out of first, switched to reverse and turned around.

Whatever he got, he probably deserved it. But later on, I felt bad about what I did. It was like I wanted those boys to do something I couldn't do. Oh God, this whole terrible mess is making me crazy too . . .

Saturday, Seven Weeks Later

He's barely bigger than Beth's dolls now.

Last week, after Marty saw that article in the *Plain Dealer* wondering "what ever happened to the incredible shrinking man," and he told Scott a book about him might be worth a lot of money, Scott, of course, blew up. Swore he would *never* do anything like that. But Marty called a friend in New York. Hooked him up with an agent who said a book would sell for at least "six figures."

Scott was the man of the house. He was supposed to take care of us, and now we're on poverty row. Scott owes us.

Tuesday, A Week Later

Scott is writing the book. They sent a contract by overnight mail and he signed it.

But I had to make a deal with him.

My friend Tina has a brother who's a photographer for that magazine, *National Geographic.* Her brother travels all over the world and he used to show us his pictures and tell us stories about how weird people are in way-off places in the world. One place, I can't remember where, some jungle place, I think . . . he told us the young mothers had this way to keep their baby boys quiet, to keep them from crying. By sucking on their *things.*

I almost threw up, but now, no matter what happens, Beth and I can make it.

Wednesday, Seven Weeks Later

The book is almost done. That's all he did every waking moment for the last month and a half. Marty says he got obsessed with it.

Fine. I don't care. Just finish it.

He typed until last week when he was getting too little for the portable typewriter (he was 21 inches tall yesterday). Too hard to punch on the keys. So he's talking the rest into a tape recorder, and Marty has his secretary typing it.

Like I said—just finish it.

Thursday, Three Weeks Later

He's almost done. And I can't help it—I'm wondering what he said about me.

Meanwhile, I just got back from the carnival. Scott was pathetic. He wouldn't get in the car. He'd met a girl from the Midway— "Tom Thumb's Sister" or something awful like that.

It's funny, even though I can't stand to be around him, I got really upset when he told me he was staying with that midget. In her tacky little carnival wagon. I can just imagine what it's like in that little wagon right about now . . .

I got so crazy-mad, I slapped him before I drove away.

But *why?*

I should be glad he did it. Now I shouldn't feel so bad about me and Marty . . .

So why do I feel like this?

Saturday, Three Days Later

The midget-thing only lasted a couple days. He was getting too little—even for her. He came back after dark, and Beth made me let him in.

Friday, A Week Later

He told me to get rid of the cat.

It's nothing new. He's been talking about it for weeks—says the cat is starting to "watch" him, and it's dumb enough to think he might be something like a big mouse.

And pretty soon Scott won't even be as big as a mouse . . .

I said no because Beth really loves that cat.

I keep telling myself that's the real reason.

Sunday, Five Weeks Later

Marty had the guy at the hobby shop modify his biggest dollhouse. The extra wall keeps the cat away from Scott. He's only 12 inches tall now, and he stays in the dollhouse almost all the time.

Beth wants to play with him, and he's afraid she might hurt him by accident.

When he said that I got really pissed—how could he accuse his own daughter of doing something like that?

Saturday, Five Weeks Later

Maybe Scott was right.

I caught Beth taking him out of his house, and he was screaming, almost crying. He's only 7 inches tall and he looked so scared.

I yelled at her, and she let him go. Angry and embarrassed, she ran to her room and slammed the door.

Later, when I got out of the shower, Scott was missing.

I checked the cat for . . . blood, but he was clean.

Beth and I looked all over the house. Even outside, but we never found him.

Monday, Four Weeks Later

Beth cried for about a week. Then she started to get over it.

I wasn't sure how I felt. Marty said it was probably better this way, and I want to believe him. It's weird to finally get what you want and not be sure it's what you wanted after all . . .

And then I found something when I went down to check the hot water heater.

A little piece of sponge. A cardboard box. Cracker crumbs stacked up in like little bricks. It was a place . . . a place for somebody small.

Somehow, he'd gotten into the cellar. And kept himself alive. I tried to think of what he must look like now. Way smaller than a little toy soldier. Sleeping and hiding in a little space.

But not just hiding. Something worse.

Not far away from his little place, among the dust motes, I found a big fat black spider. Dead. But with a *pin* stuck all the way through him.

Scott.

After something like that, was he still alive? I called his name. Heard nothing.

As I stood there, trying to imagine what it must have been like to kill that bug, I felt so bad for him. And for all the awful things I'd thought about him.

I stood there for a few minutes staring at the dead spider. And then I had the feeling I was being watched. Watched by something too small for me to even see.

It scared me and I ran up the steps and waited for Marty.

But even upstairs, I kept thinking about Scott and how he'd killed that spider. How small was he now? How small could he *get?*

Two Hours Later

Marty showed up and finished getting everything out to the car. The book money had finally arrived. Beth and I are moving to the new place . . . with Marty.

The movers are almost done. I followed Marty down into the cellar. While he dragged up the suitcases, I looked around. Careful. Trying not to be obvious. For some reason, I couldn't tell him what I'd found.

I kept hoping I would see some sign of him, but it was like looking for a single speck of dust.

I had the thought that maybe he was right there in front of me—but so small I couldn't see him. Maybe that's why I felt somebody watching me. I could have stepped on him like an insect and never known it . . . and that made me feel bad all over again.

One Day Later

We're moving in. Beth is so excited. Marty is smiling. I should be so happy, but I keep thinking of Scott.

He'd been *so* small.

I kept wondering—did he know I'd been looking for him? Did he know what I'd been feeling?

He'd been shrinking an inch every day. What happened when there were no more inches?

Two things still bother me.

Where is he now?

And what does he think of me?

She Screech Like Me

A Sequel to "Born of Man and Woman"
BY MICHAEL A. ARNZEN

When Richard Matheson's "Born of Man and Woman" appeared in *The Magazine of Fantasy and Science Fiction* in 1950, it made an immediate and astonishing impact, catapulting its author toward a major career from his very first story. Michael A. Arnzen, author of the prize-winning novel *Grave Markings* and editor of the online *Goreletter*, extends the diary of the horrifying and tragic mutant child of Mr. Matheson's tale—with memorable results.

SHE SCREECH LIKE ME

X—Father beat me off the top wood with stick when I hurt mother. He chase me into corner and hit my head. The drip spray down all over him. It shine all green on his stick like candy. He stopped and made a face at Mother and then scream and beat my legs till one feels no more and cannot move. He hit my head again until cellar turned red in my eyes and I hear squish squish squish each time his stick hits.

I angry and hurt but I see Mother alone and still where I hurt her. She is on her back just like me only by stairs. Mother not pretty like before. Crumpled purple like thing under my pillow.

Then a dark down the stairs and Little Mother is standing in door light. She screech like me.

Father stops stick.

No stick but pain keeps beating all over me. I crawl up ceiling in corner as far away from Father as I can. Legs hurt when I tuck them up and away from him. Drip is green behind me on wall. I stick on wood good.

Little Mother steps down and then kneel and cry on Mother on floor. I sorry Father says. Her face looks cold. He touch Little Mother and she run back up stairs.

She stops at light and looks at me shaking in top wood corner.

Daddy bad she says. She wipes clear drip from her nose. Daddy bad she screech and slam shut the door. I hear it lock like before.

I crawl over wood and look down at Father cry over Mother. All your damn fault he says to her. Why did you do this he screech.

His cheeks shine like window water. And he hits Mother with stick. She does not move or cry.

I pull sticky off wood and land on my bed place. Leg hurts pain slow. I have a bad anger like red light in eyes. Father no see when I grab the chain out of wall.

Father hear me though and see me and say sorry.

I screech and run at Father. I hurt him with chain like he always used stick.

Daddy bad I say until he done moving.

XX—Little Mother let me up in white room this day. Eyes hurt. Then more stairs furry with hair I don't stick to and she takes me to a room all pink and warm. She have nice bed. Soft and white. Many little live things on bed with pointy ears and tails. But they do not move. They not live. More like the furry thing under my pillow in cellar. Her little things are better—squashy and fuzzy and no crunchy or stink.

I sleep long time on Little Mother bed. Drip get cold and crusty on pillow but nice sleep. Quiet.

Later time I wake up to the bell noise I hear before when other Mothers and Fathers visit. Little Mother opens pink room door and she say hide. Please.

She holds hands together. I do not know please but she sound nice when she say it again. I look for coal but no coal to hide behind. Then Little Mother opens another door and inside is dark with scary empty Little Mothers hanging in a row. Get inside she says and run away.

I go in room and shut door. Empty Little Mothers swing on hooks. They smell like her pillow. I pull one down and slide inside. Arms tear holes but I smell like pillow now and I think I pretty like Little Mother.

I hear voices down below. Like Father voices. Scary deep talking to Little Mother. I put head on floor and I hear her say askident. Grand Mother. Please.

XXX—House empty long days. First I think it was church but no Little Mother for three times light outside. Mother and Father not in cellar. Where they go I do not know. Cellar different than before. Clean. No drip or red water where Daddy was. My bed place is gone but that is okay because I like pink room sleep better.

Bad hunger but I find eating food in room with big white cold box. Meat inside good wet and nice tearing in teeth. Stomach noisy and I laugh. Milk in a box and I wonder why box. I wear empty Little Mother when I get cold and then I sleep with little pointy ear things in bed.

Then today I hear big machine and I run down the furry stairs. I think Mother comes but it is Little Mother and she runs to me quick and laughs with squeeze and then she says hide again.

I go back upstairs but wait at top and watch.

Big Mother comes inside front door and carries stick. Very long stick longer than Fathers. So big she leans on it like a leg. Little Mother grabs her arm and Big Mother says leave me be. She looks like Mother only gray and she sound funny like door creak. I run and hide in pink room before they see me.

Later the door open. I run behind empty Little Mothers. She pokes stick inside and hurt me a little but I stay quiet.

Come on out and let me see you Big Mother says. Pretty please she say with door creak voice.

I step into light and Little Mother laugh and say awww cute.

Big Mother says nice dress and Little Mother bends over more laughing.

Big Mother drops stick and says come hug your Grandmother. What is Grand Mother I say.

Mother of Mother she says and clutches at me. And this is hug.

We stand there hug until Little Mother hugs us too and says one big happy family. I feel Grandmother go a little cold and give her a funny look.

Little Mother washes me while Grandmother makes food in room with big white cold box. I put on new Little Mother cloth she calls dress. We all eat yum at table. Little Mother seems sad and she no like food much but Grandmother is good nice to me and give me extra. We eat and my stomach makes noisy sounds and we laugh. I feel so good. Then I go sleepy fast. Little Mother too.

X—Same time but later I wake up to dark in Little Mothers room. I go downstairs and find Grandmother on long chair. She drinks out of cup and tells me to come sit on her. I climb up on her legs and look into her eyes. She is warm.

She rub my head. Tell me what happened she say.

I say about Father and stick and chain in wall and how Little Mother tell me Daddy bad and lock door.

She nods and says I knew it. I drip from eyes and she says do not worry all better. We are together now she says wiping the drip.

I look at her eyes blurry and she smiles many teeth at me. She smells good like food and pats my leg and she says I sure do make a funny Little Mother.

Where is Little Mother I say.

Little Mother not like us she say. Little Mother bad.

I hear her then. She screech from downstairs. I turn and see Grandmothers stick beside cellar door.

But Little Mother not always bad I say.

You have to trust me from now on she say rubbing my head. Please.

What is please I say.

Grandmothers face warm and smiles and then it drips while she wraps me with grey arms and hold me mushy against many chests. Mother of Mother have chest just like little live thing with tail but bigger and good smell soft like bed of pillows.

Oh you have so much to learn she say hot in my ear before she presses her mouth against the top of my head like Mother once did once and then Grandmother teaches me my name.

Everything of Beauty Taken from You in This Life Remains Forever

A Sequel to "Button, Button"

BY GARY A. BRAUNBECK

Richard Matheson's "Button, Button" (1970) presents a classic human ethical dilemma—in exchange for money, would you press a button that resulted in the killing of a total stranger somewhere in the world? Gary A. Braunbeck's sequel teaches us what we might learn from such a question—and how we might answer it. Mr. Braunbeck is the author of several popular novels (*In Silent Graves, Keepers, Coffin County*) and has won numerous awards for his short stories.

Everything of Beauty Taken from You in This Life Remains Forever

I find that I am thinking of my own mother as I write this to you, and I can't help but wonder how she'd feel, knowing that her only daughter—her *only child*—had said yes to your offer. I think she would be very disappointed in me. She worked long and hard for every cent she earned—as everything from a cashier and laundress and maid to a cable assembly worker at an electronics plant—and she never believed in taking the easy way out. Both she and my late father, as well as my late husband, possessed the strongest and most moral work ethics I've ever seen. Something like this would have broken their hearts, had they been here the other night when I finally made the decision.

It seemed so simple: unlock the dome, press the button, and receive a quarter of a million dollars in cash. Of course as a result of this action, someone whom I do not know would die, but people die every day, don't they? Some die physically, and some die in other ways. You weren't specific on that point; you merely said, "Someone whom you do not know will die."

I was awakened the night before last around three in the morning by the sounds of a loud argument coming from the apartment

complex across the parking lot. A man and a woman were screaming at each other, cursing, saying the foulest, cruelest things
you could imagine. I sat up in bed, pulled back the curtain, and
looked to make certain that the man wasn't going to strike her or
worse. Well, there was much worse, but it had little to do with
either of them.

The woman, you see, was throwing a couple of suitcases into the
backseat of an old used car, one that was in terrible shape, one that
you buy from a disreputable used-car lot or from someone who has
the damn thing sitting on their front lawn because they desperately
need the money. Those are the only types of vehicles that people
who live around here can afford, you see. But here's the thing:
standing between the woman at the car and the man in the doorway of the apartment was a little girl, no older than three, who was
crying and screaming at the two of them to stop, please, please
stop. Neither of them paid her any attention. Finally, when both of
them had stopped to catch their breath, the little girl walked toward the woman and said (and I remember these words exactly, Mr.
Steward): "Please stay, Mommy. I am sorry for whatever I did and I
promise that I will never do it again. I love you. Please do not go."
Her voice was a hoarse, spirit-broken thing to hear, and what broke
my heart the most, even more than the sound of her fear and pain,
was that this little child, this girl of no more than three, used no
contractions in her speech. It was as if she wanted to make sure that
her mother clearly understood the intent of her words. Perhaps she
had learned to use formal words in school earlier that week and was
hoping that it would surprise and please both her parents. Maybe
she'd been using too many contractions in her speech and it annoyed one or both of them, and this was her way of showing them
that she could do better. But again it made no difference. Her
mother screamed at her to shut up, as did her father, and the little
girl simply stood there crying and saying "I am so sorry, Mommy,"
over and over again. Then her mother shouted a last string of
obscenities at the man (I assume the little girl's father), the man

screamed equally foul things back at the woman, and the woman jumped into the car and sped away. The little girl, screaming and crying, ran after the car until she fell over something, and then just lay there in the filthy parking lot near the overloaded Dumpsters, choking on her tears and shouting, "Please, Mommy, come back, come back," until her voice was completely gone. No one, including me (I'm ashamed to admit) came outside to see if they could help her. The man who must have been her father slammed the door to the apartment and just left her outside. (It was thirty-five degrees, and the child was wearing no coat. In fact, I think the poor thing was dressed only in pajamas.)

In a way, Mr. Steward, I think that child died. Oh, not physically, of course, but I think a large part of her childhood died at that moment. I've no doubt things will get better and there will come a time when she's laughing at a parking-lot carnival again, enjoying the rides and cotton candy and hot dogs and carousels . . . but she will never again enjoy them as much, because a part of her will always, *always* remember the way her mother and father treated her like an annoying stray dog in the middle of the night when she tried to express her deepest feelings and found, as any child that age would, that she didn't yet have the vocabulary to articulate the emotions that no child her age should *have* to be forced into expressing. She will have fun at these parking-lot carnivals, but it will never again be the same. Every moment of joy she experiences from now on will be tempered, if not tainted, by the memory of that night, and by the hurtful hole it left in her heart and spirit. Is that the kind of death you referred to, Mr. Steward? Because if so, I think I would prefer the physical form. I know I wanted to kill both of her parents that night. I did eventually go out to see if I could help, but by then her father had come outside and carried her back in, and when I woke up the next morning, the car was back and all three of them—laughing and smiling—were heading out to do some shopping for ". . . the birthday girl."

Who was it who insisted that children are so resilient? Personally, I think that person came up with that in order to not have to face the irreparable damage many parents do to their children, the little cruelties, the unthinking hurts that are inflicted on a daily basis.

Is this the type of death you wish to perpetuate, Mr. Steward? And do you sleep better at night knowing that there are individuals who are so desperate or hateful that they will push the button on your little unit and kill another human being?

I suppose I shouldn't lay all blame on your shoulders. Though you didn't say so, I came away with the impression that you are simply, as my late husband used to put it, a cog in a larger machine. He was a soldier in WW2 and knew all about being a cog in larger machines, and killing people he didn't know. Fifty-two years we were married, and I don't know that he ever got a decent night's sleep because of the memories of the war, everything he saw, all the people he killed.

He used to tell me about something his mother would say to him when he was a child. Whenever he would get sad or heartbroken or lonely, she would stroke his hair and tell him, "Don't cry, honey, because everything of beauty taken from you in this life remains forever. If you outgrow a certain kind of happiness, that happiness, that beauty, it passes on to someone else who needs it more." He tried—we both tried—to take comfort in that thought, especially after our son began going sour on us for reasons neither of us understood. Drugs, forgery, petty theft . . . for some reason he became everything we'd hoped he would avoid. He's tried, Billy has, to get better, to get past it (he calls me every week on Sunday night, just to see how I'm doing), but I think when he was born something in him was already ruined. Is that another form of the death you spoke of? I had all but given up hope on Billy when, after his father's death, he stole Frank's medals and other WW2 souvenirs to sell, but then Billy showed up here one night in tears. He brought back everything he'd stolen and kept telling me how sorry he was, how he loved me and how he'd loved his father and I allowed myself to hope again for a little while. But then the bills came due, Frank's veteran's pension—my widow's pension—was cut off, Billy disappeared again, and I was at the end of my rope. I even considered selling Frank's medals and souvenirs myself to bring in some money because my Social Security can't cover everything and we never were able to keep much in our savings . . . and then you showed up at my door with your button unit and your promise of all that money.

I always thought I was a good person, a person who tried to do the right thing, who did her best to not bring any pain or sorrow into this world, and I always figured that on the day of my death I would be remembered as a decent-enough human being.

But would a decent human being ever have considered your offer? Would a decent human being ever have unlocked the dome? No. A decent human being would have gone right out into that parking lot as soon as the car pulled away and taken that sad little girl into her arms and stroked her hair and said, "Don't cry honey, because everything of beauty taken from you in this life remains forever."

But it doesn't remain, does it, Mr. Steward? It crumbles into dust and is forgotten and any meaning it ever had is shown to be a lie. You made me see that, made me understand that, and in a strange kind of way, I thank you for that lesson.

Because as soon as I unlocked the dome and saw the button, I realized that I don't know myself at all.

I apologize if my handwriting is getting a little shaky. I'm scared. And ashamed.

If you're reading this, then you found the envelope with your name on it taped to the outside door with the key inside. You will have let yourself inside and found this letter taped to the used button unit. I do hope you came in a timely manner. If my guess was right, then it was I who died upon pressing that button. Do please leave the envelope with the cash in it on the small mail table just inside the front door and please do not disturb my body.

By the way, Mr. Steward—aren't I a wonderful forger?

I could always copy Mom's handwriting to near perfection. She stopped writing this letter after the words ". . . I don't know myself at all."

She pressed your goddamn button, Mr. Steward, and she *was* the one who died. Leave the money and this letter on the mail table, take your button unit, and go straight to hell.

But there is one more thing I think you should know. Among those WW2 souvenirs of my father's that Mom told you about is a Luger P 08 pistol he took from the body of a dead SS officer. Dad even had bullets, and kept the pistol in good condition. It still shoots. Isn't that interesting?

So, Mr. Steward, I have only two words remaining for you, the man who took my mom away from me.

Turn around.

THE CASE OF
PEGGY ANN LISTER

A Sequel to *Someone Is Bleeding*
BY JOHN MACLAY

Someone Is Bleeding is a riveting early (1953) crime novel by Richard Matheson that, while not among his better-known works, nonetheless spawned a French film version (*Les Seins de Glace*, 1974). Mr. Matheson's tale of the murderous Peggy Ann Lister has been brought up to date—and how!—by John Maclay, editor of the classic anthologies *Nukes* and *Voices from the Night* and author of many acclaimed short stories.

THE CASE OF
PEGGY ANN LISTER

My name is Chuck Mason. At age seventy, I'm a retired Baltimore City cop, and my hobby is looking into old murder cases, all across the country, and the juicier the better. They don't need to be of the unsolved kind, that most people like me study, since often the solved ones are even more interesting. And as to the latter, I especially always want to find out what happened to the murderer.

To get on with it, the Lister case, that unfolded in 1953 L.A., had all the ingredients I love. A beautiful blonde, only seventeen at the start, who'd (a) murdered her first husband, (b) ditto her lecherous landlord, though there'd been some doubt about that, and (c) ditto her wealthy patron, who'd had mob ties to boot.

There'd been an ice pick involved for good measure, but the clincher had been, with the last murder, that the cops had found her holding the severed head! I could hardly believe that when I first read of the case, but by the same token, I was totally hooked. How could this young Peggy Ann do that, and what was more, why?

So, since I'd already studied the L.A. newspaper accounts, and even the police records I'd got through an old buddy of mine who'd left Baltimore for the Coast, I went deeper, into the trial transcript. (Isn't the Internet great?) And as I might have guessed, I found out that Ms. Lister had been pled out on total insanity, and had been sent to an institution in 1954.

So much for my need to find out what had happened to the

murderer, at least at the time. But a very intriguing note in the transcript was that one David Newton, a man in his twenties, had also apparently been deeply involved with beautiful Peggy, even supposedly married her before her arrest. And that, as an aspiring writer, he'd even written an account of the whole course of events, that he'd offered in testimony. But that, given the insanity plea, it had never been accepted.

I sure as hell had to read that account, I thought, if it still existed. So I Googled David Newton, but came up empty. Deeply disappointed, I was about to give up on the whole thing, even on Peggy in or after the institution, when a lightbulb went off in my head.

David Newton. David Neustadt! Of course! The fantastically successful writer, still alive, who must have done a reverse of the usual and changed his name back to the German, probably to distance himself from this very case.

And I was on the next plane to Florida, where I'd found out he now lived.

Key Largo is hard to get to from the Miami airport, a long drive in a rental car south, then across a bridge, then north again. The rich just fly into a small local airport on Lear jets, but that's not me.

And it's even harder to get through the gate of Ocean Reef, unless you know somebody with a million-dollar-plus property there. But a little kibitzing with the guard, and a flash of my old Baltimore badge, made him look the other way.

As I pulled up in front of Newton's, or Neustadt's, sprawling stucco house on the water, I stopped for a moment to reflect how time could amazingly change all things. A poor writer in L.A. fifty years ago, an involvement in something way off the map, and now this.

But then I walked up to the elaborately paneled front door and knocked.

And a man of about eighty, his face familiar to me from when I'd Googled again, and on target this time, opened it.

"Yes?" he inquired.

"Peggy Ann Lister," I responded.

And the look in my eyes must have made him know he'd been found out at last in some way, and he had to let me in.

Neustadt led me out to a sun porch with pastel-fabric chairs, and we sat down. He offered me a Cuban and a Havana Club, and I wasn't about to say no. And then, suddenly, she appeared.

At first, with a chill, I thought she was Peggy indeed, but in the next instant, I knew she couldn't be. Yes, a beautiful blonde, much like the old news photo, but fifty at most, not seventy or so as Lister would be.

But after introductions had been made, and she'd departed, I did pose the burning question.

"You did 'marry' her, didn't you?" I asked, hopefully with gentleness. "You've remained obsessed with her, just as I'm so obsessed with finding out why."

And Neustadt slumped in his chair as he replied.

"Yes, not to mention three times over," he replied. "That one's my third wife, all of them in a quest to find her again."

"But she was a murderess," I had to object, "and of the most extreme kind, even with insanity being no excuse. Good God, man, how in the world?!"

But just as gently, he got up and led me to a paneled library, where he took a yellowed, old-fashioned typescript from a shelf, and put it, and everything, into my hands.

It took me two hours to read it, under his ever-watchful eye. But when I'd finished, I was speechless, and I had as many questions as he had comments.

And I knew now that even he, in self-defense, had hiddenly murdered in relation to the events, which made them even more amazing. And that she'd even stabbed him, when he'd tried "only" to have sex with her.

"So she was molested at age eight, and even by her father, and so on," I began. "And that was the reason for her, to put it mildly, sexual unresponsiveness to men. But for God's sake, an ice pick, a severed head?"

And yet David spread his hands, and replied.

"You've got to remember that this was the 1950s," he said. "Before any real consciousness of child sexual abuse, and repressed memories, and date rape, and women's rights, and so forth. Indeed, if it had been now, Peggy would have just gone for counseling. And I must say, in my account, I was in advance of more enlightened times. But as it was then, she was somehow an embodiment of the extreme reaction, instead."

I absorbed that, and admitted it. But still, I sorely needed a full explanation of what, even given that construct, she had been.

And David, responding to his sensing of that in me, went on to his conclusion.

"You know, Chuck," he said, now that he was unavoidably familiar with me, "there are femmes fatales, and we usually think of them as strong women. But the most compelling of them are, as such as Marilyn Monroe proved, in the 1950s too, the vulnerable ones, the abused. The women who, in truly being so, are the ultimate 'trouble,' carrying us men before them, as we seek to protect, but also, yes, to use. But when and if these still strike out in their defense—God, I think this whole case was the first symbol, and I'm only sorry I can never publish, for legal reasons, my account of it you've just read . . ."

" 'Men—they're all pigs,' " I quoted Peggy Ann Lister's quoted words from his typescript then, not knowing what else to do. "And in one way or another," and I quoted again, " 'someone must bleed.' "

"Then and always," David Neustadt sighed, maybe enigmatically, as he finally got up from his chair to show me out of his life, that he'd so sorely worked to come to terms with . . . but possibly into mine.

I, Chuck Mason, aged seventy, a retired Baltimore City cop and hobbyist of murder cases, wherever and whatever they might lead to, then left Key Largo and him.

But before I did, I asked him if Peggy, in bodily form as well, despite his pale imitations of her as with his current wife, still survived, and if so, if he knew where I might find her. After all, in what was now surely a more severe form of my usual need to find out what had finally happened to a famous murderer, I especially needed closure.

And of course, since his obsession was indeed his life, he told me.

"You'll realize," he said, with an ultimate sigh, as he showed me to his door, "that I was lost forever, and after she got out of the institution in 1960, I picked her up in my car and proposed marriage to her again, though she refused me. You may think me insane, too, but that vulnerable type of woman, who then, well, screws you up royally, is somehow the sublime."

"As may be the case with us poor mortal males with all women," I reflected out loud. "But whatever, if she is alive, give me her address!"

To make an end to all things, the subject of the case, and the ultimate one of so much, turned out to be residing in a trailer park in Tucson. And when I flew on to there, and breathed, though still with a residual apprehension, the dry desert air, she was everything I'd also become obsessed with, and more.

When I knocked, and she opened the metal door, she was wearing a long, flowing dress, but even that didn't hide her still spectacular figure. And while she must have been seventy-plus, like me, she hadn't really aged.

True, her hair was gray now, and there were lines on her face, but that was immaterial. Could anyone imagine Jean Harlow or Marilyn Monroe, if they too had survived, being grandmotherly? There was something about this type of woman that was young forever.

And it did have to do, I thought, with the vulnerability, the early abuse and how it had formed them, even, as in Peggy's case, to the extreme. That was so evident, and amazing, in her totally unchanged, blue eyes.

"Come in," she breathed, after I'd told her only the basics of why I was there.

And I obeyed, and now I was lost forever, too.

Forget any thought about an old Baltimore cop being ready for anything that wore a skirt. Or about an aged, and insane, nymphomaniac (as I'd read so many like her were, in seeming contradiction to their early having been abused), even yet possibly leading a man on to the ultimate, and therefore most frustrating, point of refusal.

In short, in the end, and without further ado, I too took Peggy Ann Lister in my arms. And she told me she knew I was a nice man, like David Newton, and that such were so rare in this world.

But when I modestly, and I still thought rationally, offered the advice that she should finally separate such out, and, well, sleep with them as though they weren't trying to kill her (or for God's sake, she not try to kill them, as she actually had killed the less nice), her blue eyes clouded.

"You can do it with me," Peggy sighed, as she did lay aside her clothes, and I wondered at her acquiescence. "At the last, you, who must somehow be fated."

She paused.

"But when it's over," she still concluded, explaining the clouding, "I'm not guaranteeing anything!"

And as she led me to her bed, she was indeed so nudely spectacular that I didn't care. What was the end point, I reflected, in my being abstractly obsessed with murder cases, if I didn't follow the physical reality, if I'd found it?

"My dear Peggy Ann," I wound it all up, as she actually, amazingly lay back on her bed and let me into her (never mind what younger people might think about seventy-plus sex), "as the first guy you've ever taken willingly, and despite all the history and psychobabble, I just don't give a damn."

"Not even if I stab you with an ice pick afterwards?" she said then, even stating what would have been chilling to me before, but now no longer was. "Or even cut off your head?"

"Good lady," I concluded again, as I still thrust strongly, "you're insane, and I've only used murder cases as a hobby, but now, with only a few years ahead of us, haven't we come down to a point? That was then, but this is now, and does anything else really matter? I don't think even any blessed David Newton would say it did."

"So I may kill you," Peggy Ann Lister breathed, as we moved to our fulfillment. "And maybe, as things have 'progressed' over the past fifty years, you're not only into 'protection,' or 'danger,' but into 'horrific endings,' as 'S&M'?"

"My weird love," I sighed, "whatever. But for God's sake, bring it all on!"

ZACHRY REVISITED

A Sequel to "The Children of Noah"
BY WILLIAM F. NOLAN

Richard Matheson's "The Children of Noah" (1957) is a classic tale of terror in a small town with an unforgettable cannibalistic ending. William F. Nolan, author of the science fiction novel *Logan's Run* and nearly one hundred other books, wonders what might have happened if relatives of the doomed Mr. Ketchum from that tale were to come to Zachry, the town where he was last seen, looking for answers. . . .

ZACHRY REVISITED

According to the *New England Guidebook:*

> Zachry is a small community (pop. 67) situated between
> the larger towns of Brewster and Chipping along the
> rocky coast of Maine. Founded in 1850 by a sea captain,
> Noah Zachry, the town is devoid of tourist attractions
> and has only one hotel, unrated by the Automobile Club.

"Doesn't sound like much," said Bruce Lindley. He was tall, twenty-three, with a straight jaw and serious gray eyes. He replaced the guidebook in the glove compartment, leaning back in the passenger seat. "Why would your brother stop at a nowhere place like Zachry? *If* he did, that is."

Peg Lindley swept their VW Beetle through a tight curve on the ocean road. The summer sky was clear and cloudless. Below them, the Atlantic tossed up streamers of white froth against piled black rocks. The air was rich with brine.

"I'm not at all sure that Jimmy stopped there," said Peggy, "but he never reached Chipping. You heard what the desk clerks said. None of the hotels there show that he registered."

Peg Lindley was a year younger than her husband, small-boned and attractive. She drove with studied intensity.

"Maybe he decided to just drive straight through," said Bruce. He smiled faintly. "Personally, darlin', I think we're on a wild goose chase. Doesn't make sense, our driving here all the way from Wisconsin. Jim's probably snoozing under an umbrella on some Florida beach right now."

"Impossible," said Peggy. "I'm his only sister and we've always been very close. He'd never just up and disappear without telling me." She hesitated, eyes fixed on the twisting road. "I haven't said this before but . . . I don't think Jimmy's still alive."

Her husband made a clucking sound in his throat. "I hope you're wrong."

"I hope so, too," said Peggy. "God *knows* I hope so."

It was dusk when they arrived in Zachry.

The place reminded Peggy of a deserted ghost town she'd visited as a girl with her parents. The same stark sense of abandonment. The buildings were boarded-up and paint-scoured, with weeds poking through fissures and deep potholes in the pavement. The street was empty of pedestrians.

"Looks like a dead town," said Bruce.

"Not quite," asserted Peggy. She pointed to a sputtering neon sign at the end of the main street. Several of the letters had burned out:

P . R A . . S E

"It's the Paradise Hotel," said Peg. "The one mentioned in the guidebook."

"Looks more like hell than paradise," muttered Bruce. "What a dump!"

Peggy pulled the VW to a stop in front of the hotel entrance. The rose-brick façade had been bleached white by salt winds off the ocean. They walked through the dusty lobby, rife with the odor of decay, to the front desk.

The clerk put aside a yellowed newspaper and got up slowly from a cracked leather chair, staring at them through thick glasses. A break in the frame had been repaired with discolored tape.

"Do ya for?" he asked. He was small, bald, and rail-thin, somewhere in his eighties.

"We'd like to check your register for June of last year," Peg told him.

"Got none," the old man rasped.

"You don't register your guests?" asked Bruce.

"Usta. When we *had* 'em. Don't no more. Not since five year ago. This ain't no tourist delight."

Peg took a photo from her purse, showing it to the clerk. "Have you ever seen this person?"

The old man adjusted his glasses, squinting dimly at the photo. "Don't recollect the face."

"It's my brother, James Ketchum. I think he may have come here last June . . . a year ago."

"Don't recollect the face," repeated the old man.

"Thank you for your time," said Peggy, restoring the photo to her purse.

"Don't hafta thank me none," said the little man. "Time's what I got plenty of. I got nothin' but time."

And as Peggy left with her husband the old man settled back into the cracked leather chair with his yellowed newspaper.

"Where to now?" asked Bruce when they were back in the VW.

"The local police station," she said.

Bruce shrugged. "*If* they have one."

"Every town has a police station," Peg declared, putting the car in gear.

It was two streets down. A single-story weathered brick building faded by the sun. A sagging, rotted-wood sign above the door spelled P O L I C. The E was missing. The station's front windows were clouded with ancient dust. Fog was sliding in from the ocean, dimming the building's outline.

They walked inside.

"Help ya?" asked a mustached officer. He was well into middle age with his uniform loose on a bony frame. He had deep hollows in his face as he peered at them across a high desk.

"My name is Peggy Lindley, and this is my husband Bruce."

"Uh-huh," noted the officer. "If you're lookin' to stay in Zachry there's plenty of room at the hotel."

"There *sure* is," said Bruce with a tight smile.

"Ya won't like it here much. Nothin' ta do. Nothin' ta see."

"We're not here as tourists," said Peggy. "I'm trying to trace my brother. He may have been here last year." She got out the photo, passing it across the desk. "*This* man, James T. Ketchum."

The officer shook his head. "Never seen the fella."

"In June . . . of last year. He may have come here."

"Not many folks stop in Zachry. How do ya know he did?"

"He phoned me from Brewster, but we had a bad connection. Jimmy promised to call me again that same night, as soon as he reached Chipping. But he never did."

"Mebbe he just forgot."

"Oh, no. He was worried about me," she said. "I was pregnant then and Jimmy was worried. But I never heard from him again."

"So ya have a kid?"

"No, I . . ." Her voice faltered. "I had some . . . trouble at the birth, and the baby . . . didn't survive."

"Real sorry to hear that."

"The point is, Jimmy would have called from Chipping, but he never checked in at any hotel there. The only town between Brewster and Chipping is this one. He must have stopped here that night for some reason."

The policeman bit his lower lip. "Your brother . . . a fast driver, was he?"

"What do you mean?"

"I mean we got us a fifteen-mile-an-hour speed limit in town an' he coulda been stopped for speedin'."

"I suppose that's possible," said Peg.

"Tell ya what. I'll have Chief Shipley check the arrest ledger for

June 'a last year, an' if your brother was stopped his name'll be in there." He moved toward the rear of the station. "I'll just go fetch the chief."

"Thank you," said Peggy.

They waited. An ancient clock on the wall ticked out the minutes. Next to it: the frame portrait of a bearded sea captain, with penetrating eyes.

Bruce pointed. "Must be ole Zach himself." He sighed. "Jeez, what a town. Like one big graveyard. Who'd want to live here?"

"I heard that question," said a gruff-voiced man advancing toward them. He stood tall and gaunt-faced behind the desk. "I'm Chief Shipley. And as far as who would want to live here . . . well, not many. We had us a population of sixty-seven last year, but come winter the widow McComas passed on. She used to say, 'Harry, if I can reach ninety then I'm ready to make my peace with the Lord.'" He grunted. "Sarah was ninety-one when she passed, God bless her dear soul."

"We came here to—" began Peggy.

"So now," said Shipley, cutting off her words, "we got just sixty-six folks left in Zachry. Young people all gone off to the big cities. Us ole codgers is all that's left. Me, 'cept for my daughter Elmira, I'm the youngest in town!"

"I'm looking for my brother, James Ketchum," said Peggy. "The other officer, he told us you might possibly have arrested Jimmy last year in June . . . for speeding."

She showed him the photo.

"Yeah . . ." Scratching his chin. "Kinda looks familiar. I mighta seen him."

"Would you check the ledger . . . for June of last year?"

"Righto," said Shipley. "Lemme take a look-see, and we'll find out if we got us a Ketchum listed."

He removed a musty leather volume from behind the desk, opened it and flipped the pages, locating the proper month. He ran his finger down several names.

"Only time we see new folks in Zachry is when we pick 'em up for speedin' an' that's a fact," he said. "Town's pretty dead otherwise."

"So we've noticed," said Bruce.

The chief snorted. "By golly, here he is! All signed neat an' proper . . . James T. Ketchum. Doin' fifty he was. Breezed right through, so we had to pull him in."

Peggy nodded to Bruce. "I was right! I *knew* Jimmy stopped here." She turned back to the chief. "Did you fine him?"

"Not that night we didn't," said Shipley. "Ole Judge Harker, he was ailing, so we had to keep your brother here overnight."

"Which explains why he never called you from Chipping," said Bruce.

"Yep. Had him in a cell the whole night."

"Then he was fined the next morning?" asked Peggy.

"Not exactly."

She stared at the chief. "What do you mean, 'Not exactly'?"

"Well, ma'am, there was what you'd call an altercation. When we took him outa the cell in the mornin' he broke loose an' run off, jumped in his car—was a new Ford, as I recollect—an' took off like a scalded cat."

"Didn't you go after him?" asked Bruce.

"Would have. But Jake couldn't get our cruiser started. Dead battery." He gestured toward the rear. "Jake's the fella you first talked to."

"Then what happened to my brother?"

The chief shrugged. "You tell me. Last I saw, he was hightailin' it outta town in his Ford."

"But I never heard from him again!"

"Mebbe he run off the road 'tween here and Chipping," said the chief. "Real bad fog off the water. Makes the road slick. Lotsa curves. Musta been in a big hurry. Goin' fast. Likely missed a curve an' landed in the ocean. Water swallered him up. No trace left."

"That might be the answer," said Bruce.

Peggy's head was down, and she was trembling. Bruce put a hand on her shoulder.

"I've had the feeling that Jimmy was dead," she said softly.

"Real sorry, ma'am," said the chief. He checked the wall clock. "Dark now. Fog's comin' in. Dangerous for you two folks to try an' go anywhere else tonight. Why doncha bed down at the Paradise? Fix you up with the Bridal Suite. Be like you're back on your honeymoon. No charge. My treat."

"That's very kind of you," said Peggy. She turned to her husband. "Honey, I *am* tired. Maybe we *could* stay here for tonight."

"All right with me," said Bruce.

"Fine," said the chief. "You folks'll be my guests. Proud to have ya."

And he gave them a sharp-toothed smile.

Chief Shipley's daughter, Elmira, escorted them to the Bridal Suite at the Paradise. She was in her early twenties, full-figured, dark-haired, with arresting green eyes.

"This is the best we have to offer," she told them. "It's a little dusty, but I put fresh sheets on the bed."

"We appreciate that," said Peggy. She noticed that Elmira was staring at her in an odd way. It was a bit disturbing.

The suite may once have been attractive, but it was long past its prime. Strips of peeling wallpaper dripped from a stained ceiling, and the furniture was faded and timeworn. A musty odor hung in the air. Noah Zachry glowered down at them from a large oil painting above the bed.

"Looks like you've pictures of ole Zach all over town," said Bruce lightly.

"His memory is sacred to us," said Elmira. She wore a plain black dress, high at the neck, and no makeup. Her hair was tied back in a tight bun.

"Zach ever get married?" Bruce asked.

"Indeed, yes," said Elmira, keeping her eyes on Peggy. "He married a native of Africa. Brought her over here to the States

when he founded this town. They had five children together—
and we're their direct descendants. Everyone in town is related.
Like one big family."

"What was she like . . . Zach's wife?" Bruce wanted to know.

"She had . . . certain tastes," said Elmira. "She taught her
children . . . a lot."

"Thank you for your kindness," said Peg. "I'm afraid I'm just
too tired to keep talking. It's been a rough day, and I'm in desperate need of sleep. Will you excuse us?"

"Of course," said Elmira. Her dark green eyes remained fixed
on Peggy. "Sleep well."

And she closed the door softly behind her.

When Peggy awoke the next morning the bed was empty beside
her. Bruce was gone. He had left a note next to her pillow:

> *Babe:*
>
> *Got restless. Couldn't sleep. Went for a walk through
> town. And guess what I found? Jim's car in the impound
> lot behind the station. The license checked out. It's his
> all right, which means that the chief lied to us about
> your brother's running away in the Ford. He never drove
> it out of town. Something's really haywire.*
>
> *I came back to the hotel to tell you about finding
> Jimmy's car, but you were deep asleep and I didn't have
> the heart to wake you.*
>
> *I'm going to the station and face Shipley. Intend to
> get the truth out of him. Back soon.*
>
> *Love*
> *Bruce*

She had overslept. Daylight was seeping into the suite through
drawn curtains. Bruce had not returned. Hurriedly, she got up,

dressed, and went down to the lobby. The little old man was still there. He stared up at her.

"My husband . . ." said Peggy. "Have you seen him?"

"Fella that come in with ya last night?"

"Yes! My husband, Bruce Lindley. He was with me . . . in our room upstairs . . . but he hasn't come back."

"Say where?"

"Where?"

"Where he went to."

"He said he was going to talk to Chief Shipley at the station."

"Mebbe he's still there."

"After all this time? It's almost noon!"

"Go see," said the little man.

And she did.

Jake was at the desk. No, he hadn't seen her husband. And when Shipley came out of the back office he said the same thing. He hadn't seen Bruce since he'd had Elmira escort them to the hotel the previous night.

"But in the note he left for me he said—" She broke off, suddenly running out of the station to the impound lot behind the building. Frantically, she checked the six cars there. No Ford.

Could Bruce have been mistaken? No, he'd verified the license number. Jimmy's car *was* there.

The chief was standing behind her. She wheeled to face him. "Where's my brother's car?"

"Probably at the bottom of the ocean," said Shipley. His tone had altered; no longer warm and folksy. "Somewhere off the coast road."

"You *know* that isn't true! My husband saw Jimmy's Ford in this lot last night. And now it's gone."

"Just like *he* is, huh? No car, no husband." And he chuckled, a dry, rasping sound.

Jake was standing beside the chief, a white cloth in his right hand.

"'Fraid you haven't had quite enough sleep," grinned Shipley. To Jake: "I'll hold her while you do the honors."

The chief threw his arm around Peggy's neck, forcing her head back. Jake moved up to press the cloth tight against the girl's face.

Chloroform!

She went limp in Shipley's arms.

When Peggy regained her senses she found herself seated at a dining room table with Elmira, Shipley, Jake, and the little bald lobby clerk. They all smiled at her.

"Where am I?" she demanded.

"You're a guest at my house," said Shipley. "For supper."

"Bet you got yourself a real appetite by now," said Jake.

Elmira, seated next to Peggy, reached out to run her fingers slowly across the girl's cheek. "You're really . . . *very* attractive," she said softly.

Peggy flinched back. "Don't touch me!"

"I intervened on your behalf, which is why you're still alive," said Elmira. "Ever been with a woman?"

"No, no . . . Never!" gasped Peggy.

"Then you have a great deal of pleasure awaiting you," Elmira said with a sharp-toothed smile. She nodded toward the fresh-cooked food on the table. "You must be famished."

"I'm . . . not hungry," said Peggy.

Elmira set a steaming plate in front of her. "Eat. It's excellent meat."

"Well done, and spiced with Elmira's special sauce," said Shipley. "My little girl's a wonderful cook."

"Good meat," nodded Jake.

"*Real* good," said the bald little man, smacking his lips.

Peggy stared at them. "What is this all about? What have you people done with my husband? Where is he?"

"Oh, he's real close," said Jake, smiling broadly. His teeth were yellow and pointed.

"Go ahead, daughter, tell our guest what kind of meat we're serving," said Shipley.

"It's filet of Lindley," said Elmira. "Your man took good care of his body. Nice and firm . . . and *juicy*. Dig in. You'll find he's quite delicious."

"Dear God!" Peggy gasped, sour bile rising in her throat as she stared in horror at the well-cooked flesh of her husband.

COMEBACK

A Tale Inspired by "The Finishing Touches"
BY ED GORMAN

Richard Matheson's "The Finishing Touches" (1970) introduces us to a man who commits murder out of envy, in order to win his victim's widow—but the widow turns out to be more resourceful than he could ever have imagined. Ed Gorman, the prolific author of over thirty novels and short story collections, most in the mystery field (including the popular Jack Dwyer and Sam McCain series), offers another intriguing take on envy—and resourcefulness—in "Comeback."

COMEBACK

The morning of the birthday bash this dude with hair plugs and a black camel's hair coat and the imperious air only a big-time businessman exudes walks into Guitar City and starts looking around at all the instruments and amps.

A tourist. Most places you see a guy who looks like this you automatically think this is the ideal customer.

But in the business of selling high-end guitars and amps you don't want somebody who looks like he just drove over from the brokerage house in his Mercedes but will only spend a few hundred on his kid.

Some of my best sales have gone to guys who look like street trash. They know music.

I wandered over to him. I assumed he didn't know what he was holding. The Gibson Custom Shop '59 Les Paul cost a few thousand more than I make a month and I do all right.

When he glanced up and saw me, he said, "Hey, you're the guy I saw on the news this morning."

I smiled. "My fifteen minutes finally arrived."

"Well, you're going to the big party and everything. Sounds like you'll have some night. Nice that you all still get along."

John Temple had returned to Chicago on the occasion of his thirtieth birthday. This was at the end of his worldwide tour and his latest CD going double platinum. Some of the friends he'd met while on tour were flying in for the occasion. Names people around the world would recognize. "Too bad you had that falling-out with Temple, you and—What's the other guy's name?"

"McMurtin."

"Right. Temple, McMurtin and you. You're Rafferty, right?"

"Right."

"And you and McMurtin—went off on your own."

He was polite enough not to finish the rest. The well-known tale of how John Temple decided four years ago that it was time that he took his wounded voice out for a test run all by itself. Two double platinum CDs later, Temple was returning home for a press orgy of adulation.

I was working here at Guitar City. Pete McMurtin was one of the ghosts you saw standing on the sidewalk outside rehab houses shakily smoking his cigarette.

Even though he'd brought up an unpleasant subject, he redeemed himself by saying, "My son's graduating from Northwestern. He's very serious about his little band. I was hoping he'd grow out of it by now. But no such luck. He's coming into the firm but he also plans to keep playing on weekends. So I want something really special."

"Well, this is really special."

"Oh? What is it?"

I told him.

"So this is really upscale, huh?"

I smiled at his word. "Very upscale."

"And he'll need an amp. A good one."

"A good one or a great one?"

"What's a great one?"

"Well, you've got a great guitar so I'd go with a great amp—a Marshall. The Jimi Hendrix Reissue. Stack."

He grinned. "This could all very well be bullshit."

I grinned back. I knew he was going to go for it. "It could very well be. But it isn't."

"Well, I guess you know what you're talking about. This is your fifteen minutes, after all." He meant well but it was still painful. "So my son will know what this is and he'll like it?"

"He'll love it. He'll think you're the best old man a kid could have."

A hint of pain in *his* eyes now. Maybe this present wasn't just for graduation. Maybe this was a guilt present of some kind. "Then let's do it."

On my lunch hour I drove over to the facility where Pete was staying. I'd talked to the woman in charge. Natalie was her name. She had said that Pete was showing some progress with his cocaine problem and that she was afraid of what might happen if he went to the party. I had convinced her that I would take care of him. I reminded her that he listed me as his only friend. After years of living in a coke dream his family had bid him goodbye.

At one time the Victorian house had been fashionable. Easy to imagine Packards pulling up in the driveway and dispatching men in top hats and mink-wrapped women laughing their way to the front door fashionably late for the party.

Now the house was grim gray and the cars were those dying metal beasts that crawl and shake from one traffic light to another.

Natalie Evans answered the door herself. The odors made me wince even before I crossed the threshold. All the friends I've had in places like this—bad food, disinfectant, old clothes, old furniture, old lives despite what the calendar says.

"He's in the parlor. He got up and worked for three hours this morning helping to clean out the garage. I'm really hoping he can keep going this way. That's why I'm nervous about tonight."

Natalie was one of those sturdy women who know how to run just about anything you care to name. Competence in the blue eyes. Compassion in the gentle voice. She was probably just a few years older than me but she was already a real adult, something I'd probably never be.

I'd seen Pete only two weeks ago but for an unexpected moment there I didn't recognize the fragile but still handsome twenty-six-year-old who sat deep in the stained arms of a busted-up couch. The smile was still there, though. John had the voice, I had the licks on the guitar. But Pete had the classic good looks of old Hollywood. Pete had been a heartbreaker since the three of us started Catholic school together in the first grade. He played a nice rhythm guitar, too.

"Hey," he said. I could see that he was thinking of standing up but decided against it. His three hours of work had apparently exhausted him.

The parlor was a receptacle for stacks of worn-out records, worn-out CDs, worn-out videotapes, worn-out paperbacks, worn-out people. An old color TV played silently; a pair of hefty cats yawned at me; and an open box of Ritz crackers and a cylinder of Cheez Whiz had to be moved before I could sit on the wooden chair facing him. Junkies and junk food.

"I don't know, Michael."

He didn't need to say any more. The apprehension, the weariness in those four words meant that I'd done the right thing by checking in with him before tonight.

"I talked to God, Pete."

He smiled again. We'd been kidding each other since we were six years old. We knew the rhythms and patterns of our words. "Yeah, and what did God have to say?"

"He said he was going to be *muy* pissed if you didn't go."

"God speaks Spanish?"

"He could be an illegal immigrant."

He rolled his head, laughing. "You're so full of shit."

"Look who's talking, compadre."

He leaned forward, sunlight haloing his head. He'd been the most mischievous of us. I'd never seen him turn down a dare, no matter how crazy. He wasn't tough but he sure was durable. But not durable enough to stand up to a coke habit that had taken over his life six years ago. Cost him his health, purpose, hope. And it had cost him Kelly Keegan, the girl that both Pete and John had loved since she'd come to St. Matthew's in sixth grade. John walked away with Kelly and his career. She'd been living with Pete. After that, Pete's habit got even worse.

"You're strong enough, Pete. You look great."

"I look like shit."

"Okay, you look like shit. But you're strong enough."

"I really look like shit?"

I got up out of the chair, walked over to him and swatted him upside the head. He grinned and flipped me off. I went back and sat down. "You jerk-off. Now c'mon. I'm picking you up at seven and we're going to the party."

He lifted his right leg. Pulled an envelope free. Glanced at it. Tossed it to me. "From Kelly. Came yesterday."

It was indeed from Kelly. It read:

Dear Pete,

I made a terrible mistake. I still love you. Please come to the party. John'll be surrounded by people. We'll be able to talk.

Love,
Kelly

"Wow." I pitched the letter back to him.

"That's what I'm nervous about."

"I thought they were so happy. With the new baby and all."

"So did I. I mean I'm still in love with her. I always will be. But I've been so strung out I just never considered the possibility—" He lifted the letter from his lap and stared at it. "I almost feel sorry for John."

"Screw John. He dumped us. If he'd stayed with us we'd all be rich today."

"You really believe that?"

"You don't?"

"I don't know anymore. Maybe we didn't have what it takes—you know, the way John does."

"You know that's a crock, man." I'd had that same thought myself, of course. But I wasn't about to admit it. "And he sure didn't worry about you when he walked off with Kelly."

He shook his head. "But she's got to be crazy. Her kid—the whole life they've got—the money and all that. What the hell would we have to say to each other?"

"Well, there's one way to find out."

"I don't know. It just wouldn't be right."

"He didn't care about you or your habit. Not the way he left and all."

He held up a halting hand. "I'm here because I'm an addict. And you're selling guitars because the little group you put together last year didn't work out. He isn't responsible for either of those things."

"No, but remember how he wouldn't meet with us? Had that new agent of his handle everything? I just want to see him face to face."

Knock on one of the parlor doors. The old-fashioned kind that rolled back into the frame. Natalie parted the doors with a deft foot and came in carrying coffee. "I had to make a fresh pot. That's what took me so long."

"She makes great coffee," Pete said.

"Flatterer." She used her foot again, this time to drag the coffee table closer to us. She set the cups on the deeply scratched wood and said, "There you go. If you want more, just let me know."

My cup had a piece missing on the lip. I wasn't worried about glass in my coffee. The chip had been missing a long time and Natalie had no doubt washed the cup dozens of times. But it made me feel like hell for Pete. For both of us, actually, I suppose. Those old days in Catholic school, high school especially. Not the best or the brightest but we did all right with the girls and the future gleamed like a new sunrise just down the road ahead of us. So much hope and so much promise. And now here we were in this busted sad place drinking out of chipped cups.

"So I'm supposed to tell her what when you don't show up?"

"You're going anyway?"

"Hell, yes, Pete. This'll be a big deal for me. And there'll be record people there. Maybe I can make a contact."

His smile was fond. He was smiling at the same memory I'd had a minute ago. The three of us in high school and all those rock and roll dreams. "You never give up, do you?"

"Not dreaming, I don't. Maybe I'll be at Guitar City the rest of my life but that doesn't mean I have to stop thinking about it."

He laid his head back and closed his eyes. "She'll look so beautiful that I won't be able to control myself. I'll probably grab her. She's all I think about. Four years later and it still hurts as much as it did the day she told me she was leaving with John."

"But she's still in love with you."

He didn't say anything for a time. I sipped my coffee. A deep sigh. He said, "I'll go but I'll probably regret it."

Even in good suits, white shirts and conservative ties the two steroid monsters at the front door of the very upscale Regency Hall were clearly bouncers. God help you if your name wasn't on the list. The usual doormen had obviously been replaced by folks more accustomed to the world of rock and roll. And rap.

If either of the killer androids knew who we were they didn't indicate it in any way. They simply consulted their BlackBerry list and waved us on through after we handed over the invitations.

The hall was the preserve of visiting artists, classical musicians, noted scholars. The lobby held a discreet Coming Attractions board. Chamber music was the next attraction. Few of the people in the lobby looked as if they'd be here for that particular event. The trendy hairstyles (female and male), the chic clothes (female and male) and the number of visible tattoos (mostly male) spoke of different musical pleasures. Dreadlocks, male rouge, cocaine eyes. Not your typical chamber music crowd at all.

Pete stood tight against me. He was the child afraid to leave his parent. I could almost feel him wanting to do a little shapeshifting.

"I shouldn't have come here," he said.

And with that the joyous evening began.

John took the stage to a standing O and then went immediately into generic humility. He thanked more people than ten Oscar winners. Nary a mention of Pete or me. No surprise there. He was saving the moment for Kelly. And it was quite a moment. Four years and a kid later she was still the pale Irisher redhead of almost mythic beauty. The emerald cocktail dress only enhanced her slender but comely shape.

John, my generation's Neil Diamond, in theatrical black shirt and tight black jeans, gave her the kiss everybody wanted to give her. I saw Pete look away.

"This is the reason I'm up here. I was going nowhere in terms of my career until my true love Kelly agreed to marry me. And that gave me the strength to break away and go on my own. I really mean it when I say I wouldn't be on this stage tonight without this woman."

I wondered how many people in the audience understood what "break away" meant. Break away from Pete and me. Bastard.

Kelly didn't reach for the stand-up mike so John leaned it toward her. "C'mon, honey, just say a few words." And as he said this, on a huge TV screen suspended from the right corner of the stage, was a sunny photograph of Kelly holding their two-year-old daughter Jen. The kid was almost as much of a beauty as the mother.

Pete tugged at my arm. "Let's get outta here, man. I can't take this."

I whispered so nobody else around us could hear. "I'm tempted to go backstage and lay him out. Just break him up a little."

"Yeah. And then I'd come visit you every weekend in jail—if they'd let me out of the halfway house."

He turned, starting toward the door but I grabbed him. "Just a few more minutes, Pete. We got nothing else to do, anyway."

"I'd rather be back at the house."

Invisible speakers boomed "Happy Birthday" so loud there was no point in trying to talk. Everybody was singing along and then this five-tiered cake was wheeled on stage. John went back into generic humility for the next few minutes as he cut the cake and served Kelly the first slice. This was when the other rock stars appeared, four of them, encased in their arrogance and privileged clowning.

Then dancing and liquor and dope of all kinds broke out. The party was officially on.

Pete managed to leave my side before I could stop him. There was a crowd at the door and he somehow eeled through it. I had to bump between two big important bellies to catch him just as he reached the front door and the androids. I could feel the belly owners glaring at me.

I grabbed him by the shoulder and spun him around. One of the androids had been facing inside. He lurched toward me.

"No problem here," I said.

Pete saw that he was eager to waste me so he said, "Everything's cool. No need for any trouble."

Disappointed, the android stopped, glared at me and then went back to his post.

I half dragged Pete into an empty corner of the lobby. "Where the hell were you going?"

"Where do you think? Watching her up there—"

"It got to me, too, Pete."

"Not in the way it got to me. You hate him and that's different from me being in love with her. You just want to hurt him."

"I want to kill him."

"That's what I mean. That's different. You don't know what I'm going through." I'd seen him cry before, too many times, trying to kick coke. But these tears were different, not harsh but gentle, sad as only Pete could be sad.

"Aw, man, I'm sorry."

"So could we just leave?"

"Sure. We'll get a pizza."

He smiled as he brushed a tear from his cheek. "All that fancy food inside and we're going to get a pizza?"

"Yeah. Better class of people, anyway."

He saw her before I did. There was a stairway leading to the balcony. She descended it concealed by a group of much larger people. He said "God" and that was when I saw her, too.

And that was the moment when all the corny moments in all the corny movies proved to be not so corny at all. Her recognizing him; him recognizing her. It was really happening that way. Them stunned by the sight of each other. And all else falling away.

If she said goodbye to the important people around her, I wasn't aware of it. She simply left them and floated across the lobby to us. To Pete, I mean. I doubt she was even aware that I was there.

He was the old Pete suddenly. The bad drug years fell from his face, his eyes. And it was all ahead of him, the great golden glowing future. And when she reached out and took his hand, I saw that she wanted to be part of that future. That she knew now how bad a mistake she'd made taking up with John. That despite her marriage, somehow she and Pete would be together again.

She tugged him away from the corner. She still hadn't said hello to me or even let on that she knew I was there. I didn't care. I was caught up in their movie dream, happy for both of them. And happiest of all that the retribution I'd wanted to visit on John was now far more crushing than a few punches could make it. He was losing his wife. They were gone.

For the next twenty minutes I drank wine and listened to conversations between people who were—or claimed to be—in the music industry. The anger was coming back. I wanted to hear my name instead of John's. I wanted those chart sales to be mine. I wanted the tour they were discussing to focus on me. John should be working at Guitar City. Not me.

But at least Pete was getting something out of this night. All the way back to grade school he'd been the one she'd loved. And now maybe it was finally going to happen for them.

"Are you Mr. Rafferty?" She was an officious-looking blonde in the red blazer that Regency Hall employees wore.

"Yes, I am."

"John would like to see you in his dressing room."

"John Temple?"

"Why, yes." She gave me an odd look, as if maybe I was stoned and not hearing properly. Was there any other John who mattered here tonight?

"What's he want to see me about?"

She'd been trying to decide if she found me tolerable or not. She'd just made her decision. Not trying to hide her irritation, she said, "I'm just doing what he asked me, Mr. Rafferty. I'm not privy to his thoughts."

"Aw, God. I'm sorry. I'm just a little surprised is all."

"Well, there are a lot of people here tonight who'd be happy to visit with him in his dressing room. Consider yourself lucky."

She didn't have anything more to say to me until we reached backstage and the row of three doors off the left wing of the stage. She knocked gently on the center door and said "Mr. Temple?"

"Yes."

"Mr. Rafferty is here."

"Great. The door's unlocked."

She stood back for me. I wondered if she could tell how angry I was at hearing his voice. Four years of rage, of betrayal. I wanted to rip the knob off and flatten the door on my way inside where I'd grab him and begin beating him to death.

But he was quicker than I was. He stood in the open door, all black-clad rock star, smiling camera-big and camera-bright. He'd learned that smirking with your mouth made you enemies. Now he tucked his smirks into his dark eyes. He took a step forward and I thought he was actually going to give me a Hollywood man-hug but he obviously sensed that that might not be such a good idea so he settled for waving me in. The small room held a large closet, a makeup table with the mirror encircled by small bright bulbs and several vases stuffed with red congratulatory roses.

"Close the door, would you?" he said.

"You want it closed, you close it."

He walked over to the dressing table and hoisted a bottle of Jack Daniel's Black. "I'm sure you'd rather have this than all that sissy-boy wine they're serving. You get some Jack, I get the door closed. That's how the world works, Rafferty."

I kicked it shut with my heel.

"Nice to know you've grown up," he said, not looking at me, pouring each of us healthy drinks.

"What the hell you want to see me about?"

The eye smirked as the hand offered me my drink. "We didn't leave on the best of terms. Maybe I feel guilty about things."

"Oh, man. Spare me this crap, all right? You dumped us because you knew we were going to get a contract and then you'd have to share the spotlight with us. You wanted it all your own."

The sharpness of his laugh surprised me. The contempt was bullet-true. "God, Rafferty, do you really believe that? Please tell me that's not what you really think."

But before I could say anything he went on.

"I stayed a year longer than I should have. I stayed because we went all the way back to grade school. I stayed because we were friends. But Pete's habit got worse and worse and you—" He paused.

"And me? What about me?"

I noticed that the smirk was gone. The gaze was uncomfortable. "You're not the greatest guitarist I've ever worked with."

"I was good enough to write songs with." But the whine in my voice sickened me as much as it probably pleased him.

"You'll notice I've never recorded any of those songs. Never played them on stage. Never tried to sell them."

"So you called me in here to tell me what a genius you are and what losers Pete and I are?"

"I called you in here to have a drink and to say that I'm sorry for how things were left. It's natural for you to think of me as a bad guy. But I had the right to do what I did. A lot of people leave groups and go out on their own. I didn't commit any mortal sins."

"Maybe not. But you helped destroy Pete."

"Pete was already destroyed. It was just that neither of you would admit it then. I've kept track of him. In and out of rehab. Every time the stays get longer. Every time there's a little bit less of the Pete we grew up with."

The words came out. I didn't say them. In fact I was as shocked as John had to be. "Well, right now there's enough left of him to be off alone somewhere with your wife."

There was a flash of deep pain in the eyes. "I'm well aware of that, Michael. One of my people has been keeping an eye on her for me. Kelly and Pete are in a small office off the balcony. I'm trying not to think about what's going on."

Again he spoke before I could.

"I could stop them. But she needs to get it out of her system. She thinks she's still in love with him. Her one true love. I have every-thing I've always wanted now but I'll never have her the way Pete had her. Maybe when she sees him tonight, sees that he's not who he once was—" He shrugged. "But that's kidding myself. She loves the idea of Pete. She knew he was a junkie and that's why she went off with me. But she can't get rid of this idea of him." He tapped his forehead. "She won't see him as he really is. He'll be the old Pete to her."

I wanted to think that this was just a performance. That way I could enjoy it as simple bad acting. But I knew better. As much as I hated him I knew that he was telling the truth.

"That make you happy, Michael?"

"Yeah. It does. The one thing you can't have. That makes me very happy."

And then the smirk was back snake-quick in the eyes. "You like it at Guitar City, do you? I'm told that you're their best salesman."

"Screw yourself."

"You didn't answer my question, Michael. Are you happy at Guitar City?"

The girls don't come as easy as I thought they would. You see all these reality shows where girls will do anything to sleep with rockers. But I do all right. A lot better than I was doing before John added me to his band. The money's pretty good, too. I own a '57 Vette and when I take it back to the old neighborhoods you'd think the Irishers were having St. Patrick's Day.

The touring was cool for the first year but now it gets to be a drag sometimes. John's letting me play on the next CD. He says that'll keep us in LA for at least six months. Cool by me.

Kelly has pretty much willed me out of existence. Even when I'm forced to stand close to her she won't acknowledge me in any way. Everybody in the band notices, obviously. I think they feel sorry for me.

She only came after me once. This was after a gig in Seattle. She'd had a few drinks and right in front of John she slapped me and said, "I know where he got the coke, Michael. You gave it to him. More than enough to kill him. And I know who put you up to it." She was staring right at John when she said it.

The word is she's staying with him because of the kid. And that may be true. But maybe she's like the rest of us. You know, the whole rock and roll thing. She's the belle of the ball, "The Nicole

Kidman of Rock" as *People* called her recently. And maybe that's how he keeps her. She wouldn't be as hot if she divorced him. More number-one double platinum CDs. Not even her beauty can match that.

The last time I went back to Chicago I stopped by the halfway house where Pete had last stayed. The woman Natalie? I gave her a check for $2,500 to help with the bills for the house. I thought she'd be real happy about it but she handed it back and walked away.

Late at night I feel bad about it sometimes. But as John always says, maybe we did him a favor. I mean it wasn't like he was ever going to have a comeback or anything.

AN ISLAND UNTO HIMSELF

A Variation on "Disappearing Act"
BY BARRY HOFFMAN

"Disappearing Act," · Richard Matheson's memorable 1953 tale, consists of a journal written by a man whose every acquaintance is disappearing around him—literally. In "An Island Unto Himself," Barry Hoffman—author of the "Eyes" series of suspense novels (*Eyes of Prey, Hungry Eyes, Judas Eyes, Blindsided*)—presents a strikingly different take on the idea.

An Island Unto Himself

Don looked at his watch, then looked at a clock in the lobby of the CNN Building to verify the time. 8:35. He had an appointment with his assignment editor at nine. *Shouldn't be a problem*, he thought to himself. He was early, as always. Punctual to a fault, he would grudgingly admit. Most of the time he arrived far too early, while the person he had an appointment with invariably arrived late or kept him waiting. Common courtesy was certainly lacking, he'd think, as he shook hands with whomever he was to meet. Seldom did they ever apologize for their tardiness. Arriving "fashionably late" had become the norm. But Don would get butterflies in his stomach even at the thought of not being punctual.

Now he waited his turn in line at the CNN security desk, which reminded him of the lines at airports. Ever since 9/11 and, later after an anthrax scare aimed at network anchormen, security had been tightened severely both at airports and at major news organizations. And those in charge of security seemed to take a perverse pleasure working as slowly as possible. Hell, he saw a well-known anchorman at the front of the line now being scrutinized. Like Wolf Blitzer might be a terrorist.

Still, Don got to the front of the line at 8:46. Plenty of time to get to his meeting with minutes to spare.

"Hi, Charlie," Don said to the balding overweight man whose

security uniform bulged at his waist. Charlie usually gave him a perfunctory glance and ushered him through.

"Can I see your ID, Sir," Charlie said. It wasn't a question.

"Charlie, it's me, Don. Don Woodson."

"ID, Sir."

"Is this some kind of joke?" Don asked. Why the hell was Charlie treating him like a total stranger? Usually . . . no, *always,* there was some playful banter on Charlie's part. A quip about his wife, who seemed forever pregnant. Seven children and counting. An anecdote about one of his children. Or a comment about how the weather was up there, where Don stood. At six-foot-five Don towered over the far smaller man. Charlie might joke about Don's height, but he was civil enough not to mention the scars that tattooed the left side of Don's face. The now faint lines resembled a tic-tac-toe board. A Palestinian suicide bomber had blown himself and a dozen others to bits when Don had been in an Israeli restaurant four years earlier. He still suffered occasional headaches from the concussion he'd sustained. That, and glass shards that now decorated his face were constant reminders that he was always surrounded by death in his work. Plastic surgery could do just so much. Now he stared at Charlie who refused to acknowledge him. "You act as if you don't know me."

"I don't," Charlie said. "Look, I need to see your ID or you'll have to get out of line."

Don sighed. Charlie must be having a bad day, he thought. Don searched his pocket and was chagrined to find he had no photo ID. His wallet had money and both a library card and credit cards with his name on them, but no driver's license. No photos at all. Could he have left them at his apartment? Rather than argue Don got out of line and decided to call his editor. He looked at his watch. 8:54. With any luck he'd still be on time for his briefing on his third trip to cover the war in Iraq. It would be his second trip to Baghdad, where sectarian violence was at its worst.

"Jean, this is Don," he said, when Tom Spooner's secretary picked up her phone. "I'm in the lobby. There's been some kind of foul-up. Can I speak to Tom?"

"Your name, please," Jean said, without greeting.

"Don. Don Woodson, for Christ's sake. Tom's expecting me for a briefing."

"I'm sorry but Mr. Spooner has no appointment with a Don Woodson," Jean said.

"There must be a mistake, Jean. Look, just let me talk to him."

"Your name again?" she asked.

"Cut the crap, Jean," Don said, his anger building. "Look, you're Jean Darcy. Short red hair, blue eyes. You just got contacts because you felt glasses made you look old. Unlike most women you like beer, not wine. We've tossed back a few in Tom's office." Don realized he was talking fast, as if the woman on the other end of the line would hang up at any moment. "You have a piece of chocolate or a donut, then think you have to go on a diet. And . . . oh, you have a tattoo of a serpent on your . . . your left shoulder. Am I right?"

"How do you know—"

"Because I've known you for five years," Don said. "Shit, we even slept together once. That's how I know," he said lowering his voice so others couldn't hear, "about the *other* tattoo you have. The one on your inner thigh. A butterfly. Now let me talk to Tom."

"But . . . I don't know you. I've never heard of a Don Woodson, much less slept with him . . . you," Jean said, sounding flustered. "I'm sorry, I can't—"

"Fuck it," Don said, cutting her off. He disconnected. What had he done to piss Jean off? he wondered. Maybe mention of their one-night stand hadn't been appropriate. But that had been over a year ago. Don had been completely upfront with her when he noticed her flirting with him. They'd gone out and ended up in bed. He had told her his life didn't allow for commitment.

They hadn't slept together since and neither had mentioned the night until today. Don knew his comment had been in poor taste, but it was petty of her to not allow Don to speak to her boss because he'd been crass.

Don decided to wait for Tom. If Don was obsessive about punctuality, Tom was equally rigorous when it came to sticking to his schedule. At noon, rain or shine, he went to a deli three blocks from the CNN Building. No matter how busy the restaurant was, there was always a table for their best customer. Tom had his cell phone in case there was an emergency back in the newsroom.

Don was across the street from the deli at 11:45. At 12:10 Tom entered. Don waited a few minutes then went inside the deli and took a seat across from his assignment editor.

"I'm sorry I missed our appointment this morning," Don began, seeing Tom taking a bite out of a roast beef sandwich. "Security wouldn't allow me in and then Jean—"

"Do I know you?" Tom interrupted, his mouth still full.

"This is getting fucking ridiculous," Don said, a bit too loud. Several customers were staring at him. He lowered his voice. "Okay, I'll play along. Of course you know me. Don Woodson. Crack photo journalist. Whenever the shit hits the fan in some far corner of the world you send me on the next plane to cover the story." He turned his left cheek towards his friend, showing his scar. "You sent me to Israel and I came back with this souvenir. I'm told you never left my bedside the three days I was in a coma. Now let's cut the crap and—"

"But I really *don't* know you," Tom interrupted. "Never saw you before. Never heard of a Don Woodson. Never sat by your bed while you were in a coma, though I'd like to think I would have if one of my people was hurt on the job. You must be confusing me with—"

"You've been my assignment editor . . . my *friend* for six years," Don said, trying to remain calm. "What the fuck's going on?"

"Let me see your press card," Tom said.

Don took out his wallet. Cash, credit cards. No license. No press card. "I . . . I must have left it on my bureau at my apartment," he said meekly.

"Really," Tom said, and Don could hear the sarcasm in his voice. "Before you go to bed each night you take your press card out of your wallet?"

"Look, I know it sounds—"

"Lame," Tom finished for him. "I don't know what your problem is, but I assure you this is the first we've met. Now, if you don't mind, I don't want to have to call the manager to—"

Don got up. "Forget the charade, Tom. I don't know what the fuck's going on, but you have my number. Call me when you want me to go back to work."

Don stormed out. Fled, he'd later admit to himself, and walked to a park two blocks away. Sitting on a bench he replayed the entire morning in his head. Charlie, Jean and now Tom said they didn't know him. He had no photo ID. No press card. He considered the possibility someone was playing an elaborate joke on him, then tossed it aside. How would the ringleader have gotten his license and press card? No, something was wrong. He'd have to prove he existed.

So, how do I prove I exist? he asked himself. *You're a reporter, simpleton, how would you prove anyone existed?* he answered his question. Soon he came up with a plan.

He went to a nearby library, made his way to a bank of computers and sat down in front of one. His hand was shaking as he Googled his name. There were loads of Don Woodsons, he saw with relief. He scrolled down looking for himself and his relief turned to despair. Doctors, lawyers, ministers, even an article from a scientist named Don Woodson about how cow dung could be used instead of gasoline to fuel automobiles. But not a single mention of photo journalist Don Woodson. He was certain there had been numerous stories about his injuries and recovery when he'd been reporting in Israel and become a victim of a suicide bomber. He found stories about the bombing itself, but no matter how he phrased the query he couldn't locate one story about himself on either Google or three other search engines he tried.

He then logged onto the CNN website and searched for himself, to no avail. He went to the CNN library on the website and looked for stories he had reported on and photographs that he had taken. None. *What the hell is going on?* he wondered. He abandoned the library.

Next he went to his bank. He attempted to withdraw fifty dollars from the ATM outside. A message flashed across the screen telling him no such account existed and he should go inside to seek the assistance of a teller.

Seated across from an assistant manager he explained his problem.

"The ATM and your teller," he said pointing to a spindly young woman with a bad case of acne, "both tell me I have no account here. Problem is I've been banking here for ten years and have ample cash in both my checking and savings accounts."

"We'll take care of this quickly," the assistant manager said. She looked like a matronly school teacher who could solve all his woes. She typed in his checking account number and frowned. "I'm afraid there is no such account," she said.

"You mean it's been closed?" Don asked.

"No, there has *never* been such an account."

He told her his savings account number and she frowned again after she had typed it in. He gave her his ATM card. Another frown.

"Wait. I have a safety deposit box here. I even have a key," he said, holding it aloft for the woman to see.

She took him to the back of the bank and had him both sign his name on a computer screen and place his thumb on another screen which would read his thumbprint. Don remembered he'd gone through the same procedure whenever he put something into the box. He couldn't recall ever having taken anything out. This time she sighed, after he'd gone through the process. Neither his signature nor his thumbprint had been recognized by the computer.

"I'm sorry, but maybe you have mistaken us for another bank."

He could have argued with her but he knew it would have been fruitless. Instead he went back to his apartment. He still had a list of a dozen other ways to prove he existed.

Getting off of the elevator he saw Jerry Newfield, a doctor who had been his neighbor for seven years.

"Jerry, how's it going?" Don asked.

The man gave him a blank stare.

"Don Woodson from apartment 304," he said, seeking to jog the man's memory.

"Ah, you must be the man who just moved in," Jerry said, with a weak smile. "I don't recall us having met yet," he added and held out his hand.

No, Don wanted to yell. We've definitely met. He wanted to tell Jerry about the affair the man was having with his tennis instructor. A *male* tennis instructor. He wondered what Jerry's wife would have made of that. But he said nothing. No use in alienating the man. He shook Jerry's hand then made his way to his apartment. Would his key work? he wondered. When it did he sighed in relief. Then thanked his lucky stars when he saw the apartment was no different from the one he'd left that morning.

He went to a bookshelf and pulled down his college yearbook. He turned to the page with his photo. It hadn't been very flattering, but all he cared about now was to see it staring back at him. It wasn't there. There was no blank spot where his picture belonged, just a photo of someone else in his graduating class. He pulled out a high school yearbook. He wasn't in that either. He also couldn't find himself in group photos of the high school newspaper or swim team, both of which he'd been a member.

"Fine," he said out loud. He looked at his list, then shook involuntarily. He'd call his parents. Hell, he owed them a phone call. He'd been back in the States for four weeks since his last assignment in Iraq and had spoken to them just once, two days after his return.

His mother answered the phone. Thank goodness, he thought. He recognized her voice. His parents existed. *He* existed.

"Mom, it's Don. I'm sorry I haven't called—"

"You must have the wrong number," his mother said.

"*No*, it's Don. *Your son*," he said, and once again he knew his voice was rising. He heard his mother call for his father and then their voices became muffled. She must have put her hand over the receiver while she spoke to his father, he thought.

"Who is this?" a man—*his father*—asked.

"Dad, it's Don. Your son," he said, feeling foolish.

"How . . . how could you be so cruel?" his father said, both anger and hurt in his voice.

"What have I done, Dad?" Don asked.

"Don't you dare call me *Dad*," the man said. "We have no children. Call again and I'll contact the police." His father hung up the phone.

For the first time Don considered he just might have gone insane. Maybe he wasn't Don Woodson.

It was then he remembered his journals—six books in which he had written what had happened to him as a photo journalist. Impressions and anecdotes behind the photos he took and the film he shot for CNN. He smiled as he recalled how he thought he'd use the journals when he wrote his memoir. He'd been full of himself when he'd started. Yet even when he realized his life hadn't been extraordinary enough to merit an autobiography he continued to express his inner thoughts in his journals. He had a doozy of a tale to tell now.

He found the books where they belonged. Hands, shaking, he took down the most recent journal and opened it. Scanning the pages he felt like jumping for joy. The journal was filled with entries just as he recalled them. Here was proof he had taken the photos and shot the film he couldn't locate.

He read some of the most recent. He relived his last trip to Baghdad. He read how he'd ignored the violence and his refusal to photograph the Iraqi civilians killed or maimed in the carnage. Money shots often shown on television or in newspapers and magazines. Instead he had focused on the soldiers—a National Guard unit recently called up which had just arrived in the country. Poorly trained and many without proper equipment, he had captured *their* terror. They hadn't signed up for this and had no idea how to cope with what they encountered. They literally feared for their lives and their sanity. He had captured their horror and confusion. It was what Don was noted for.

His existence was validated—at least to himself. Still, he had to find others to prove that this too wasn't a figment of his addled mind. On a night stand next to his bed was a tattered phonebook. While he now stored his phone numbers in a BlackBerry, this one, in his own handwriting, contained most of the numbers his electronic phonebook stored. He had calls to make.

He called doctors, including the plastic surgeon who had done wonders on his scarred face. He called his dentist of over fifteen years and even a shrink he'd gone to after he'd gotten out of the hospital. He had had recurrent dreams of the Palestinian suicide bomber. In each he saw different victims being dismembered by the blast. In each he saw the face of the bomber smiling at him before blood, bone and tissue took its place as he exploded his bomb. He saw the window from the glass hurtling towards his face. Sometimes he'd even dream when he was awake. That was when he knew he definitely needed professional help. While he still had the occasional dream of the carnage, the psychiatrist had helped him immensely.

The responses to his calls were invariably the same.

"I don't have a patient named Don Woodson."

"Could you check your records?" Don asked.

Always there was a sigh, but the physician or secretary relented. "I'm sorry, but we have no records for a Don Woodson."

He called colleagues who, while not friends, knew him well. Not any longer. He shook his head, his eyes closed, as one after another feigned having no idea who he was.

Finally he was down to one last name, a professor at NYU he considered his mentor. He was the man who had given him direction. The man who had given his photos a unique voice. Don recalled a meeting with the man; small in stature, with a receding hairline and horn-rimmed glasses. Don had given Carl Westman his dissertation—a portfolio of forty some-odd photographs.

"Don, these are technically excellent. Even extraordinary. Your use of shading, sunlight, backgrounds for your subjects, composition, well, that and more are as good as any I've ever seen," Westman said. "But, and I hate to sound harsh, they are instantly forgettable. I've seen the same photos dozens of times before. Not as good as yours, but there's nothing memorable."

For a moment Don had loathed the man. He was being told in the same breath he was an exceptional photographer yet his work was instantly forgettable. "I don't understand," Don had said, exasperated.

"Here, look at this child you captured holding onto the leg of a fireman. The boy seems to have lost his parents."

"Yes, they perished in the fire," Don had said with enthusiasm. "The expression on his face speaks volumes."

"Seen it . . . dozens of times before," his professor had said. "But what of the fireman? We don't see his face at all. Is it filled with compassion or does it lack any emotion at all because the man has seen the same scene so many times before? That's what could make your photos stand out from the multitude of others. Your talent is indisputable. You're just not taking the right photographs. Forget about the victims . . . at least the obvious ones. It's what every photographer focuses upon."

He stood up and went to a shelf and removed four books, then handed them to Don. "There are some classics in these books. Look at them so you don't replicate them. Come at your subject matter in a way that's unique. With your technical proficiency you could then create masterpieces of your own. Shoot firemen, policemen, even the throngs that gather at such tragedies. Let your photos tell *their* story. Their fear. Their trepidation. Their emotion or lack thereof because they're burned out, possibly, or maybe they've learned to become emotionally detached to survive. And there are so many different emotions on the faces of those who gather at a crime scene or tragedy. Hell, at a fire you could capture the face of an arsonist. They tend to want to see their handiwork."

Don had nodded and smiled. Differentiate himself from the

crowd of photographers who populate a fire or crime scene taking the same vapid photographs.

"I'll give you a two week extension, if you wish," his professor had said, as if reading Don's mind. "Or, I'll give you an A now because your work is clearly superior to that of any of your classmates."

Don had taken the man's challenge and when he returned two weeks later with a new portfolio of just a dozen shots the man had smiled. "These tell stories that are far more interesting than any you've taken before." He took off his glasses. "This, Don," he said, tapping the photos he'd laid out on his desk, "is why I teach. So much mediocrity parades before me I sometimes want to quit. But knowing my words got through to you and seeing what you've accomplished makes it all worthwhile."

Don had kept in touch with Westman over the next fifteen years. His professor was now seventy-five and semi-retired. He was a guest lecturer at NYU, physically unable to teach full-time. Don had sent him photos from his various assignments. Westman enjoyed those far more than the film footage, even though he told Don his films were equally powerful. At first Westman had critiqued Don's photos and offered suggestions. Westman's notes changed after Don had photographed the aftermath of Hurricane Katrina. "I have nothing more to offer," his letter said. "I looked at your photos and cried for half an hour. They are *that* good. *That* moving."

Don had received similar letters after he'd sent Westman photos from Afghanistan and Iraq. If anybody remembered Don it was Westman. And a few weeks before, when he had visited the man at his home he was overwhelmed to see an entire wall in Westman's living room adorned with Don's photographs.

Don was about to call Westman when he decided to visit him instead. A widower for twenty years now, Westman had had Don over numerous times to look at and discuss Don's work.

Don was aware he was holding his breath when he knocked on

Westman's door and waited for the man to answer. He had had butterflies in his stomach the entire way over.

"Can I help you?" Westman said, when he opened the door.

Don was crushed, but then thought it might have been Westman's glasses, which appeared as thick as old-fashioned soda bottles. It was also late afternoon. Maybe . . .

"It's Don. Don Woodson," he said.

"I'm sorry—"

"You don't recognize me?" Don asked, wondering if his professor had gone senile. "The name means nothing to you?"

Westman shook his head.

"I was your student. You're my mentor," Don said. "May I please come in?" he asked, remembering the wall filled with his photos.

Westman shrugged. "I don't get many visitors these days." He ushered Don in.

Don went to the wall that held his photos. The wall was bare. "My . . . my photos were here just a few weeks ago when I visited," Don said, crestfallen.

"I've never had photographs on this wall," Westman said. "Are you sure you haven't mistakenly—"

"No, no, *no!*" Don said, not wanting to hear the same tired words uttered yet another time. "Just give me a moment of your time. Please hear me out."

Again Westman shrugged and told Don to take a seat.

Don told Westman he had been a student in his class. He told the professor how he'd influenced his work . . . his *life*. He told him of the letters they'd exchanged over the years and the many photos he'd sent him. "Does *any* of this register with you?" he finished.

"It's what I *would* have said to someone with talent, but no direction," Westman said. "I've had a number of technically proficient students but they all went for the money shot—the photo of a poor victim that would grace the front page of a newspaper or the cover of a magazine. I never had a student you describe, though it would have made my life complete. I'm sorry, but I don't remember you."

There was nothing else for Don to ask, to say, so he thanked the man for his time and left.

He walked around the NYU campus, if it could be called a campus. Buildings with a few small parks, all you could expect in New York City. He decided to see a shrink. He had two reasons. First, someone to pour out his story to who might be able to sort out the problem and offer advice. But there was a second reason that was equally important. If he went back to the same psychiatrist the next day and was recognized, then he would know he wasn't crazy.

He couldn't go to the therapist he'd gone to after the suicide bombing in Israel. His nurse had already told him he had never been a patient. He recalled the name of a psychiatrist a soldier had seen after his first of three tours in Iraq. His parents had paid for him to see someone not connected with the military. A fresh set of eyes, so to speak. While young, the woman had done wonders for him. When ordered back for his second tour he'd told Don he no longer felt like damaged goods.

Don walked uptown to 63rd and 7th Avenue. It was 6 p.m. He doubted the woman would be in, but he had nothing to lose. No place else to go and certainly no one else to see.

The door to Eileen Tilghman's office was unlocked. There was no receptionist, but Don could see a light in the office of a partially open door. He knocked and was told to come in.

He was staring at what first appeared to be a teenager. Eileen Tilghman *was* young. And gorgeous. She wore a pants suit, she but had taken off the top. The top three buttons of her blouse were undone, exposing ample cleavage. He breasts were high and firm. She didn't have a beautiful face, but her delicate features were pleasing to the eye, as was the brown hair that wended its way halfway down her back. A woman he definitely wouldn't forget.

He introduced himself and told him the soldier who had mentioned her. She nodded in recognition.

"And you're here to . . . ?" she began, without finishing the question.

"I've got a problem. A serious problem that needs immediate attention," Don said. "I know it's late and I have no appointment, but . . ." And now he didn't finish.

Dr. Tilghman looked at her watch, then shrugged. "I have no plans for the evening, so why not? Sit and tell me your problem."

"You don't have a date?" Don asked, wondering why this woman so fascinated him.

"I seldom go out."

"Oh, you're not into men," Don said.

Tilghman laughed. An infectious laugh, Don thought. "I'm not a lesbian. I . . . I . . . well, if you're going to be my patient we might as well get this out of the way at the outset. I'm thirty-four—"

"Get out!" Don cut in. "You don't look a day over—" Don began, but now Dr. Tilghman cut him off.

"Fifteen? Eighteen? Twenty-one?" she asked. "Simply put, I have a condition. I don't age as most people do. Now it's a liability—adults telling their innermost problems to a *teenager*," she said making quotation marks with her fingers. "But think of it this way: when I'm sixty I'll probably look thirty, if that. *Then* I'll have more dates than I can handle. So, tell me what has you seeking therapy at six in the evening?"

Don told her about his day. "I don't know what to think," he concluded. "Am I crazy? Or do I really not exist?"

Dr. Tilghman looked at her watch. "I seriously don't think it's the latter. You very much exist, Mr. Woodson. Our session's about up and I need time to process all you've told me, but if you want, I can squeeze you in tomorrow." She walked him to her secretary's desk and he saw her write his name in her appointment book. "Please bring me one of your journals tomorrow along with any photos, if you can locate them."

He looked at her again—at her breasts, to be precise—and thought himself a dirty old man. *Telling my problems to a teenager,* he mumbled to himself.

He went home to his apartment. After a shower he felt exhausted. And why not? he thought. He'd been going at this all day non-stop. He looked in the bathroom mirror as he prepared to brush his teeth. He expected to see a haggard visage staring back at him. Instead he was staring at himself as he looked in his late twenties. There were no bags under his eyes. Laugh lines were far less prominent. He shook his head. He must be more tired than he thought.

He sat on his bed and started reading one of his journals. I do exist, he thought. At least I *think* I do. He closed his eyes and slept.

He didn't get up until close to noon the next day. As soon as he was awake the enormity of his situation hit him hard. For the hell of it he called Tom Spooner. Jean answered and confirmed for him the last day hadn't been a figment of his imagination.

No, she didn't know him. No, he didn't work for CNN. No, he hadn't had an appointment with Spooner the day before. And, yes, she remembered his call from the previous day. Harass her again and she'd contact the authorities, she told him and hung up.

His appointment with Dr. Tilghman was at 1:30 in the afternoon. He'd finally learn the truth. As he approached her office the desire to flee was almost overwhelming. What if she didn't recognize him?

He went up to Dr. Tilghman's secretary. "Hi, I have a 1:30 with the doctor," he said. He gave her his name.

The woman, probably older than the psychiatrist, was nondescript to a fault. *But she existed*, a voice in the back of his mind retorted.

"I'm sorry, there's no appointment for a Mr. Woodson."

He sighed. "I was here last night. I saw Dr. Tilghman write my name in."

The woman turned the appointment book towards him and pointed to 1:30. "Blank, as you can see."

Don tried to control his rage. Or was it panic? he wondered. He kept his voice at an even keel. "Look, won't you just ask Dr. Tilghman to come out and verify our appointment? *Please.*"

The secretary was about to say something, then picked up the phone instead. She had a brief hushed conversation with, Don assumed, Dr. Tilghman.

A moment later the therapist came out of her office.

"Dr. Tilghman," Don said. "Please tell your secretary we have an appointment."

"I have no idea who you are," she said.

Don bit his lower lip before replying. "Please, give me five minutes," he said, hearing the pleading quality of his voice. "I *know* you're free now. Just five minutes."

She shrugged. "You're right, I am free. Come on in."

"Before you say a word please listen to what I have to say," he asked, when they were seated. When she didn't respond he went on. "I was here last night, just after six. You saw me for an hour. You had on a suit like you're wearing now, but it was brown and you'd taken your . . . jacket off. Your top three buttons were unfastened. You're thirty-four, you told me, although you look to be a teenager. A condition, you said. And you joked that while irritating now when you're sixty you'd look like you were thirty and have plenty of dates. Now how would I know that about you if we hadn't met . . . last night?"

"A good question, but I recall no such session last night and I certainly have no recollection of ever meeting you. Still," she said, checking her watch, "if you want, I'll listen to your problem."

"You did that, too, last night. Looking at your watch. Several times."

"A habit," she said. "Want to tell me what's bothering you?"

"Sure, but it won't do any good. I'll tell you. We'll make another appointment and when I appear you won't recognize me."

"Let's give it a try, Mr. Woodson."

He repeated his story, then handed her his journal. "Last night you asked me to bring in a volume of my journal. You also asked me to bring in some of my photos, but they've . . . they've vanished. But the journal is proof—"

"That you wrote about Don Woodson, a photo journalist," she finished for him. She read several pages, then handed the journal back to him. "I'm certain you wrote it," she said, with a smile. "The question is, is it fact or fiction? Have you created some other identity for yourself due to some trauma or is it one of a number of what may be multiple personalities?"

"You're saying I'm schizophrenic?" he asked.

"Not at all. *Not* after one session."

"Two," he said, adamantly.

Her phone buzzed, startling him. Dr. Tilghman didn't pick it up.

"I'm afraid I have another patient," she said. "Let's schedule you for another session in . . . say two days. I'm sure we'll get to the bottom of this."

"And I'm just as sure when I return you won't remember me. My name won't be on your appointment book. Actually, you *have* clarified all I need to know. Another session won't be necessary." He got up to leave, then stopped. "I know this might be out of line, but you won't remember who told you. You're a gorgeous woman, but you hide yourself from the world because of your condition. You immerse yourself in your work . . . just as I did. Take off your jacket, unfasten a few buttons on your blouse. You don't want to wait until you're sixty for dates. You can have plenty now. Hell, you may even find love. Expose yourself, so to speak. You're no teenager." Before she could reply he left.

He went back to his apartment. He sat on his bed and thought about his life. He thought he'd been content, but the past two days had opened his eyes. He had sacrificed relationships and commitment for work. He had no wife. No children. Relationships were one-night stands, like that with Jean, to meet physical needs. In work he'd been a voyeur, observing from the outside without becoming engaged. To those he photographed he *didn't* exist. Those who looked at his pictures in newspapers or magazines saw only his subjects, unaware of his existence. There was that word again, he thought. "My life has been a waste," he said aloud. Maybe whatever he was experiencing was a wake-up call. "Get a life," he said aloud. At thirty-five it certainly wasn't too late. What if he tried to start all over again?

He decided to write all of the last two days in his journal. He'd commit it all to paper and thus close the book on his life and start anew. Pun intended, he said to himself.

He began writing frantically. Twenty minutes later he went to get a drink of water. He looked into the bathroom mirror. He hardly recognized himself. He was no older than twenty. He recalled the night before when he'd looked into the mirror he'd thought he looked younger than his thirty-five years. He had dismissed the notion as suffering from fatigue. Now he looked younger still. He had no idea what it meant, but he knew he had to complete his journal before . . . well, before he couldn't.

Half an hour later he found it difficult to find the words he wanted or string a sentence together. He stared at the page he'd just written and saw a number of words misspelled. Much of the page was the gibberish of a child. Soon after, he no longer wrote letters, but drew crude pictures. And then everything went dark.

He opened his eyes and instinctively he knew he was in his mother's womb. He'd have another chance . . . a chance to do things right.

There's something I have to remember, he told himself.

Something important.

Something . . .

Eileen Tilghman took out the duplicate copy of her appointment book from her desk. She stared for a moment at Don's appointment, erased it and put it back.

VENTURI

A Tale Inspired by "Legion of Plotters"
BY RICHARD CHRISTIAN MATHESON

In his introduction to this volume, Ramsey Campbell describes Richard Matheson's 1953 tale "Legion of Plotters"—the story of Mr. Jasper, who believes there is a "secret legion" devoted to driving him mad—as "a seminal study of paranoia." Mr. Matheson's son, Richard Christian, joins this celebration of his father with a powerful variation on the theme. The younger Mr. Matheson is an acclaimed short story writer and television and film writer/producer.

VENTURI

"When did you first notice this?"

"Week ago," said David. "Three days after the fire."

"Any pain?"

"No."

The doctor's gloved fingers probed shoulder blade. It was soft, egg-sized; under skin.

". . . saw the fire on TV. Did you have to evacuate?"

David watched smoke swarm the medical building, tall flames lashing, wanting in.

He looked at the doctor.

"You still up in that canyon in Malibu? I hear they don't give you much time to get out."

Banshee winds hammered the glass, black plumes muting sun. The room darkened, the doctor's face a feral shadow.

"I had fifteen minutes. You take what you can." His mouth was dry. Body numb. "My house didn't burn. But the neighborhood's gone." He felt ill. "Thirty-eight houses."

The doctor stopped. Tried to picture it. "My god."

Dense smoke suddenly filled the examination room; gushing through vents; seeping under doors. Grimy ash swirled; sick snow.

"Fire creates its own wind," said David, ". . . it's called the Venturi Effect."

The doctor's breathing deepened.

"The flames feed on themselves. Like a frightened animal."

"*Venturi . . .*" the doctor repeated.

David could see his next door neighbor's house clawed by apricot blades, cooked black. "Got to ninety-six miles an hour on my hill."

The doctor fell silent. "Awful. Gotta be exhausted. Getting any sleep?"

"Not really."

He nodded, re-washed hands. Voice apothecary calm. "Far as I can tell, this thing feels like a muscle spasm. Tension."

Smoke snaked around the doctor, luscious pleats of it fingering his neck, sliding between lips and teeth.

"I want you to take hot showers. I'll give you some muscle relaxant. It'll ease up."

David heard winds outside moan louder.

"Let's just watch it. Call me if anything changes."

"Like what?"

The doctor scrawled on prescription pad. "You look exhausted, David. You gotta get some sleep. These'll help."

"I can't sleep. It's fire season." His eyes were red with exhaustion. "Anything could happen."

The doctor looked outside. Smiled, told David it was a nice day. "Weather guy says it may even rain."

David heard axes smashing through doors and quietly left the office.

4:47 P.M

The freeway couldn't breathe.

Drivers hunched. Eyes eating; devouring. Watching mirrors; lips sewn in disgust. Exhaust pipes fuming; vile, chrome mouths.

David felt his shoulder blade. Wanted whatever was in there to die.

2:17 A.M.

The folded chair was in a carpet of soot.

David sat on his deck, surrounded by charred mountains that smelled like wet, dead cigarettes. Their burnt flesh rose from shore; soft, black cameos, looming and silent.

He sipped coffee. Scanned his dead neighborhood; grey casket streets. It had been days since he'd slept and his bones felt wrong; aching, drilled with holes. He yawned, eyes bloodshot. Watched insomniac sea. Surf broke far below; pale blades on ink.

" . . . *the meridian where conscious and unconscious meet,*" the Swedish widow up the street had told him, days before she died in the '97 firestorm, trapped in her house, chased by red infuriations.

He stopped, mid-swallow. Smelled smoke.

Somewhere; maybe close; the first sign death neared. It was everywhere; the warm, charcoal breath. Those who hadn't survived fires didn't notice the hateful, uninvited scent of it. Billowing, citric welts, rushing closer, making birds shriek in terror, trees bend.

He heard groaning red trucks curving up his narrow road, tires crunching, blinded by smoke. Seventy foot flames swaying in the ravine like burning kelp.

Then, nothing.

He searched with binoculars, found distant Los Angeles skyline, scanned surrounding hills. Nothing unusual. He breathed in, deeply, as leaves began to rattle in his sycamore. Closed fatigued eyes. He'd taken the shower and muscle relaxant but no sleeping pill; closing eyes would be a fatal mistake.

He breathed in, again. Maybe he'd imagined the smoke. He needed to be careful; after a fire, everything smelled of it. He tried to distinguish, isolating nuance, turning his head to find it.

Smoke.

The world was filling up with it; choking, flesh sweating, slick with fear. Flames crawling horizon, gobbling. Raving gusts of it, moving in for the kill. To sleep was to die. Awaken to sirens, evacuations. Screams in the night.

There was no stopping it.

It just got worse.

Boxes filled with personal belongings thrown into frantically idling cars. Children panicked, crying. He could see his Collie, Jack. Ears flat, as the crackle of burning hillsides drew him, and he ran, whining, scared, into fevered skirts of smoke. David had heard his howls, pleading for a way out.

Then, nothing. Just houses and creatures and trees burning as flames took them like fast cancer.

He felt sick to his stomach. Remembered when he'd first seen the house, nestled atop mountain, overlooking a trance of water and land. Despite its helpless perfection, perched calmly in the middle of a fire path, he'd bought it. It had nearly burned in a '94 firestorm that took two hundred hillside homes; a hot, windy afternoon, when the sky bloodied to third degree burn. The owner had decided to stay, as her world went red and black; listening to flames getting closer; starved for helpless things. She'd slit both wrists and, as they slowly drained, applied makeup and taken a cool bath.

At this elevation, the death winds found everyone.

He stared into the night.

Listening for sirens; desperate calls for help. Santa Ana winds began moving across the hills like rabid gangs and he saw himself on fire; insides blazing, smoke filling his throat like a chimney; drifting from his dying mouth. Ash silently fell and he thought he saw smoke spiraling just over one hill; furious crows of it moving closer.

He could hear ghouls in cars, racing up his narrow road, hungry to see the decimation. Cigarettes in idiot mouths. Teenagers on the beach, burning driftwood, paying no attention as embers twinkled fatally away. Hikers making campfires.

Arsonists. All of them.

He grabbed for his binoculars, again, and gasped as the rise on his shoulder blade moved. He instantly shed jacket and T-shirt to check and, to his shock, found more rises, on upper arm, forearm and chest; apricot-sized mounds, sheeted by flesh.

He rushed into the dark house, turned on the light and stood before bedroom mirror.

There were *more*.

He hesitated, afraid of what they might be and, after a moment, carefully poked at one on his chest. The rise responded, pushing outward, slowly straining against skin until finally splitting it open; a wound in reverse. David gasped at sharp pain as, one after another, the rises pushed, tearing through his flesh, each now visible in its own raw, puckered socket, slowly orbiting.

Lids lifted and the eyes stared intensely at him; brown like his own, unblinking, whites shining. They seemed neither trapped nor accusatory and each began to stare, alertly, in different directions, searching for something.

He felt them covering his back, blood trickling where they'd erupted, and frantically sifted through his hair to find more. When he touched them, the lids tightly shut, gradually, re-opened; watching, pupils dilating. The ones on his forearms and palms studied the room, taking everything in with a detailed scan.

It was exhaustion; the trick of a traumatized mind. He knew it; thought about calling the doctor.

But it was pointless. He'd recommend sleep, a hospital. There was no leaving the house now; death was everywhere. Hot winds howling, fire galloping closer.

Coming for him.

He moved out onto the deck, stared at pewter sky, heard sirens in the distance; bleak arias. Tree branches shuddered and he was sure he saw vicious orange coming over the hill, mowing toward sea.

He stripped off the rest of his clothes, saw more eyes covered him; vigilant, unblinking stares that swept the hills and ravines for danger. His arms slowly outstretched at his sides, to allow them

unimpeded view and, as they surveyed horizon with restless de-
tection, he began to calm.

He stood, naked in warm, ominous winds, fears gradually easing,
as the scores of eyes kept watch and his own slowly closed.

QUARRY

A Sequel to "Prey"

BY JOE R. LANSDALE

Richard Matheson's 1969 tale "Prey" made its biggest cultural im-
pact when it became the climactic segment of the 1975 TV movie
Trilogy of Terror—Karen Black's desperate struggle against the
Zuni fetish doll, "He Who Kills," is a highlight of television history.
In "Quarry," Joe R. Lansdale—the Texan "Mojo storyteller" behind
Freezer Burn, Bad Chili, and some twenty other novels and
collections—posits that there are more Zuni dolls out there, just as
ready to kill. . . .

QUARRY

There had been better days in his life, and as Jeff drove home from the court house, the convertible top down, the wind blowing through his hair, he tried to put all that had gone before out of his mind and think about the book he was writing. He was at least two months behind on the deadline, and it seemed to him that if he doubled up, by working weekends, which he did not normally do, he might be able to make it.

Now that Brenda had left he should have plenty of time, fewer interruptions.

Brenda. It always came back to Brenda. It had been hard to concentrate on much else the last few months, and though he thought he should be angry and glad to be rid of her, all he felt was empty and sad and lonely. She always said, in spite of his financial success, that he was a loser who didn't know a thing about being a man. He could write books, but he wasn't like the men she knew, like her father and brother. Football players, hunters.

He sat in the dark in front of a word processor and made up stories.

"Not a manly profession, Jeff," she told him.

Considering she was always glad to spend his money and was now expecting more from the divorce, he was a little uncertain about her belief system, but still, it hurt to be considered a wimp.

Try as he might to put Brenda out of his mind, thoughts about the book wouldn't come. He needed to finish it, turn it in, get his other half of the advance and keep his publishing schedule, but it was more than a little hard to concentrate.

On the way home he stopped by the antique and curiosity shop. He had ordered a few things for the house from antique buyers who promised him some nice surprises. It had been exciting to him at the time, the idea of hiring someone to find him some new and interesting pieces for their new home, but now it was his new home, and if Brenda's lawyers handled things correctly, it might be her new home.

The shop was on the outskirts of the little community of Falling Rock, not real far from his home. The building was nestled in the mountains as securely as a tick in a fat man's armpit. It was backed up against a rock face and the front of it stuck out close to the highway. There were all manner of odds and ends out front, and these items were more junk than antiques, but inside the shop, which was as huge as a warehouse, there was old furniture, paintings, weird art objects. The place was called OLD STUFF AND ODD STUFF, and it was operated by a gay couple.

They were anything but stereotypical. Jason was about forty and was a body builder and had a macho swagger. His mate, Kevin, taught Mixed Martial Arts Combat Fighting, and had won a number of championships. They had bought the place from a cranky old man and his crankier old wife about a year ago. Jeff had always liked antiques and odd art objects, and had frequented the shop for years. The success of his books worldwide had given him the money to buy all manner of things. Colorful rugs from Morocco, tables and chairs hand made in the Appalachians, primitive art paintings from the Southern states and the Midwest.

As he pulled into the gravel drive out front of OLD STUFF AND ODD STUFF, he thought maybe he ought to cancel his order. He could use the money. Six months ago, he was a millionaire, and though he might still be considered one as of this moment, a lot of his money had already gone to lawyers, and soon more would be heading there, like a cue ball for a pool table pocket, ready to drop out of sight.

But the problem was he had asked Jason and Kevin to hand pick him a few items, and he had already paid half down. He knew Jason and Kevin well enough to know that they had gone to considerable trouble to find the items for him, had spent the last month looking high and low for just the right objects.

He decided the thing to do was to bite the bullet.

Inside Jason greeted him with a handshake and a pat on the shoulder, and for a moment Jeff felt better. He always enjoyed Jason and Kevin's company. Jason, as usual, looked as if he had just stepped off the cover of a magazine, and Kevin, as usual, was in sweats with tennis shoes.

They talked briefly, and he sat and had a cup of coffee with them. After they had gone through the coffee, the pair walked him around the place, showed him a few primitive art pieces, three of them paintings, one a "sculpture" they referred to as "found" art. It was made with odds and ends, an old transistor radio, a little statuette of Elvis, a cell phone, and some lightbulbs, all of this encased inside a wooden box. It was unique and interesting. The phone's insides had been replaced with a battery, and when you punched the call button, it played Elvis singing "Don't Be Cruel" and the lights lit up and the statuette of Elvis bobbed from one side to the other.

"That I like," Jeff said. "Best thing yet."

"No," Kevin said, and his eyes seemed to light up, "I don't think so. We have a very fine and different piece for you."

Kevin took Jeff by the elbow and guided him to a shelf at the back of the place, and on the shelf, in a black box, about twelve inches high and six inches wide, perched on a little platform inside the box, was a very strange thing indeed.

It was a kind of doll, dark as a rainy night with a shock of black hair that looked like dyed straw; it stood up from the doll's head as if it had been charged with electricity. Its body was skeletal and its mouth was open, revealing some jagged, but sharp looking teeth. It had a little spear in its hand. Its hands were large for the rest of its body, the knuckles each the size of a shelled pecan. Its long fingers were tipped with sharp fingernails. There was a small coil of black rope hanging from a hook on one side of its leather belt, and on the other side was a miniature dagger the length of a sewing machine needle and the width of a fingernail file. The doll was sexless, smooth all over. It stood on a little platform about two inches high. As he got closer, Jeff saw that there was a chain around the doll's neck, and on the little chain a placard that read: HE WHO KILLS.

"My god," Jeff said, "it's wonderfully ugly."

"Isn't it?" Kevin said. "There's a little scroll inside the stand."

Kevin slid a sliding door aside on the platform beneath He Who Kill's feet, and took out the scroll. It was bound with a black ribbon. He gently removed the ribbon and opened the scroll. He read what was written on it: "This is a Zuni fetish doll, He Who Kills. He is deadly and ever persistent. The chain holds his warrior spirit at bay. Remove at your own peril, for he is a strong and mighty hunter."

"Isn't that just the thing?" Jason said. "This is very rare. There are only a few, and this is the only one we've ever seen. We've heard of them, and they have a story around them, about a curse and all, but considering the kind of fiction you write, we thought that wouldn't be a worry for you."

Kevin rolled up the scroll and bound it with the ribbon and replaced it in the compartment inside the platform. Jeff grinned. This was just the sort of thing he would love to have on the mantle. A nice conversation piece. He'd have to do some research on it.

"Guys, I like it all," Jeff said.

"Good," Jason said, "we can deliver it day after tomorrow."

"Let me pay up, and take the doll with me," Jeff said. "You can deliver the rest."

"I told you he'd like it," Jason said. Then to Jeff: "Isn't that doll just the bomb?"

"The atomic bomb," Jeff said.

At home Jeff got the good scissors out of the kitchen drawer and sat at the kitchen table and cut loose the wrapping Jason and Kevin had put around the box. He dropped the scissors on the table and took the doll out of the box and turned it over and looked at its back. It was polished there as smoothly as it was polished all over. It seemed to be made of some kind of light wood, or perhaps bone. He wasn't sure exactly. He tapped it with his knuckles. It sounded hollow . . . No. There might be something inside. He got the feeling that when he tapped, something shifted in there. He had heard a sound, like the beating of a moth's wings.

He laughed. The soul. The mighty hunter's soul shifted. That was the sound.

His dog, Fluffy, the poodle—his wife's name for their pet—trotted over, reared up on Jeff's knee, looked at the doll and growled at it.

"Don't worry, Fluffy. I won't let him get you. Besides, he's got his chain on."

Jeff touched the tip of the little spear, jerked his finger back. It was razor sharp. His finger was bleeding. He stuck it in his mouth and sucked. Damn, he thought. That thing is dangerous.

Jeff sat the doll on the table, pushed back his chair and studied it carefully. Its features were very fine, and the eyes, he couldn't figure what they were made from. They didn't look like beads, or jewels, clam shell maybe. White clam shell with small black dots painted in the center.

"I should turn you loose on my wife," he said.

He stood the doll upright on the table, went into his study, turned on his computer, typed in ZUNI FETISH DOLL, HE WHO KILLS. As he typed, Sofia, his tabby, climbed up in his lap.

He stroked the cat's head with one hand while she watched him work the mouse with the other. Maybe she thought it was a real mouse, and dad had trapped it, holding it down for her to eat.

He smiled and looked at what he had brought up on the screen.

It was a photograph of a doll like the one he had. He skimmed the reading material. Apparently, only three of the dolls were known to exist. They had a kind of cult story about them, sort of like the Hope Diamond. Whoever owned the dolls met with a bad end. This was the reason they were popular, the story that went with them. Owning a doll that supposedly had a curse attached to it was the cool thing to have, or so it seemed.

He studied the photograph of the doll on the screen. It was very much like his doll. No. It was exactly like his doll. The photograph had been taken in the nineteen thirties by an anthropologist. The doll was called a Zuni doll, but there seemed to be some question as to if it meant the Zuni Indians. There was also some question as to where the chains and the little placards around their necks, written in English, had come from?

No one seemed to have any answers.

Jeff was about to switch to another site, try and find more information. He figured that the dolls had been made in modern times as curios, and a legend had built up around them for sales purposes. He doubted they were Zuni or that they were ever found in a cave. But, it would make a great story. Maybe a novel. Sounded more interesting than the one he was working on at the moment, and—

There was a crashing noise, and then Fluffy yelped in the kitchen.

When Jeff entered the kitchen he discovered the doll was missing from the table. He was immediately mad. Fluffy. That damn dog had grabbed the doll. She was bad about that sort of thing, climbing up in the chair to eat out of plates, get hold of anything she could grab, just to make sure she got attention, good or bad. The crash he had heard had most likely been his expensive doll, and worse, it was probable Fluffy had already begun to chew on his rare property.

Jeff noted that the sliding glass door to the garden was cracked open. He had opened it when he first came in with the doll, then left it open for the cat to come inside. He pushed the glass door wider and looked out at the garden inside the high walls that surrounded it.

There wasn't much moonlight tonight, and what light there was appeared gauzy, as if cheese cloth had been thrown over the quarter moon. Jeff went out into the garden and looked at the tall plants that made the place look like a little patch of tropical forest. Shadows draped between the plants like plaited ropes of black satin.

He and his wife had planted these, and it occurred to him that what she had said about never loving him was probably not true. She had loved him. She had loved him when they had made the garden. Now she didn't and she was saying she never had. The plants gave him comfort that once they truly had loved one another, made him feel less like an idiot.

The doll. Fluffy. His mind came back to the problem at hand. He was about to venture out into the garden, to see if Fluffy had gone out there, when he heard a noise in the house, a dragging noise.

Jeff stepped back inside and shut the door.

"Fluffy," he called.

He went around the table, and as he did, something shiny caught his eye. He looked down. It was the necklace with the placard for He Who Kills. Jeff bent down and picked it up and examined it. He was certain now that what had happened was the doll, perhaps when Fluffy bumped the table, had tipped over and fallen to the floor, losing its necklace. It had fallen on Fluffy, hence, the yelp. And then Fluffy, vengeful and dog like, had grabbed it and carried it off and was probably in the living room, behind the couch, chewing its head off.

Jeff called the dog again, but nothing.

He went into the living room, pulled up sharp. There was a dark red swipe of blood beginning just as he stepped into the living room. Jeff studied the swipe, saw that it wiped across the wooden floor and disappeared behind the couch.

He took a deep breath, and careful not to step in the blood, went behind the couch and let out an involuntary cry.

Fluffy was there.

He was lying in a puddle of blood . . . and there was the doll's little spear sticking out of the side of his neck. It had penetrated an artery and Fluffy had bled out in seconds. Jeff bent over the dog, took hold of the little spear and pulled it free.

And then there was a crackle and the lights went out.

Moving through the dark, accustomed enough to his home to make his way about, but not so accustomed to avoid bumping his knee on the edge of the couch, Jeff managed to cross the living room, stumble down the hall, to the closet. There was a fuse box in the closet, and he had some spare fuses inside, and he needed light. His stomach felt queasy. His heart was beating fast. He still had the little spear in his hand.

There was a bit of moonlight coming in through the back sliding door, across the kitchen and down the connecting hall. It fell into the hall where he stood, near the closet, making a little pool of glow. It wasn't much, but it made him feel better, being able to see something.

The closet door was open. His cat, Sofia, was standing outside of the closet, making a strange sound. The hair on her back stood up like quills.

He stepped into the closet and felt around for the flashlight he kept on a shelf, found it, and turned it on. The fuse box was open, and there were old shoe boxes stacked all the way up to it.

What the hell?

He thought again of the little spear. He looked at it with his flashlight. The blood on its tip was already drying, growing dark. He put the spear on top of the fuse box and took a deep breath. He looked at the shoe boxes again.

Someone, or something small had stacked them to get at the fuse box, which, now, as he flashed the light on the box, he saw had been wrecked. Someone . . . or something . . . had savagely ripped at the guts of the box and torn them out. But what had been used, and who . . . or what had done such a thing?

He had an idea, but it wasn't an idea he could completely wrap his mind around. It just did not make sense.

And if it was the doll—there, he had said it—how would it know to do such a thing?

Instinct?

Experience?

Oh, hell, he thought. Don't be silly. There's a perfectly reasonable explanation for all this, it's—

Jeff heard something, like a roach caught up in a match box. He turned the light around and around on the floor of the closet. Nothing. And then he saw the little black rope. It was dangling from the closet shelf, being slowly drawn up.

Swallowing, Jeff turned the light onto the shelf.

And there was the doll, just pulling up the last of its rope. The rope was clutched in one oversized hand, and the scissors that had been on the table were clutched in the other.

The doll leaped at him.

Swatting at the doll with the flashlight, he knocked it to the side, against the closet wall. It was such a hard strike, that after he hit the doll, his flashlight traveled into the edge of the closet doorway and came apart in an explosion of glass and batteries.

Jeff leaped backwards out of the closet and slammed the door.

Suddenly there was a savage yell inside the closet, and then the tip of the scissors poked through the wooden door and missed his knee by less than an inch. Jeff staggered back. In the faint moonlight he could see the tip of the scissors being driven through the door again and again, in a paced rhythm of strikes.

My God, the little beast was a psycho.

And then the stabbing stopped. Jeff stepped back, thinking. Okay. Okay. He's in the closet. It will take him awhile to work his way through the door, even as relentless as he seems to be.

The doorknob began to shake.

My God, he thought. It has leaped up and grabbed the knob, and he's hanging there, trying to open the door.

Don't just stand here, meathead, he told himself. Do something.

Jeff grabbed a chair from the kitchen and stuck the back of it against the knob. There, that would hold him.

He rushed into his study, opened up his desk drawer and got the .38 revolver out of it. He wasn't a great shot, but he had been known to hit targets with some regularity at the range. He also had another flashlight in the drawer, a smaller heavier one. He clicked it on.

The doorknob continued to shake furiously, and then he heard the chair jar loose and fall to the floor. He rushed out of the study, into the hallway. The closet door was cracked open. Plenty wide for it to get out.

Was it out?

Or was it still waiting inside?

Something ran between his legs and Jeff jumped. He twisted, the flashlight in one hand, the gun in the other, saw something darting across the floor. He fired off a shot. There was a screech that he knew was his cat. He had missed her, but the bullet had slammed into the wall next to her. She had darted into the living room; he could see her shape just as she turned the corner.

Idiot, he told himself. Calm down. You're going to shoot the cat, or yourself.

Save the five left in the gun for the doll.

The doll!

Was he dreaming? This was crazy. A doll come to life, chasing him through his own house, killing his dog?

Ridiculous.

He was about to pinch himself when there came a ferocious

yell, and then a screech from the cat, the sound of something tumbling, something falling, breaking, the terrible yells of the doll, a kind of high pitched, "Eeeyah! Eeeyah! Eeeyah!"

Jeff made himself move toward the living room. Each step was an ordeal, but he made it. The screeching and the high pitched Eeeyah continued the entire time. When he looked into the darkness of the room, he saw what at first appeared to be two tumbling shadows, but the shadows stopped rolling, and what he saw was Sofia, lying on the carpet, not moving. The doll was standing over the cat with the scissors upraised. It bent forward and examined its quarry, made a satisfied sound.

The doll turned its head and looked at Jeff.

Jeff raised the revolver. The doll came skittering across the carpet at a wild run, the scissors raised high in its hand.

"Eeeyah! Eeeyah! Eeeyah!"

Jeff fired the gun and the sound of it in the living room was foreign and wrong to his ears, but he couldn't stop shooting. Each shot missed. He heard glass break. A thud as a bullet imbedded in the couch, and then the doll was right on him. He fired, and this time he hit it. The bullet knocked the thing winding and he saw something dark fly up from it. It lay facedown on the floor next to his dead cat.

He took a deep breath and dropped his hand to his side, clutching the empty revolver as if trying to strangle it. He pooled the flashlight beam around the shape on the floor. The thing raised its hand, the one with the scissors in it, and jammed them into the wood flooring, pulled itself forward a pace. It lifted its head, and looked at him. The eyes glowed in the flashlight beam like flaming match heads.

It put one knee under itself and started to stand.

Jeff could see that one of its large hands was missing a finger. That's what his bullet had hit.

And that wasn't good enough.

Jeff threw the empty, revolver and then the flashlight. Neither hit its mark. He made a run for it, back down the hall, through the linking hall, across the kitchen and out the sliding back door and into the garden. He could hear the thing running behind him, still in the house, but coming fast. The sound of its feet running was like a soft drum roll. It came on yelling that horrible war cry: "Eeeyah! Eeeyah! Eeeyah!"

The garden was thick with plants and they rose up high, staked out professionally on posts. They gave the garden a jungle atmosphere, gathering in shadows, laying them deep within the greenery.

He darted into their midst, peeked around a twisty bit of plant growth, saw the thing coming through the open doorway, into the moonlight. It paused, lifted its head and sniffed the air. It turned to the side, made a few steps. As it crossed in front of the glass doorway, he could see its reflection in the glass. The reflection was huge, and wavery. It whipped and twisted like something being cooked alive on a griddle.

My god, Jeff thought. The glass is reflecting its soul. The soul of the hunter, He Who Kills.

Easing behind the foliage, resting on his knees, Jeff tried to get his breathing under control. Certainly He Who Kills would have heightened senses. He kept breathing like he was, the thing would hear him.

When he had taken a couple of deep breaths, he started to move again.

All of the long wide rows were crisscrossed with little narrow rows so he could move the wheelbarrow and gardening equipment about. He used one of the small crisscrossing rows to enter one of the wider rows, moved down it until he reached the wall that surrounded the garden. It was about twelve feet high, and it occurred to him if he could get over the wall, maybe the doll could not. But there was no time to consider that seriously. He would have to bide his time and think that one over, find a way to manage his way over twelve feet of substantial rock wall. But right now, he had to hide. He skulked through the rows as silently as he could manage. He could hear the doll moving through the garden,

carelessly pushing foliage aside, yelling its war cry, and then . . .
Everything went silent.

Jeff squatted in the middle of a row, breathed through his nose,
long, deep breaths, and listened. Nothing. Not even a cricket.
Then, he thought he heard the snapping of a plant. No. Maybe
not. There was a gentle wind blowing. It could move things
around. It could fool him, way his nerves were on edge.

The snapping again.

He wasn't sure what he was hearing. He looked down the row,
saw that it was the one that ended at the water faucet and hose. The
thick, coiled yellow hose with its squeeze handle and nozzle shone
dully in the moonlight. It looked like some kind of metal-headed,
yellow anaconda. It lay next to the compost pile. The compost pile
was up against the wall, and it was made of neatly arranged rail-
road ties with a tarpaulin thrown over it, weighted at the edges with
bricks. If he could run and put a foot on the ties, he might be able
to make a jump, grab the top of the wall with his hands and pull
himself over.

It was iffy. But he couldn't stay here. The thing would find him
eventually. There were only so many places to hide.

He decided to make a break for it.

Jeff was about to run for the compost pile, leap for the wall, when
a shadow fell across the row. The shadow came from the connecting row, and it was undoubtedly the shadow of He Who Kills. It
looked like the shadow of something gigantic, but it was definitely
the little warrior. The shadow writhed and vibrated as if powered
by electricity. The thing was standing in the connecting row, and
all it had to do to find him was step forward slightly and turn its
head his way.

Jeff held his breath. The shadow gradually moved away, growing
smaller, going in the other direction.

Stooping, easing down the row, Jeff came to the connecting row and paused. He got down on his hands and knees and slowly peeked around the edge of the thick vegetation.

Nothing there.

He crossed the openness where the rows connected, made it to the other side, and then there was a flash as a limb on one of the plants snapped toward him at about knee height. And then he felt terrible pain in his kneecap.

He Who Kills had rigged a snare. The miniature knife the doll carried had been attached to a limb with a cut of the rope, bent back and let go.

Involuntary cries leaped from Jeff's mouth as he grabbed at the limb, jerked the needle-like knife out of his knee. He Who Kills sprang from the enclosure of the greenery brandishing the scissors, yelling, "Eeeyah! Eeeyah!"

"You devil!" Jeff said, and kicked at the doll. It dodged. The scissors were plunged into Jeff's foot. Jeff screamed. The scissors came down again, and again, ripping into Jeff's legs as he tried to dart past the little monster.

He finally managed to dodge around him. Limping, he made for the compost pile. He Who Kills attacked the back of his legs, driving the scissors in deep. Jeff yelled and wobbled toward the compost pile, managed to reach the water hose. He snapped it up, swung it around and hit the doll with the nozzle. It knocked the doll back about ten feet. Jeff lifted the hose and squeezed the lever on the nozzle. Water blew out in a hard, fast stream. He used it on the doll in the manner a firefighter might use a fire hose on rioters.

The water kept knocking the doll down, and the doll kept getting up.

Jeff turned, tossed the hose over the top of the wall, pulled back, and the hand lever attached to the nozzle hung at the summit.

He leaped onto the compost pile, jerked the hose taut, and began to climb, his feet against the wall, his hands moving up the hose like a pirate climbing the rigging of a sailing ship.

When he reached the top, he stretched out on the wall and looked down.

He Who Kills was clamoring up the hose with the scissors in his teeth. Jeff grabbed the nozzle, pulled it loose, flipped it back into the garden, sending the little monster sprawling.

He dropped to the other side of the wall, and in considerable pain, limped toward the garage. He looked back. The hose nozzle was flying up in the moonlight, hanging on this top of the wall. He Who Kills was stealing his method, and he was coming after him.

He saw the shape of the doll on the top of the wall just as he reached the garage door.

Locked.

He didn't have the garage door opener to work it. It was inside the car which was inside the garage.

Jeff stumbled around the side to a low hung window, used his elbow to drive into one of the panes and break it. He knocked loose glass aside, reached through the missing pane, got hold of the lock and flipped it. He pushed the window up and squeezed through.

He felt a sudden moment of panic. He had trapped himself in the garage, and he wasn't even sure he had his keys.

He felt for them as he moved toward the car. He had them. He managed them from his pocket and hit the device that unlocked the car doors. He got inside and looked through the windshield and saw the shape of He Who Kills climbing through the window. He hit the door lock switch. He looked around for the garage door opener.

And then it hit him, and he felt his stomach roll. He had taken it inside. He was going to refresh the batteries. It was lying on the kitchen counter. Getting out of the car, going back into the house didn't seem like such a good idea.

Not with that thing out there.

He took only a moment to consider, stuck the key in the ignition. He Who Kills appeared, rising up over the hood of the car. Then it was standing on the hood.

Jeff jammed the car in reverse, hit the gas and sent He Who Kills flying.

The car struck the door and knocked it off its hinges, sent it hurtling across the drive and out into the connecting street. He had always loved the fact that his house was isolated, on a street he had built, where there were no neighbors. But right then he wished he had someone, anyone he could turn to for help.

But there was only himself to depend on. He was on his own.

He backed the car over the door, out into the street, jammed it into drive. Just before he punched the gas, he looked in his side mirror. He Who Kills was running rapidly toward the car.

He stomped the gas. The convertible leaped with a growl. He turned on the lights.

He checked the mirror again.

It was coming, bathed in the red glow from the car's rear lights. Running ridiculously fast behind him. Closing.

It seemed impossible that it could be running that fast.

He let out a laugh. Impossible. Of course, it was impossible. Everything that had happened from the time he bought the doll was impossible.

Except, it was happening.

He gunned the engine harder, checked the rearview mirror. No doll.

He let out a sigh of relief, took the road past the dark community of Falling Rock, down toward the city. The car wound around one curve after another, the mountainous terrain little more than bumps and valleys of darkness.

And what about the doll? It was out there, running around. What did he do about that? Who would believe him? People would think him crazy, and he could hardly blame them.

But I'm not crazy. I'm fine. I'm all right.

His legs began to ache where He Who Kills had attacked him. He was losing blood. He felt a little dizzy.

He rounded a curve. Now he could see more than dark bumps and valleys, he could see city lights, way off in the distance, down in the lowlands, like someone had turned on a wadded up handful of Christmas lights.

There was a hard metallic sound.

Jeff checked his rearview mirror. He felt the blood drain out of his face and his stomach turn sick. He Who Kills was on the back of the car. He was stabbing the scissors into the convertible's trunk with one hand, burying its claws into the trunk with the other. It was using this hand over hand method to crawl toward the back window of the car.

The damn thing had stayed after him, maybe grabbed onto the back of the bumper, or had worked its way along beneath the car. He didn't know how, but it had stayed after him and caught up with him, and now it was coming for him, and all he could do was watch it move toward him in the rearview mirror.

Whipping the car left and right, Jeff tried to shake the doll, but no luck. It hung tight, like a leech. It jerked the scissors free, leaped and landed on the roof of the convertible. He could hear it up there, scuttling along.

The scissors poked through the ceiling, were withdrawn, poked again. The roofing began to rip in a long strip, and then the face of He Who Kills jutted through the slit and let out with its wild cry of "Eeeyah! Eeeyah! Eeeyah!"

He Who Kills dropped through the slit, onto the front seat. It ran across the seat in a fast scuttle, striking out with the scissors, burying them in Jeff's shoulder. Jeff groaned, swatted at the doll, knocked it back against the front passenger door, sent it rolling onto the floorboard.

The demon still had the scissors; nothing seemed able to dislodge them from its grasp. It jetted across the floorboard and stabbed at Jeff's feet, causing him to lift them, then jam his right foot back down on the gas.

He whipped the car hard right when another blow from the scissors went deep into the side of his calf. It was too late to swerve back. He was heading right for a guard rail. He moved the wheel some, but not enough. The car hit the railing, tore it apart with a horrid screech of metal against metal, and then the machine was flying through the air. It went for some distance before hitting the side of the mountain, blowing out its tires. The drop was so terrific, so violent, that Jeff's door was thrown up, and he was thrown from the car, sent tumbling head over heels down the side of the mountain until he smashed up against a lump of rock that knocked the wind out of him. He felt something shift in his back, and then the pain started.

The car kept going. It sailed down the mountainside, bouncing, throwing up sparks. It appeared to head deliberately for one old, dead, lightning-struck tree that jutted out from the side of the mountain like a deformed arm. The convertible slammed into it and burst into flames.

Jeff, crawling painfully around the rock he had hit, saw the flames whip up and scorch the night air. Blood ran down his face, into his left eye. He wiped it away with his sleeve. He watched the car burn. Good, he thought. I got him. I got him.

Out of the flames he saw something moving. He Who Kills. The doll started running up the hill, directly toward him. It still held the scissors. It blazed like a torch.

"No," Jeff said aloud. "No."

The doll was halfway to him when Jeff dislodged a rock about the size of his fist and threw it. It was a lucky shot. It hit the flaming hunter and knocked him down.

But, it wasn't enough. Still decorated with flames, He Who Kills got up and came running up the hill again.

Jeff tried to dig another rock out of the ground, scratching and pulling so hard his fingers bled. He got it loose, looked up. The doll was almost on him . . . And then its legs burned out from beneath it. It fell, facedown. Flames licked off its smoldering corpse.

The hand holding the scissors shot out and stuck them in the ground. It pulled itself forward. It lifted its head and opened its mouth and flames licked out of it. It raised the scissors again, struck out, driving them into the dirt. It was coming for him, using the scissors to lurch toward him, inch by inch.

Jeff lifted the rock, rose to a sitting position, felt blood running down his legs, face and shoulder. "Come on," he said. "Come on, He Who Kills. Come and get some. You and me. Come on!"

The doll struck out with the scissors again, pulled itself forward another inch as the flames that bathed it slowed and blackened and turned to smoke. It struck one more blow with the scissors, and—

—the doll ceased to move. The smoke from its scorched body twisted up and became thick and full. The smoke took on the form of a savage face; the mouth opened and the smoke face jumped toward Jeff, yelled, "Eeeyah!" Then the smoke swirled rapidly skyward.

Jeff could still see the shape of the face in the smoke, but it had begun to spread and flatten. The smoke thinned and rose high and clouded Jeff's vision of the already murky quarter moon.

He looked back down at the doll. It had come apart. The burnt arms and legs and head had separated from the torso. Tendrils of smoke trailed off of its pieces.

"I won!" Jeff said. "I beat you, you monstrosity. If that isn't manly, nothing is. Nothing."

Laughing, he lay back. The last of the smoke faded away. The cloud cover faded as well. There was just the scimitar moon left, floating up there, nestled amongst the stars, bright and shiny in a clear, clean sky.

RETURN TO HELL HOUSE

A Prequel to *Hell House*
BY NANCY A. COLLINS

Hell House (1971) is perhaps Richard Matheson's most terrifying novel. It tells the story of Belasco House, a classic haunted-house setting invaded by four psychic investigators, one of whom, Benjamin Fischer, has been there before—he was the sole survivor of an earlier attempt to learn the house's secrets. Now Nancy A. Collins, author of the popular Sonja Blue vampire series, tells the story of Benjamin Fischer's first horrible encounter with the notorious "Hell House."

RETURN TO HELL HOUSE

As the taxi drew closer, Ben could see a small knot of reporters gathered around the white picket fence surrounding the tidy front yard and garden of Alida Crowder. Although the time and place of the meeting was supposedly known only by a handful of people, he did not require assistance from the spiritual plane to know who had tipped off the press.

"Was this really necessary, mother?" he groaned.

"This is important news, Benjamin," Mrs. Fischer replied. "You're the youngest medium ever to take part in such an experiment. There's nothing wrong in letting the world know that you're about to solve one of the biggest supernatural mysteries of the modern age! Besides, the more people know about you, and the miracles you can do, the more they will believe in the movement."

"There he is: there's the Ghost Boy!" one of the reporters shouted as the cab pulled up to the curb.

Ben hated being called Ghost Boy. But ever since the article in the *Saturday Evening Post,* when he was eleven, he had been unable to shake the nickname. As he stepped out of the cab, one of the reporters moved to block his path.

"Ben! *Bangor Daily News!* Is it true you're going to Hell House?"

"His name is *Benjamin*, not 'Ben,'" Mrs. Fischer said sternly as she emerged from the taxi. "And if you mean *Belasco* House, yes, my son has agreed to be part of Professor Fenley's investigation into the phenomena associated with that location."

"Professor Fenley? I heard it was Dr. Graham and Dr. Rand

who got the grant from Hale University to conduct research at Hell—uh, Belasco House."

"That might very well be true, but it was Professor Fenley who contacted us. The Professor and I have known one another for years. We're both members of the American Spiritualist Church, you know."

"Mrs. Fischer! *New York World-Telegram*! Aren't you concerned for your son's safety?"

"What is there to be concerned about?" Mrs. Fischer said with a disparaging laugh. "I have every confidence in my son's abilities. Besides, I'll be accompanying him . . ."

"*Mom!*" Ben said, grabbing her arm.

The reporter from the *World-Telegram* gave Mrs. Fischer an odd look as he jotted down short-hand notes. "Given what happened in 1931, I thought you, as a mother, might be worried something might, well, *happen* this time."

"Of *course* something will happen!" Mrs. Fischer laughed. "That's the whole point of Benjamin being part of the team! He is the greatest physical medium of this or any age!"

"Do you think Belasco is *really* dead?" the reporter from the *Bulletin* asked. "The courts pronounced him so four years ago, but no one has yet to find his body."

"That is one of the many questions I expect to answer in the next week," Ben replied, as he ushered his mother through the gate into the front yard. "Now, you really must excuse us—we're keeping the others waiting."

The interior of the Crowder home was as modest as its front yard. While the furnishings were not cheap, neither were they ostentatious, with much of it dating back to the Spanish-American War. Seated on a caned-back occasional chair in the front parlor was their hostess, Mrs. Crowder, her hands folded in her lap.

She was a fraile-looking woman, with long, steel gray hair

braided into a single coil and pinned to the nape of her neck. Although her face was lined and wrinkled, it was obvious Alida Crowder had once been a woman of exceptional beauty. As Ben entered the room, her faded blue eyes flashed from behind her spectacles.

"You said nothing of a child being involved, Dr. Graham."

"I'm *not* a child, Mrs. Crowder!" Ben replied heatedly. "I'll be sixteen in a few months!"

"Seeing that you're here in the company of your mother, you are still a boy in my eyes," she countered. "Although, I daresay spending a week in Hell House could very well change that."

"Young Mr. Fischer is not like any other fifteen year old you're likely to meet, Mrs. Crowder," Dr. Graham assured her. He was a sturdily built man in his early fifties with a salt-and-pepper beard and piercing gray eyes. "I'm certain he'll be able to hold his own."

"Perhaps," Mrs. Crowder said, eyeing the young medium as if guessing his weight. "Emeric had a particular dislike of children— at least those of the male gender. He was like the god Uranus, devouring the young before they could grow strong enough to overthrow him." She pointed a bony finger at Mrs. Fischer. "I have never had children—that ability was denied me, thanks to my first husband's abuse—but I appeal to you as such: do not allow your son to set foot inside Hell House."

"I appreciate your concern, Mrs. Crowder," Gladys Fischer said, squaring her shoulders. "But I have no intention of seeing any harm befall my boy. I'll be going with him to make sure of it."

"You'll be staying at Hell House as well?" A look of genuine alarm crossed Mrs. Crowder's face. "Then in that case, you should take your son and run as fast and far as you can from the Matawaskie Valley."

"Mrs. Crowder!" Dr. Rand said sternly, getting to his feet. He was a stout, older gentleman with snowy white hair. "While we appreciate you allowing us access to the mansion, Dr. Graham and I do *not* appreciate you trying to scare off the members of our team!"

"That's what you say now," Mrs. Crowder sighed. "If it was up to me, you wouldn't be allowed any further than the front door! But I need the money your university is paying me for the privilege of investigating my ex-husband's den of depravity."

"I realize that your ex-husband is a painful subject for you, Mrs. Crowder," Professor Fenley said sympathetically. He was a tall, thin Irishman, with copper-red hair starting to turn to white gold. "But as you are one of the few people who were intimate with Belasco who is still amongst the living, I was hoping you might enlighten us as to the nature of the man?"

"The fact that Emeric named me as the executrix of his estate should tell you everything you need to know about the man. I left after three years of marriage, denying all rights to his fortune, simply to be free of his cruelty and evil mind. Yet now I find myself inexorably linked to his foul legacy. Lumbering me with the maintenance of that monstrous pile of stone is his idea of a joke, you see.

"I was on the stage in New York when we first met. I specialized in untouched virgins—what they called an ingénue. I suspect that—and the fact his own mother was an actress—is what drew him to me. Emeric had this perverted desire to corrupt that which was unstained. He delighted in revealing the worm in the bud. It bolstered his low opinion of the natural world and man's place in it.

"He once told me you could only judge a man's character by his perversions, since virtue could be so easily faked. I am not proud to say that in the three years I spent married to that man, I was witness to, and an occasional participant in, debauchery on a grandiose scale. Nowhere near what was indulged in once he built the house—but still bad enough to make me fear for the destination of my immortal soul now that I'm older.

"I consider myself lucky, in that I am amongst a handful of his former lovers who escaped with both my life and mind intact. The majority were not so fortunate. That includes poor, bedeviled Myra. It was his blatant flaunting their affair that ultimately spurred me to leave him, you know. I had tolerated the other indiscretions—and they were legion—during our short marriage, but openly taking your own sister as a mistress . . ."

"Mrs. Crowder! *Please!*" Mrs. Fischer gasped, a scandalized look on her face.

"Spare me, Mrs. Fischer," Mrs. Crowder said sourly. "You are willing to risk your son's life and sanity, yet you're afraid of him hearing the truth about the man who raised those horrid walls? Believe me, incest was merely the tip of the iceberg for Emeric.

"After he wearied of her and cast her aside, as he did all the others, she continued to follow him about, like a pathetic little puppy dog. She went into seclusion with him at Hell House, and never came out alive. I heard she became a heroin addict. In any case, she died of an overdose in 1923, six years before Emeric pulled his little disappearing act."

"He sounds like an absolute monster," Grace Lauter said with a shudder. A tall, attractive woman in her early forties, her pale blonde hair was starting to turn to silver at her temples.

"That he was," Mrs. Crowder sighed. "Still, he was not without his charisma. He could be very charming, when the mood struck him. He was also the most intelligent man I have ever known. Arguing with him was fruitless. No matter if you were solidly in the right, he would find some way to twist things around so that you ended up accepting his opinion. What little I've seen of that dreadful Mr. Hitler on the newsreels reminds me far too much of Emeric for my liking.

"Emeric was as cruel and depraved as he was beguiling. He took no pleasure without some pain being attached to it—preferably another's. I left him before his 'dream house' was built, thank goodness. I firmly believe that's the only reason I was able to escape him. As it was, I spent the next three years in a sanatorium, mending what was left of my nerves. Once I had sufficiently convalesced, I was lucky enough to find my second husband.

"Mr. Crowder was nowhere near as handsome as Emeric, nor as rich. And, I must admit, there were times I found him more than passing dull. But he was a good and kind man, and proved a tonic for my battered psyche.

"As for Emeric's second wife, Rose—also a stage actress—she was not so lucky. Once she entered Hell House, she never escaped it. She killed herself in 1927. As executrix of the Belasco estate, I ended up in possession of her journals." Mrs. Crowder pointed to a stack of leather-bound volumes resting on the desk in the corner of the room. "They will tell you what you need to know about what went on in Hell House those last few years—far more than any newspaper clippings could."

"If you are so fearful of what might happen, Mrs. Crowder—why are you allowing another investigative team into the house?" Grace asked.

"Emeric was a man of immense vindictiveness and even greater patience. Every night when I go to sleep, as soon as I turn out the light, part of me fears that I will see him standing there at the foot of my bed. I want to know if he's *really* dead. And, if he *is* dead, I want to know whether he is trapped within that house. If that is the case, I will breathe easier knowing, should I find myself in hell, I have one less devil to worry about."

The next morning the members of the expedition headed north out of Boston. Since Emeric Belasco had built his "private Xanadu" in one of the most isolated parts of Maine, virtually a stone's throw from the Canadian border, it would take the better part of two days to reach their destination.

Dr. Rand and Grace Lauter rode with Dr. Graham in his Studebaker, while the Fischers accompanied Professor Fenley in his Packard. Bringing up the rear was Dr. Rand's assistant, Mr. Carlyle, who drove a rented panel truck containing the group's equipment and Benjamin's spirit cabinet.

As they traveled through Massachusetts and into Maine, Benjamin found himself growing increasingly excited. He'd never been on such an extensive road trip before, at least not in a proper touring car.

Although it was still September, the air had already taken on a damp chill more reminiscent of winter, and the closer they got to the Canadian border, the colder it got.

"I remember when the 1931 team left to come up here, nine years ago," Grace said, pulling her car coat tighter about her body. "The expedition was put together by Professor Vladimir from the Society of Psychical Research. There was also Dr. Melrose, physician out of Boston, and Vivian Benton, a highly-regarded physical medium who had worked with Dr. Coover at Stanford. The fourth member of the group was Simon Wagner, a mental medium famous for his work with Dr. Rhine at Duke University."

"How is it you know so much about the previous expedition?" Dr. Rand asked.

"I knew Simon Wagner."

Dr. Graham raised an eyebrow. "How well?"

"Well enough to know he'd never rape a woman, much less kill her."

"Yes, well, I'm sure we'd all like to believe the best of those we count as friends, Miss Lauter," Dr. Rand said. "But there is no way of truly knowing what lurks within the hearts of others . . ."

"Perhaps, but in Simon's case I have no doubt. You see, he had no sexual interest whatsoever in women. It's why I broke off our engagement."

"Ah!" Dr. Graham said, his eyebrow climbing even higher. "What else do you know about the 1931 team?"

"I know that within two days of setting foot inside Hell House, Vladimir and Melrose stabbed one another to death during a quarrel, and that Simon attacked Miss Benton. They later found him stumbling around nude in the theater. He'd driven nails into his eyes. He was promptly shipped off to Castle Rock Asylum. Less than a year later he was dead—he somehow managed to swallow his tongue.

"I went to visit him in the asylum, not long before he killed himself. To see such a glorious mind as his overthrown—it is something you never forget. That is why I was so eager in responding to your letter, Dr. Graham. I feel that I owe it to poor Simon to prove that he wasn't responsible for what happened."

Graham and Rand exchanged glances, but neither man said anything as they continued towards their final destination.

"It's been a long time since we've seen another car, Professor," Mrs. Fischer said nervously. "Are you sure we're not lost?"

"Quite sure, Gladys," Fenley reassured her. "I drove up here a month ago, shortly after the initial meeting with Mrs. Crowder, to make sure the generator was in working order and the house properly aired out—or, at least, as much as possible, considering there are no windows."

"No windows?" Ben frowned. "Why would someone build a house without windows?"

"Oh, it started out with windows," Fenley chuckled. "Belasco may have been an iconoclast, but he wasn't *that* extreme. Not at first, anyway. I was looking through the journals of the second Mrs. Belasco the other night. According to her, her husband bricked up the windows after an influenza epidemic killed several of his guests."

"Why on earth would he do that?" Mrs. Fischer asked.

"He seemed to believe that the sickness had something to do with the Matawaskie Valley fog. At least that was his excuse for sealing up the house. His wife was of the opinion he didn't want the habitants to be reminded of the world outside the confines of the house. Which is why, I suspect, she committed suicide three months after the last brick was cemented into place."

"You mentioned a generator—do you mean to say that the house isn't on the county power lines?" Mrs. Fischer asked.

"Afraid so. Nor is there phone service, although I've been told there is a private switching board within the house."

"What about running water?"

"The plumbing's fine—the toilets flush, and the hot water heater works. Everyone should be reasonably comfortable."

"I assume that there are enough rooms to go around?" Mrs. Fischer asked. "If not, Benjamin and I are accustomed to sharing . . ."

Professor Fenley shifted about uneasily. "Yes, well . . . About that . . . I'm afraid there's been a misunderstanding. You're not going to be staying at Belasco House with the rest of the team. However, we *have* made provisions for you at the Caribou Falls Inn . . ."

"But I *always* accompany Benjamin on his sittings—!" Mrs. Fischer protested indignantly.

"Yes, we're all aware of that; but in order to prove to the world what we record at Hell House is authentic, it's necessary to remove any hint of collusion or fraud from the picture . . ."

"Professor Fenley!" Mrs. Fischer gasped. "Surely *you*, of all people, aren't accusing Benjamin of being a *fake*?!?"

"No! Of course not, Gladys!" Fenley said quickly. "I have no doubts as to the authenticity of your son's gifts! It's just that it will be necessary to prove our findings to skeptical minds. As it is, we're taking a huge chance by including a spirit cabinet as part of the research equipment . . ."

"It's *him*, isn't it?" Mrs. Fischer scowled. "It's Dr. Rand: he doesn't believe in the soul's survival after death. To him it's all magnetic energies and quantum physics! But he doesn't have any problem using my boy to try and prove his scientific mumbo-jumbo!"

"It's not *just* him," Professor Fenley admitted uncomfortably. He glanced at Ben, and then quickly looked away. "We're concerned that your presence at Hell—I mean, *Belasco* House, will prove too distracting. Benjamin's under a great deal of stress to perform. We don't need him worrying about your welfare on top of everything else. As I said, you'll just be up the road, in the village. You can come to see us on Day Three."

"What's so special about Day Three?" Mrs. Fischer asked.

"We've brought two days' provisions with us. Carlyle will be bringing fresh supplies on the third day, as well as retrieving whatever notes that have been taken for transcription."

"But Benjamin has *never* had a sitting without me being present! This is *outrageous!* Benjamin isn't going to agree to it, are you, dear?"

"Mother, *please*," Ben whispered, his cheeks turning bright crimson.

"I'm afraid this isn't something that can be negotiated, Gladys," Fenley said, his voice growing stern. "If Benjamin insists on having you accompany him into the house, I'm sure we can make do with Miss Lauter."

"Grace?" Mrs. Fischer sniffed haughtily. "Ha! She's as unstable as that crazy ex-boyfriend of hers! I'd like to see them turn their backs on my Benjamin in favor of that woman! Benjamin could channel rings around her any day of the week, isn't that right, dear?"

"I appreciate your position, Gladys," Fenley said. "But if Benjamin refuses to work under the conditions put forth by the team, then Dr. Rand & Dr. Graham will only pay you a fraction of what was agreed to."

"They can't do that! You're the team leader, Ambrose—you can tell them to change their minds!"

Fenley laughed humorlessly. "I'm more along the lines of a paid consultant, I'm afraid. I might have helped put Nelson and Edgar in touch with Benjamin and Miss Lauter, but they're the ones who got the grant from Hale University. They can do whatever they like. You signed a contract with them, as Benjamin's legal guardian, that says as much. Or did you not read the fine print? The devil's in the details, you know."

The First Day:

After the grueling seven-hour drive north from Bangor, the Matawaskie Valley looked like a massive witch's cauldron full of seething green mist. As the Packard began its descent into the fog-shrouded valley, Ben could see why someone might consider the fetid air harmful to their health.

He turned to look out the back window of the car as the sun was swallowed whole by a rolling cloud of grayish-green vapor. Although it was two o'clock in the afternoon, it might as well have been dusk.

"Is it *always* like this?" he asked.

"Far as I can tell—yes," Fenley replied dourly. "Although the locals tell me that during the summer months it isn't quite as gloomy. Then again, summer around here only lasts six weeks."

As they made their way to the floor of the valley, the fog grew thicker, until all that was visible of Dr. Graham's Studebaker ahead of them were the taillights, which glowed like the eyes of a devil.

About ten miles outside of Caribou Falls the Studebaker veered off the main road and headed down a private black-top drive that appeared on no maps of the state, and never would. About a mile down the narrow drive they came to a locked gate. Dr. Graham stopped his vehicle and got out, fishing around in his tweed jacket for the key ring Mrs. Crowder had given him.

Dr. Rand hopped out of the passenger seat of the Studebaker and helped his research partner push open the heavy metal gates wide enough to allow the panel truck through. A half-mile later, they came to a large gravel parking area at the edge of a narrow concrete bridge. Ben could barely see the outline of the mansion on the other side.

"Come on, everyone—this is as close to the house as we get," Professor Fenley said.

Ben looked down at the tarn that separated the house from the rest of the estate. The water was the same lifeless gray-green as the fog-shrouded sky above it and smelled of rotting vegetation. As he peered into its cloudy depths, he thought he saw something with thick, stumpy limbs wriggle across the slime-coated bottom and slip underneath a rock.

"Wait up, son!" Dr. Graham called out. "We need to unload the truck first!"

Suppressing a shudder, the young psychic hurried to rejoin the others.

"Be careful with those crates," Dr. Rand said as Carlyle tipped the loaded hand truck onto its back wheels.

"Don't worry, Doc," his student assistant grinned. "I moonlight for a moving company to help with my tuition." As he crossed the footbridge with his burden, he grimaced in distaste. "Yowza! Does this place stink!"

"I doubt Emeric Belasco came here for the water," Dr. Rand said, glancing down at the fetid bog.

Belasco House was a huge Victorian mansion built from massive blocks of dark gray stone that seemed to emerge from the swirling mist like some huge sea beast rising up from the floor of the ocean.

"It's blind," Carlyle said.

"What do you mean?" Rand frowned.

"It's got no eyes," the student said, nodding to the blank walls of red brick that were all that remained of the house's windows. "It can't see."

"Nevertheless, it knows we're here," Grace Lauter said ominously. She turned to Ben, who was standing nearby, staring up at the building with a mixture of fascination and disgust. "Can you feel it?"

"Yes," he whispered. "Yes, I can."

"What is it like?" Dr. Rand asked.

"It's like when you see a wild animal in your yard," Grace whispered. "You stop what you're doing and become very still, trying not to scare it away, so you can get a better look at it and figure out if it's dangerous or not. Right now the house is being very, very still."

―――――――

"There you go, Docs," Carlyle said as he rolled the last load of supplies up the wide porch stairs and into the cavernous entry way just inside the massive double doors. "You want me to help you set everything up?"

"We can take it from here, thank you," Dr. Graham assured him. He glanced at his wrist watch, then at the darkening clouds congealing over the valley like a bruise. "You better leave for Caribou Falls with Mrs. Fischer. It'll be night soon, and you don't want to be on the road in this fog once the sun goes down."

Ben stood in the middle of the gravel drive and waved goodbye as the truck bearing his mother pulled away. Mrs. Fischer did not smile or return her son's wave, but instead glowered at Dr. Rand, who was busy helping Dr. Graham unload suitcases from the trunk of the Studebaker.

Ben felt a twinge of guilt for misleading his mother as to the reasons behind her being sent away. While it was true the good Drs. Graham and Rand were not thrilled by the prospect of having a "stage mother" underfoot, it was actually Ben's idea to keep her from entering the house. As eager as he was to exert his independence, Ben was unwilling to stand up and tell her that to her face. He was still enough of a child to be fearful of risking his mother's wrath that he found it easier to place the blame on someone else for his decisions.

He was almost sixteen years old—it was time for him to start doing sittings by himself. He would never shake the "Ghost Boy" label if he continued to travel with his mother. As a child he had been content to play the part his mother had planned for him since birth: savior of the Spiritualist Movement. But as he'd grown older, he had begun to chafe under her stewardship. He was becoming increasingly interested in finding a way to convert communicating with the dead into a way of life—and a profitable one, at that. He'd had enough of taking bus rides to sittings and living in furnished one-room apartments. Was it so horrible that he wanted to use his gifts to buy a car for himself and a house for his mother?

After Hell House, he would be able to put the "Ghost Boy" moniker behind him forever. He could name his price and have it met without anyone blinking an eye. No more two-day trips on the bus. No more shabby rented rooms. No more meals at Woolworth luncheon counters. It would be nothing but first-class accommodations from here on in.

All he had to do was crack the house's secret and discover the truth about its sinister master, Emeric Belasco. But as Professor Fenley had pointed out, he wasn't the only psychic on board. If he wanted to claim the glory that came with solving the riddle of Hell House, he would have to act fast and decisively. Coming in second in a two-person race wasn't an option.

"So this is the dreaded 'Hell House,' huh?" Dr. Rand said, standing in the enormous entry way of the mansion. "Looks more like the Knickerbocker Club than a private residence, if you ask me."

"At least the generator is still working," Dr. Graham said as he flipped the walk switch, illuminating bulky Victorian-era furniture and walls covered by faded tapestries.

"This house was never intended to be a home," Professor Fenley said as he walked across the hardwood floor. "It was built as a combination resort and petrie dish, where Belasco could conduct his social experiments without fear of interruption or censure."

As Ben stepped over the threshold he felt like a swimmer caught in a current far stronger and swifter than expected. He glanced at Grace Lauter, who was standing in the middle of the foyer, scowling up at the ceiling, and then quickly looked away.

Grace's head abruptly whipped about, a look of surprise on her face. "Did you hear that?" she whispered hoarsely, looking to Ben.

"Hear what?" Rand asked. He fished a small notebook out of his breast pocket, checked his watch and began to jot down notes.

"Voices—those of young girls," Grace muttered distractedly.
"How young?"

Grace tilted her head to one side, an intent look on her face. "I'd say adolescent. Certainly no older than fifteen, sixteen years old."

Dr. Rand and Dr. Graham turned to stare at Ben, to see if he was experiencing the same phenomena. The boy's cheeks flushed and he shook his head. They weren't inside the house five minutes, and Grace was already on record as claiming to have some kind of contact. If he wanted to get anywhere, he was going to have to hustle.

"I'm a physical medium, not a mental one like Miss Lauter," he said defensively. "I need my spirit cabinet."

"Very well, we best get started then." Dr. Graham turned to Professor Fenley. "You were here before, Ambrose—where do you recommend that we hold our experiments?"

Professor Fenley pointed across the foyer to a huge archway six feet deep. "The Great Hall seems a natural enough base camp," he said. "According to Rose Belasco's journals, it's where her husband held his nightly orgies."

"*Nightly?*" Dr. Rand said with a chuckle. "Humbug or not, I have to hand it to the old boy's stamina."

At ninety-five by forty-five feet, the Great Hall was about as cozy as the waiting room at Grand Central Station. It stood two stories high, with walnut paneling extending the first eight feet, with the rest built from blocks of roughhewn stone. At the far end of the room was a colossal fireplace big enough for a man to stand inside, with a mantle made of antique carved stone depicting cavorting fauns and nymphs.

In one corner of the room was an ebony concert grand piano, while the center of the room was dominated by a huge twenty-foot-wide table ringed by sixteen high-backed chairs. Above the meeting table hung an equally immense chandelier.

Using the hand truck and dolly left behind by Carlyle, the team ferried their equipment into the room. Ben and Professor Fenley set about putting together his spirit cabinet, placing it at the end of the large table.

Made of wood, the cabinet was seven feet high, six feet wide, and two feet deep, set eighteen inches above the floor atop a pair of sawhorses. A wooden curtain rod with heavy velvet drapes hanging from brass rings was placed between the crossbars, so that the medium could sit revealed or be hidden from view if needed. As they were putting the final touches on the spirit cabinet, Dr. Rand frowned and looked around the room.

"Where is the kitchen in this damnable barn? We need to put up our supplies."

Dr. Graham pulled a folded piece of paper out of his jacket pocket. "If the map Mrs. Crowder gave me is to be trusted, you should be able to reach it by going through the dining room," he said, pointing to an archway on the opposite wall of the Great Hall. "There should be a set of swinging doors that lead directly to the kitchen."

"Good enough," Rand grunted, hoisting a large cardboard box full of provisions. "Would care to join me, Miss Lauter?"

"Of course, Doctor," Grace replied, picking up a bag of groceries.

She followed Rand through the archway, entering a cavernous dining hall only slightly smaller than the room they had just left, dominated by a forty-foot-long table and an immense fireplace with a Gothic mantle that stretched all the way to the ceiling. They crossed the polished travertine floor and pushed through a pair of swinging doors into the kitchen.

The kitchen at Hell House resembled those found in restaurants accustomed to preparing meals for numerous guests. All the counters were stainless steel, as was the double-sink, triple-oven stove, and the industrial walk-in freezer. In the middle of the room was a huge steam table. Dark-paneled, glass-fronted cupboards lined the walls, filled with stacks of crockery and stemware, as well as rows of bottled spirits.

"I guess I shouldn't be surprised Belasco wasn't one for Prohibition," Rand said sarcastically.

"I don't think he had much respect for the Laws of Man," Grace agreed, setting down the bag of groceries on one of the steel countertops.

"Being this close to the Canadian border must have been useful in that regard, at least," Rand said as he began shelving the cans of tinned food. "Maybe that's where the old bastard escaped to after everything went to hell in here."

"You genuinely believe Belasco is still alive?" Grace asked.

Rand shrugged. "I'm not sure he's still amongst the living now—egomaniacs like Belasco usually don't disappear without a trace for years on end—but I don't think he died here with the others back in Twenty-Nine."

As Grace opened one of the cabinets, she stopped then quickly turned around, as if trying to catch someone sneaking up behind her. She glanced over at Rand, who was watching her with a slightly amused look on his face.

"You didn't hear that?" she asked. "It was those girls again . . . they sounded like they were standing right behind me. They called me by name."

Rand fished his notebook back out and briefly jotted down the time and location. "Very interesting, Miss Lauter," he muttered under his breath. "Very interesting indeed."

By the time Grace and Dr. Rand returned to the Great Hall, the others had finished setting up the spirit cabinet, as well as the rest of their equipment. A large Magnetophon sat on the opposite end of the meeting table, its huge metal reels threaded with magnetic tape in anticipation of the evening's séance. Next to the table stood a large Bolex 16mm film camera mounted on a tripod, pointed at the spirit cabinet. Arranged along the table top itself were a barometric pressure gauge, a free-standing thermometer, a chronometer, and a hygrometer.

"Now that we've got everything set up in the Great Hall," Dr. Graham announced, "I think we should take a brief rest before dinner and this evening's sitting. From what I've been told, there's no shortage of guest rooms upstairs."

"Sounds good to me," Dr. Rand grunted.

They left the Great Hall and returned to the foyer, picking up their individual suitcases before climbing the staircase to the second floor. At the top of the stairs was a long balcony corridor open to the floor below. To the right, behind a heavy balustrade, was a lengthy line of bedroom doors set into the paneled wall. To the left was a single door, far larger than the others.

"What's that?" Benjamin asked, pointing at the double-sized door. Not only was it twice as wide as the others, it was twice as high, as if designed to accommodate a giant.

"That was Belasco's room," Professor Fenley said.

"Really?" Ben grinned. "I want to see."

"It's locked. When I was here last month, we couldn't find the key to open it."

"Are you sure about that?" the young psychic asked as he gave the knob a turn.

Professor Fenley frowned. "I swear that door was locked tight last time I was here."

"I don't doubt it was," Graham replied as he followed Ben into the darkened room.

Graham flicked on the overhead lights, revealing the personal quarters of the master of Hell House to be more along the lines of a duplex apartment than a simple bedroom. The lower portion was a lavishly appointed sitting room with a polished teakwood floor. To the left was a curving stairway that led to the second floor sleeping quarters, which were partially obscured from casual view by a waist-high wooden partition that jutted out over the room below like the prow of a ship.

The furnishings in the sitting room were handsome, if out of date. A Tiffany stained-glass lamp sat on a dresser, alongside a pewter art nouveau figurine of Pan playing his pipes. Next to the dresser was a barrister bookcase filled with leather-bound volumes.

Ben moved forward to get a better look at the titles printed in faded gold leaf along the spines of the books, only to freeze in mid-step. Sprawled at his feet across the floor was the nude body of a woman laying face down, a tangle of long blonde hair obscuring her face. As he watched in mute horror, a halo of blood welled up around the woman's head and radiated outward across the floorboards. He instinctively stepped back as it spread towards his feet.

Despite his shock and revulsion, Ben's eyes were drawn towards the woman's bosom and buttocks. However, whatever titillation he might have received from seeing his first "real" naked woman was overwhelmed by the revulsion he felt at the sight of the bite marks across her shoulders. Whoever this woman was, she had been horribly brutalized before being tossed over the balcony.

He looked up at the others, wondering why they didn't seem surprised to find the body of a dead woman in a house that had supposedly been sealed for the last nine years. Unless, it suddenly occurred to him, he was the only one who could see her . . .

"Do you hear that?" Grace asked, tilting her head to one side.

"What? Is it the girls again?" Dr. Rand asked curiously.

"No," she said. "It's not them. It's something else . . . it's coming from up there." She pointed at the lofted section of Belasco's personal quarters.

As Grace climbed the stairs, the sounds that at first seemed like the grunting of beasts, transformed themselves into the moans of a couple engaged in vigorous sexual intercourse. Upon reaching the top of the stairs, she saw a huge Louis XIII bed with elaborately carved columns and the initials "E.B." worked into the center of the headboard in bas-relief. It was from this bed that the sounds seemed to be emanating.

She could plainly see a naked man and woman on the bed. The woman was on her belly with her hindquarters raised, her face buried in a pillow. The man was on his knees behind her, pounding away with the finesse of a jackhammer. From the violence of his strokes, the woman's partner seemed more interested in using his penis as an instrument of punishment than pleasure, even his own.

The man suddenly whipped his head about to leer at Grace. She gasped in horror, automatically covering her mouth with her hands. Simon Wagner grinned at her, blood welling like scarlet tears from the raw, red holes where his eyes used to be.

"I fucked the shit out of the bitch, Gracie," he cackled, continuing to pump away like an obscene clockwork toy. "She called me a fag, said I was less than a man. I showed her! When I'm finished, I'll show you, too!"

Choking on a strangled cry of revulsion, Grace closed her eyes, turning her back on the monstrous vision before her. Her pelvis struck the balcony partition and she felt herself start to topple forward. Her eyes flew open as she grabbed the railing to steady herself, only to see Ben's horrified face looking up at her from the sitting room below.

Ben Fischer looked up from the dead woman at his feet and was shocked to see a pale man's face with brilliant green eyes staring down at him. The man's face was contorted into a look of undisguised loathing. Ben blinked and the man's features disappeared, to be replaced by those of Grace Lauter's, who appeared extremely frightened and badly disoriented.

Grace looked around, like a sleepwalker startled from a dream, as Professor Fenley and Dr. Graham hurried up the staircase after her.

"Are you all right?" Fenley asked, steering her away from the edge of the balcony. He tried to maneuver her towards the bed, but she shook her head and refused to go any further. "You looked like you were in a trance . . ."

"I saw . . . I saw . . ." she tried to find the words to describe what she'd witnessed, but she was afraid she might vomit if she did.

"What *did* you see, Miss Lauter?" Dr. Graham prodded as he took her pulse.

"Something . . . awful," she muttered.

"Someone was killed in this room," Ben said, his voice floating up from the floor below. "A woman."

Dr. Graham walked over to the balcony and looked down at the youth. "How do you know that?"

"I saw her body," Benjamin said, pointing at the floor.

"Is it still there?" Dr. Graham asked.

Benjamin shook his head. "It disappeared the moment it seemed Miss Lauter might fall."

"Why don't we leave this room for later," Professor Fenley suggested as he escorted a badly shaken Grace back down the stairs. "We all would benefit from freshening up before we continue."

"You're absolutely right, Ambrose," Dr. Graham agreed.

As he closed the door behind him, the doorknob slipped out of his hand, as if someone on the other side of the door had quickly jerked it shut. Of course, that was impossible. It was just negative air pressure, that was all.

Except that the house was hermetically sealed.

As he followed the others in the direction of the guest rooms, Graham patted the breast pocket of his jacket, making sure his flask was still there.

Dinner that night was a humble affair, compared to the magnificent feasts once served in the dining hall. Instead of fine French foods and savory sauces, Hell House's most recent guests dined on hot Spam and fried egg sandwiches with canned fruit cocktail salad on the side.

As they were finishing their modest repast, Grace turned to fix the scientists with a curious stare. "If you don't mind me asking, Dr. Rand, since you and Dr. Graham don't believe in the existence of spirits, what is it, exactly, you are trying to prove with your investigation into this house?"

"I'm sure you're familiar with the phenomenon known as *igniis fatuus*—fool's fire," Dr. Rand said. "That's when the rotting vegetation in bogs generates methane gas, creating 'ghost lights' that resemble flickering lamps that seem to move about on their own accord. In that case, what has been perceived as supernatural has turned out to be a natural event imperfectly perceived.

"Dr. Graham and I are of the opinion that 'hauntings' are much the same thing: misinterpreted natural phenomena. We are of the opinion that psychic energies are released under particular circumstances, and that these energies build up over time. Given the proper situations, the minds of 'sensitive' individuals, such as yourself and young Ben, react with these stored energies on a subconscious level, resulting in what the layman perceives as 'ghosts' and other such supernatural phenomena."

Dr. Graham nodded in agreement. "If we can prove that there is such a thing as a psychic energy field, the next step is to move from unintentional exploitation to conscious and deliberate manipulation. Think of the advantages to the human race if we could harness such power!" he said excitedly. "Hitler already has a very advanced parapsychology unit conducting experiments along the lines of what we're trying to do here. I can tell you, the Führer would give his mustache to have access to Hell House!"

"So, if I understand your analogy correctly, Ben and I are the equivalent of struck matches being introduced to a house full of gas fumes."

"I wouldn't put it quite so crudely," Rand said uncomfortably.

"I just hope you're prepared to handle the consequences," Grace said as she pushed herself away from the dining hall table.

"You and Dr. Graham might not believe in spirits, but I do. And I resent the implication that what I saw today was anything I *wanted* to see. I assure you that the force that powers this house is very real, and it is certainly not born of any living mind."

"Are you ready, Ben?" Dr. Graham asked.

"Yes, sir," the boy replied, holding his wrists out to the physician. He had changed out of the clothes he had been wearing earlier and into the close-fitting black turtleneck sweater and tights he always wore during séances.

Dr. Graham took the length of rope and tied the young psychic's hands securely, while Dr. Rand tended to his feet. Once they were convinced the youth was securely bound, they lifted him up and placed him on the chair inside the spirit cabinet.

"Please turn out the lights," Ben said. "It must be dark in the room if I'm to contact the spirit world."

"We need some light in order to record what happens," Dr. Graham reminded him.

"Very well," Ben nodded. "Use the red light, then."

Professor Fenley leaned over and switched on the Tiffany lamp in the middle of the table, the incandescent bulb of which had been replaced with one painted red. When the overhead light was turned off, the room was bathed in a dim crimson glow, like that of a photographer's dark room.

Dr. Rand and Dr. Graham took their place at the table alongside Professor Fenley and Grace, who were sitting in a semi-circle facing Ben. Set in the middle of the table was an aluminum cone with holes at both ends. Although called a "trumpet," it looked more like a megaphone than a musical instrument. Dr. Rand flicked a switch on the nearby Magnetophon, and its reels began to turn.

"First séance at Hell House, commencing at exactly nine sixteen o'clock, on September 25th, 1940," Dr. Graham intoned. "Benjamin Franklin Fischer is serving as the medium, with Dr. Rand, Grace Lauter, Professor Fenley and myself in attendance."

"I must warn all of you," Ben said, his manner extremely serious for someone so young, "the trumpet must not be touched, except when you are told it is safe to do so. If you touch the trumpet, you run the risk of getting a bad shock, and possibly giving me one as well. I'm ready to begin."

Grace nodded her understanding and began to recite the Lord's Prayer, which the others took up as well. As they chanted the protection prayer, Ben's head and shoulders began to droop, until he was completely slumped in his chair.

The boy's jaw dropped open, and a pale object, resembling the questing pseudopod of a snail, emerged from his gaping mouth. As the others watched, the membrane unraveled itself like a length of gauze bandage.

"Ectoplasm begins to manifest at exactly nine twenty-two," Dr. Rand whispered, watching in amazement as the material blindly groped its way out of the spirit cabinet and onto the table top, humping towards the spirit-trumpet like an inchworm. The ectoplasm wrapped itself around the narrow end of the trumpet and began to lift it into the air.

"The spirit is forming an artificial voice box within the mouthpiece so it can converse with us," Grace explained in a whisper. "We should be able to hear from Ben's spirit guide momentarily."

As if on cue, a masculine voice resonated from inside the trumpet, speaking heavily accented English: "*Me Shi Kwan-Chiang. Royal physician to Zhou Wuwang. Me bring greetings from ancestors.*"

"Greetings, Shi Kwan-Chiang," Dr. Graham replied in the kind of overloud voice usually reserved for the hard-of-hearing. "You honor us with your presence."

"*No honor in this house—only shame.*"

"What do you mean, Shi Kwan-Chiang?" Dr. Graham asked.

"Not good here. Take boy and leave."

"Shi Kwan-Chiang, what can you tell us about the spirits that haunt this house?" Professor Fenley asked the spirit guide.

"This house mouth of dragon. Very hungry dragon. Many spirits here. Many sick. They pluck sleeve, ask me to heal them, too sick to know they are dead."

Dr. Graham leaned over and whispered something to Dr. Rand, who quietly left his place at the table to go stand behind the movie camera. A second later the wind-up 16mm began to whirr. The trumpet swiveled in mid-air, like the needle on a compass, pointing its bell at Rand.

"What is noise?"

"It is only the sound of a machine, Shi Kwan-Chiang," Grace said quickly.

"No. Not that," the spectral voice said with a hint of irritation. *"Other noise. Like roaring of tiger. It comes closer."*

Grace frowned. "I don't understand, Shi Kwan-Chiang—what do you mean?"

The voice of the long-dead Chinese physician suddenly grew panicked. *"He comes! The giant comes!"*

Before anyone could quiz the spirit guide any further, a strong wind suddenly filled the room, lifting the heavy tapestries like they were chintz curtains, and rattling the measuring equipment arranged across the tabletop. The camera tripod suddenly began to topple, and it was all Dr. Rand could do to keep it from smashing against the floor.

Accompanying the fierce wind was a guttural howl, like the bellowing of an enraged bull. Grace cried out and clapped her hands over her ears, as did the others. The trumpet snapped its ectoplasmic tether and began to spin out of control like a leaf caught in a whirlwind, striking Dr. Graham's temple with the wide end of its bell before flying across the room and landing in the crackling flames of the fireplace.

Nelson Graham put a hand to the side of his head and stared in dazed surprise at the blood on his fingers. Raising his eyes, he saw a green, glowing mist filling the air above the table, directly opposite Ben in the spirit cabinet, who was still slumped over in a deep trance.

"God, the stink!" Dr. Rand exclaimed, staring at the shifting cloud of greenish mist hovering above their heads. "It's like an open sewer!"

"More like the bog," Professor Fenley said, wrinkling his nose in distaste.

There was a rattling noise as the huge table began to tremble, causing the recording instruments arranged across its surface to topple and roll off onto the floor. It was as if someone—or some *thing*—was trying to lift the massive piece of furniture from underneath, like Atlas balancing the world on his shoulders.

"Ben! Wake up!" Grace yelled, trying to make herself heard over the roaring sound that seemed to come from every part of the room.

"No! Don't stop him!" Dr. Rand snapped. "This is genuine poltergeist activity! This is what we came here for!"

"You don't understand—we're all in danger!" Professor Fenley said. "Whatever is within this house is using him as a portal!"

One of the statues in the room toppled over, as if shoved by an unseen hand, and one of the heavy leather-bound volumes lining the bookcase on the opposite wall suddenly flew across the room, striking Dr. Graham in the shoulder hard enough to knock him off his chair. Within seconds the air was filled with flying books as the rest of the shelf was emptied by some invisible force.

"Take cover!" Fenley shouted, narrowly avoiding a set of encyclopedias.

Dr. Rand crawled over to where Dr. Graham lay sprawled on the Persian carpet, clutching his shoulder blade. "Are you okay, Nelson?"

"I think my collarbone is broken," Graham replied between clenched teeth. "What the hell is going on, Edgar?"

"I'm not sure—it seems to be some kind of poltergeist."

Apparently no longer satisfied with simply hurling books around the room like a discus thrower, the force that had invaded the séance began tearing their pages out and tossing them into the air like confetti. As Rand brushed the shredded paper out of his hair, he looked up to see the greenish mist suspended above the table congealing like the skin on boiled milk, until it was the shape of a human hand reaching out for the bound medium.

Professor Fenley jumped to his feet and hurried towards the archway leading to the grand hall, only to have his way blocked by a heavy ottoman. Fenley lunged over the piece of wayward furniture and hit the switch plate on the wall. The chandelier overhead blazed back to life, banishing the murky red light and shadows of the séance.

The results of the lights being turned back on were instantaneous: the roaring stopped abruptly, as if someone had lifted the needle off a record; the heavy table slammed back down onto the ground, narrowly missing Dr. Rand's foot; and the phantom hand dropped onto the tabletop, splattering like a child's water balloon on contact.

Ben raised his head and looked around with bleary eyes, a confused expression on his face. "What's going on? Why are the lights back on?"

Grace hurried forward and untied the young psychic's hands. "Do you remember any of what happened after you went into the trance?"

"Shi Kwan-Chiang appeared, and then . . . and then . . ." Ben frowned as he struggled to recall what occurred next. Normally when he went into a trance his consciousness hovered just above his physical body, allowing him to observe everything in the room as if he was at the picture show. But all he could remember was utter blackness, as if his mind had been filled with ink.

"Something came through, didn't it?" he whispered.

"Something tried," Grace replied grimly. "It nearly destroyed the room and attacked Dr. Graham."

"I don't understand," Ben said as he massaged the circulation back into his wrists. "Shi Kwan-Chiang normally protects me from harmful spirits . . ."

"That's it! I've had enough of this spiritualist nonsense!" Dr. Rand said angrily as he helped Dr. Graham onto a nearby sofa.

"Edgar—don't!" Graham said, grabbing at his comrade's sleeve. "There's no need to make things worse by antagonizing the others."

"I don't care, Nelson!" Rand replied. "I'm tired of pretending to pay lip service to their hogwash!"

"What are you going on about, Dr. Rand?" Professor Fenley asked stiffly.

"This bunk about ghosts and spirit guides is utter horseshit! The sole person responsible for what happened here tonight is sitting right there!" he said, pointing at Ben.

"Are you suggesting Ben *deliberately* used his powers to attack Dr. Graham?" Grace gasped.

"Not consciously, no. I think he simply tapped into an unexpectedly large pocket of psychic energy, and it got the better of him. Everything that happened was a material manifestation of things he expected to occur."

"But you heard Shi Kwan-Chiang's voice yourself!" Grace protested. "You heard what he said about this place being full of spirits unable to move on!"

Rand turned to look at the young medium. "Tell me, Ben— haven't you ever asked yourself why an ancient Chinese doctor would communicate in English? Granted, it is pidgin English, but English nonetheless—without a single word of Mandarin or Cantonese?"

"But the voice . . ."

"Yes, I *heard* the voice," Rand said with a wry smile. "And I recognized it as belonging to Sidney Tolar—better known as Charlie Chan."

Ben blinked, his initial confusion gradually giving way to self-doubt as he listened to the scientist's words. He'd never really thought about it before, but now that Dr. Rand mentioned it, Shi

Kwan-Chiang *did* sound an awful lot like the famous matinee detective.

"That's quite enough, Edgar," Graham said, wincing as he got to his feet. "There's no need to upset the boy. I think we've done quite enough for our first day. I say it's time we call it a night and retire to our rooms."

Ambrose Fenley sat down in the chair next to the fireplace in his room and opened one of Rose Belasco's journals. Although the others didn't seem to deem the diaries important, Fenley felt they provided insight into the mind and personality of Emeric Belasco, and he was a strong believer in getting to know his enemy. He had no doubt that Belasco was not only dead, but the one responsible for the attack during the séance. During his lifetime Belasco had been extremely possessive of his private little fiefdom, and he saw no reason for him to act any differently now that he was dead.

The volume he was holding was bound in calfskin, with a hand-sewn spine. The pages were covered in a fine, feminine hand, the ink having faded from black to pale blue over the years. Instead of reading chronologically, he simply let the journal fall open at random.

April 8th, 1924

Emeric continues to ignore me, preferring to spend his time with his precious new favorites, Dr. Tarr and Prf. Fether. They are insufferable boors, and the only guests as convinced of their godhood as Emeric. I guess that is because they are surgeons and accustomed to holding life and death in their hands. Their conceit amuses Emeric a great deal. Prf. Fether is notoriously fond of laudanum. I must remind myself never to fall sick when they are here.

He flipped the book open to another, earlier passage.

August 20th, 1923

They found Myra dead in her room today. I cannot say I am surprised. The needle was still lodged in her vein. At least we are spared her continuous, pathetic attempts to win her brother back into her bed. She really was a sad little creature toward the end. Hard to believe she and Emeric had the same parents.

Fenley closed the journal and exchanged it for another, allowing it to fall open in the exact same manner.

June 15th, 1926

If my time within this house has taught me anything, it is that there is no depth too low to which I will not sink. Every time I believe I have fallen as far from grace as humanly possible, Emeric devises some new means of proving me wrong. Take yesterday's "Feast of Cupid"— yet another of his themed "events." Everyone was to dress as one of the great lovers of history. I came as Cleopatra. Emeric simply came dressed as himself, of course.

When I arrived downstairs, I found the grand hall full of costumed guests, drinking and making merry. Emeric had a troupe of circus dwarves shipped in and dressed them all as Cupid. There were dozens of them waddling about on their bowed legs, costumed in diapers with artificial wings strapped to their backs, armed with miniature bows and arrows. It was all quite amusing, at first, and everyone laughed.

I started off drinking champagne, but somewhere during the evening I switched to absinthe, as did the others. That was about the same time when the first few couples began to shed their clothes. I remember standing around with the others, watching Margery Pettijohn suck Judge Fitzsimon's cock while Evangeline Crutchfield licked her pussy. I can clearly recall how ridiculous the judge looked, with his huge belly overshadowing his tiny little dick.

I looked up and saw Emeric staring at me from across the room with those shining green eyes of his. He was smiling like he used to, and I thought maybe, just maybe, he wanted me again. My heart fluttered in my breast like a bird at the possibility. Even after all that has happened between us, after all that he's done to me—I still hunger for his touch. God help me.

After that things get . . . foggy. The next thing I know, I'm on my back in front of the fireplace. It takes me several moments to realize where I am—and that I'm not only naked, but that someone is inside me. I assume it is my husband and I start to moan and respond—then my vision clears and I see Emeric sitting on the divan beside me, smoking one of his Havana cigars, watching me with a cruel smile on his lips.

I raise my head to find one of the dwarves atop me, leering at me as he paws at my breasts with his tiny hands and stubby fingers. My first instinct is to scream and push the horrid creature off of me, but the look of reproach in Emeric's eyes keeps me from doing so . . . Instead, I lay back and allow him to continue. Once the dwarf finishes, he is replaced by another Cupid. And then another. And so it went throughout the night.

Throughout it all I stared into the face of my husband, hoping for some glimmer of approval. However, once the last of his stunted rapists finished with me, he stood up without so much as a word to me, to go off in search of fresher meat.

I have washed myself six times since then, trying to make myself feel clean, without any success. Sweet Jesus, Savior of Us All, give me the strength to free myself from the hold this man has on my soul and let me walk out of this house and into the safety of Your arms.

Fenley shook his head in dismay. What a horrid influence Belasco was on those in his world. He seemed to take a particular pleasure in degrading those who adored him, as if punishing them for daring to see something in him worth loving. Fenley got the distinct impression that Belasco was the kind of man who could not look at a flower without dwelling on the fact it grew in manure.

Fenley had never known the man, and, judging from what little he had read about him, was damn glad of it. If there was one thing Fenley despised, it was men who mistreated women. And Belasco was the worst of the lot, judging by how he treated his wives and sister.

"I don't care if you stood six foot five or not," Fenley said defiantly to the empty room. "What a stunted, shriveled little man you must have been."

When he stood up to go to bed, something fell out of the journal, landing on the rug at his feet. As Fenley bent to pick it up, he saw it was an old rotogravure photograph of a woman dressed in a formal-length red velvet gown, with auburn hair swept atop her head. Although her face was obscured by a Venetian-style carnival mask, Fenley recognized her as Rose Belasco. His heart went out to this beautiful, deeply conflicted woman. Perhaps, in the morning, he'd talk to Ben Fischer about another sitting—this one designed specifically to make contact with Rose Belasco.

There had been no knight in shining armor to help her escape, all those years ago. But he would prove that chivalry, unlike Emeric Belasco, was not dead.

Ben lay in the dark and told himself he had no reason to be frightened. The naked man hanging by his neck from the light fixture in his room was not real. According to Dr. Graham and Dr. Rand, his unwanted roomie was simply something conjured forth from his subconscious by the psi-energy within the house.

Under normal circumstances, had he woken up in the middle of the night to find something like that in the room with him, he would have summoned Shi Kwan-Chiang to his aide. For the last three years he had relied on the ancient doctor to guard him from forces intent on harming him. But if what Dr. Rand said was right, and Shi Kwan-Chiang wasn't a "real" spirit, but merely a figment of his imagination, given voice and form by some amorphous psychic energy field, then that meant he'd never had anyone protecting him in the first place.

The rope from which the dead man dangled made a groaning noise as the body twisted ever so slightly in the air, slowly rotating so that its black, bloated face was pointed in Ben's direction. Suddenly the dead man's eyes flew open, staring at him with unalloyed malice.

Ben's hand shot towards the bedside lamp. The second the light came on the dead man winked out of sight. Ben heaved a sigh of relief and fell back against his pillows. Maybe he ought to go ahead and sleep with the light on. Just to be on the safe side.

Nelson Graham grimaced as he tried to make himself comfortable. Edgar had helped him rig up a sling for his right arm and propped up several pillows so he wouldn't put too much pressure on his clavicle, but the pain was making it difficult for him to get to sleep.

He removed his flask from the bedside table and shook it. There was barely a swallow of whisky left, not even enough to take the edge off. Still—it was better than nothing. He upended the flask, savoring how the liquor burned its way down his throat and into his belly.

As he returned the flask to its hiding place, he glanced across the room at the bookcase arranged against the wall. The shelves were lined with various bits and pieces of Edwardian bric-a-brac, but what caught his eye was the glint of light off cut-crystal.

"I'll be damned," Graham muttered under his breath.

Sure enough, sitting on the third shelf was a square-bodied crystal decanter, complete with stopper. Although unlabeled, he could see it was three-quarters full of some kind of green liquid. Setting his teeth against the pain, he reached up with his good hand and took down the container, setting it on the octagonal table in the middle of the room.

He removed the stopper and sniffed the contents, which smelled strongly of licorice. With a start, Graham realized what he was holding in his hand was absinthe, which had been banned in the United States since 1912. Even though he was completely alone, he instinctively glanced about to make sure no one was looking.

Normally he preferred whisky, but he was willing to give any-thing a try once, especially if it might blunt the pain in his shoulder enough for him to get some sleep. He needed some rest if he was going to continue his experiments with the boy in the morning. Al-though they'd gotten far more than they'd planned for during the first sitting, the results were very promising. After all, Benjamin was young and not as set in his beliefs, which meant he was going to be far more suggestible and easier to work with than Miss Lauter.

Besides, after all he'd endured earlier, who could begrudge him a little nip before bed?

―――――

The Second Day:

Grace Lauter sat in front of the vanity table as she brushed out her hair. Her room was relatively small, by Belasco House standards, with a single canopy-top bed and an ornately patterned Oriental rug covering the floor. She glanced at her wrist watch, which assured her it was just past midnight, since it was otherwise impossible to tell whether it was day or night inside the house.

She had not wanted to participate in that evening's sitting, but since another medium was needed to insure the session was controlled properly, she'd had no choice. Not that she had been of much help, in the end.

Even though she disagreed with Dr. Graham and Dr. Rand's beliefs and tactics, she was in no position to pack up and leave, even if she wanted to, as she desperately needed the money they were paying her. Then there was the matter of clearing Simon's reputation.

Grace . . .

The voice outside her bedroom door startled her so badly she dropped her brush. In truth, she didn't really "hear" anything—it was more like she somehow *knew* what was being said, like when someone speaks to you in a dream. She got up off the bed and padded over to the door, pressing her ear to one of the panels.

"What do you want from me?" she whispered.

Help . . .

"Who are you?"

Violet . . .

Iris . . .

"There are two of you?"

Yes . . .

Sisters . . .

"What can I do to help you?"

Follow us . . .

Please . . .

Grace returned to the nightstand and retrieved her flashlight. As she slid on a pair of slippers and put on her house coat, she paused for a moment, wondering if she should tell the others what she was doing, but quickly dismissed it. There was no talking to Dr. Graham and Dr. Rand about what she was experiencing. They were men of science, not faith. They were more interested in things they could weigh and measure and calculate, as opposed to the intangible. With a physical medium like Benjamin, they could record direct voices and photograph manifestations. But when it came to mental mediumship, there was no way of knowing if the voices she heard and visions she saw were anything more than delusions.

She stepped out into the corridor and spotted a small flicker of pale purple light retreating down the hallway, away from the stairs. Tightening her grip on her flashlight, Grace hurried after the ghost light, being careful not to make a sound as she hurried past the rooms of her teammates.

The pale glow flitted through the gloom like a drunken firefly, occasionally splitting itself into two separate points of light, as it led her past rows of shut doors, each one identical to the one before and after. She finally found herself at the end of the corridor, staring at a blank wall of bricks where a window used to be.

"I don't understand," Grace said. "What are you trying to show me?"

In answer, the ghost light settled into the tulip-shaped wall sconce across from where she stood. Grace reached out and pulled the light fixture towards her like the arm on a slot machine. There was the sound of hidden mechanism engaging, and a portion of the paneling opened, revealing a narrow stairway. Without hesitating, she climbed up the steeply angled stairs.

The attic room was roughly the size of one of the guest rooms, but with a much lower ceiling, due to the severely pitched gables. As she played the beam of her flashlight about the room, she espied a gaily painted toy chest tucked against the wall. Grace frowned. Could this have been a nursery? From what she had learned about Emeric Belasco, he had precious little use for children, even his own.

She spotted a pull-chain dangling from the middle of the ceiling and gave it a tug, not really expecting it to work after nearly twelve years of neglect. To her surprise, the bare bulb above her head flared to life. As her eyes adjusted to the light, she gasped aloud, covering her mouth with her free hand.

The secret attic room was a grotesque parody of a child's nursery, its walls covered with obscene murals depicting scenes from famous storybook tales, as envisioned by a perverted madman. Mama Bear and Baby Bear tore at the flesh of a shrieking Goldilocks while Papa Bear impaled the dying child on his engorged penis; a rabid Big Bad Wolf mounted a terrified Little Red Riding Hood from behind, burying its slavering fangs deep into her neck and shoulder; a leering Captain Hook forced a frightened Peter Pan to fellate him while menacing the eternal boy with his deadly namesake; Prince Charming grinned demonically as he raped Snow White's lifeless body in its glass coffin, watched by a group of eagerly masturbating dwarves.

The crib and playpen in the nursery, as well as the hobby horse in the corner, were all oversized, obviously designed for the amusement of adults, not children. Grace walked over to the toy chest that had first caught her eye and flipped open the lid. Instead of teddy bears and wooden trains, she found a jumble of leather corsets, sculpted leather dildos, and other "toys" that had no place in a child's playroom. She bent down and picked up the cat o' nine tails that was lying on the top of the pile, holding it from her at arm's length as if it was a rotting fish.

"Why did you bring me to this horrid place?" she asked aloud, unable to hide her revulsion. "What are you trying to show me?"

He brought us here a long time ago . . .

Now we cannot leave . . .

No escape . . . no freedom . . . no respite . . .

Damned to serve him forever . . .

And ever . . .

Without end . . .

"Were you servants?" Grace asked, a sudden glimmer of understanding lighting in her eyes. "Did you come here to work, only to be used as prostitutes? Was Belasco a white slaver?"

As if in response, there came a gentle sigh and Grace felt what felt like a kiss upon her cheek. She smiled and gently touched the side of her face with the tips of her fingers, then hurried back down the stairs.

First thing in the morning, she would tell the others what she had found. She could hardly wait to see the look on Dr. Rand's face when she revealed the secret passage and hidden room that she could never have possibly known about otherwise. That should put a potato in Dr. Rand's skeptical tailpipe.

Edgar Rand scowled at the tape recorder sitting on the table before him. He'd been in a hurry to get the machine to his room, so he could play back the recording made during the sitting. He was particularly interested in listening to the conversation with the so-called spirit guide, but what he found on the tape was not at all what he'd expected.

Instead of the voices of Grace Lauter and Dr. Graham, all he heard was a murky, mumbling sound, without any distinctive voice of words to catch the ear. He fast-forwarded the tape, hoping to find some trace of the séance—surely the noise from the poltergeist attack would have registered? When he got to the end of the tape he rewound it and played it again, but still all that was audible was the muted mumble. It was like listening to a recording of Grand Central Station during rush hour from the bottom of a swimming pool.

What was it Ben's spirit guide had said about the room being filled with numerous spirits unaware they were dead?

Rand shook his head. No. That was utter foolishness.

There was any number of sane reasons for why the tapes sounded the way they did, such as a faulty microphone, or perhaps the tape somehow becoming demagnetized. Nelson might have the patience to coddle Grace and the boy, but he certainly didn't. He had dedicated his entire adult life to the service and understanding of science and the natural world, and he sure as hell wasn't going to let a little thing like a defective recording trick him into believing in something as patently ridiculous as ghosts.

"I learned how to make this while in the Army," Professor Fenley said with a laugh as he put a plate of chipped beef on toast down in front of Ben. "It's not pretty, but it'll get the job done. Would you care for some, Nelson?"

"No, thank you," Dr. Graham said. The physician's face was haggard and his eyes looked puffy and bloodshot. "I think I'll stick with black coffee for the time being. By the way, has anyone seen Miss Lauter? I thought she would be downstairs by now."

"Do you want me to go check on her?" Ben asked.

"There's no need of that," Grace said as she walked into the dining room, smiling as if she hadn't a care in the world. "Good morning, everyone!"

"You seem to be in exceptionally good spirits today—no pun intended," Dr. Rand observed.

"Yes, Dr. Rand, I *am*. And the reason is because I have proof that there are indeed surviving personalities trapped within this house, not merely a mass of undirected psychic energy."

"I assume this involves the girls you keep hearing?" Rand said dubiously.

"As a matter of fact, it does," Grace replied cheerily, determined not to let the chemist ruffle her feathers. "Last night they came to me, begging for help. I learned that they are sisters named Iris and Violet. They originally came to this house looking for work as domestics—but ended up being forced into sexual slavery by Belasco."

"It certainly sounds like something he would do," Fenley grunted. "The man was an ogre."

"Do you have any proof of this?" Dr. Graham asked.

"They showed me something only someone intimately familiar with his house would possibly know about: a room hidden in the attic, accessible only through a secret passageway on the second floor."

A sudden hush fell across the room.

"You don't believe me?" Grace challenged. "Then come see for yourself." She turned and walked briskly back out of the dining room, without pausing to see if the others were coming or not.

"What the hell," Rand muttered, draining the last of his juice.

The others followed the medium up to the second floor and down the long, gloomy corridor, until they were all gathered in the dead end with the bricked-up window.

"So where is this secret passageway of yours?" Dr. Rand said, his arms folded over his chest.

"I'll show you," Grace said, standing on tiptoe. "All you have to do is tilt the light fixture towards you like so and . . ." She gave the wall-sconce a tug, but it refused to budge. She frowned and gave it a second, harder pull, but it still didn't move.

"And *what?*" Dr. Rand asked impatiently.

Grace stepped back from the wall, staring in confusion at the light fixture. "I don't understand . . . It worked last night. I must have miscounted the doors . . . I know it's here somewhere! It opened for me last night—I climbed up the stairs to this room— this horrible room, covered in the most disgusting pictures imaginable . . ."

"Perhaps you're mistaken?" Dr. Graham charitably suggested. "We were *all* very tired last night. You probably fell asleep and had a particularly vivid dream . . . ?"

Grace shook her head in stubborn protest. "No! It was *real*, I tell you!" she insisted, fighting back tears of frustration. "Iris and Violet led me here . . ."

Dr. Rand rapped his knuckles against the paneling on the wall.

"There is no secret door, no hidden staircase, no mysterious room, Miss Lauter. Just as there are no ghosts of defiled twin sisters haunting this house. Now, if you'll excuse us, Dr. Graham and I will be spending the rest of the day escorting Ben about the mansion, to see if we can generate any further responses."

"Are you sure that's a wise thing to do, given the violence of the reaction you got last night?" Professor Fenley asked.

"We appreciate your concern," Dr. Rand replied tartly. "But we came here to get results, not tiptoe around like a bunch of cat burglars. This house is just that—a house. The only power it has over us is what we give it. It's just that simple."

Benjamin stared in open awe at the gilded, renaissance-style proscenium stage at the bottom of the sloping, three-aisled floor. The room was designed to seat an audience of one hundred, with walls covered in antique red brocade, with silver electric candelabra set every ten feet. The floor was covered in thick red carpets, and wine-red velvet upholstery covered the seats. He'd never set foot in a commercial movie house this swanky, much less one built inside a private home.

"Look at this place," Dr. Rand said, shaking his head in disbelief. "Belasco certainly spared no expense when it came to his hobbies."

Dr. Graham nodded in agreement. "From all accounts, he fancied himself a patron of the arts, and encouraged his guests to perform for his amusement. Legend has it he even went so far as to recreate the martyring of the early saints by having some poor girl fed alive to a big cat he kept starved in the cellar."

Rand grimaced. "Lovely."

"Are you picking up any vibrations from this room, Ben?" Dr. Graham asked.

"Not really. It's actually kind of flat." He angled his head back, to try and pick up some kind of etheric signal. "Hey—what's that?"

he asked, pointing up at the square cut into the brocaded drapery covering the back of the theatre.

"It looks like a projectionist's window," Dr. Rand said.

"That sounds likely, seeing there's a movie screen built into the stage," Dr. Graham observed. "I wonder how you get up there?"

"Look—over here!" Ben said, pushing aside one of the draperies, revealing a small door.

They climbed the narrow stairs into the cramped confines of the projectionist's booth. Dr. Rand flicked on his flashlight, illuminating the old film projector bolted to the floor.

"There's a movie threaded onto the take-up reel!" Ben said excitedly.

"I wonder if this thing even still works," Dr. Rand said, flicking the switch on the side of the machine.

To everyone's surprise, the projector's carbon arc lamp sprang to life and the reels began to turn with a loud rattling noise. A beam of light stabbed through the view port, spilling out onto the screen below. Suddenly the trio found themselves staring at an extreme close-up of an erect penis plunging into the mouth of a young girl. Ben's cheeks turned bright crimson, but could not bring himself to look away.

"My goodness!" Dr. Graham said, quickly turning off the projector. "I think we've seen enough of that, thank you!"

"It seems Belasco enjoyed filming his orgies," Dr. Rand chuckled. "There's a whole shelf of them over here." He played his flashlight over the collection of dusty film canisters as he read the titles out loud: "*The Last Days of Pompeii, 120 Days of Sodom, The Lustful Turk, Salome . . .* something tells me none of these little epics would meet the Hays Code."

"We didn't come all this way just to watch Belasco's stag reels," Dr. Graham said sharply. "Let's move along, Ben—assuming you're ready."

"Huh? Oh, yes, of course," Ben replied, trying his best to hide the erection tenting his pants.

The next room on their list was the chapel, which was directly across the hall from the theater. Although Graham and Rand entered ahead of him, Ben found himself unable to cross the threshold. He tried to will himself to step inside, but something kept him from moving his legs.

The room was low-ceilinged, with enough wooden pews to seat fifty worshippers comfortably, all of them facing an altar, on which rested a large leather-bound volume and a silver chalice. Above the altar hung suspended a life-sized, flesh-colored representation of Jesus on the cross. The big difference between this crucifix and every other one Ben had ever seen was that the Christ figure gracing the Belasco chapel was completely nude and sporting an enormous erection.

"Good God," Dr. Rand whispered as he stared up at the blasphemous relic.

"God had very little to do with Emeric Belasco's world, it would seem," Dr. Graham said darkly. The physician looked around the interior of the chapel, suddenly aware that the young medium was nowhere to be seen. "Ben—why are you standing in the hall?"

"The house doesn't want me here," Ben replied, a slight quaver in his voice.

"It's not a matter of what the 'house' wants, Ben," Dr. Graham said reassuringly. "It's not alive. You're just picking up on negative energy, that's all. Come inside, son. There's nothing to fear."

Although every nerve in his body was screaming at him to turn and run away as fast as he could, Ben took a deep breath, closed his eyes, and stepped into the chapel.

The moment the young psychic's foot touched the aisle between the pews the floorboards began to groan and the wrought-iron Spanish-style chandeliers hanging from the ceilings started to sway like incense burners. The chalice atop the altar suddenly started hopping about like a jumping bean.

Ben stood frozen in the middle of the aisle, staring fearfully at the obscene crucifix, which was rattling so loudly it sounded as if it was trying to break free of its moorings.

"I don't know about this, Dr. Graham . . ."

"Don't pay any attention to what's happening, Ben," Dr. Graham said, trying to keep his voice as calm as possible in order to comfort the nervous teen. "You simply have to remember that *you're* the boss here, not the house."

With that, the chalice on the altar leapt across the room as if hurled by an angry hand, and struck Dr. Graham in the mouth.

Professor Fenley hurried into the Great Hall, where Dr. Graham was reclining on an antique fainting couch in front of the fireplace. In one hand he held a bowl of ice cubes, in the other a fresh kitchen towel.

"Here, this should help with the swelling," he said.

"Thank you, Ambrose," Graham said gratefully. He quickly wrapped the ice in the towel and applied it to his split lower lip.

"How do you feel, Dr. Graham?" Ben asked solicitously.

"I'm afraid I'm going to be restricted to a liquid diet for the rest of our stay," Graham sighed. "Once we leave, I'll have to get a couple of stitches. I'd do it myself, but the old adage, 'physician, heal thyself' doesn't apply in situations like this."

"I'm *really* sorry, Dr. Graham," Ben said. "I never intended for you to get hurt—you have to believe me."

"It's not your fault, son," Dr. Graham sighed.

"Well, that's *one* thing you and I agree upon," Professor Fenley said angrily. "It's not Ben's fault because Ben didn't have *anything* to do with what happened in the chapel! Dr. Graham, I've held my tongue up to now, but I really must protest your use of the boy in these reckless experiments! Ben's too young to realize the danger you're putting him in—not to mention the risk to the rest of us!"

"I'm not a child anymore, Professor Fenley!" Ben protested. "I can take care of myself."

"Benjamin, I remember when you had to sit on telephone

books just to reach the table during séances. I know you're a capable young man. But Hell House isn't like anything else you've dealt with. You're out of your league. We *all* are. Miss Lauter was right. Hell House is like a leaky stove, and you're in danger of blowing us all to kingdom come!"

"Speaking of Miss Lauter . . ." Dr. Rand said, looking about the room. "Where *is* she?"

"She's locked herself in her room," Fenley replied. "Not that I blame her, after the way you spoke to her earlier today. There was no need to humiliate her."

"The woman is clearly delusional, Fenley," Rand said tersely. "Frankly, if either Nelson or I had known about her personal involvement with one the members of the 1931 team, we would never have brought her on. She's determined to prove that there are multiple hauntings going on within this house because it's the only way she can accept what happened to her ex-fiancé. It's far easier to believe in evil forces from beyond the grave than to admit someone they cared about was capable of rape and murder."

Grace sat in front of the vanity table, staring listlessly at her reflection. She felt like such a fool. She had been so eager to rub Dr. Rand's nose in the truth, she had succumbed to the exact same arrogance she found so distasteful from him. Now she had completely destroyed what little credibility she might have had with the others. After this morning's stunt, she must look like a hysteric, desperate for attention. After the fiasco with the secret door, she was too embarrassed to show her face in the common area downstairs. She would wait until everyone was asleep and sneak downstairs and fix herself something to eat later. Until then she'd just lie down and take a nap . . .

As she stood up, she heard the same soft, feminine sigh as the night before. She turned to look behind her, but saw nothing. Although the room appeared empty, she knew she was not alone.

"Why did you trick me like that?" Grace asked, unable to hide the disappointment in her voice. "You made me look like a fool in front of the others. I can't help you if I can't show the others that the things you tell me are real. They think I'm crazy. You have to give me some proof of who you are, do you understand? Only then can I help free you from this place."

There was a moment of silence, and then the door to the room swung open of its own accord. Grace looked out into the hallway and saw the same ghost lights as before trailing down the corridor, but in the opposite direction. She hurried after her phantom visitors, only to come to a halt at the head of the stairs.

She could hear Professor Fenley arguing with Graham and Rand somewhere below. She peered cautiously over the balustrade, to make sure there was no one standing in the foyer who might spot her, before tiptoeing past to the other side.

The door to Belasco's room was standing slightly ajar. Taking a deep breath, Grace stepped inside the room, turning on the lights as she did so. In the second before the electric chandelier came to life, she saw the twin ghost lights making their way up the curving staircase to the lofted bedchamber.

Upon reaching the top of the stairs, Grace was relieved to find the bed empty of its previous occupants. She glanced around the loft, trying to figure out what it was that Iris and Violet were trying to show her. Her attention was caught by an antique wardrobe that stood seven feet high and four feet deep, set against the back wall.

As she opened the armoire, the odor of mothballs that rose to greet her was nearly enough to make her gag. One side of the double wardrobe consisted of a series of shelves, while the other was a hanging space reserved for suits and coats. She began pulling open the drawers of the clothes press, searching for something to prove to the others she wasn't wandering the halls at night talking to herself.

She found what she was looking for in the form of a metal box hidden underneath a stack of neatly laundered silk shirts. She pried off the lid and shook out its contents onto the nearby bedstead, and was rewarded by the sight of dozens upon dozens of old photo-graphs. Her initial excitement was dampened, however, upon real-izing they were all pornographic in nature.

Grimacing in distaste, Grace sorted through the jumble of faded sepia-tone snapshots. Although few of the people in them were wearing clothes, she could tell from the hairstyles on the women that the majority of the photographs had been taken dur-ing the Twenties, although there were some that seemed to date back as far as the 1900s.

Judging from the collection before her, Emeric Belasco was a compulsive shutter-bug, keeping pictures of his guests enjoying his hospitality in every position imaginable, much like a boy col-lecting baseball cards. Not all the pictures were of anonymous libertines, however, as she recognized at least one or two famous politicians, as well as a couple of silent film stars.

What captured her attention, however, was a snapshot of two young girls standing posed in front of what she recognized as Belasco's bed. The girls were identical twins, no older than six-teen or seventeen, dressed in leather corsets and black boots laced up to the knee. They both had dark hair, which one wore in a Dutch bob while the other's was finger-waved; outside of this difference, it was impossible to tell one from the other. The girl on the left brandished a cat o' nine tails in one hand, while her twin on the right stood with her hands on her hips, proudly bran-dishing the artificial phallus strapped about her thighs. What Grace found genuinely disturbing was not their youth or their manner of dress, or even their attendant props, but the fact both girls were openly smiling at the camera, their eyes gleaming with excitement. They did not look at all like the unwilling sex slaves Grace had imagined them to be.

There was the sound of a whip cracking, and Grace looked up to find one of the twins—the one with the Dutch bob and the cat o' nine tails—blocking the stairway.

"Which one are you?" Grace asked, trying not to let fear show in her voice. "Are you Iris or Violet?"

The ghost did not answer, but instead smiled in a way that made Grace's stomach twist into a ball of anxiety.

"I'm here to help you and your sister, as you asked. You have nothing to fear from me."

Grace gasped as what felt like fingertips brushed against the back of her head. She spun around to see the second twin lounging on the bed, watching her through heavily lidded eyes, a bemused expression on her face. Grace quickly averted her eyes from the over-sized, oiled-leather dildo jutting from the girl's crotch.

"Why have you chosen to show yourself to me in this manner?" she asked them plaintively. "This is how Belasco made you, not as you *truly* are."

As if in answer, the twin guarding the stairs tossed back her head and laughed. Her sister rolled onto her hands and knees atop the bed and began crawling towards the frightened psychic, like a panther stalking its prey.

Grace closed her eyes and began breathlessly reciting the Lord's Prayer. She flinched as what felt like a hand touched her hip, and then traveled upward to cup one of her breasts. Crying out in alarm, she staggered backward, only to tumble onto the mattress. Disoriented, she opened her eyes and saw a male figure looming over the foot of the bed. At first she thought it was Simon, but then she realized he was far too tall. With a surge of terror, she suddenly realized who she was looking at, even as Violet and Iris giggled like demonic school girls.

We are here to serve him forever . . .

And ever—without end.

"I think I'm going to call it a night, if it's all the same to you, Ben," Professor Fenley yawned as he pushed himself away from the chessboard.

"What? Giving up already, are you?" Ben laughed.

They were the only ones left downstairs in the Great Hall. Due to his most recent injury, Dr. Graham had retired to his room relatively early, while Miss Lauter had not even bothered to come downstairs for dinner at all. Dr. Rand had briefly amused himself by plunking the keys on the grand piano, only to finally give up and retire to his room as well.

"It's almost midnight," Fenley said, pointing to his watch. "Men my age need their beauty sleep. As you can tell, I've been slacking off of late. You should be thinking of turning in as well."

Ben shook his head. "I'm not tired. I think I'll sit up for a little while longer."

"Suit yourself. Although I wouldn't wander around down here alone, if I were you. Haunted or not, this house isn't safe in the dark."

As he headed back to his room, Fenley paused in the hallway to check on the tray of food he had left outside Grace's room earlier that evening. The humble meal of tomato soup and grilled cheese was still sitting where he'd left it, apparently untouched. He sighed and shook his head. So much for the world of faith and the world of science uniting to solve one of the great mysteries of the twentieth century.

Fenley changed into his smoking jacket and sat back down in front of the fireplace to continue his study of Rose Belasco's diaries. As before, he let the book drop open randomly. As it turned out, the entry proved to be one of the last in the journal, written in an extremely shaky hand.

March 30, 1927

I have been delivered, courtesy of Dr. Tarr, as Prf. Fether is no longer with us, having recently succumbed to either laudanum or influenza, I'm not sure which. He whisked it away almost immediately, per Emeric's orders. I saw enough of it to know it resembled its father, whichever one he was. Whether it will join the others in Bastard Bog, I do not know. When I asked him of his plans, Emeric said something about veal, and then laughed. In any case, its end will be soon and its suffering behind these walls brief. I envy it.

Fenley shuddered and quickly closed the book, appalled by the passage he'd just read. As he set the journal aside, he heard what sounded like a woman sobbing in the hallway outside his room. Thinking it might be Miss Lauter, he hurried to the door. "Grace— is that you?"

Although the hallway was empty of any sign of Grace Lauter, Fenley spotted movement out of the corner of his eye. His heart leapt as he glimpsed what looked to be a woman dressed in a long red velvet dress hurrying down the stairs.

In all the years he had dedicated himself to the spirit world and its practices, Ambrose Fenley had never actually seen a spirit outside the boundaries of a séance. He knew that for one to show itself to someone besides a sensitive such as Ben or Grace was exceptionally rare, and indicated an attempt at communication by the deceased. He followed after the retreating figure, careful to keep her in his line of sight.

The woman in red reached the foyer, only to disappear under the overhanging staircase in the direction of the corridor that led to the theater and the chapel. As Fenley followed after her, he glimpsed Ben Fischer sitting in the great hall, playing a game of solitaire. To Fenley's relief, the youth did not look up from his cards as he hurried past.

The corridor under the stairs was dimly lit, but he could make out the figure of Rose Belasco standing just outside the door of the chapel, as if waiting for him. As he drew closer, she ducked inside.

Standing between the rows of pews, he saw her kneeling before the altar. Even though he had seen the blasphemous "chapel" on his previous visit, Fenley was still taken aback by the sight of the obscene Christ hanging above the altar like some pagan god. As he drew closer, Fenley could see that her shoulders were trembling, as if wracked with sobs.

"You have nothing to fear from me, Rose," Fenley said gently. "I mean you no harm. I just want to help free you from this earthly prison. I've read your journals, Rose. I know what your husband put you through. I understand that what happened to you wasn't your fault. Belasco was the one responsible for the evil that happened in this house, not you."

Fenley was standing so close to the ghost the tip of his shoe was almost touching the hem of her dress, which was spread about her like a fan. The scent of dead roses and overripe plums radiated from the apparition, threatening to overwhelm his senses. He could see the graceful arch of her neck, as pale and perfect as that of an alabaster Venus, seeming to invite the stroke of a loving hand.

"If I can understand and forgive your trespasses, Rose," he whispered as he reached out with trembling fingers, "surely Our Lord and Savior does too, and would not deny you a place in His kingdom."

The woman crouched before the altar whipped her head about, snapping her teeth like a rabid dog, her mouth and chin smeared with blood. Fenley looked down and saw the body of an infant with its throat torn open cradled in her arms. Strangling on a cry of horror, Fenley turned to flee, only to see the door of the chapel slam shut.

Something knocked his legs out from under him, sending him sprawling across the aisle between the pews. As he struggled to get back up, he briefly glimpsed the silhouette of a tall man standing in front of the altar. Before he could look too closely, he heard a shrieking noise and turned to see Rose Belasco running toward him, her fingers hooked into claws, hair flying about her head like a nest of angry snakes, and her lips pulled back into a death's head grin.

Stifling a yawn, Ben set aside his game of solitaire. He had lied to Professor Fenley earlier about not being tired. The truth was he had not slept well the night before. However, he was in no hurry to return to his room and the company of the hanged man dangling from his ceiling. He could always change rooms, he supposed, but he doubted whatever waited him elsewhere was much better. He also refused to break down and move in with one of the older team members. If he wanted to lose the "Ghost Boy" image, he was going to have to start acting like a man—not that he'd been given much of an opportunity to do so before now.

Thanks to his "gift" and the fact his mother was constantly dragging him from one séance to the next, Ben never had much of a chance to be around girls his own age. Not that he wasn't interested.

So far wandering around the Belasco mansion had been a unique form of torment, since everywhere he looked there seemed to be a statue or painting or some other kind of decoration depicting sexual activity. He felt like he'd spent as much time trying to hide his near-constant boner as he had serving as a psychic Geiger counter for Dr. Graham and Dr. Rand.

But now that he was finally alone, he found his thoughts turning back to the movie projector in the theater. Although he had only glimpsed a few seconds of the film before Dr. Graham turned off the machine, what he had seen had remained in the back of his head all day. In fact, he couldn't stop thinking about it, and how he might be able to find a way to see even more.

From what he'd observed, turning the projector on and off wasn't that difficult. The only thing that seemed genuinely complicated was threading the film through the sprockets, but since that was already taken care of, there really wasn't much to worry about on that end. Where was the harm in sneaking another peek? It's not like his mother would find out.

The Third Day:

Dr. Graham hurled the empty decanter across the room, causing it to shatter against the fireplace. The pain from his split lip, coupled with that from his broken collarbone, was making what was already a difficult situation increasingly intolerable. The way things were going, he would have to leave the house for medical treatment once Carlyle arrived with the fresh provisions.

Now, to make matters worse, he'd run out of alcohol. The absinthe was about the only thing that made his discomfort manageable. But where could he find more of it? Perhaps there was a liquor cabinet in the dining hall or the kitchen?

He glanced over at the alarm clock on his bedside table. The hands were straight up on the dial. Surely the others wouldn't begrudge him a little midnight tipple? After all, he *was* injured.

As he crossed the foyer in the direction of the kitchen, he did not see anyone downstairs, even though all the lights were still burning in the great hall. He pushed open the metal-faced swinging doors at the end of the corridor off the main entry and entered the kitchen. After ransacking the cabinets, he finally found an unopened ten-year-old bottle of Canadian whisky stashed behind a sterling silver punch bowl.

Graham sighed in relief as he cracked open the seal. He wondered for a moment if he should try and find a glass, then shrugged and drank directly from the open bottle. The sweet, full-bodied whisky tasted just like nectar, and instantly spread its relaxing warmth throughout his body.

As he wiped his mouth on the back of his hand, he noticed light shining from under the double swinging doors that opened onto the dining hall. Emboldened by the alcohol coursing through his veins, he pushed open one of them and looked inside.

Although all the lights were on, the dining hall was as empty as the kitchen. The only thing that seemed out of place was the covered silver tray placed at the head of the table, the chair to which was slightly pushed back, as if whoever seated there had suddenly been called away.

Graham wondered what could possibly warrant such a fancy presentation. So far all their meals had consisted of little more than canned meat and heated tins of soup, with the odd sandwich thrown in. He casually wedged the bottle of whisky inside his sling in order to free his good hand, and lifted the cover off the tray.

Lying on a silver platter, trussed like a prime rump roast, was a baby. Or something *like* a baby. Its head was overlarge, the forehead bulging in such a way that the right eye was sealed behind a lump of bone and gristle, while its limbs seemed abnormally stunted, even for those of an infant.

As Graham recoiled in horror at the cannibal feast set before him, the baby dwarf opened its good eye and began to slowly crawl off the tray and onto the table, humping its way towards him like snail on a garden wall.

The cover dropped from Graham's numbed fingers, ringing like a gong as it struck the floor. With a strangled cry of terror, he fled the dining hall, tears streaming down his face. He was so frightened he did not notice the figure before him until he collided with it.

"*Jesus H. Christ, Nelson!*" Dr. Rand growled. "Watch where you're going, damn it! You nearly knocked me down!"

Graham was shivering so hard he looked like he was vibrating in place. "Horrible—so horrible!" he managed to sob.

"What's horrible?" Rand's eyes narrowed as he spotted the bottle tucked inside the sling. "Where did you get that? I thought I told you no liquor while we were here!"

"I know I promised," Graham whimpered. "But I needed it for the pain. You can't expect a man to suffer, can you?"

"Damn you, Nelson! I *thought* you looked hung over at breakfast!"

"I'm sorry, Edgar—"

"Never mind that," Rand sighed wearily. "Just go back to your room and *stay* there until I get back."

"Where are you going?"

"I'm going to search for Fenley and Ben."

"Aren't they in their rooms?"

"I thought so, but when I went to check on Ben, he wasn't in his room. The bed didn't even look slept in. I thought he might be with Fenley, but his room was empty, too. I came down here to look for them, then I heard a god-awful clatter coming from the dining hall."

"I saw something in there. It was awful."

"I'll be the judge of that," Rand snorted.

"No! Don't go in there!" Graham said, trying to block his friend's path. "It's too terrible!"

"Get a grip on yourself, man!" Rand snapped as he pushed past him. He glanced inside the dining hall and shrugged. "There's nothing here. It's empty. Now do as I told you and go back to your room."

Graham nodded dumbly and shambled off upstairs, carrying the bottle of whisky cradled in his arms like a beloved child.

Edgar Rand cursed under his breath as he watched Graham stumble up the stairs. Nelson was a good man, although he had a bad weakness for strong drink. He should have known that the pressure would get to him eventually. Still, that was no excuse for getting stinking drunk the minute things started to get difficult.

It wasn't like Rand didn't understand the stress they were under. Head of his department or not, he could pretty much kiss any chance of ever being taken seriously by his peers good-bye if he came back to the university empty-handed.

Here they were, barely sixty hours into their week-long stay and one of their two mediums had locked herself in her room, his research partner was drunk as a skunk, and the remaining two members of the team were wandering about after midnight in a darkened mansion the size of Carlsbad Caverns. Right now he felt like the only sane man in a house full of lunatic children.

Fishing his flashlight out of his coat pocket, he headed across the entry hall in the general direction of the theater. However, before he reached his destination, he heard what sounded like male voices coming from the adjoining corridor that led to the ballroom.

Before he could reach the chapel, he heard what sounded like male voices coming from the adjoining corridor that led to the ballroom. Changing direction, he walked sixty feet down the hallway before spotting an immense archway on his right.

Rand stepped into the cavernous room, the heels of his shoes ringing loudly against the parqueted oak floor. The beam from his flashlight swept about the room, briefly illuminating the lofty, richly brocaded walls and red velvet draperies, as well as the musicians' alcove at the far end of the room.

"Hello?" he called out. "Anyone in here?"

As if in response, there came a tinkling sound high above his head. Rand pointed the light at the paneled ceiling and saw the three immense crystal chandeliers swaying gently in some sourceless breeze.

As Rand turned to leave, he was grabbed from behind by a pair of strong hands. As he cried out in alarm, a rag stinking of ether was clamped over his nose and mouth. The last thing he saw before he collapsed onto the floor was the silhouette of a tall man standing framed against the archway.

Rand was not sure if he had been unconscious for minutes or hours. One second he was in darkness, the next he was lying flat on his back, staring into a blinding light. He tried to sit up, but it felt as if his arms and legs had been strapped down to some kind of gurney. As he struggled to free himself, a voice spoke close to his ear.

"He's coming out of it."

Rand looked up to see a man looming over him. Although the bright light made it difficult for him to make out detail, he could see whoever it was looking down at him was dressed in a surgeon's gown and mask.

"What happened?" Rand asked. "How did I get to a hospital?"

The surgeon did not reply, but instead turned and motioned to someone standing outside Rand's field of vision. A moment later a second figure, his face also covered by a surgeon's mask, stepped forward.

"We're almost finished, Emeric. Just one more to go."

"What are you talking about?" Rand snapped. "My name's not Emeric. Who are you people? Where am I?"

As he lifted his head to get a look at his surroundings, he caught a glimpse of himself. His lower torso was covered by a white cloth stained with blood. The surgical drape was folded back, revealing a freshly sutured stump where his right leg used to be.

"My leg! What have you done to my leg?" Rand wailed.

"It's right here, Emeric," the second surgeon said, holding up the withered, spindly appendage like it was a prize-winning fish. "You needn't worry—we'll soon have you outfitted with something far more suitable for a man of your stature."

"Just lay still and let us finish," the first surgeon said as he pushed Rand back down onto the operating table. "Is there any more laudanum?"

"I just used the last of it," his companion giggled.

"That's what I was afraid of," the first doctor sighed as he picked up a gore-covered surgical saw. "I'll make this as quick as possible. It should only take a minute or two."

Ben stood in the close confines of the projectionist's booth as the movie unspooled behind him, watching through the viewing port at the naked people writhing on the screen.

He watched intently as a man dressed in elegant evening clothes stretched out across the same fainting couch Dr. Graham had laid earlier on that evening. The man opened his breeches to expose himself to the camera. A young naked girl with short, dark hair set in finger waves stepped into the frame and knelt between the man's outspread legs, sucking on his erect organ while she fondled both him and herself.

Ben fumbled with the front of his trousers, sliding his hand inside his underwear as the man on the couch maneuvered the girl so that she was lying facedown across the chaise lounge, her bare posterior pointed toward the camera. The young psychic groaned, barely able to contain himself. He was so excited he was on the verge of release after only a couple of strokes. Just as Ben felt himself start to orgasm, the man on the screen picked up a bamboo cane and, with a malicious grin, brought it down again and again across the girl's buttocks, covering her bottom with welts until blood ran down her thighs.

As appalled as he was by the violence, Ben was too close to orgasm to keep himself from climaxing. Disgusted with himself and what he had just witnessed, he quickly turned off the projector. After wiping his hands and straightening his clothes, he hurried down the stairs.

As he walked toward the exit, the screen on the stage abruptly flickered back to life, filling the theater with a ghastly light. Ben turned to stare back up at the projectionist's booth, but the view port was completely dark. Baffled, he looked back at the screen.

The man and the woman were gone, replaced by a mass orgy scene shot in what looked to be the Great Hall. Naked couples and trios occupied every possible piece of furniture and spilled out across the floor. Every possible sexual combination and position seemed on display, moving with the clockwork precision of a Busby Berkley dance routine.

However, what caught Ben's eye wasn't the acres of naked, fornicating flesh, but the figure of a tall, powerfully built man, dressed all in black, standing on the far side of the room, observing the debauchery around with the dispassionate air of a medieval king watching his jesters cavort for his amusement.

As Ben stared up at the screen, the tall man began to walk across the great hall towards the camera, moving with an odd, stiff-legged gait as he stepped over the libertines rutting on the floor. As the tall man drew closer to the camera, his face filled the screen, revealing a broad forehead, short jet-black hair and a goatee. With a start, Ben realized that he was looking at Emeric Belasco, the diabolic lord and master of Hell House.

Belasco grinned at the camera, revealing white strong teeth, and reached out as if to adjust the lens. As he did so, the movie screen suddenly began to bow outward, as if something on the other side was trying to push its way through. Ben turned and fled the theater. He had no interest in sticking around to see how the picture might end.

He was halfway to the foyer when a figure suddenly staggered from one of the adjoining corridors, throwing its arms about his neck and shoulders. After a couple seconds of panicked flailing, Ben succeeded in freeing himself. His attacker slumped against the wall, only to slide down onto the floor. When Ben saw who it was, he gasped in shocked surprise.

"Dr. Rand!"

The chemist lay on his back, staring up at Ben with a horrible, pleading look in his eyes. One half of the older man's face was contorted into a rictus mask of horror, while the other was completely slack. Rand tried to lift one of his arms, as if in supplication, only to have it drop back down like so much dead weight. His jaw worked for a long moment, but all he could muster was a slurred: *"Grrrraaahammm."*

Ben nodded his understanding. "I'll go get him, Dr. Rand. Don't worry—I'll be right back." He sprinted up the corridor and into the foyer, taking the stairs two at a time.

"Dr. Graham! Open up!" he shouted, banging on the door as hard as he could. "It's me! Ben!"

After a long moment, the door cracked open just enough for Ben to see the physician's bloodshot eyes.

"What do you want?" Graham snarled, his breath redolent of whisky.

"Something's happened to Dr. Rand. He's been hurt really bad."

Graham paused for a long moment, wobbling slightly, before finally throwing the door the rest of the way open. "Very well. Take me to him."

Ben led the physician back downstairs, to where Dr. Rand lay sprawled on the floor. Graham's shoulders slumped as he saw his friend's contorted face.

"Help me with him. He's had a stroke."

The two men picked the chemist up off the floor, one under each arm, and dragged him back to the foyer, where they placed him on an overstuffed divan.

"Edgar—it's me, Nelson," Graham said as he knelt beside his friend. "What happened? What did you see?"

Dr. Rand struggled to raise his head to speak, but his paralyzed lips and tongue could not form the words he needed. He lifted a palsied hand and tried to point at his useless legs, but the effort proved too much for him. With an awful groan, he fell back dead, a look of horror on his face.

"Damn it, Edgar!" Graham sobbed as he staggered to his feet. "Why did you insist on bringing us to this mad house? We should never have come here! Mrs. Crowder was right—this place is Hell on earth. And everyone who enters it is damned!"

"So—at last you understand. Too bad it's too late to do us any good."

Ben and Graham turned to see Grace Lauter standing on the landing of the stairway, staring down at them with a look of numbed devastation on her face. Her blouse and skirt were torn, and her lips looked bruised and swollen. In her right hand she held something made of silver, although Ben couldn't tell exactly what.

"Miss Lauter, are you okay?" he asked nervously.

Grace shook her head. "I'll never be okay ever again, Ben," she replied. "Simon was right. This place, and everything in it, is unclean. Including us."

The medium raised her right hand and drew it across her throat from ear to ear. A heartbeat later, a thin red line materialized, followed by a spray of arterial blood. Grace's eyes rolled back into her head as her knees buckled, sending her tumbling down the steps until she came to rest at Dr. Graham's feet.

"What are we going to do?" Ben whispered fearfully.

Graham said nothing, but instead bent over and removed something silver from Grace's lifeless hand. Even though it was covered in fresh blood, Ben could still see the monogrammed "B" on the handle. Graham let the straight razor drop to the floor and turned towards the front door.

"I've got to get out of here," he mumbled.

"Where are you going?" Ben asked in alarm. "Dr. Graham? Wait! Don't leave!"

Oblivious to the boy's pleas, Graham yanked open the front door. A frigid gust of air swirled into the entry hall, bringing with it the stink of the stagnant tarn that separated the house from the driveway. Without so much as a second glance back, Dr. Graham stepped out into the cold Maine night.

The moment the physician crossed the threshold, the heavy wooden door slammed itself shut with the finality of a tomb.

"Dr. Graham! Come back!" Ben shouted. He grabbed the doorknob, but it refused to turn. The door was locked tight.

Nearly on the verge of tears, a distraught Ben returned to the foyer. He tried to pretend the bodies of Dr. Rand and Miss Lauter weren't there, but it was hard ignore the slowly expanding pool of blood spreading out from Grace's head.

Dr. Graham had deserted him. Dr. Rand was dead from a massive stroke. Grace had killed herself. That left Professor Fenley unaccounted for. Surely *he* would know what to do.

Ben headed back down the corridor, checking the ballroom and chapel for any sign of the spiritualist, but without any luck. Swallowing his fear, he pushed open the door to the theater, half expecting to find Emeric Belasco waiting for him on the other side. Although he was relieved to find the screen empty and the theater dark, Professor Fenley was nowhere to be seen. That just left the lower level of the house.

Ben headed down the stairway directly across from the chapel, which ended in an anteroom fashioned of natural stone. To one side of the room was a door leading to the wine cellar, while at the other end hung a pair of swinging metal doors with porthole windows, through which could be glimpsed an indoor pool.

Pushing open one of the swinging doors, he saw Professor Fenley crouched at the edge of the pool, scooping up handfuls of the murky water and splashing it onto his face and upper body. Whatever hopes Ben had of finding a responsible adult to make him feel safe were dashed when he realized that not only was the professor naked, but muttering under his breath over and over again: "*Unclean, unclean . . .*"

"Professor Fenley?"

Fenley started as if he'd prodded with a hot poker. He jerked his head up, staring at Ben with eyes devoid of reason. Ben could see the older man's body was covered with numerous ugly scratches and what looked to be bite marks. Ben carefully backed away, leaving the madman to his toilette.

He was so overwhelmed he was nearly paralyzed with fear. He was now truly on his own. All the adults in the house were either dead or mad. It took all his strength just to climb the stairs back to the main floor. For the first time in years, he wished his mother had come with him.

"*Benjamin!*"

Ben stood in the hallway outside the chapel, unsure as to whether to believe his ears.

"*Benjamin Franklin Fischer!*"

It *was* her! He was sure of it. Ben hurried in the direction of the voice and saw his mother standing in the foyer. He was so relieved to see her he didn't ask himself what his mother was doing in a locked house in the middle of the night.

"Mom!" he said, weeping tears of relief. "I'm so glad to see you!"

Gladys Fischer turned to scowl at her son, freezing him in his tracks before he could embrace her. "Don't give me that 'so glad to see you' bullshit, you ungrateful little bastard! I *know* what you've done! You should be *ashamed* of yourself! It's bad enough you touch yourself, but now you're trying to get rid of me! *Me!* Your own *mother!*" She reached inside her purse and pulled out a tissue, which she used to daub at her eyes. "You think you're such a hotshot, such a *big* man! You think you don't need your mother anymore! You're going to leave me, *aren't* you? Just like your no-good father did!"

"No, Mom—that isn't true," Ben said defensively.

"Don't *lie* to me, you little *fucker!*" Mrs. Fischer snarled, her eyes flashing pure, unadulterated hatred. "Don't you *ever* lie to your mother! I know you're planning to walk out on me, just like that use-less drunk Graham walked out on you!"

"How do you know about Dr. Graham?" Ben asked, taking a cautious step back from his mother.

"I know a *lot* of things, little boy!" the thing masquerading as Gladys Fischer said with a malicious grin. "I know that you like jerking off to girls getting what's coming to them. I know that when you play with yourself late at night, you do it as fast as you can, because you think I won't wake up and hear you. But I *do* hear you, Benjamin. I lay there listening and think about how *good* it would feel to have you inside me, back where you belong!"

"Shut up! You're *not* my mother!" Ben shouted, clamping his hands over his ears. "Go away and leave me alone!"

"I'm not going *anywhere*, Benjamin," the thing chuckled, its voice dropping in timbre and register. "And neither are *you*. We are going to spend a long, *long* time getting to know one another. And once you start to bore me, maybe, just *maybe* I'll let you kill yourself, like all the others."

Ben's eyes rolled back into his head as he dropped to the floor and thick streams of ectoplasm began to pour from his mouth, nose and ears. Within seconds the viscous, gray-white material had qua-drupled in size, sculpting itself into the form of a regal-looking Mandarin.

Shi Kwan-Chiang, former physician to the Emperor, turned to face the tall, menacing figure that stood framed against the arch-way of the Great Hall.

"Am I supposed to be *afraid* of you?" the dark man chuckled. "You're not even real."

"I have *always* been real," Shi Kwan-Chiang replied, no longer sounding like Charlie Chan, but more like an older, more mature version of Ben's own voice. "I am the boy's power. This is merely how he chooses to perceive me. And the boy is mine, not yours."

The entire house began to shake from its rafters to its foundation. The chandeliers in the dining hall and ballroom began to dance and jingle, as if they were trying to free themselves from their mounting hooks. The projector in the theater toppled from its pedestal, smashing to pieces on the floor. And in the chapel, the lewd crucifix swayed like a piñata, while a wall panel behind the altar began to crack.

The dark man roared in rage as he melted into the shadows of the house. A foul wind that reeked of death and decay whipped through the entry hall and down the corridor and into the chapel, slamming the door shut behind it as it went.

Alida Crowder sighed as she stared at the house keys sitting on her desk. Things had gone badly at Hell House, although not quite as horribly as the '31 investigation. At least this time there were survivors, if you wanted to call being reduced to catatonia and raving lunacy "surviving."

According to the report from the state police, the Fischer boy had escaped by the skin of his teeth. Luckily, his mother had talked Dr. Rand's assistant into driving up to the house earlier than scheduled. They found the poor boy lying comatose on the front porch, completely nude. He regained consciousness only long enough to scream and vomit blood as he was loaded into the ambulance. The last she heard, he was still at the hospital in Caribou Falls, in a semi-catatonic state. God only knows what horrors he'd endured during the three days he'd spent inside that awful place.

They found Dr. Graham's body in the woods surrounding the estate. He had apparently gone outside for some reason and gotten lost in the fog, only to die of exposure. Dr. Rand and Miss Lauter's bodies were inside the house, just inside the entry way. Although Rand had died of natural causes, the same could not be said for poor Miss Lauter.

As for that nice Professor Fenley, he was found wandering around the lower level of the house, hopelessly insane. It looked like the poor man was going to spend the rest of his life at Medview Sanatorium.

She prayed the Fischer boy would eventually recover, although there was no way he could ever be the same again. She knew that more than anyone.

She had lied to Mrs. Fischer that day in the parlor. She knew all too well what it was like to be a mother, and to lose a son to Hell House. The shame of abandoning her only child in exchange for escaping with her life was such she had never dared speak about it to anyone, not even Mr. Crowder.

The old woman opened the top drawer of the desk and swept the keys to Hell House inside. The next time she went to the bank, she would place them in a safety deposit box and leave them there. No matter how badly she needed money, she would never allow anyone inside that house for as long as she lived. She had enough blood on her hands already.

"Please forgive me," she whispered as she locked the drawer. "Forgive me, Daniel."

CLOUD RIDER

A Tale Inspired by *Collected Stories*
BY WHITLEY STRIEBER

Richard Matheson's *Collected Stories* (1989) should be valued for just what it is—a testament to the talents of one of the great story-tellers of our time. In describing his Mathesonian tale for this volume, bestselling writer Whitley Strieber (*Communion, The Coming Global Superstorm, The Grays*) comments: "It is more inspired by Richard's body of work than by a specific story . . . I got into his work, the *Collected Stories*, and it just sort of formed on its own." Readers will be delighted that it did so!

CLOUD RIDER

They gathered the little, innocent clouds, bringing them together until they were great and dangerous, and the sky became electric. On the ground, men watched and wondered. Crows dropped to fenceposts, unwilling to fly in hurting air. Back in the hills, lynxes took to caves and coyotes huddled silent. Dogs went under beds and under houses.

So high that it could not be heard, a lone luxury jet crossed the sky. In the lit luxurious tube, smelling faintly of leather and excellent things, men in shirtsleeves conferred jovially as they ran numbers on laptops made like jewelry. They were rich, and the moment this plane touched down in San Jose they were going to be very much richer.

The plane was owned by a player of the first order, a man who could drop a million dollars at a Macao casino, and did from time to time, just to show others what it was to be truly, truly rich. He had come out of the dirt of China, this man. He remembered smashed earth floors and stooping to the green relentless rice, and watching the fungus eat his skin. When he slept, he saw the faces of his dead, those he had loved and those he had fought.

The plane hummed, a perfect machine, cared for with the devotion that comes from very large paychecks.

"There is a storm," he said in English.

"Yeah, and this is a jetstream," his Chief Financial Officer for North American Operations muttered. Then he looked up from his laptop and said, "Sir, I think we've made two billion dollars on this day."

They had made more, he knew. He said nothing. Nobody fully understood his business except him. But this acquisition would cause Triad Software in Shanghai to run out of alternatives. They, also, would sell, and at a price that was good.

A sound came, not loud, but not normal. He detested airplanes. He pressed the intercom button beside his seat. "What was that?"

"Lightning across the bows," came the cheerful reply from the co-pilot. "Not an issue."

Americans. Trusters of machines.

The plane was watched by careful eyes, its strobes flashing its position. They lined up across the sky, all twelve of them. In unison they raised their long wands, and as they did so the air around them crackled with energy. The plane was much faster than they were, moving as straight as a leaf in perfect wind.

In a graveyard far below, a new stone announced a new name, "Roger Lempert, 1983–2010. And the truth shall make you free." Briefly, the stone was lit by something flaring in the sky, blue light from above. An owl, which had been standing in a tree nearby, went off on her silent work. In the hills, the coyotes began to bicker, and the lynx to hunt. The crows fluttered their wings and slept their wary sleep.

Alarm! Alarm! Alarm! "Jesus!" From the intercom, a voice screeching with terror. 'What is this?' Then Mike, his copilot these six years, "We're losing it, buddy."

"Run fire on two! Run fire on one!"

"Running fire. No good."

"Mayday mayday mayday—"

They watched the white pieces of it fluttering down like insects on a summer evening, white moths in the light of the moon. An easy wave at the sky collapsed the little storm they had made.

Mr. Robert Wang, as he called himself, would not be completing his acquisition after all, so they went, each one, to his own great home, some in the Montana wilderness, some in the eagle's nests of the very rich in New York, some to Malibu and Santa Barbara, and one flying with slick excellence, the best of them, to his tower in Chicago, there to sleep in his marble office, a place as cold as his ice-bound heart.

When he awoke, he sat a long time in meditation, did Mr. Ronald Trask, in the orange robe of a Buddhist monk, as the sun spread over the city below him and he heard his traders coming in from their miseries and debaucheries.

The office murmured through the morning, an occasional shout marking a disaster or a triumph. But it didn't matter. None of it mattered.

Last night, Wang's death had made Charlie Forsyth a lot of money. Even as they'd worked the sky, Ron had seen a chance for himself this weekend. Extraordinary chance. If all went as he was determined it would, by this time next week, he would make a truly extraordinary sum. He would make one billion dollars.

He waited until the wheat pit was just about to close. Then he slid into the T-shirt and shorts his staff was used to seeing him wear, and went out to set his trap.

Chris Booker had struggled all day with a couple of nasty looking oil trades. He was far, far south when the market closed, so he had the weekend to think about the losses he was piling up for the most brutal boss—and the richest—in the whole hedge fund scam. It was a clear afternoon, bell-clear and warm in Chicago, just an edge of autumn touching the air. Wheat would close next. At least he had a decent short position there. With the harvest coming in huge, wheat was due for a limit down week.

He wished he cared, but he did not care. He'd been a damn fool to become a trader. What bothered him was that every dollar you made came out of somebody else's pocket. You might be celebrating down at Henry's, knocking back shots in triumph while the guy down the bar was knocking them back in despair. He'd go home busted, because his money had migrated to your pocket.

The way of the world, sure, but he wanted to grow things, to make things that were new. His was a creative nature, and he knew now that he should have jumped at the chance to take the farm when mom had offered it to him. He'd be married to Maggie now, instead of trying to figure out how to ask her to marry a struggling futures trader who probably didn't have a future. Meanwhile, his younger brother Mark and his wife Julie were making a great success of the old place, and Julie had little Mark Jr. already in the oven.

His mind wandered to the spreading fields of wheat that had now been in their family for a hundred and three years. He could imagine the crews on their combines, the golden grain piling up in the silos.

It was going to be a big harvest, for sure, the kind of harvest his dad used to call a "racer," meaning that you had to race to beat the glut. The faster you got your wheat to market, the more it would be worth, so the whole family would turn out, running the machines day and night, and he remembered the rich smells of night harvesting, and the wheat a faded gold sea under the moon. You couldn't rely on the traveling harvest crews. If you were going to race, you had to harvest ahead of the crews.

Chris had told Mark a week ago to get moving, if he wanted to beat the market.

Chris had knocked around the futures business for a few years before landing here at the System Fund. It was a hedge fund based on a trading system worked out by a Really Bright Guy, the boss of bosses around here, the one guy in a T-shirt and shorts. He enforced a strict dress code just so he could flaunt his power by breaking it. He was that insecure. He needed that much reassurance. Ronnie-Boy Trask was the inventor of the mysterious system and your garden variety laid-back easygoing super-dominant office dictator. Stalin with a Buddha blanket in his closet.

He only looked like a surfer inexplicably cast onto the shores of Lake Michigan. He was not exactly Mister Niceguy, and had rung the hundred million dollar bell at least four times to prove it.

In short, Ron was a monster. The way he looked at it, though,

he was nice. It was the market that was the monster. In most offices, traders were insulated from their day to day balance sheet.
Not here. Ron didn't dish out bonuses. What he did instead was
to give you a nice, thick cut of the meat. Thing was, if you lost
money, you went in hock to the firm. There were guys around here
living on penny draws while they tried to dig themselves out of
million dollar holes that only got deeper. But for the losers there
was always Heaven's Gate, the washroom window that had claimed
David P. Leydecker and old Charlie Orf, who'd sailed off into the
sunset just a year ago, and whose estate was now being dragged
from his widow's desperate hands to pay his debt to dear old Ronnie Boy.

"Still here?"

"Ron!"

"You're gonna drop in an order to buy ten thousand contracts
July Wheat at 289 right now."

Chris laughed.

"I'm not laughing, buddy. Do it, we got three minutes to the
close."

"But—Jesus!" July had been selling hard all day, and it was
going to get killed as soon as the fed's crop condition report hit
the wire on Monday morning. For every point wheat lost on
Monday, the firm would lose half a million dollars—and all of it in
Chris's account. "Ron, I'm in a short on wheat. And if you want my
advice—"

"Wipe the short, it's stupid. Do my trade now."

"We'll get hosed!"

"Do I need to get a goddamn gun?"

Chris sent the orders in. The short covered at a pitiful profit,
and then the enormous long position worked. "Filled at 287.25,"
he said a moment later. Or rather, a very sad man using his mouth
said it. Whereupon Ron strolled off to another workstation. Soon,
Mel Stockton was yelling and writhing. What in hell was Ron up
to? Was he intentionally bankrupting the firm? Some sort of Zen
thing? The Buddha stuff was all fake, Chris knew. Nobody as evil

as Ron could have even the slightest interest in Buddhism or any other religion. Chris's theory was that Ron did it for the desecration. Maybe prayer made demons feel holy.

As Chris watched, his big buy moved the market up to 288.50. It hung there for a couple of squawks, nothing happened, and it found its close at 286.75. "Oh, good," Chris muttered to himself. With his wheat short ruined, he'd had a miserable week, going negative a hundred and sixty grand. But now you had to plant him in the minus column, big time. And on Monday, megadeath.

"Guess I'm gonna pack in my shit for the day," he said to nobody in particular. Most of the other traders had already started their weekends. Lucky bastards, they hadn't been around for Hitler's Little Helper to pick on.

But not Mel Stockton, who sat as rigid as a corpse staring at his charts.

"Drink?"

"He just forced me into the greenback," Mel said, his voice soft. It was awe, it was sadness. Unlike Chris, who could lose thousands of dollars a minute, Mel's ultra-leveraged foreign exchange operations could crater spectacularly. FOREX traders had been known to burn a million bucks in a second. Not here, of course, not yet. Or—

"Position holding up?"

Mel giggled. There was a touch of insanity in the tone of it. Chris stepped back. When would some trader Ron had destroyed show up in this office with a shotgun? Had to happen.

"Let's see, I've been in the trade for four minutes and I am down . . . one hundred and six grand. Damnit. Ron! Ron, I'm gonna liquidate!"

Ron called from the open door of his office. "Do it and you quit."

"Then I quit!"

"But your debt doesn't, boy-o. Remember that."

"We could kill him," Chris said.

"That'd help." He stared at his screen. "*Shit.*"

Ron came out. He was long, Ron was. A long face, long arms

and hands. Behind his back, they called him a lot of things, but the meanest and truest was "spider." "The system is never wrong," he said in his voice, which, in contrast to the wiry appearance of the man, was smooth and deep and could reassure a burning man that the fire wouldn't hurt.

Up close, Ron smelled like spice. It was a personal odor so odd that Chris had researched it and found that the odor characteristic of schizophrenics was caused by something called trans-3-methyl-2-hexenoic acid, and was more of a chemical smell. Ron tried to disguise his odor with cologne, but they only made it worse. He didn't date. As he put it, 'I hire everybody, especially women.' He had a display wife living on a vast estate up the lake, or maybe in Palm Beach, who knew at any given time?

"I have to tell you, I don't believe there is a system. You're the system."

"This hedge fund is built around it."

"This hedge fund is built around making you a whole lot of other people's money."

"That, too. I'm goin' to Skokie to screw my new honey," he said as he strolled out.

They watched him close his office door.

"The air," Chris said, taking a deep breath. "Suddenly it's . . . lighter."

"Fuckin' oughta liquidate this thing," Mel muttered.

"Do it!"

"It's down a hundred and sixty-two grand, so if I pull out, I am outa here owing the spider six figures. So no, that I cannot do."

Chris went back to his own hole, sat down and stared for a while at the lifeless wheat chart on his monitor. Then at the picture of Maggie. She wasn't a goddess but—yeah, well, actually she was.

He heard Mel decamping, crashing through various doors.

"Let's torch his office," Chris called after him.

"Yeah, yeah." Unlike the futures pits, FOREX never closed. The insane trade would eat Mel second by second all weekend. Poor damn guy. Here in the Mid-World Tower, they were high atop the city, and Chris could see all the way to Waukegan in the north. To the east across the lake, the sky was beginning to turn to deep blue. It was time to go down to Henry's and knock back a shot for every c-note he'd lost, and for his lost career and ruined life, and then head over to Maggie's folks' place and sit out on the wide front porch with her and explain to her that there was no longer any point at all.

"G'night, Ron," he called into the vast office that dominated the south side of the floor the hedge fund occupied. "Hope you die soon."

What was his game? Why did he want to lose money? Who knew, maybe it was some complex psychological thing of the sort that needed solving by a psychiatrist. But what would a farm boy know about that?

He struggled down Market, wishing that there was at least a single cloud somewhere on the horizon, but the weather was absolutely perfect, and every exclusive, incredibly costly private forecast they bought said the same thing as the National Weather Service: ideal harvest conditions out at least two weeks.

By a week from today, the position he'd been forced to take could be down by a million bucks. More.

Henry's was a dingy place, but famous among traders and beloved to them. It offered beer, beer nuts, burgers that had undoubtedly been dug up somewhere and gigantic, bathtub-like drinks, which was what kept the trade coming back. No watered booze here.

He pushed open the door with the crazed glass that reflected the immeasurably dreary mirrored chandelier inside, and heard singing. Some damn pit was celebrating a week of successfully ripping the public's money.

The hell with it, he abandoned Henry's and struggled on to the El, dreading, as he always did, the long climb up into its stratospheric hell. Heights did not amuse. Being in the building was fine, but not lurching around on some windblown steel platform, and worse, riding the trembling rails that swept ever so far above the traffic.

Give him a subway any day. Loved New York, except there was no chance there of catching a whiff of corn tassel on a summer night, and the girls didn't have Juicy Fruit breath, poor benighted creatures. Eastern girls were as smooth as oatmeal. Midwestern girls crunched like apples. New York honeys glowed soft, while Illinois and Iowa girls glistened tight. When you slept with them, you slept with somebody. New York girls surrounded you like smoke and then were gone.

He rode the screeching, whining El to the north end of the line, calling Mags on his cell as he got off. "On the street," he said.

"Hey, great. I expected later."

"Got any food for a hungry traveler?"

"You bet we do, fella."

As he was closing the cell, he noticed a text message waiting. The El must have drowned out the warning beep when it arrived. He feared that it was some kind of vicious parting shot from the spider, but it turned out to be from Mark. "In racer. Bring troops."

All hands were needed for the harvest, which meant finally teaching Maggie how to run a combine. It wasn't hard, just loud, but she was an Iowa girl, so it would be in her blood. Also, a good test. She wasn't marrying the farm, but close enough to it to need to be comfortable with its life.

He texted back, "On way. Max poss bods 2."

Maggie's mom and dad would have come, but her dad was nursing a major ski bump from their trip to Aspen last week, and, as Chris knew but would never say, her mom's hair was too big to survive wheat chaff, which turned to paste when you tried to wash it away. You had to brush it out dry, and there went the coiffeur. He was too nice a guy to do that to an unsuspecting big hair lady.

As he walked along Maple, the street lights came on. Kids in car coats and mittens played in front of one of the spacious, beautifully kept old homes. A Daschund yapped frantically at boys tapping a soccer ball. The evening news was on TVs up and down the street, and he could hear the WGN weather man crowing about the fabulous week ahead.

Out on the farm, he'd have to be happy about it, and that was going to be hard. He was no actor. Smile and die, smile and die. Thing was, he wanted to take his bride to something more than his fairly decent Near North Side apartment. He wanted a house out around here. A million dollar house, and the promise of good schools. Not a huge dream, he didn't think.

He turned up the driveway and paused, drinking in the glow of light from inside the house. It was cold now that the sun had set, and autumn-evening quiet. Above the high roof, a single blue star shone. Jupiter, he thought. To the west, the sky had that deep orange color that comes when the air is dry enough for dust to rise from autumn fields. In other words, it was your absolutely perfect harvest sunset.

But how could he want anything else? Mark's livelihood depended on the next week being as benign as nature could make it. Then he'd sell his wheat, probably a full week before the big boys came in to drown the market in the fruit of their labor.

Ron pitted people against each other. Discord made him money, so he claimed. Feuds energized him, the more bitter the better. But how could he know that what he'd done this afternoon would make Chris hope his own brother's harvest—and all the other harvests, for that matter—would fail?

Maybe the vicious bastard *had* known. He was aware of the farm. Not in detail, but he knew that there was one somewhere in Chris's family. Maybe he was sucking a pipe with his honey right now, chuckling about the two brothers he was forcing to tear each other's hair out.

Vicious, vicious bastard.

He could see Maggie and Babs in the kitchen. Eight-year-old Robbie was there, too, sampling. Charlie would be back in the den with his older boy, Kevin, watching the evening news. The great weather, blah blah. In fact, from now until the market opened on Monday morning, everyone would be excited about the great weather. And after. On and on, until Chris had been crushed like the miserable little bug that he was.

He went up to the kitchen door and knocked. Then, suddenly, he was in the bright kitchen and inhaling the smell of a standing rib roast just being drawn from the oven, and Robbie said, "Great weather for your bro!"

"Fabulous. He's got a racer going, too, so—hey, wait a minute—why don't you and Kev come, too? Ever run a combine?"

Babs said, "Robbie has basketball." Kevin, however, proved to be more than willing, so as the roast was carried out to the dining room, Chris texted Mark that there would be one more. It was vastly less romantic, of course, having the kid along, but hey, it was harvest time. Anyway, being around a pre-teen was good practice. All exposure to the little brothers was okay by him. Anyway, he enjoyed them both. Good guys.

"Great weather for your brother," Jack said as he came in from the news. "Not a cloud for miles."

"We're going down to help with the harvest," Maggie said.

"How much is he gonna bring in, anyway?"

"We're looking at your proverbial bumper crop this year, looks like."

"So that means that prices come down."

"Well, they'll drift downward until the crop report, then they'll crater, pretty much."

"Which is why your brother races his crop. But doesn't everybody do the same thing?"

"Whoever can. But most of the business relies on custom crews, and when the harvest is big, it slows them down. The little guy's got a lot against him, but at least he can move fast."

Grace was said, then plates of food passed. Dinner in this house was a formal family affair, no TV, no kitchen casual. There was a dining room and it was put to use. He liked this, liked it a lot. He wanted a dining room, and well-defined family customs. He wanted the kind of love that filled this house, and his heart.

After dinner, Babs and Maggie made a care package for the road. On the way, roaring along in Maggie's sweet Lexus, Chris drank coffee and ate donuts still hot from the deep fryer. Kevin ate roast beef sandwiches.

They drove for two hours, then made a gas stop in Parnell, just the other side of the Iowa border. While Kevin was in the men's room, Chris kissed Maggie. They spoke a little of love, and walked away from the gas station, into the darkness of the road.

"What a lot of stars," Mags said.

"You've been in the city too long."

"That's for sure."

"Something's troubling you, Chris."

He wanted to tell her, but he didn't want to ruin this beautiful moment. He took her hand in his, absorbed the purity of her presence beside him. Then, before he could stop himself, let alone understand himself, he heard himself say, "Marry me."

He took a deep breath. Another. Wished he had a drink, big. Then his heart started banging, because he couldn't afford for her to say yes, couldn't bear for her to say no.

She smiled the smile of the ages. "Sure I will, Chris, oh, *sure I will.*"

"Uh. It's—"

"We'll do it Christmas. A Christmas wedding." She threw her arms around him and kissed him hard, and from the direction of the gas station there came clapping, a little slow not to be ironic. "Kevin is not a romantic," Maggie said with a giggle in her voice. "Not quite yet."

They walked slowly back to the car, agreeing, as they went, not to tell him. She wanted the two of them to tell her parents together, and Kevin would call them on his cell immediately.

As he strapped himself in and started the car, Chris wondered if he would be in bankruptcy when they made their little announcement, or merely dead broke. He was insane. Controlled by impulses. A fool.

He drove on, deep into the night.

The farm was far from any main road, out in the vast flatness of eastern Iowa. Long before they reached it, they saw the bright lights of the combines in the fields. "Mark's not very far along," Chris said.

"That's not like him."

"He must've had a breakdown. I'm glad we came."

He pulled around behind the barn and drove as far into the cut field as he could. They walked through the cuttings, through the rich, deeply familiar scent of the grain and the broken stems, a smell for him associated with security and love and deep home. There were two combines running, with Mark in one and Judy in the other, and their roar wiped out every other sound. As they got closer, Kevin put his hands over his ears. Mark, from long experience, jumped up on his brother's cab and banged on the door.

The big machine stopped, which Judy saw, and stopped hers, also.

Suddenly, silence, soon filled by the ratcheting of late cicadas and the whisper of the night wind in the wheat.

"Hey, there," Mark said as he swung down. "We've got the machines if—" He stopped. He was looking to the west. "Hey," he said.

Chris followed his gaze—and saw that the moon had just disappeared. "What the hell?" Then he saw lightning on the horizon, and heard a long, trembling roll of thunder.

"Goddamn," Mark muttered.

Then, in another flash, they saw a towering incredible mass of clouds.

"No," Mark said. Judy came close to him.

The wind that touched them now was colder, heavier, coming straight out of the storm. As if it knew that disaster was building, the wheat trembled, great waves sweeping through fields lit by lightning.

"NO! Damnit NOOOO!" Mark threw his lucky cap to the ground.

"What's wrong?" Kevin asked Chris.

"That storm is what's wrong." He knew weather. He knew,

specifically, *this* weather, and there had been not a trace of any front, squall line or even a disturbance anywhere from Illinois all the way out to Idaho and up into Alberta. And not one forecast had predicted it. Just Ron Trask and his crazy "system," which was just some damn psychosis of his.

So what was this? Where had it come from?

"I've got exactly eleven acres in," Mark said. He turned on Chris. "Why *in hell* didn't you warn me?"

"Mark, when I left the office, this wasn't there." Mark was going to be ruined, but, because of Ron and his system, the hedge fund might make a million dollars on Monday.

"It had to be there!" Mark shouted. "What were you thinking?"

"It wasn't!"

But it was here, and now the wheat bent low. Lightning cracked across the near sky.

"Look," Kevin shouted. He pointed toward the storm.

The flashes were continuous, the clouds were boiling, but there was nothing to make anybody point. "What?" Julie asked.

"I—oh, there they are again!" When Kevin pointed this time, Chris saw a line of dots racing ahead of the storm.

"What the hell?"

Mark ran toward his combine and climbed into the cab. Chris followed him. "Mark, there's too much lightning."

"I'm gonna lose my harvest!"

"It's too dangerous!"

He started the combine. The hard set to his eyes told Chris that this brother he knew so well would not be stopping it. The big windshield flashed blue as lightning streaked overhead. Then there was an explosion of thunder and a flash so bright it hurt. "Mark, for God's sake!"

Mark put it in gear, and there was nothing Chris could do but jump down. Julie went to the combine and slapped the door. When he ignored her, she began running beside it. "Mark! Mark!"

But he roared off into the wheat. When Julie started for her own combine, Chris grabbed her shoulders.

"Leave me alone!"

"Julie, don't take the risk!"

"My husband is taking it!"

Another flash brought one of the most terrifying sights in nature: the massive wall of an oncoming windstorm so violent that it was kicking up huge masses of dust. It wasn't more than a few miles away, and bearing down on them.

Those winds could be seventy, eighty miles an hour, fast enough to cause a combine to blow over, crushing the driver in the cab.

"Mark! *MARK!*" Julie screamed, abandoning her own combine and running off down the row he was harvesting. He was headed straight for the storm, but with the combine's huge lights glaring into the wheat ahead, there was no doubt in Chris's mind that his brother could not see his peril.

The wind wall appeared again, in another flash of lightning, and now you could also hear it, a crazed, deep hissing, getting louder. All around them, the wheat was shaking.

"What do we do, Chris?" Maggie shouted.

He took Maggie by the shoulders. "Lie down. Claw the dirt." He shook her. "Claw it!" He took off running after Julie and Mark, and saw before him the combine with its brilliant lights, and ahead of it stretching from earth to the beyond, a great wall of blackness, and behind them both a running woman, her legs pounding.

At five months pregnant, she was not going to catch the combine, slow as it was, and Chris was soon beside her, then in front of her, then he was in the combine's wake, his feet pounding, his chest catching fire, as the coarse, thick dust poured down his gasping throat.

The lightning was continuous, the storm blasting straight toward them, the combine roaring. He could see Mark's shadow inside, the shadow of his brother—"MARK! MARK! MARK!"

The wind swept the wheat, sending a fusillade of chaff into Chris's face. Then the combine shuddered, stopped, and got blasted by what must have been one of the most powerful straight-line winds ever to cross this prairie. As it swirled around him, Chris thought it must be clocking an easy hundred and twenty, and pieces of the combine were flying off and bounding away into the dark.

Then it was gone, the wind and most of the combine. The front had passed. Silence came, and the hiss of little rain. Cicadas started again. Chris got to his feet. "Mark! Julie!" He ran a little bit, then suddenly thought—"MAGGIE!"

This silence—he recognized it. It was the silence of death.

"MAGGIE!"

"Hey, Bro."

"Oh, Jesus, Jesus, you got it, you went up with the combine, Mark." He threw his arms around his brother.

"I jumped off the damn thing."

"Oh thank God, thank you God."

In the distance, then, another voice, piping, shrieking, the voice of a terrified elf—then he realized that it was Kevin and cold claws came around his throat. A moment later, another blast of lightning, and in it he saw two figures, their faces gray, eyes like dead sockets—but they were alive, they were running this way, and it was Kevin and it was Maggie. He went toward the flickering, running shadows, and he threw his arms around Maggie and smelled her fear and her life, sharp, rich—and then saw in the light of another flash, her stricken eyes. He said, "Mark's okay, he's right here," and she said, "we can't wake Julie up."

At that instant, hail flooded out of the sky, a torrent, a cataract, smashing the wheat, hammering the people, causing them to duck and shelter under their arms while Mark howled in the wild wilderness of it, bellowing for his wife, begging God, finally kneeling, his face tormented, hail slamming it and the white body he was holding in the sweeping flood of mean stones, in the evil flashes.

The storm went growling eastward, wrecking the vast harvest land, crushing the wheat and the corn like a great fist, wrecking fields from Canada to Missouri, cutting the yield in half, killing people, smashing homes and whole towns, until it spent itself, finally, along the old Appalachian massif.

Saturday morning dawned in gold and sorrow, and slow black trucks ran the narrow roads between the farms, carrying bodies out.

Maggie stayed with Mark that day, while Chris drove Kevin home. On the way, Kevin asked, "Did you see them?"

Chris watched the road passing, the old road that he'd driven the first time he'd ever driven, that he had taken to school and, at the last, to college and the life he knew now.

He didn't need to wait for the market to open to know that Ron had blessed him with riches. There were ten thousand bushels in his account, and wheat was going to be limit up all week. That would put a million dollars a day into his coffers, and he would keep 10 percent of that. While they buried Julie and Mark saw the farm ruined, he would be making a hundred thousand dollars a day.

"Did you see them?"

"Who?"

"There were a bunch of them. In front of the clouds. You could see them in the lightning flashes."

"Birds?"

Kevin shook his head. "Something is wrong, Chris."

"Yeah, Julie's been killed!"

"Something is *wrong*."

Chris might have asked him what he was getting at, but the weight of his grief stopped his voice. Julie had been a glorious, wonderful girl, and he had loved her from afar from the day Mark first brought her home to meet the family.

Where had that damn weather come from? It was being called a freak of nature, but that wasn't enough. He wanted answers, damn it. Why hadn't the National Weather Service even suggested the possibility, let alone any of the specialists? What were the bastards worth, any of them?

Mark and Julie didn't have a plot anywhere. Why would a couple of kids in their twenties have a plot? So they took her first to the Laurel Funeral Home in Mayville, where Chris gazed on her cold body, and wondered at the meaning of death, and did the dead fly off somewhere, or was there nothing there?

Mark moved with the curious, gliding motion of a dreamer. He'd lost all but about eighty acres, plus what he'd gotten in before the storm. It was enough to pull in about sixty grand. That would keep the farm for a few months, but then he'd have to go short on his mortgage. He figured that the bank would give up on him in about January.

He moved like a man in a nightmare, with the softness and speed that danger brings. Kevin asked him, during the little service at St. George's Episcopal, "Did you see them?" Beryl had leaned down and whispered to him, but he had persisted. "Did you see them?"

Mark looked at him as if he was from another planet, speaking an unknown language, irrelevant to grief and so to him.

Old Pastor Charles officiated with his one eye gone to a stroke and the same *gravitas* he had brought to services ever since Chris could remember. The continuity of life that he represented was so powerful that Chris almost loved him. He felt that the ceremony was real, that it was about these people and this place, the good holding one another against the storms and all that befell them. There would be weeping.

They took her to Oakview Cemetery, and buried her beside mom and dad. Her folks had wanted her with them, but she belonged here and they knew it, and now her father bowed his bald head and her mother wept in the quiet way that marks the grief of the strong. She'd lost Taylor in Baghdad, so now she had one left, her young daughter Tara, who stood proud and blond beside her mother, like a stalk of wheat herself, and Chris thought, looking at them all, that this America would never end, that somehow people like these would always find their way.

On its way down, the coffin creaked and sighed, reflecting, Chris imagined, Julie's eager restlessness, her ceaseless quest for more, for better, for the zest of life.

It was Wednesday when he returned to work. He saw that his

account was an astonishing three million seven hundred and eighty thousand dollars up, and not only that, the sudden shortage of grains had caused the dollar to go through the roof, too, so Mel would be up big time, too. And yet, Mel's desk was empty. Not that he wasn't in, it was emptier than that.

Counting it all up, he thought that Ron would be looking at a ten million dollar week, and he went into his office to congratulate them both, because a significant piece of that was going to be his.

Ron was the same as always, kicked back in dungarees and boots because it was too cool now in Chicago for shorts and flip-flops. Chris crossed the huge office, went around behind the enormous glass desk, and held out his hand.

Ron looked at the hand, then up at Chris, his eyebrows raised.

Chris withdrew the hand. "How did you ever call that?"

"I'm busy making people money," Ron said, looking toward his monitor. "It's what I do. But not you, fella."

"Only four million bucks so far this week. Less my trivial commission, of course." He wouldn't tell him about Julie, and he would use some of that astonishing windfall to put Mark back together. All would not be well, but all would not be lost. And, in the end, it was the storm that had killed Julie, not Ron. All Ron could be blamed for was saving the farm.

Ron had leaned back in his chair and was looking at him. Just looking.

"What?"

"Do you seriously think that I'm gonna give you any ten percent of a trade I set up myself? You're not risk tolerant, Chris. You're not effective."

"I took the trade in my account. And the risk!"

"Kicking and screaming all the way. And the rest of your work—it's boring, Chris."

"I make money. Mostly."

"But not interesting money. Not useful money. Which gets me to something I've needed to do for a while, but I don't like to do it, so I put it off and I guess that makes me a bad boy. But I've gotta do and get it over with, Chris. I'm sorry."

"You're sorry?"

"Truly, I am, because when I have to let a guy go, it's because I made a mistake, and I don't like to make mistakes."

"You're firing me?"

Ron gave him a smile, big and bright. Did the man also have too many teeth?

"This is about you keeping my commission. It's not about my work."

"If you'd brought me this trade and convinced me to take it, you would've earned that obscene commission. But all you did was push a button, and guys don't get six figure paydays for pushing a button, not in my operation."

Like everybody, he hated Ron, but not enough to do anything about it, not until now. He took a step toward him. Ron looked up at him out of eyes that had gone lazy and knowing. Chris told himself that he wasn't going to do this, that he didn't hit people, but he kept on going, he couldn't stop himself.

"This'll make a good video," Ron said. He nodded toward a dark object in a corner of the ceiling, obviously a camera. "Interesting to the police."

"Just tell me one thing, Ron. How in hell did you call that trade?"

"The system."

"No system is gonna tell you that freak weather is on the way. When we took that trade—"

"I took it."

"I took the fucking risk! In my account! If it had gone south, I would've been in hock to you for the rest of my damn life, but instead you owe *me* money, so I'm fired."

"Fucking sermons in fucking church, please. Now get out of here."

If he swung at him, Chris thought he would not stop until he killed the guy. As if on its own, his open hand moved toward Ron's face. It was uncanny. He couldn't stop himself. But he had to. He'd end up broke *and* in jail, because Ron would not forgive.

To avoid battering the guy's brains out, he snatched up what looked like a black paperweight made from a hockey puck and hurled it at him.

The thing hit his shoulder and cracked open, and some sort of substance splashed out, black and thick. The can or whatever it was smashed against the wall, leaving a large black spatter.

"Get out of here!"

As Chris turned to leave, he noticed two things—first, the arm that had the liquid on it seemed to be fighting Ron, as if it was trying to rise, but he was holding it down with his other arm. The second thing was equally strange: the liquid that had hit the wall was dripping, but not down. It was moving upward, as if the room had somehow inverted.

Chris picked up the burst tin. "Cloud Rider," it said on it. "What the fuck is this?" On the back, "Lempert Pharmaceuticals."

"I said get out!"

Chris touched some of the stuff. It was dark, the consistency of molasses. "You some kind of an addict, I hope?"

"Leave!"

"Oh? Because I busted your stash? What *is* this shit?" He rubbed it between his fingers. It was a little sticky, not a lot. Smelled slightly sweet, spicy. "It's your damn perfume! God, what drek."

"GET OUT!"

"Oh, my, the little spider is—oh. I hurt your arm. So sollee!"

The arm that had the goop on came up like it was floating, like he was some kind of damn ballerina. He looked at it hanging there beside him.

Chris looked at it. "Uh . . . can I help you?"

"I'll kill you, I swear to God, I WILL KILL YOU!" His face was blazing, practically purple, his eyes gone to tiny dark jewels, his characteristic mean smile transformed into a searing grimace.

It was serious, Chris realized. This man would indeed kill. Was about to kill. He turned and got the hell out of there.

As he was stuffing his few personal items into his trashed out old black briefcase, Ron came out. Now the arm was pushed down in the belt, up under a sweater.

"Where's Stockton?" Chris asked Henry Culler, the trader who sat in the next cubicle, who had facial warts and so wore a beard. Traded fungus or some damn thing. His friends called him Hen. Hen was intent on something, and ignored him. "Hello?"

"He resigned," Hen snapped. "Cleared out his desk on Monday."

"Resigned or gotten fired. The dollar rose with food supplies so tight, so that greenie position he had must've made a fortune."

"Dunno. Look I got work—"

"On the Hoffman-Winters website? What're you doing, applying for a real job?"

Hen cracked his gum. "I've been told to set up a big-time position in short-term puts, and the market's thin, so I'm looking for stockholders, then I'm gonna get an option principal to write us some of these stupid and insane losers."

"Puts on Hoffman-Winters? They own the Sears Tower, they're not in any trouble."

"My point exactly."

His crap safely bagged, Chris headed out—and came face to face with the glowering Ron. "You're after the Sears Tower, aren't you?"

"What're you talking about?"

Chris pointed at him. "You got an angle, don't you?"

Shrugging, Ron went back into his office. Chris headed for the door—but stopped. He had to have it out with the bastard, he just could not leave him with a total win. Ron needed a beating.

But Ron was not in his office, which was odd because he hadn't come back out through the only door. "Killed yourself, I hope? Estates are easier to sue." He crossed the opulent marble floor with its alternating black and white tiles, and went to the huge old desk, Spanish, supposedly, sixteenth century. A fake, Chris had always hoped, considering that it had set the spider back half a million dollars.

"Hiding?" Chris moved deeper into the broad space, going toward the windows and the hideous fake statue of Aphrodite the monster had brought back from the Great Art Acquisition Trip. What was it made of? Not marble, any moron could see that. Most of the guys figured it for some kind of exotic plastic. So far, Ron hadn't noticed the cigarette burns inflicted on its ass, which faced the window. Cigarettes don't melt ancient Roman marble, Ronnie boy.

Where *was* the fuck? He needed killing was what he needed, but a good fucking up was what he was gonna get, and he *was* going to get that. Chris picked up the two cans of Cloud Rider on the scumbag's desk—and noticed something he hadn't before, which was that they were so light that they seemed, actually, *too* light. What kind of metal felt like a feather?

There was a shuffle and Ron's latest bimbo-cum-secretary—emphasis on the cum—leaned in. "He's not in," she said.

"*What*? I'm stunned." He turned to her. "What is this stuff?" He held out one of the black hockey pucks of a can.

"Dunno. Stuff."

He pushed it back into his pocket. Then he took the other one and pocketed it, too. Who knew, maybe it was something illegal. Maybe he could give it to the DA and get the spider put in a spider hole.

"You shouldn't oughta take his stuff."

"Nobody cares."

"He'll yell at me."

"You oughta quit. Job like this is bad for a nice kid like you."

"I'm a whore daylighting till I ditch the clap. So don't 'nice kid' me, please."

"What a world . . ." He noticed light coming out of what he'd always assumed was a closet behind Ron's desk. The door opened onto a stairway that led to the roof, which he immediately took. Maybe push him off. An accident, tragic.

Momentarily blinded by the sunlight, he paused at the top of the short flight of steps . . . and felt heat in his pocket. Stuffing his hand in, he found that the cans were now warm. He took one out and held it in his open palm, and discovered that it was not only hot, it had a curious sort of movement to it, first one side lifting off his palm, then the other. In a few seconds, it was floating just above his hand. He stared at it. What kind of damned thing was this? Next chance he got, he would sure as hell Google Lempert Pharmaceuticals.

Without the slightest warning, somebody was there. A man in black clothing—shiny black, like a wetsuit. The man's head was covered by a black helmet, his face hidden behind a gleaming black plastic bubble. The man had something in his hand—a tube. Metal, with a dark gleaming business end.

What was this, an alien? "I'm a friend," Chris said as he backed away from the guy, backing toward the door.

When the man moved the stick through the air, it crackled and hissed. Nasty, very damn nasty. Chris backed closer to that door. Then the man raised his hand, raised it high, and pointed the thing directly at the sky.

Was Chris seeing this? What was he seeing?

A shadow came, and Chris saw clouds. A storm forming right overhead. What in hell? Then a rumble, soft, then louder and *wham wham wham wham* lightning bolts hit the roof, hit to Chris's left and he bolted, and another one struck, and he threw himself backward and went tumbling down the steps and heard above him a roar of pure rage.

The figure came to the top of the stairs and stood there a moment, his hands on the door frame, legs spread wide. Chris thought the guy was going to leap down on him, but instead he leaped *up* and Chris saw the impossible happen—the man went sailing off into the sky. Not like some jerk wearing a paraglider in an updraft, either. He went clean, just him and the wetsuit and the concealing helmet.

Chris got the hell out of there, and he did it fast. As he dashed out of the office, he grabbed the stuff he'd bagged at his workstation, his lucky Spongebob, his pen set that Maggie's folks had given him for Christmas, his box of Red Hots, candy of the gods and traders, made right here in Chicago.

For a couple of seconds he hammered the elevator buttons, then grew afraid that the alien or whatever it was would appear at the window at the end of the corridor. Damn thing could fly, recall. So he took the stairs down instead, leaping them three at a time. What had happened? *What*? People don't fly, it's impossible. They do not! But that guy—and where was Ron? Holy God, was *that* Ron?

On the way down, he texted Mel, got a message back. "Henry's. On way." Meaning that he was at Henry and on his way to being blind drunk.

The interior of Henry's was black mahogany, its ceiling still yellow from the old days when it was filled with smoke. Dad's lung cancer had cured Chris of smoking before he started.

Mel was in one of the back booths. He looked tiny and vulnerable, a little, withered old man. On Friday afternoon, he'd been thirty. He looked eighty.

Chris slid in across from him. "He's into something really weird and really evil."

No response.

"I have proof."

Still nothing. He took one of the two cans of Cloud Rider out of his pocket and put it on the table. "This is gonna be the weirdest thing you have ever seen."

Mel's eye opened a bit, regarded the hockey puck. "Whassit?"

"I just came here to tell you, this is gonna take him down. Do you understand?"

Mel picked it up. Shook it. Frowned. "Why's it so light?"

"We shall see, my friend. We shall see. I just want you to know this. What this bastard is into—it's truly, truly evil. In that can is a hell of an invention, and he's using it for the worst possible purpose."

Mel knocked back his drink, tapped the glass against the table. "Wake me when I'm dead," he said as Lucy the heavenly barmaid restored his glass. Lucy was a goddess to traders, soft and hard at the same time, following her considerable pair wherever they took her.

Mel tossed the can of Cloud Rider into the air. It turned slowly, then drifted down and settled in his palm.

"Take that outside, out from under all the weight of ceilings and roofs and iron girders, and you have to hold it down. That can is full of stuff that wants to fly."

"Ah. I get it. I'm behind in my drinking. Lucy! Lineup!"

"How did he call Katrina? Remember that? Twenty million dollars in puts on the insurance industry? You know what he took out of that? At least a hundred million. How did he call that storm when it was just a Cape Verde hurricane, answer me that? I'll tell you. *He made it into a killer.*"

He recalled the moment when Kevin had pointed to those strange dots in the sky, scudding before the storm like gulls. And Julie's voice came to him, bubbling with laughter, and her funeral in the gray morning, in the stillness.

"This is insane."

"That blizzard in '09—how did he call that? We did, God, eleven million in natural gas futures in two days. Tell you what Ronnieboy has. He has an inside track on acts of God, is what he has. He creates them."

"He's got loads of that crap. Cloud Rider. Couple cases of it. Thought I'd give him some last Christmas, just because he's already got so much. Not for sale, though."

"Where does he have this?"

"Supplies closet. Behind the ball point pens and the trader's notebooks and old shit nobody uses anymore. I thought it was some kind of potted meat at first. I tried to eat some of it. Tastes like shit, make me froth like some kinda sick dog."

"We buried my sister in law because of that storm."

"You're shittin' me."

"And my brother stands to lose our farm now that I can't bail him out." Chris had to stop. His voice had been crowded out by a sob he didn't care to utter.

He touched his buddy on the cheek, then, embarrassed, drew his hand back. But the emotions were there. In fact, these were among the most powerful emotions he had known since he'd first realized how much he loved Maggie. They were deep, a hunger that who and what was good in the world might prevail. "I will fix this," he said. He didn't know how, and nothing he could do could ever bring Julie back, but—well, the first thing was to get out of here with the two cans of Cloud Rider he had, and wait until dark and then—actually, he had no idea. Avoid getting killed, for sure, because Ron was going to be after this stuff, and trying hard, and with all the resources at the command of an evil billionaire, there was no telling what he be capable of.

He lived in an apartment where you could hear but not see Wrigley Field during the season. He'd learned to gauge the disappointment of the Cubbies fans by the sound of the roars of despair, and could usually tell from the decline into a flattened murmur exactly when the game was irretrievably lost. Ah, but the soaring of the ball, and the thrill as it hit the wall and got lost in the vines, which turned the other team's single into a triple. But what would Wrigley be without the beloved vines?

He crept down off the El the same way he always did, clutching the ever so flimsy rail and wishing to God you couldn't see through the damn steps.

Nothing seemed amiss as he passed the Barnes and Noble, then the inexplicable shop called Necktie Show that had opened up next door. No doubt a guy in his situation should look for suspicious vehicles, but all he saw was a mid nineties Explorer and a dead Beetle with an elderly hippie standing beside it gnashing into her cell phone. There were a few parked cars, nothing odd, except maybe that old LeBaron with the peeling landau roof. That was the sort of car that hoods from Cicero might drive when they were doing hits. They went for big trunks, obviously.

Then he stopped. Or rather, his feet did. Just stopped. His front door was two hundred feet away. Marty the doorman was at the curb helping Mrs. Arnold with her groceries. All was well.

He turned and ran like hell, and as he careened around the corner he heard the growling of an engine, and knew without looking that he was the target of an oncoming car which was large but not the LeBaron. The thought crossed his mind, "nobody looks up," and he did look up, and saw in the fluffy afternoon clouds four black dots just exactly like the ones that had scudded before the storm.

He ducked into the Barnes and Noble. The Starbucks was in the back, and behind it was the poetry section and the door to the stockroom. So he had a means of escape.

"Excuse me," he said to a guy massaging a Mac. "I urgently need to go online for a second. Could I pay you ten bucks for that privilege?"

The guy looked up at him. Silent. There could be a lot of reasons for such a request that weren't good.

"Just do me this. Google the name Lempert Pharmaceuticals."

He worked his keyboard. "There's a Lempert Family Foundation. Rumanian. And a guy, not connected. Anthony Lempert. An inventor. There's a Wikipedia entry. He was an exotic materials designer. But he's dead. Man, he wasn't even thirty."

"How did he die? Does it say?"

"Apparent suicide."

So that was a dead end, quite literally. Ronicide would be more like it, was Chris's guess.

So now what? That bar the figure on the roof had pointed at the sky—it had called up a storm right there, right over them, immediately. He knew storms, how they worked, and he also knew that this thing must have superheated the air somehow, causing it to go racing up in a column where it had hit the freezing cold stratosphere, and presto, a mini storm. So what might the figures in the sky do now? They had been watching him, tracking him, so that their ground forces could close in.

Ron and his friends were magicians, but their magic was real.

A blue Escalade slid past slow, windows up, shadows inside. Too slow, too near the curb. It kept going, at least until it was out of sight. But then, just past the end of the building, it stopped.

Of course it did, they knew for certain that he was in here because he'd been seen from above and his position radioed down. They dared not actually drop on him during the day, because this would obviously cause a huge sensation.

He threaded his way among the shelves of books until he found the doors to the stock room, then headed back and through to the loading dock, then returned to the street. Despite the thin foliage, he stayed as much under trees and awnings as he could. He hailed a cab. Did Ron know about Maggie? He didn't think so. He'd certainly never taken her to one of the compulsory-attendance office parties, with the poisonous shellfish and the cheap beer. He'd sooner throw her into a furnace. But had he ever mentioned her name? Written it down anywhere? Called her on a company phone?

The answer could be any damn thing, so he couldn't go near her house. Anyway what if, despite his best efforts, they *did* follow him to her place?

No, he couldn't go anywhere near there. Not even in that direction. So he had a few friends—Frank Thompson, for example. They went to Dugan's now and again to watch Browns games, both being secret—very secret—fans of that benighted team. Browns, Cubbies, Bulls. All had been in their glory days when he was a kid, when the only thing that matters to a ten-year-old fan is winning, and certain types of people—like him—pick their teams for life.

He needed a private place to experiment with the goop. If you didn't eat it, then did you slather it on? That could be, and suddenly he knew what it was, that an obscure legend was true, that there really was a witches' salve, and it had indeed enabled them to become night flyers.

A cab sulked past. No cabs, it could be a trap. He walked until he found a building with an open front door and the doorman busy, and he slipped in.

Like all the other fairly nice places around here, it was a fairly nice place, and he knew exactly how it worked. There was the doorman. Somewhere in the bowels of the thing, there would be the super. There would also be a laundry room, a boiler room and possibly a disused kitchen in the basement.

He found the fire stairs beside the elevator and went down. Soon enough, he was in a hallway, narrow, the ceiling low, with a light that had turned on when it sensed his movement. Same deal as an apartment building in Paris. If you didn't move, the lights went out on you.

The sloshing of washers told him where the laundry room was. He entered it and found behind it just what he needed, a disused room, maybe an old coal room. Fairly clean now, though, if you considered spiderwebs a sign of cleanliness.

He closed the door, found he could bolt it and did. The light was your classic single bulb that looked like it had been personally put together by Edison himself. So now, open the Cloud Rider.

It wasn't hard. The tins were so thin that he could have torn them open with his teeth. As it was he used the tip of a Bic pen. Ruined the pen, but the stuff came oozing out. He had seen what it did to Ron's arm, so maybe it was to be applied to the body. Maybe it *was* witches' salve. Somewhere along the road, he'd read that they had rubbed this stuff on their bodies. In any case, Mel had put some in his mouth at one point, and he hadn't gone anywhere, had he.

He untucked his shirt and took a gob of the stuff about the size of the end of his thumb, and rubbed it on his chest.

There was no delay. The effect was immediate, and so spectacular that for a moment he was disoriented, trying to figure out what he was looking at.

Then it came clear—he was staring close up at the ceiling, because his chest was pressed against it. His legs dangled heavily, and his arms. It was as if his chest was pinned to the ceiling, pinned and glowing like it had be slathered with Ben-Gay, and the sensation was spreading, and as it spread, more and more of him lifted to the ceiling.

Finally, he was pressed against it so hard that he had to fight to turn his face aside. When he did, though, he became aware that he was not alone in the room. A man had entered, and was going through a box of some sort. He couldn't quite see, but the clanking told him that he was looking for a tool. Under his breath, the man was singing to himself. Then he was just below Chris, the top of his head perhaps a foot under him. If Chris had been able to lower his arm, he could have touched the top of the guy's head.

People do *not* look up. They just don't. When the man left, he turned out the light and closed the door. Wonderful. Chris inched his way along the ceiling until he found the wall, then felt downward. Problem was, going down felt exactly like going up used to feel, and how in hell was he going to climb a wall? He tried bending at the waist, but it was the same as raising your feet from your waist would be—really hard. And anyway, there was nothing to push against. His feet swept clear air. He could reach down and feel the top of the door jamb, but that was about it.

Rule one: do not put this stuff on inside.

In the end, Chris was trapped in the dark room for so long that he actually fell asleep. When he woke up, though, it was because something was tapping the back of his head. For an instant, total disorientation. Then he remembered where he was and he groaned. Would he starve to death up here? What would happen.

Again, the tapping. He pushed against the ceiling and found that the ceiling was no longer there. He felt into the clear darkness, then felt below him—and pushed something away. Or rather, he pushed himself away. He was hanging above the floor, just floating like a balloon with perfect balance between weight and lift.

A tap, and the floor was gone. He flailed and found the door and the light switch beside it and turned on the light. He was rolling in the air like a swimmer underwater. He didn't feel exactly weightless, but astronauts in the various space stations appeared like this when they were filmed.

He opened the door onto the basement corridor and floated down it, drawing himself along the wall with his hands. At the far end he found a fire stair that went all the way to the top of the building around a column of air. By pushing against the banisters, he could float upward easily, and he moved smoothly from floor to floor. He was aware that there was a growing gulf below him and looking down would be a whole lot worse than the El, so he did not do that.

"Hey!"

He'd just passed a guy heading toward a trash chute with his garbage.

A head appeared two stories below. "Hey!"

The garbage gushed out like a fountain, cascading down into the depths. "Building inspector," Chris yelled.

"Aw, *shit*," the voice wailed, as the guy realized that his garbage was festooned down eight flights of banisters.

Chris was far above him now, approaching the skylight at the top of the stairwell, still pushing himself gently upward every time he began to drift down.

"You got a harness?"

"Yeah! Inspecting the walls." He pushed open the skylight and went out. From below there came another bark of amazement.

But Chris was outside now. It was dark, too, with a full moon, but as far as being seen was concerned, it still beat broad daylight all to hell. He scudded along the roof, his toes just touching the tarpaper. He wanted badly to tell Maggie about this, but he knew that he had to keep his head. Any move toward anyone he loved endangered that person, and he intended to take this thing all the way, which meant getting the bastards who were perverting this miracle behind bars and releasing the secret to all mankind. What wonders might unfold then, he had no idea. But that was the whole point of the marketplace, wasn't it?

This worked, he was beginning to see, pretty much like a balloon. It made you lighter than air. Presumably, you could control your altitude and the duration of your flight by varying the amount of it you rubbed in. It didn't take much, either. He had been pinned against that ceiling for hours, and he'd used just a tiny amount of the stuff, maybe two grams.

The door to the roof opened and three men came striding toward him, the guy from the stairwell, a black man in overalls, probably the super, and a cop.

"That's him," the tenant said.

"Sir," the cop said. "Do you have a city credential?"

Chris ran. He didn't know what else to do. Behind him, he heard the familiar cry of "freeze, police," then the pounding of feet. He came to the edge of the roof and, dear God, he launched himself into the air.

The roof wheeled below him, then the street with its row of streetlights, and then he was gliding downward, in an easy arc. He was going pretty fast, but not too fast, he didn't think. He crossed above the trees that lined the street, then settled roughly onto a roof on the opposite side.

Three figures stood across from him. The cop had his hat off, and was running his hand through his hair. The tenant was jabbering away.

Chris couldn't think what to do, so he bowed like a stage magician and went to the back of the building. He was heavier now, he could feel it, but it wasn't difficult to jump to the alley below.

As he sailed downward, he found that by shifting his weight he could control his movements a good deal. However, he could not vary his speed, no more than a balloon can. To do that, he would need some kind of a propulsion device, a motor of some kind.

Leaving his pursuers to wonder what they had actually seen, he made a gentle landing, which caused an old lady across the street to applaud as her two tiny dogs yapped frantically.

He stepped back into an alley. He was going to try this stuff, big time and right now. He took some of it out of the open can—not a lot, just enough to make a spot on his chest about an inch in diameter.

Walking up and down the alley, at first he noticed no change. But then his legs began to feel as if they were dangling from his torso, an odd and completely new sensation. He likened it to how it might feel to be dangling from ropes like a marionette. Next, his feet ceased to impact the ground and began scraping it. He pushed off—and suddenly he saw the towers of the Loop in all their drama and splendor.

That one little gesture had caused him to rise a good two hundred feet into the air—and he was still rising. He windmilled his arms and legs, which did nothing but cause him to tumble through the air. For a time, he was inverted, which caused the weird illusion that the world, instead, had turned upside down.

He bent at his torso and twisted himself until his feet were pointing downward—and, in doing this, looked down.

He was a good thousand feet up. And he screamed. He couldn't help it, the cry just literally erupted on its own. It echoed off across the night, and he had to force himself to tear his eyes from the ground. Seeing the tiny cars, the roofs of buildings, the glimmering myriad of city lights below the dark outlines of his own feet was just too much to bear. From this day on, the El would be a piece of cake.

When he raised his eyes, he found himself staring at the awesome immensity of the Sears Tower. He'd been moving toward the Loop, and he realized why—the buildings created a updraft that brought air in from all around them. He was floating just like a balloon at this point, with no clear idea how to control his movements.

The tower came closer, and fast, and soon he could make out office furniture in lighted windows, and here and there a tiny figure. How small our vision is. None of those people could even begin to imagine the miracle that was unfolding out there in the dark.

And then he thought, "the Sears Tower," and realized that Hen had been setting up a put position on the ownership company.

Ron was going to do something to this tower. He moved closer, and as he did, he found that shifting his weight altered his direction quite efficiently. In fact, he could tack like a sailboat, and considerably increase his speed by working his angles.

The stars above, the buildings whirling past around him—it was the most glorious experience possible. He was a bird, soaring, sweeping across the roof of a skyscraper at an altitude of three feet, then across the chasm beyond without the slightest sense of falling. Turning into the wind, spreading his arms and thrusting his head forward and he went up, rising beyond the roofs and above the honking horns and rumbling traffic of the city, into a night silence more profound, and a beauty greater, than he had ever known.

Souls on their journey must see the world this way, and he thought of Mark and his lost Julie, and Maggie and their future, and the sterling wonder of this secret that he was about to give to the world.

Ahead, he saw the Mid-World Building. Counting floors to eighteen, he saw lights. The System Fund's offices were still active, which was odd because traders generally closed down with their markets, and the markets were over for the day.

With so little experience of flying, he had hardly any sense of speed, and so made no effort to slow himself down until the lit windows of the System Fund offices were right in front of him. He turned, he fought, he strove not to hit them, but he did hit them and hard, sending a flash of pain through his shoulder. He tumbled head over heels, attempting to brake himself against the glass. He gradually regained control, his back to the glass. He was looking north now, up the lake, across the ocean of lights and the great darkness that marked the presence of the water.

Slowly, still struggling with his control, he turned around, preparing to push off and get the hell out of there.

Staring through the glass at him were six of the ominous figures, all in identical black clothing, all in black helmets and full-face visors. All carried the aluminum wands. All were looking straight at him.

He put his feet up to the glass and pushed out and up, and went sailing so fast the wind howled in his ears, sailing at an angle upward. When he was able to twist and turn enough to see where he had come from, the figures were emerging onto the roof, and taking off in his direction.

Sparks shot across their bodies, and they used the wands to spark the air and drive themselves even faster. Small thunder ripped and snickered as they sped toward him. Behind him, there was a steady clicking noise, getting quickly louder. Then it was below him, and he saw that he was two feet above the top of one of the twin television antennas that stand atop the Sears Tower.

The Sears Tower. The puts. The cloud riders, already assembled and ready.

Whatever they were going to do to this tower, they were going to do it tonight.

He snagged the tip of the antenna—and found that his buoyancy made it hard to control himself. His body, which had always wanted to seek the ground, now sought the air. Struggling, fighting, he got himself down onto the antenna, crouching on it like some kind of gargoyle. Slowly, he worked his way in between its crossed girders, until he was actually inside the structure of it.

At first, there was only silence, the whisper of a small wind, the distant rumble of Chicago all around him. Then, growing louder, there came another sound. It was a little like the crackling of a trolley's pantograph as it crossed electrical points, this sound, and it came from the swiftly rising bodies of the cloud riders—or so Chris was calling them. Cloud riders, after the substance they used and the evil they did, using the weather as a weapon. For his part, he was a flyer, and if he lived out this night, he vowed that he would not be the only one.

They swarmed the sky now, the cloud riders, their electrified suits snapping and giving off small blue lightning as they moved. They were beautiful, sleek and athletic, their movements a ballet in the sky—for him, if he was found, a dance of death.

Now Chris saw why Ron meditated. It was not Zen. In fact, it wasn't Buddhism at all, but some kind of martial exercise, because only somebody with that kind of physical discipline could look the way these people looked in the air.

They came to the roof of the building and began circling it. He saw that they were looking for him. Of course they were, he would be a number one priority. The fact that he'd shown himself like that would not be ignored.

Faintly, he could hear voices. They had radios in their helmets, of course.

Then one of them turned toward him. The gleaming faceplate reflected the antenna. He glided closer. Chris was cold and his shivering was shaking the antenna. Had he been spotted? No, the figure turned and drifted backward, apparently bracing against the antenna to damp his motion so that he could observe the sky more clearly. "Gone," he said. Male voice, sounded about thirty. In other words, a man in his prime. "Yeah," he said, responding to a radio message that Chris could not hear.

Chris saw that his wand was in a sheath along his leg. This sheath looked to be leather, tightly fitted to the fabric of the suit he was wearing. He couldn't hide here forever. Any one of them could spot him at any moment. He was unarmed, cold as hell, and when they did see him, he would be helpless.

The sheath was about five inches from his right hand. The question was, would its owner notice the removal of the wand? The weapon was Chris's only chance to live through this night, he was convinced of it. The thing was powerful and multipurpose, and who knew, maybe depriving them of one of the things would at least reduce the impact of whatever they were about to throw against this building.

Then he heard, ". . . guard the armory? Why?"

What armory?

". . . not goin' back there."

So the offices of the System didn't only house a supply of the flying salve, there were weapons there, too.

"Okay!"

With a rattling hiss and a shower of blue flashes, the group of them shot off at truly incredible speed, disappearing in an instant into the sky. These people were *good*, and they were also in a hurry. So maybe they were on a schedule. Maybe weather conditions or some other factor made speed essential. Or maybe it was a feint. Perhaps they'd realized that he was hiding somewhere and they were hoping he'd expose himself by trying to move.

So he would climb down the interior of the antenna, then pull himself across the edge of the roof and shove off *downward*. He could assume that their helmets were equipped with night vision equipment, radar and GPS, so once they spotted him, he knew that he would not escape.

Unless, of course, he could give himself a fighting chance by raiding their armory.

It was slow work staying inside the antenna, as slow and hard as it would have been to climb upward, and by the time he reached the roof itself, he was covered with sweat and breathing hard, and in danger of losing his footing and "falling" right back up to the point of the antenna—which, he suspected, would leave him at risk of injury or death.

He was climbing through the antenna's anchors when he saw, far off across the dark vastness that marked Lake Michigan, a small flicker.

It was them, and he knew what they were going to do to this building—about the only thing you *could* do to something as substantial as this skyscraper with the weather. They were going to break its back with a monster tornado. Right now, they were out there over the lake creating the kind of massive supercell that would be needed to generate such a storm. It would have to be the largest tornado ever recorded, beyond category five, with God knew what sort of windspeeds. Three hundred miles an hour, maybe more.

Gutting the top fifty stories of this structure would result in an insurance nightmare. Tomorrow, the puts Ron and his friends had bought would bring them millions.

Chris launched himself straight at the older, lower Mid-World Building. Twisting, fighting the roaring air, he managed to get into a feet-first position. Faster he went, and faster. The windows, still lit, came closer and closer—and then there was a crash and glass splintered and spiked him in a dozen places, and he was sliding across the ceiling of the office, frantically ripping out ceiling tiles to break his momentum.

Below him, he saw cubicles gliding past, including his own, which was already refilled by another hopeful sucker. He could see a picture of a family on the desk, and a stack of portfolios of some kind. He hit the window on the far side so hard he almost went through it, but the glass, although it cracked, stopped him.

All right, now where was this armory? Not in Ron's office, not unless it was behind a secret door. He climbed along the ceiling, turning and looking down—and realized that he wasn't going to have any trouble finding it at all, and for a remarkable reason—the walls didn't connect with the ceiling, which was because the chamber itself had no door.

This way, no matter how hard they might look, Ron's staff would never find it. As he clambered along, he saw, also, that it was nearly empty. There was one black suit, though, and two of the wands. Enough. Also, the entire room was designed so that everything could be used from above. The suit was stretched between two wires, and he was easily able to get into it. His clothes under it made it lumpy, and also there was a burned tear in it. Somebody had been struck by lightning, looked like. The wand, when he moved it even slightly, emitted a crackling sound and a smell like the purified essence of electricity. This was one nasty toy, and he wished to hell he had one damn idea how to use it.

Torn or not, the suit still worked, because as soon as he was in it, he suddenly had literally masterly control of his movements. He'd been bobbing around like a balloon. Now he was under control. However he positioned himself, this was how he stayed. But how did you propel yourself? He could more-or-less slide along in midair, but not speed like the others did. Maybe this suit was indeed broken.

He lifted the helmet out of its upward-facing rack. This wasn't just a helmet, it was a control center, and as soon as he put it on, he was all but in another level of reality. A continuous readout gave him his position on a map that was visible in his left eye. He hit a chin switch and the darkness disappeared. Night vision glass. Nifty. Must cost the earth, too, this stuff. Had to be full of microscopic light amplifying diodes. This was a generation beyond night vision goggles, for sure.

As he crossed the office again, he saw all the phones. Maggie would be wondering where he was. She'd be worried. Mark would need his brother. He'd be worried.

Chris crossed above the desks easily, but at a maddeningly stately pace. He moved through the broken window, noticing with pleasure that Ron's fake Aphrodite was on the floor in a thousand pieces, a small but delicious blessing.

Now he hung eighteen stories above the street. Looked down. From inside this rig, it wasn't so hard. He felt absolutely solid and stable. But how did they move out like that?

He writhed, he twisted himself, he bucked—nothing. He could ply along at the pace of a swimmer. A little faster, maybe. He'd been better off just in his jeans.

So maybe the key was, the suit had to be in contact with your skin. It was electrostatic, after all, that he could see from the sparks and sheets of static the suits generated when they moved.

He unzipped the suit and worked his way out of it. Then he pushed open his faceplate and got a sleeve in his mouth. The suit sure as hell didn't float in midair. Now he emptied his pockets of his wallet and his two cans of Cloud Rider, and got them down into the pouch on the suit's hip, opposite where the wand was carried. He pushed off one of his great Converse sneakers and watched it tumble away into the darkness of Lower Righter Street, fortunately abandoned at this hour. Maybe a couple of parked trucks, compliments of the printer across the street, that would be it. The rest of his clothes followed it the shoe, until he was buck naked in the cold. If he dropped this suit, he was in a lot of trouble, but he got it on successfully.

Okay, now he felt a tingling all over his body, that and cold air coming in through the tear. When he twisted to the left, he ended up going around in a circle, whizzing so fast the world became a blur. He threw his arms wide and the spin gradually stopped. So what happened if you vomited into one of these things?

The light changed. To be specific, it got darker. But why? The moon had been high in the sky when he'd come back here from the Sears Tower.

He raised his head—and shot upward so fast it was literally dizzying. It seconds, his ears were popping, oxygen was hissing and the suit had become toasty warm—and he could see below him the entire city, laid out in a vast pattern of lights that hugged the toe of Lake Michigan.

He must be at least ten thousand feet up, and it was ungodly wonderful, the most extraordinary, most freeing, most joyous feeling he had ever experienced. How could you use something like this for greed and doing harm? This was poetry, this was, the dream of flight in its purest form.

Lightning flickered to the north and he glimpsed, far out over the lake, what looked at first like the mushroom cloud of an atomic explosion. He turned toward it. Leaned toward it. Started to move, then to move faster, then to literally streak in the direction he was leaning. The suit shuddered around him, spreading electric flashes.

Then he heard a voice, just a snatch of one. Radio. Low power so it wouldn't be noticed by folks with scanners. Probably on an exotic frequency to boot.

"We have topping. Topping at level thirty-six."

"*Hit the core, god damn you! Go higher!*" Ron's voice.

"We're hitting it!"

"*Harder!*"

"Shut up, you shit."

Nobody liked him, it seemed, not even his friends.

"God, I'm in the draft!"

"Who's in the draft?"

A scream, then, and among the worst Chris had ever heard. Somebody was trapped in the storm's updraft.

"Past forty!"

"Drop out, drop out!"

"I can't, I—oh, God, fifty!" Another scream, this one savage with pain and fear. Death cry.

"You got it high enough, Ron? High enough for you? That's a good man up there!"

"George. Talk to us, George."

Silence. Chris was close to the clouds now, very close, and he could see, here and there, circular red pulses going into the storm's wall where members of the group were hitting it with heat bursts. The theory behind what they were doing was well established. They were using heat to create artificial thermals, which developed into much larger ones when they reached the cold upper atmosphere. The technological wizardry came from what made these wands tick. He would find out, he was determined, but now it was time for him to break up this little party.

"We lost George!"

"Shit, shit! What do I tell Chrissie?"

"Nothing." Ron's voice again.

"Yeah, we're supposed to be fishing together at my camp in B.C."

"So think of something! Fricking Indians ate him. We got clouds to move, gentlemen."

"And lady."

Who was *that*? A billionairess willing to tear up the sky like this? If they were all billionaires. Maybe they worked for people, some of them.

No, these were the owners. Had to be. The potential for blackmail was too great. The only people who knew about this were—

—a bolt of lighting flashed past his head.

Okay. What was that?

A whoosh of really hot air.

"What in hell are you doing?"

"That's him, you stupid fuck!"

"That's—who *is* that? Martin?"

"That is the little shit from my office in Martin's suit. Must be cold in there for you, little boy. Let's see if we can improve things."

From straight on, the oncoming heat pulse looked like a speeding bolus of pure sunlight. Hot, very hot.

Chris turned his face upward, and began to move. Faster. The fireball came closer. He moved faster still. The fireball loomed, huge now. He could feel the heat right through the suit. The fireball was on him it was hissing, it was touching his feet—and he pulled them up and it passed just beneath him, and he heeled to the left and dove toward the storm.

And toward Ron. Right toward him. He could see Ron aiming the wand, bringing it to bear even on his speeding figure. Without any real idea what would happen, he squeezed the handle of the wand he'd brought.

There was a clap of thunder and the world went wild, the storm, the sky, the distant waters of the lake spinning so fast they were a blur. In the blur, another fireball glided past.

Chris got himself under control. He was no more than a thousand yards from the roiling cloud face, and now he could see other members of the group turning his way, aiming their weapons.

Not knowing what this might mean, he darted into the clouds. At once, a female voice began counting altitude. He was going up, and fast.

He felt the wand, trying to find its settings, because it must have them—and indeed, they were there. The handle worked like the shifter on a motorcycle. Four settings. He tried the next one—and this time, a burst of light shot out of his wand. It went deeper into the clouds, though, not in the direction of any of the riders. As it penetrated, Chris saw shafts of rain, great mountains and valleys of cloud, the blur of wind shears, and, as it penetrated the base of the storm, the black waters of the lake far, far below.

This was a monster, this was, and it was going to cause fantastic destruction. He realized that the puts in the company that owned the Sears Tower were probably just one small part of what was going down here. This thing was going to shatter an entire city, causing billions and billions of dollars worth of damage and God only knew how much death. Every way there was to profit on knowing that in advance, these people had to be involved. First rule of the markets: if you can predict, you can win, no matter what.

The numbers kept reeling off, twenty-one, twenty-one five, twenty-two. He was rising at a very fast clip. Oxygen hissed in his ear, but how long? And the suit was so cold it felt like he was burning. No wonder its owner had stayed at home. You didn't want to be out here in a torn suit.

He tried throwing himself backward, but there were just more clouds. He turned. Clouds. Turned again. More clouds.

He was lost—and then he saw a faint glow enter the clouds, grow brighter, then very bright, then disappear in a frenetic crackle of lightning.

They were still heating the thing, still making it bigger.

He knew now that this was going to be the most terrible tornado in history.

Then one of them was right in front of him. Rising with him.

"You done good, little man," the radio crackled. "But now it's time to go."

It was Ron's voice and Ron was about to fire straight at him, so Chris aimed the wand and crushed the pliable handle as hard as he could.

Heat enveloped him, the whole world turned white—and then it was black again, blacker than night. The helmet's mask had been burned out. Raising the visor brought a blast of thick, stormy air and a sound, not in the radio, in the sky, and he saw a man dancing in the void, covered with flares and flashes, blue flames speeding along his arms.

Chris watched, sick with horror, as the fire spread through Ron's suit and consumed him. Twisting and flailing, he moved upward, drawn by the storm's powerful winds, until he appeared like a meteor in the clouds, a burning brand that left a smoke trail as it rose higher and higher, a smoke trail that was torn away by the wind.

Chris tried to follow him, but the winds were growing, surging, pulling him first up and then down. No matter the miracle of the suit's propulsion system, the storm was stronger. He'd come up here to stop this evil and point the perps toward jail, not to see men get themselves burned alive, no matter how much they might deserve it.

Chris could hear a voice in his ear, but the winds were drowning it, so he pulled the visor back down. It had recovered from the flash, and he could see again, and, in the silence that now enveloped the helmet, also hear.

"Ron!" the speakers snapped. "Ron, come in, guy!"

For the first time, Chris spoke. "I'm afraid he's had an accident."

"*Bastard!*"

Three dots converged on him from different directions. He retreated to the towering face of the storm and dived. Going down worked just like gaining altitude would, if you weren't dosed with Cloud Rider. Going down was slow.

Not for them, though, they were experts and they came after him one hell of a lot faster than he could go. He turned and fired again, and this time a series of flashes came out of the wand, and caught two of them, and they went spiraling off into the cloud base. One of them, he saw, dropped his wand, and it went down into the dark and was gone. Cloud Rider only worked on living bodies. What you dropped, fell.

Somebody punched him hard in the gut, and now he went down so fast that the cloud base literally sped into the sky—and then he hit something that felt as hard as a wall, but it was water, and he found himself floating in Lake Michigan, then under the lake in a roiling mass of bubbles. Then he broke the surface and shot upward as fast as he would have shot downward without Cloud Rider. Two more fireballs were launched at him, but he was moving too fast, and they passed him again.

He shot carefully and quickly, drawing on his skill as a hunter of pheasant and quail. But he didn't use the fireballs, he had no intention of doing that again. He used the pulses of light that hit you like a giant fist, and knocked two of his pursuers deep into the clouds.

They called to one another, many voices, at least eight. "Break off, break off!" "We gotta do this!" "Christ, I'm in the core, I'm in the core!" Then, a cry of rage and alarm: "We lost the damn storm!"

Chris felt a surge of hope—but then he saw that the front face of the storm had changed. It was no longer a billowing mass of clouds, but something he had never witnessed before, a cliff, sheer and unimaginably vast, like the face of a gigantic wave that reached to the top of the sky.

But the light—what was lighting it? Not the moon, the moon was too far north and west. The storm was blocking out the moonlight.

"Run, guys! Course west southwest, fast or this thing is gonna tear us apart!"

The speeding dots broke off their engagement with Chris and shot off toward clear air. As Chris turned, watching them, trying to count and be sure they were all leaving and this wasn't some kind of a trap, he had the shock of his life. He was a few hundred yards from the Loop, the buildings were huge before him. He'd been backing before the storm, they all had, and now the thing was coming onshore. The storm was being lit by the city itself. He dashed up to a nearby building—the Ritz Carlton. A woman stared idly out as she brushed her hair. "Run," he screamed, "Lady, RUN!" She continued brushing, her golden hair shimmering.

He heard the long, wailing note of a siren, then many sirens. He saw the woman turn, look at a red light that had begun flashing on her ceiling—and then he saw her pick up the phone. He groaned inwardly.

His mind raced with thoughts. How could he break this storm?

His only tool was the wand. It had the ability to generate heat and the ability to move clouds with shock waves. It could generate electricity.

The heat. If there was enough energy in this thing, he could maybe reduce the power of the storm. To do that, he'd have to go all the way to the top of the clouds and apply heat there. If he was lucky, this would slow down the convection that was driving the thing enough to transform it back into a normal squall. Thing was, though, the experts had run like hell, and at least one of them had already been carried too high.

He had a decision to make right here, right now. Did he try to break this thing at the cost of his own life, or did he run? In his mind's eye, he saw Maggie. He saw her grieving, her and Mark. Then he saw, far below, people gathering on the pier, people looking up and pointing at the storm.

He raised his head and the suit shuddered and sparked, and the oncoming face of the clouds began to slide past.

"Eleven," the altimeter said. Nice voice. Female. Reminded him of his Honda. "Eleven three." Yeah! He was going up fast. "Twelve." He fingered the wand. He had to get heat right across the top of the thing, however high it was. "Fourteen."

It was colder here. He began to hear a faint hiss behind his head. The suit carried oxygen, but it couldn't be much. Time was against him.

Something bulged out of the clouds, a long, seeking tendril. He saw that it was a tornado, not a large one. "Fifteen. Fifteen five."

The front face of the Ritz melted away as the wind hit it. "NOOO!"

"Seventeen."

He twisted, strove with all his might, trying to make his body language speed the suit up. This was how it worked, he had seen the others doing it. But why not for him?

The air coming in the rip was now so cold it felt as if it was burning him. "Twenty-six."

Christ, he wasn't even near the top of this monster.

Rumbling. Another tornado, close, pressing out of the storm front.

Huge! Black death, oncoming, and the city below it, the lights shining, the sirens wailing, traffic on the highways getting clogged, the city beneath an avalanche of hail.

"Thirty-six."

The oxygen gave a burp, then started hissing again. Once it was gone, he had only seconds.

The suit heater was failing because of the tear. His whole body was getting cold. He was rising up the outer wall of what was without question the greatest and most terrible tornado ever spawned, and it was crossing into the Loop right now.

Then he was soaring, he was soaring in the stars, and below him there was a vast, white range of low hills that stretched off into the dark.

The storm top!

He raised the wand and checked the setting on the handle, making certain that the glowing red LED on the grip was lined up with the one on the body of the device. The fireball setting. He squeezed the handle and three of the fireballs crossed the sky . . . and just disappeared into the immensity of the clouds and the dark.

This was ridiculous, he was too small, he could not save the city.

But men had made this storm.

And then he saw, directly below him, the dark mouth of a whirlpool. For a moment, he was confused. What was this?

Then he knew—he was looking *down* into the tornado—and he could see its glowing electric walls, the rushing of its winds, and in the wind, traveling round and round like a dancer, an eighteen wheeler, its lights still on.

He fired heat down into the funnel. Fired more. Again and again and again. Thankfully, his oxygen had not stopped.

"Fifty-two." Jesus, he was at fifty-two thousand feet, here! "Fifty." What? "Forty-five, forty." It began counting down like an unwinding altimeter because that's what it was, and nothing he did would stop it, and he was dropping directly into the maw of the tornado and he knew why—the one thing he had not anticipated, *the Cloud Rider was wearing off!*

"Thirty-five."

The walls of the tornado were closing around him now. Again and again he fired into it. Whipping past in the fireball light he saw the twisted remains of the Ferris wheel from the pier, seats from Soldier Field, cars, trucks, signage and people, yes, people were dying, he was not preventing all deaths or right now any deaths.

Now he was being snatched at by the wind, his suit being pulled and torn more. "Twenty-eight."

Whoosh!

Silence. Sheets of rain passing him. Debris dropping toward the streets far below.

He let out a whoop of sheer joy. He hadn't killed the storm, but he had killed its heart, because the tornado had just collapsed, its wind surfaces aloft heated to the point that the deadly whirling ended.

Chicago was out there, most of it still intact, gleaming lights, traffic, people. "Ten. Danger of descent. Danger of descent."

He had to land. Or maybe he was already dropping too fast. Maybe he had to die.

But then the secret of Cloud Rider would die with him, and that must not be, it *must not be*!

"Nine." He twisted, trying to find his bearings, to find some place he could land, but he was already over the North Side, and so low that he could hear horns honking, could hear the warning sirens still wailing.

Then wind took him, and he blew fast across the city, blew tumbling in the hail and the rain.

Six. Danger. Danger."

Gaining some control of his fall, he turned north again. His hands were heavy now, and his feet. "Leaving four."

It was no use, he was crashing. He had been trying to reach Maggie's but he would not succeed.

Well, that was okay, he'd saved most of the city from the storm, which was now just another muttering autumn disturbance, sheeting rain and hail, and giving a few lake steamers exactly the kind of hell they expected this time of year.

But he must not die, not with the secret of Cloud Rider.

He had to get the remaining bastards a ticket to Joliet, he had to marry Maggie and give Mark all the help a brother could offer. He had to *live*. "Leaving one. Warning. Leaving one. Overspeed. Slow down. Overspeed."

He fought to reach the Cloud Rider in the suit's thigh pocket, but he couldn't do it. Below him, streets—familiar ones. He saw the El, saw the broad street he took to Maggie's. He'd come closer than he realized and now she'd see his broken body, she'd wonder for the rest of her life what bizarre thing had happened to him.

He'd been arching his back, pointing his face upward, trying to get the suit to help him, trying to somehow navigate.

There was a flash, and for an instant, he thought they'd gotten him after all—but then he understood that he was on a roof. He was on a roof and he wasn't dead! He was *not* dead. Yet. The roof was steep, the ground was far away.

His weight was normal. The Cloud Rider had worn off. Then he saw, in the front of the suit, a neat pouch. That's where he should have put his extra can, but he hadn't noticed it before.

Climbing carefully, clutching the spine of the roof, then inching down along the shingles, he got to an attic dormer. "Sorry," he muttered as he busted a pane and unlocked it. He'd come back and pay them.

Only when he was inside the tiny attic room did he realize just how cold he had been. He fumbled around, saw a bed, realized that this was a finished room, but dusty and unused.

Leaving his faceplate down, he went to the outer door of the room and opened it.

A short hallway led to stairs, which he took. Opening the next door, he found himself in an upstairs corridor papered with old-fashioned floral wallpaper. There was a clear run to more stairs—narrow, probably back stairs that led to the kitchen. What time was it? No idea. Late, though, dinner would hopefully be over.

Maybe the kitchen was empty. Maybe he had a shot at getting out of here without being seen.

A short, sharp sound made him turn around.

There stood a woman, young, in a skirt and blouse, brown hair, fists obscuring her face.

"I've taken a wrong turn," Chris blurted.

The woman's face flushed, her chest heaved. She'd sucked in a massive breath. It was going to come out in the form of an unholy loud cry for help.

He raised his visor. "Could you direct me to the nearest El Station?"

She gasped. Gasped again. Lowered her hands—and he saw that it was Maggie.

"Oh!" It was all he could say. "I've been trying so hard to get here!"

"Oh my God. My God, what're you doing in a wetsuit?"

Her dad's voice from below: "What's going on up there?"

"Nothing, Daddy!"

"Something is." He would not care to find Chris up here.

"It's fine!" she shouted. She grabbed his wrist and pulled him into her room.

"I can explain!"

"The wetsuit?"

"Everything. The whole thing." She started to talk again, but he put a hand over her mouth. "In time," he said, and he kissed her. She melted into it, for a moment, but then broke away.

"Chris, you need to explain right now! Where did you come from, and *what is that wetsuit?*"

"Honey, this is a long story. It's a real long story, and I'm gonna need some time with it before I tell it."

She searched his eyes. "Okay," she said at last. "You have time. Some."

He embraced her again, and this time she did not pull away, but rather sank into his arms in a way she never had before. Without saying it, without really even understanding it, the peril of this night had brought them into one another's deep hearts. While he longed for her on the battlefield of the storm, she sweated for him as the tornado approached, and their fear one for the other turned a young love affair into a permanent matter of the heart.

He felt the future flying toward the two of them, him and his Maggie, its promise and its peril flying toward them, and toward all the world.